Mayhem, Murder

and the PTA

By Dave Cravens

To my first fan.

I hope I did you proud.

0.

"What exactly did you expect to happen, Parker?"

Parker Monroe closed her tired hazel eyes and pinched the bridge of her nose as though to keep it from exploding. *This is a mistake,* she thought. *A joke. A dream – a nightmare.*

The forty-year old red head and Pulitzer prize winning journalist for the *American Times* took a deep breath. She opened her eyes to lock with those of her editor, Jerry, a fifty-something divorcee hemorrhaging money from his two kids still trying to "find themselves" in an ivy league school. Jerry's eyes didn't express anger so much as abject terror. He simply couldn't afford screw-ups like the one he'd just printed a million copies of, let alone the re-tweets and shares online.

Ever defiant, Parker straightened her posture. "What I expected was for Senator Hammers to be hauled away in handcuffs," she explained.

Jerry threw his hands in the air. "Jesus, Parker, you're lucky they're not hauling *us* away in handcuffs!"

Parker paced across the office's hardwood floor. Yes, her source vanished before supplying the documented proof he'd promised over the phone. Yes, it was risky trusting him without the usual verification. Yes, she put her magazine's reputation on the line to scoop *Drudge, the Post, the Times* and all the other hacks who moved at the speed of emojis. But Parker hadn't won a Pulitzer by playing it safe.

Jerry's only sin was trusting Parker enough to go along for the ride.

"We've already retracted the story," Parker assured her boss. "We'll issue an apology. Let's not blow this out of proportion."

Jerry shook his head. "That's not going to do it. I've got every lawyer and member of the board making my ass red. Defamation.

Slander. Personal distress. It's all over cable news." Jerry turned off the circus of talking heads on the TV's behind him, weary of the endless scrolling text that announced variants of: *American Times'* *"bombshell" blows up in own face!*

"Fuck cable news," Parker spat. "And defamation? Try this headline: Senator Hammers can go choke on a dog's dick! How's *that* for defamation?"

"Classy, Parker, you talk to your kids with that mouth?" berated Jerry. "Hell, you even see your kids these days?"

Parker's face flashed red hot. "What is that supposed to mean?"

Jerry took a deep breath. Normally he didn't dare poke the momma bear. But it was high time he said something. "Listen, I know how hard it's been since Kurt died."

Parker's ring finger suddenly ached. She adjusted her wedding band around the swollen skin. "That was three months ago, it's got nothing to do with--"

"You never talk about it. You took like, what, a week off to grieve? You hire a nanny, so you can come back to work while your kids—"

"Leave my kids out of this."

Jerry waved Parker off. "No, no, this is my fault. I should have never allowed you to come back so soon. I thought it might help you cope, but you weren't ready!"

Parker summoned her calmest voice. "I'm fine. My kids are fine. Nothing has changed."

"Everything has changed!" Jerry exploded. "Jesus, if you can't look at your own personal situation then look at your work! I used to have this spitfire reporter who chased down every lead, talked to every witness, verified all her facts and triple checked her goddamn sources before going to print!"

Parker swallowed. "Used to?"

4

Jerry sheepishly looked down at his desk. "They want blood, Parker. They want a sacrifice. You wrote the story."

"So, you're firing me."

"The board has agreed to call it a suspension."

Parker allowed herself a chuckle. "For how long?"

"Indefinite."

"So, you're *firing* me. Let's just call it what it is." Parker kicked her toe into the leg of the desk. "No, it's bullshit. *That's* what it is." She smiled deviously as a new, delicious thought popped into her head. "I will fight this, Jerry."

Jerry laced his hands onto the top of his perspiring bald head. "Of course. I told the board you would." He turned around to look out at the Chicago skyline framed by his 82nd floor window. "All you're going to do is make it worse."

"*So* much worse!" Parker insisted. "I'll countersue! Then we'll get all the nasty facts out about what a douche bag the Senator is! While he's floundering in the court of law, I'm gonna fuck him straight up the butt in the court of public opinion!"

Jerry spun around, his face contorted. "I don't even know how to process that."

"Uh, yeah, because it's gonna be raw and nasty!"

"Stop!" Jerry held out his hand. "Okay? He played you, Parker. For all we know your 'source' was a plant. You got beat!"

"I'm not your employee anymore!" Parker shouted. "I will blow the lid off every shady deal Hammer's ever had in his silver spoon-fed inbred life and America will thank me!"

Jerry sighed. "If I were you, I'd stay low for a while."

"That's not my style. I'm doing this, and there's not a thing you or anyone can say to make me change my mind!"

"Excuse me, Ms. Monroe?" a meek voice asked from behind.

Parker spun around to glare at the young millennial who carefully poked his head around the glass office door. "What?" she blasted.

"Um, I hate to interrupt," the millennial winced. "but no one's been able to reach you on your cell."

Parker seethed. "That's because I turned it off. I didn't want to be reached. See how that works? If I don't pick up, stop calling." She pressed on. "There was a time, long ago, before your mom tore up the backseat of a Volvo with your dad, when children didn't have cell phones. Adults were able to converse without being interrupted by Game of Thrones ring tones, poop emoji texts, or Instagram photos of your lunch!"

The millennial rolled his eyes. "Yeah, wow, *thanks* for that. I'm a better person for it." His head retracted behind the door, only to immediately pop out again. "Oh, and by the way? There's an emergency regarding your daughter."

Parker's heart skipped a beat. "My daughter?"

"They've been trying to get a hold of you for the last hour. I couldn't think of a good emoji to properly express that, L-O-L, so I thought I'd just tell you in person, hash-tag: you condescending bitch."

Parker's mind went blank. She instinctively reached for her phone to turn it on.

After a quick boot, several text rings piled on.

Where are you?

I've tried calling twenty times!

Emergency!

Call me back, NOW!!!

911!

Why aren't you calling back?!?!?

6

Parker's heart thumped against her chest like a trip hammer as she pressed to dial home. She carefully placed the phone to her ear. A hysterical whimpering bled out the speaker.

"It's Parker," she stated in her calmest voice. "Tell me what happened."

1.

3 months later...

"Mom, stop falling asleep!"

Parker snorted as her eyes shot open. She clutched the steering wheel to jolt her Toyota Highlander back onto the moonlit freeway along the Mojave Desert. Parker violently shook her head. "I wasn't," she stopped mid-sentence to taste the dryness of her mouth. *Yuck. What did I eat for dinner?* "I-I wasn't sleeping," she protested. *Cheetos. I ate a bag of Cheetos.*

"Yes, you were!" argued Maddy, the eleven-year-old portrait of pre-teen angst who sat in the front passenger seat. "Your eyes were closed!"

"It's called blinking."

"You could've killed us!"

"Don't tempt me." Parker shot her oldest daughter an angry glare.

Maddy folded her arms and shot one back.

Still haven't forgiven me yet, have you, Maddy?

It had been three months since the "Chicago Incident." Parker had made two huge mistakes that day, the first of which got her fired—that was the good news. The trauma of the second created a rift between Parker and Maddy the size of the Grand Canyon. Still, it could have been worse. *Nobody died, right?* Parker didn't blame Maddy for being angry. But how long was it going to last?

I've packed up everything we own and am moving across us country to start over. Maddy, can't you appreciate that? Can't you at least see I'm trying to change?

Parker glanced in the rear-view mirror to check on the others. Her bushy haired six-year old son, Drew, used his plush Pokémon as a pillow. Ally, her golden-haired toddler of two years was slumped over, sound asleep in her car seat. Every square inch of the enclosed space behind them was crammed with plastic sacks, suitcases and backpacks stuffed with life essentials – toothpaste, semi-clean underwear, toys, comic books, magazines, cereal boxes, shoes, umbrellas and Maddy's piano music.

"…and in other news, Senator Hammers continues his assault on American Times magazine months after the firing of senior journalist, Parker Monroe…" squawked the radio.

"Turn that shit off," barked Parker.

"Mom, your language," grumbled Maddy as she pressed the radio's button.

"What—you mean, English?"

"Why do you swear so much?"

"Maddy, it's just how I talk." *And everyone I used to work with.*

"*I* don't get to talk like that."

"When you turn forty and have three kids, talk however you want."

Maddy slumped further in her seat. *"Dad* never talked like that."

And there it was, the daily comparison Maddy slung at her mother to make her feel small, inadequate and lonely all in one strike. Parker's husband, Kurt, had given up his music career to be a stay at home father, and bonded with the kids in ways Parker only dreamt of. Parker worked overtime winning the bread, but Kurt knew how each kid liked to have it toasted, sliced and buttered. Kurt's sudden death traumatized the entire family in the obvious ways, but now, six months later the not so obvious ways kept surfacing.

Angry, Parker clamped her mouth shut as she adjusted her wedding ring to ease the throbbing pain of her finger. She was careful not to lash out and undo the minutia of progress she'd made with her daughter these past few weeks. "Why don't you close your eyes and get some sleep?" suggested Parker. "We've got a few hours before we hit Grandma's."

Maddy refused to look at her mother. "If I fall asleep, who is going to wake you up?"

Oh, you little shit, don't make me pull this car over.

Maddy turned away to stare out her window, but the night had long since swallowed the California desert in black velvet. Only the sparse train of headlights and brake lights on the freeway offered any distraction, and Maddy had tired of them hours ago.

Parker cringed at the idea of starting their new life like this. "Okay, I tell you what," she relented. "How about a game?"

Maddy shrugged. "What kind of game?"

"You play your cards right, a profitable one."

"Go on."

"To help break me free of my deplorable habits--anytime I swear in front of you, I will pay you one dollar."

Maddy tilted her head. "Five dollars."

"Fuck *that*."

Maddy's index finger lashed out toward her mother. "Ha! You owe me five dollars!"

"I never agreed to five dollars!"

"Come on! One dollar isn't going to do anything, and you know it!"

Parker reluctantly nodded. "Fine. Whatever. Five dollars," she held up her finger to mark an addendum. "If, and only if, you agree to pay me five dollars if you don't address me as 'Mom, The Almighty.'"

"What?"

"I want some respect, damnit! I'm tired of all the pouting, and the eye rolls and stuff!"

"Mother!"

"Noooooooooo, 'Mom, The Almighty! Now, *I've* got five dollars in the bank!"

"Noooooooooo, you swore twice! I'm still five bucks ahead!"

Parker allowed herself a chuckle, maybe the first in months. She looked at Maddy hoping to catch her in a half smile – none surfaced. "Okay," said Parker. "You're five bucks ahead."

Bribing. That works with kids, right?

Parker studied her daughter's face as she continued to stare out the front window. This was the first tearless moment they had shared together in weeks. A small victory to be sure, but a victory nonetheless. Then Parker's eyes suddenly widened. "Oh *shit!*" She slammed on the brakes, throwing their bodies at the mercy of their seatbelts. The Highlander violently shook and skidded to a halt. Ally and Drew stirred in the back, trying to recover from a rude awakening.

"What? What is it?" screamed Maddy.

Parker leaned ahead to look past her daughter out the passenger window. "We missed our exit."

Maddy took several quick and short breaths. Once her pounding heart had settled she grinned at her mother. "You owe me *ten* dollars!"

Parker threw the Highlander in reverse and slowly backed up along the road's shoulder, earning angry honks from the passing cars. She pulled forward onto the exit ramp. "You know I'm out of a job, right?"

2.

Cruising through the empty streets of Oak Creek...

at three in the morning marked a surreal homecoming for Parker Monroe. She'd spent her first eighteen years of life trying to escape the stifling suburbia hell. At a population of fifty thousand in the foothills thirty miles north of the Mexican border, it was neither a big city, nor a small town, nor largely Hispanic or white, nor vastly rich or hopelessly poor, only decidedly average in every way. Parker despised average, which may be the only trait she had in common with her mother, Valerie.

Even from down the street, Parker could see her mother, sitting on her porch's bench swing, beaming like some perfect, twisted angel. Despite the ungodly hour, Valerie projected the confidence of a movie star, with a grace and poise that eluded her only daughter. Sixty-two years of age had done nothing to slow the tall brunette down, her shapely body and toned skin seemingly impervious to the sagging hands of time.

Parker pulled into the familiar driveway of the five-bedroom detached home. Valerie's eyes tracked her daughter's SUV like a hawk, only relaxing when Parker finally waved to her. Valerie smiled, and stood up from the bench, leaning the broom she'd held in her lap next to the front door.

"It *is* you!" Valerie greeted with her arms outstretched. "I wasn't expecting you so late. Why didn't you call?"

Parker shushed her mother as she stepped out of her SUV, pointing to the three sleeping children. "Maddy finally dozed off," whispered Parker. "We got another late start, so I thought we'd push through the night." She embraced her mother with a heavy squeeze.

13

"My," Valerie's postured stiffened as she took a sniff. "You are ripe!" She pulled back with a smile and massaged her daughter's arms. "Oh, and there's more of you to hug than I remember."

"Wow, thanks, it's good to see you too, Mom," said Parker. She had no desire to recant her recent weight struggles at three in the morning. "Were you waiting on the porch this whole time?"

"Of course," answered Valerie in a tone that implied any mother worth their salt would have dutifully sat for the additional eight hours until their child's arrival. "I was expecting a minivan. You gave me a startle when you pulled up in that—"

"Highlander. Why a minivan?"

"When you said you bought a new car, I figured you got something practical."

"I did get something practical," argued Parker. "And I would never buy a minivan. Ever." *It screams 'mom' and I've got enough in my life screaming at me.* Parker hunkered down on the porch swing with a yawn. "God, I'm tired." That's when she noticed the "broom" that Valerie had stood up was not a broom at all. "Holy fuck, Mom, is that a shotgun?"

"Twelve gauge, dear."

"Is it loaded?"

"What use is a gun that isn't?"

Parker's jaw dropped. The statement was a stark reminder of Valerie's political tendencies and her love of the NRA. "Were you expecting trouble?"

Valerie smiled. "No one ever expects trouble, Parker. But for the love of Helen Mirren, I'm a wealthy, attractive woman sitting alone on her porch waiting for a daughter who was supposed to arrive eight hours ago and never bothered to inform me she'd be late."

"Ah," Parker nodded. Her mother never swore, she only invoked the names of famous women she respected. "But now that my *kids* are living here you're going to keep all that locked up in the gun cabinet like you promised, right?"

"Of course," said Valerie, picking up the shotgun. She glanced down affectionately at the gun in her hands.

"Great," said Parker, lifting her aching bones off the bench. She rubbed her eyes as she looked back to her sleeping kids. "Everyone is beyond bath-worthy. We'll let them sleep in, then hose them off for lunch."

Valerie laughed nervously. "Lunch? Aren't you forgetting something?"

Parker snapped her fingers. "Right! I need to borrow twenty bucks." She'd already dug a considerable swearing hole before Maddy had passed out.

"Parker, tomorrow is the first day of school," reminded Valerie. "Well, today is, technically."

"What? No, school doesn't start until the 22nd."

"Correct."

"That's--" Parker checked her phone, prompting a slap to her own forehead. She'd been all turned around going from central time to mountain time to whatever time over a three-day drive that somehow became four days. *Where did I lose a day?* Parker eyed the mountain of life she'd jammed in the back of her car. "Holy shit! School starts in five hours!"

3.

I just mommed the shit out of this morning!

Parker tossed two plates of scrambled eggs, toast and bacon onto the kitchen table before her drowsy son Drew. Her toddler, Ally, wiggled in delight in her high chair at the sight of food.

That's right, I also verbed the shit out of 'mom.'

"Breakfast is served, people!" Parker proudly announced. She couldn't help but relish in her own miracle. In the past five hours, not only had she unpacked the entire car, showered or bathed all her kids, pillaged five different suitcases to find clean clothes and press them, but she'd also managed to clean up and get *herself* ready before making breakfast. All that, and still twenty minutes to spare before leaving for school.

Drew poked at the rubbery eggs before lifting the burnt toast to examine it like a forensic investigator. "Time of death," he glanced at his Power Rangers digital watch. "6:55am. Carbon scarring would indicate excessive burning."

"Oh no!" gasped Ally, slapping her round cheeks to mimic shock. It was one of three phrases she could articulate, along with "What?" and "Thank you!"

Parker patted Drew on the back. "If the eggs are a little overdone, try the bacon," she suggested.

Drew's eyes nervously bulged at the crispy black thing on his plate. "That's bacon?"

Parker ignored the comment. She leaned out of the kitchen to yell up the stairs. "Maddy, are you coming down for breakfast or what?"

"I'm coming!" Maddy answered for the fifth time.

"You bet your ass you're coming," mumbled Parker. She had just pulled off the super-mom feat of all feats, and there was no way she was going to let her oldest make them late for the first day of school. Looking to optimize her time, Parker headed for the sink to get a start on the dishes. She wrenched her wedding ring off her swollen finger and set it to the side, only to catch her ghastly reflection in a dusty window.

Parker hardly recognized the woman who stared back in a faded Bon Jovi t-shirt. The morning's sun practically shone a spot light on her streaks of grey hairs and laugh lines. Her cheeks looked rounder. At least her bloodshot eyes matched the bags beneath them. *When did all of this happen?* She wondered where the lean, athletic, no-nonsense journalist was hiding and if this new stranger had eaten her.

Valerie stepped out from behind her daughter to join the portrait of reflection. Parker couldn't help but to shake her head at the sight. Though twenty years older, Valerie remained a testament of confidence. "Are you sure I'm your daughter?" asked Parker.

"The one and only," Valerie squeezed her daughter lovingly. It was a rare display of pure, unbridled affection that took Parker by surprise. "Why don't you finish getting ready? I'll do the dishes."

"I *am* ready," insisted Parker.

"Oh," Valerie pulled away. "Sure. So, you are."

Parker rolled her eyes. Maybe the exhaustion was finally catching up to her, but her mother's judgment suddenly felt like a crushing weight. Parker tried to shake the feeling off. *What is wrong with me?* She waved her hands. "I'm sorry," she apologized. Her hands fumbled for her wedding ring on the counter. "I just--" Parker grunted. "Huh."

"What?"

"It's my—" Parker's face contorted. "My ring." She grunted again, trying to force it on. "Gahhhh, it won't fit!"

"Maybe, run it over some cold water," Valerie suggested.

Parker turned the faucet on, blasting her finger with ice cold water. To her dismay, her finger was too swollen to give in. Pain shot up her arm. "Shit! Why won't it go on?" Her breathing hastened. "Damnit, I need it to go on! Come on!"

"Try some soap."

"I am, Mom, it's not working!" Parker found herself shouting. She didn't mean to, she simply couldn't help it. "My fingers are just too—" She winced. "Swollen!"

"Swollen?"

Parker closed her eyes, feeling the tears welling up. "Thick! Large! Fat, okay? My fingers are too fat! *I'm* too fat, and I can't get my damn ring back on! I just want—" Parker let out a loud roar as she bloodied her ring finger to no avail. The ring would not fit. Parker looked up to the ceiling. "It's stupid, but, I just wanted Kurt to be here for the kids' first day, okay?"

Valerie wasn't used to seeing her daughter so vulnerable, but the exhaustion, the travelling, the coping the everything—it had all caught up. She massaged Parker's shoulders, helping the moment to pass. "Kurt *is* here," she reminded. Valerie gently guided Parker's chin to look at the two young children sitting at the kitchen table. They were the two most beautiful things Parker had ever seen, joined by a third, Maddy, who finally strolled in with her backpack in tow. Out of all of them, Maddy's brown eyes and square jaw were the most like Kurt's.

Parker smiled and wiped the tears from her face. "Thank you," she said. "I'm sorry, I don't know what came over me."

"Life came over you." Valerie started in on the dishes. "It happens."

After collecting herself, Parker jammed the wedding ring on her pinky. She turned to her kids, summoned the few remaining watts of energy she had spared over the past twenty-four hours and pumped her fists in the air triumphantly. "You guys ready for the first day of school?"

"Yeah!" shouted Drew, hoisting his fork up. The maneuver flicked bacon bits into Maddy's eye.

"Drew!" bellowed Maddy.

"Oh no!" added Ally.

Drew shrugged and went back to eating.

Maddy wiped the debris off her face and stormed over to her mother. "We're not going to be late, are we?"

Parker threw her hands on her hips in a mocking fashion. "Um, we were all waiting on *you*, so thanks for catching up."

Maddy threw her hands on her hips to mock her mother. "*Um*, you're not dressed."

"I *am* dressed. I'm rocking Bon Jovi today. He's gonna help me unpack bags and work out after I drop you off at school."

Drew raised his hand as if to practice for the first grade. "But normally you look good!" he argued. "I mean, you used to wear suits, or dresses and stuff."

Parker clutched her heart, reeling from the blast of honesty. "Yeah, well, that was when I was working. Remember, when I got fired, and we moved across country to live with Grandma, so I could focus more on doing, you know, mom things?"

"You mean *Daddy* things."

Parker smiled. Up until now, all her kids knew of the domestic life was Kurt. "Well, Mommies do them too."

Drew looked puzzled. "So, who did all those things for you? Your mommy or your daddy?"

"My Daddy couldn't," answered Parker. "He died before I was born. So, it was all Mom for me."

"How did he die?"

Valerie left her dishes, as if suddenly relishing the opportunity to explain the family history. "Well, you see," she said as she approached the table. Valerie wiped her hands on a towel as her mind drifted back forty-some years. "When I first met your grandfather, we fell madly in love. We loved each other very, very, much," she explained. "But we had waited until the night of our honeymoon to show each other *exactly* how much."

Both Drew and Maddy looked at each other in utter confusion.

Parker slapped her forehead. "Oh God." She knew this story very well but had never thought about the context in trying to explain it to children.

"And that night," continued Valerie. "I loved your grandfather, very, very, very, very much."

"Please stop."

"I filled him with so much of my love that his heart couldn't take it – and it burst."

Drew's jaw dropped. "Like – exploded? No way!"

"And he filled me with—"

Parker stepped in like a coach trying to call off a bad play. "Alright, Mom! Thank you! We don't need the play by play."

Valerie arched a brow. She smiled. "Anyway, nine months later your mother was born."

Maddy didn't know exactly what had just happened but decided things had gotten way off track. "So, why can't you look nice for our first day of school?"

Parker had to work much harder to smile now. *Because, giving birth to a child after forty made my metabolism take an elephant-sized shit!* With the added stress of losing Kurt, trying to juggle a full-time job while being a single parent – eating right and exercising just wasn't a priority. But all of this seemed way too much to explain to an eleven-year-old. Instead, Parker shot a glance at Valerie. "Did you put her up to this?"

Valerie raised her hands into a "don't shoot" pose, to which Drew immediately took notice and quickly formed his fingers into a gun.

"Grandma! Pow! Pow!" shouted Drew as he pretended to shoot Valerie.

Valerie clutched her heart and smiled. "Ohhhh, right in the heart! You got me!"

"Oh no!" Ally added, more concerned than ever.

Drew aimed for Maddy. "Maddy! Pow! Pow!"

Maddy held up her hand to deflect the imaginary bullets and stomped her foot. "Can we focus here, people? This is about mom's awful wardrobe!"

"Don't be rude," Parker shot back. "And that's 'Mom, the Almighty.' You owe me five bucks."

In a rare display of solidarity, or in an effort not to get pummeled later by his older sister, Drew suddenly joined Maddy's plea. "But Mommy, you look so pretty when you dress up. Will you change? *Please*?"

Parker sighed, looking at the clock again. It was twelve minutes before they had to leave for school. She had to admit her sweat pants and Bon Jovi t-shirt had seen better days. "Fine. You know what? You're right. It's my first day of school too, and it wouldn't hurt to make a better impression. Give me ten minutes to change."

4.

Twenty-three minutes later...

I look like an extra in an 80's themed porno.

As Parker screeched her Highlander around the street corner, she couldn't help but to stare at her cleavage in the rearview mirror wondering if it was too much for a school setting. Her navy dress suit and white blouse were bursting at the seams, amplifying every curve and fold on her body, but she couldn't help it. It was the one nice looking outfit she could squeeze into in the time she had. Despite the adrenaline rush, Parker tried to breathe slowly, for fear one of her shirt buttons might fire into the windshield and spill her boobs out onto the dashboard. She glanced at the clock – 7:32am.

Parker stomped her foot onto the accelerator.

"Are we late?" asked Maddy. Her fingers firmly dug into the passenger seat's armrests.

How could we possibly be late, when it took me twenty minutes to cram myself into this skirt?

"We're in hot pursuit!" Drew gave the thumbs up from the seat behind. He enjoyed the tight turns and the roar of the V6 engine.

Parker gritted her teeth as she rounded another tight corner. She remembered enough about Oak Creek to know that the Elementary school should be after the next bend. At her current speed, they'd have no problem flying in to the parking lot on time, but it was going to be close. "Shit!" Parker slammed on the breaks, jostling her two passengers. Parker was thankful Ally had stayed home with Valerie.

"Shit?" asked Drew. "What's a shit?"

Our morning is about to take one, thought Parker. And yet --
"Really? You've never heard me use that word before?"

"It's a bad word," answered Maddy, glaring at her mother. "Don't repeat it."

"Your sister is right, don't repeat it, it's just—" Parker frowned at the endless line of stopped cars waiting to make a left turn into the school's parking lot up ahead. An equally long line of cars approaching from the opposite lane were also waiting to enter the lot. It was as though every parent in town had decided to arrive at precisely the same time for the first day of school. *Go figure.*

"Is this going to make us late?" Maddy whined.

"Cool it, Maddy, all these other families are going to be late too."

"So, we *are* late!" The confirmation was all Maddy needed to justify a freak out.

"Mom said 'cool it', Maddy!" shouted Drew.

"Shut up, Drew!"

"Quiet! Both of you!" Parker yelled, a little too loud this time as the top button of her blouse popped off and hit the dashboard. She bowed her head. Losing that single button might have just promoted her from 80's porn extra to the starring role. Parker scanned the surrounding area. Traffic wasn't moving, she was at the end of a long line, and the last thing she wanted was to initiate a huge "Mom-Fail" on her kid's first day in a new school by making them tardy. *That's the word, right? Tardy? Stupid word.* Parker quickly formulated her plan of attack. "We're going to park and walk the last few blocks."

"Park *where*?" blasted Maddy. "The streets are full of cars!"

"Umm, *duh*, we're going to park right *here*," she sneered as she pulled into the first driveway of the house on the street corner. It was a small two-story home painted a bright lime green that

23

appeared as though its occupants were already off at work. At least, that's what Parker hoped.

"Do you know who lives here?"

"I'm pretty sure Grandma knows them," Parker bluffed. Though the statement couldn't be that far off from the truth. Valerie Parker, the woman who had killed her husband with sex was a legend in Oak Creek. "Besides, we'll be back and gone before they know it. Let's go."

The trio pounded the sidewalks with a brisk pace, rushing to catch up with the mass of families heading to school grounds. Parker checked her phone -- two minutes to spare. She rechecked the school registration email. "Alright, Maddy, we're going to drop you off at your classroom first," she informed with confidence and authority. "Then Drew, you and I will go to your classroom. You'll stay with your classes and meet at the playground for the flag assembly greeting thingy, and boom, we're golden until pick up time."

"Do I have piano lessons after school?" prodded Maddy.

"Maddy, I haven't even found a teacher yet."

Maddy sulked in disappointment.

"We've lived here six hours, Maddy!" Parker explained. "I know how it important it is, just give me some time, okay? Maybe ask your music teacher if he knows anybody when you see him in class."

Luckily, Maddy's homeroom was a short but crowded stroll away. As with most of the classrooms, it featured a side door that opened directly to the playground area. Parker gave her oldest an awkward squeeze before sending her off to the care of Ms. Brandy, a middle-aged hipster in a long flowing skirt, and curly hair and an excess of beaded necklaces.

Maddy stopped halfway into the classroom and looked back at her mother. "You're gonna be here, right?" she asked. "At the end? For pick up?"

Parker forced a smile. "Of course!"

"You won't forget?"

Parker's insides wrenched into a knot, which were already under plenty of punishment from the tight fit of her under-sized pencil skirt. "Maddy—this isn't Chicago. Let's make it a fresh start, okay? *Please?*"

Maddy gave a slow nod. Without another word, she turned and disappeared into the classroom.

Drew tugged at his mother's skirt. "She's still mad at you about Chicago," he explained.

"I got that, thank you," said Parker.

"She's dealing with a lot of change and misses her friends."

Parker blinked in astonishment as she looked down at her little man. Drew's poignant comments between fart jokes could make him sound like it wasn't his first trip around life's merry-go-round. "What about you? Don't you miss your friends?"

Drew shrugged. "We had a big blowout over Pokémon Go." He hung his head, as if in mourning. After a brief respite, he looked up to his mother hopefully. "But, this is first grade. I'll make new friends."

Parker nodded. At least she hadn't entirely screwed up one of her kids – yet. "Let's get you to class."

5.

"Welcome students. Welcome parents. Welcome all, to another fabulous year of learning at Oak Creek Elementary!"

A lot had changed at Oak Creek since Parker's own elementary days. Twenty years of renovation, demolition and addition had transformed the campus into a mish mash of modern architecture. But the one thing that had not changed was the shrill voice that blasted over the PA system to greet Parker and the hundreds of students and parents who were packed shoulder to shoulder onto the hot black tar of the playground. The voice belonged to a small, petite elderly woman who stood proudly at the microphoned podium that dwarfed her. Karen Heller still wore her jet-black died hair pulled into a tight ballerina bun and donned a stiff, tweed suit.

"Holy hell," Parker gasped under her breath. "That crazy old chick is still alive!"

"Shhhhhh!" a baby-faced mother angrily glared at Parker and pressed her finger to her lips.

"Relax," Parker assured her. "*Old Yeller Heller* gave the same speech even when I went to school here." To prove it, Parker matched the next refrain of Heller's speech, word for word.

"—Your children are the future of our community," Heller started.

"Our nation," Parker recalled from memory, matching Heller's cadence perfectly. "And our world." Parker put her hands together to fain prayer and sell the sincerity to the baby-faced mother.

This performance did little to impress Baby-Face, who angrily pushed her stroller away.

Of course, when Parker was a kid, Karen Heller was only *vice* principal at Oak Creek Elementary. Forty years later, Parker assumed she'd been given the top spot of Principal. Parker assumed the younger, Latina woman, sharply dressed in magenta standing behind Heller just off to one side might be the new vice principal. She wondered if this woman might pray for the day Heller finally combusted into ash like a vampire exposed to too much sunlight, so that she might earn her own battlefield promotion.

Heller droned on, as Parker continued to recite her speech. "We owe it to our children to ensure they can learn in a safe and productive environment." they spoke together.

Parents joined in a chorus of "Shhhhhh!" to shame Parker into silence.

"Fine!" Parker shot back in an excited whisper. Feeling the focused heat of stares, she retreated deeper into the playground when her phone suddenly blasted with the chorus of "Living on a Prayer."

More angry glares and "Shhhhhh's" followed Parker as her fingers fumbled for the phone in the mousetrap that was her purse. Not wanting to attract any more attention, Parker slinked further toward the back, hoping the derelict parents that likely hung out there might be more tolerant of her antics. When Parker detected the rude whispers of other folks on their phones, she knew she'd found a safe space.

Parker glanced at her missed call. It was Jerry, her former editor from the *American Times*, now playing the role of the dickhead who didn't fight for her job. Parker stared at his number angrily, when her finely trained ears tuned into some gossip trading behind her.

"No, no, no," a man whispered. "She's a *clumsy* kind of hot. Like in an Amy Schumer, or Meghan Trainor kind of way."

Parker's eyes burned. *Who are they talking about?* She didn't want to turn her head and let on she was eavesdropping. She slowly lifted her phone, thinking she might use the reverse camera for a subtle peek.

The man continued. "The way that skirt is hugging her ass? Yup. I would tap that!"

Oh hell, thought Parker. *He better not be talking about me.*

Heller's voice droned on. "—which is why we encourage all parents to become a part of our school. Join the PTA. Get involved with your children."

Parker was barely paying attention to Heller anymore, only the whispers behind her. A woman joined in.

"Are you kidding? Her skirt is crying it is so stretched right now! And that top is practically strangling her," the woman corrected. "The ensemble is at least three sizes too small. Ten bucks says she shows up tomorrow in a t-shirt and sweat pants."

That's what I was going to wear today!

Parker's phone suddenly vibrated in her hand from another incoming call, startling her into dropping it. The phone rattled on the black top as Bon Jovi informed everyone they should 'take his hand, because he swears they'll make it this time.' Parker cursed as she bent over to pick up the phone, hoping she wouldn't split her skirt in half.

"Oh, wow, thank you for that view," whispered the woman sarcastically.

"It's gonna be a great day!" said the man.

They are talking about me!

6.

In a fit of righteous anger...

Parker turned off her phone, tossed it in her purse and spun around with a clenched fist to greet her judges. The first was a tall, thin man with a thick moustache, a Hawaiian shirt and skinny jeans who looked like a poor man's version of Magnum PI. The second judge came in the form of a bleached blonde bombshell with an orange tinted tan. The woman's athletic build hinted that her choice of expensive active wear wasn't just for show. She was in tip-top shape. But if it came down to a brawl, Parker calculated Blondie wouldn't expect a hard punch to the boob followed by an eye gouge.

For now, Parker chose to unload on the unlikely pair with her words. She started with the Blonde. "You won't like the view when I ram my foot so far up your ass you'll be coughing up Jimmy Choo's for a week." And then to Mr. Moustache. "And you! Meghan Trainor? Are you fucking kidding me? You're old enough to be her father!"

The ends of the man's moustache curved up into an alarmingly white smile. "But never too old to be her 'daddy,' am I right?" He lifted his hand in hopes to receive a high five from anyone who might be listening. "Don't leave me hanging now."

"Gross!" giggled the blonde. "Glory, you are hopeless!"

Glory – is that this creep's name?

Glory and the blonde could barely contain their giggling despite the sheer anger radiating off Parker's body. When the pair finally realized Parker wasn't smiling, they tried to settle down. "Oh, relax, we're just having fun," explained the woman. "We know we're terrible people. We judge *everyone*. It's just how we pass the time when Heller goes off on one of her—" the woman paused. Her eyes lit up as she studied Parker's face. "O-M-G! Parker? Parker is that you?"

Parker squinted. Strip twenty years off the blonde, lose the tan and change her hair to a deep brown and you had – "Julie Kimball?" gasped Parker. Julie Kimball was Parker's classmate for nearly every grade in her academic career, beginning with Oak Creek Elementary. They were never close friends but became well acquainted having spent so many years going to the same schools.

"It is you!" squealed Julie at the top of her lungs. The squeal was so loud that Principal Heller stopped her speech mid-sentence, punctuated by a loud microphone squawk that nearly deafened the entire audience.

"Is there a problem back there?" asked Heller, stretching over her podium to see to the back of the playground. "I heard a commotion. Do you need assistance? I heard some kind of scream."

All eyes turned to look at Glory, Julie and Parker. Parker sighed. *Please don't lump me in with these two.*

"No scream, just a squeal of delight! Sorry!" yelled Julie. "Ran into an old friend! Everyone, this is Parker Monroe!" Julie lifted her hand over Parker's head to point down on her. "She's new here! Kind of! Be sure to give her and her family a warm Oak Creek welcome! That's *Parker Monroe*! Remember that name! Sorry! Carry on! Carry on!"

Heller nodded. "Thank you for that delightful introduction Ms. Kimball," said Heller. "And as for you, Parker Monroe—*welcome back*."

The words nearly sent chills up Parker's spine. Those were the same words Heller would use during Parker's visits to detention. Parker's list of offenses was long and distinguished, not the least of which was coining Heller's nickname: "Old Yeller Heller."

Does she remember me?

30

Principal Heller moved on with her speech. "As I was saying—"

Parker shook her chills loose as she turned back to Julie. "Holy shit, Julie, what are you doing with this creep?" She jammed her thumb in Glory's direction.

Julie laughed. "Glory? Oh, he's harmless. And he's the best plumber in town. That's how we met."

"I'm good with the pipes," added Glory. "All kinds of pipes."

Parker couldn't help but to notice Glory taking long peeks at her over-exposed cleavage. Parker tried to pull her suit jacket together and button up, but the tight fit made it impossible. She settled for a verbal swipe. "Oooooh, a plumber with a moustache! How original."

"Ouch," said Glory. "But I won't take it personally. In fact, I'm going to put you on my personal list to earn a special Glory discount for all your plumbing needs. You're welcome."

Parker had to swallow whatever bit of breakfast she had just regurgitated.

Julie grimaced. "Wait, is this some kind of MILF discount list?"

"I have a very complex ranking system." Glory raised his phone, proudly displaying a list of names and numbers. "Don't worry, you're on the list."

Julie wagged a finger at her friend. "First, I am disgusted you keep such a list. Second, I better be at the *top* of that list, because I don't work out three hours a day to come in second at anything."

"—and so, let us all work together for a brighter future. Have a great first day of school everyone. You are dismissed!" Heller finally concluded.

Julie pumped her fist into the air like a cheerleader, pretending as though she'd heard the entirety of Heller's speech. "Gooooo, Oak Creek!" Then to Parker. "I gotta say goodbye to my kids. Let's get

31

coffee sometime!" And just like that, Julie and Glory disappeared into the dispersing body of parents, leaving Parker to shake her head.

What the hell just happened?

Parker wasn't sure if seeing Julie again was a blessing or a curse, even without the Glory factor. Regardless, if Parker was to slam-dunk her first-*first* day of school experience as a doting mother she'd better say goodbye to her own kids. Parker scanned the crowd to see if she could catch one last glimpse of either of her kids as they walked with their class lines to their homerooms. There, in the distance was Maddy, who glanced back for a split second before she turned away.

Is she pretending she didn't see me?

Maddy disappeared around the corner.

Parker turned to the first-grade lines and spotted Drew in the middle of his. He didn't see her. Determined to end the morning on a high note, Parker raised her hand and shouted. "Drew!" she waved. "Drew!"

Drew finally heard his mother's call and turned to smile at her.

The smile melted Parker's heart and wiped away all the awkwardness of the morning. Not wanting the moment to end, Parker decided to play the same game she saw Drew and Valerie play earlier. She raised her hand and positioned her fingers into the shape of a pistol and aimed at her son. "Pow! Pow!" she popped excitedly.

Drew laughed and aimed back with a pair of his own finger guns. "Pow! Pow! Pow!" he shouted back.

Parker clutched her heart, determined to secure the Oscar nomination this time with an over the top performance that would make Jennifer Lawrence jealous. "You got me!" she cried and laughed.

Drew laughed as he continued to shoot his mom.

"You got me again!"

Thank you for that, Drew.

Parker waved goodbye one last time and turned to leave the playground, only to find the small but rigid form of Karen Heller blocking her way. "Oh!" Parker greeted in surprise. "Hello there!"

Principal Heller slowly folded her arms. "Ms. Monroe," she greeted coldly. "I'm afraid I need you and your son need to come with me."

7.

"We have a zero-tolerance policy for guns,"

explained Principal Heller from behind her large oak wood desk. The perfectly square office was not the one Parker remembered from her youth, but Heller's steely gaze of unwavering judgment was all too familiar.

Parker sat in a smaller chair alongside Drew, whose wide-eyes and trembling shoulders were the only clues he hadn't yet died of shock. Despite her son's terror, Parker kept her cool and armed herself with her best version of a charming smile to help clear up whatever was going on. "No guns at school," she concurred. "I completely agree. So, what is the problem?"

Heller kneaded her hands together and placed them on her desk. "You and your son shot each other with guns."

Parker's smile widened. "We *pretended* to shoot each other with our fingers."

"Fingers that were made to look like guns."

Parker couldn't help but to have a small chuckle. "Sure, but they weren't actual guns. We were just playing."

"Zero tolerance includes all guns, Ms. Monroe," argued Heller. "Even play guns. A gun, is a gun is a gun."

"Except when it's not a gun, and it's a hand with fingers." Parker aimed her fingers at Heller to illustrate the point, but quickly realized it only served to irritate her more. She clumsily transitioned her hands into jazz hands. "I can do many things with these fingers, see?" Parker deftly arranged her fingers into various puppets. "I can make a rabbit with ears. A duck. A heart." *I can even flip you the bird if I wanted to.*

34

Heller sighed. "Did you not shoot at your son, Ms. Monroe? Did he not gleefully fire back? In front of everyone on my playground?"

"Well, in a manner of speaking, I suppose we did, but it's no more dangerous than a metaphor or a song." Parker snapped her fingers as she attempted the chorus to an old favorite. "You know—'shot through the heart, and you're too blame! You give love—a bad name!' Yes? No? That ring a bell? Bon Jovi? Surely you've heard of Bon Jovi?"

Heller's cold eyes did not so much as blink.

Parker sat back in her chair, which felt tinier by the second. "Maybe that was before your time." *You know, the Dark Ages. I shouldn't have snapped. Who snaps to a Bon Jovi song? That's lame.*

"Zero tolerance, Ms. Monroe," chided Heller. "Guns are not allowed in any form, even in play form, and *we* don't want to encourage guns in a school setting. Both you and your son violated a strict rule. An example must be made."

Drew carefully leaned over to this mother and whispered to her out of the corner of his mouth. "Am I in trouble?"

"What? No!" Parker insisted. Her blood began to boil. "Don't be ridiculous!" Parker clenched her fist. She'd tried being polite, but that didn't seem to be getting her anywhere. It was time to ratchet things up. Parker straightened her posture and leaned forward, ready to tear into Heller when Heller's cell phone suddenly buzzed alive.

The principal glanced at the screen. "I must take this." Her wrinkled, liver spotted claw of a hand put the phone to her ear. "Yes?"

Parker could hear a muffled voice responding.

Heller's eyes darted anxiously from side to side. "You found a car parked in our driveway? A Toyota Highlander?"

You gotta be shitting me.

35

The muffled voice on Heller's phone continued.

"It's blocked you in?" asked Heller, her tone growing icier with each word. "No, I didn't tell anyone they could park there. Yes, I understand you're late to the doctor's. But what can I do about it? Call the Sheriff. Report it. Have it towed. I don't know what else to tell you. Yes. Call me when it's done." Heller pushed a button to end the call, and then looked around as if searching for a place to slam the phone into a cradle like the good old days. When she couldn't find one, she drew in a deep breath and retrained her eyes back on Parker, who offered a nervous smile back.

Fuck! There goes my moral high ground.

Drew shifted in his seat. "Mom, that sounds an awful lot like—"

"Some people," interrupted Parker as she patted Drew on the back – hard. "Parking in driveways they shouldn't. Soooo rude. You're going to have it towed, huh?"

"Why—is it yours?"

Parker froze, and then did her best to look offended by the suggestion.

Heller watched Parker like an FBI interrogator waiting for the pupils to dilate. Finally, she let out a sinister chuckle. "I'm only kidding, Ms. Monroe. I think you'd be smarter than to do that."

Parker titled her jaw awkwardly as though recovering from a strong right jab.

"You were always a bit of a spitfire, Ms. Monroe." Heller looked at Drew. "Your mother used to cause me quite a bit of trouble during her time here."

"She did?" asked Drew.

"I would hate to see you fall in the same pattern. We don't allow guns in school young man, pretend or otherwise. But you're new, so I'm going to let you off easy with a one-day suspension."

Drew's eyes popped open. "Suspension? What is that?" he asked his mother. "Is that bad?"

8.

Parker exploded out of her chair.

"It's his first day of school!" she spat. "Hell, it's his first day of elementary! Ever!"

Heller's smile faded. "There is no need to raise your voice, Ms. Monroe. I am not the one who demonstrated such awful judgment. Guns are a serious offense."

"Mom?" Drew cried, his eyes welling up with tears.

Parker swallowed her words to keep from raising her voice. "Principal Heller, Drew did nothing wrong. He was only following my lead in a silly game we play at home."

"Ms. Monroe, I have no authority to punish you, other than to inform you of the error of your judgment, poor behavior and even poorer choice of wardrobe for a school setting."

Parker clenched her fist. "I lost a button, okay?" she explained. "Listen, Principal Heller, I'm begging you, give Drew some kind of warning, or community service or whatever you want, anything, *anything* but starting his academic career with a suspension! Surely, as someone whose job it is to develop young minds you can see how much over-kill this is!"

Heller blinked. Was she considering the idea? Before she could answer, there was a knock at the door. Heller's eyes darted to the young Latina woman in magenta who casually strolled into the office as though she owned it. Parker recognized her as the woman who stood behind Heller during the Flag Assembly. The woman was immaculately groomed, and her suit was in the same cut as Parker's − only it fit her young, slender frame perfectly. "Vice Principal Heller," the woman greeted. "I'm sorry to interrupt, but I need my office back to make some important phone calls."

Parker's eyes widened. *Holy fuck! Vice Principal Heller?*

If Heller were capable of blushing, this might have been the moment. But instead the ends of her wrinkled mouth turned slightly downward into a frown. "Principal Mendez," she greeted. "Ms. Monroe and I were just discussing the inappropriate behavior displayed by her and her son on school grounds."

"I'm sure you've been very thorough," said Mendez. "Have you met with Mr. Bernstein like you said you would?"

"No," Heller replied coolly.

"Then I guess we both have things to do," decided Mendez. "I'll finish up with Ms. Monroe." She gently leaned toward Drew with a smile. "And it's probably time this young man went to class. We don't want you to fall behind on your first day, now do we? Vice Principal Heller can show you the way before she follows up with Mr. Bernstein." She turned to Parker. "Ms. Monroe, I'd appreciate it if you stayed a moment after the others leave."

Relieved, Drew smiled and wiped his tears away. "Thank you, Ma'am."

"Off you go," said Mendez. Then to Heller. "Both of you."

Drew gave his mother a squeeze before grabbing his Plants vs. Zombies backpack and heading to the door to wait for Heller. The vice principal slowly stood up from the desk and walked over to join him, not so much as glancing in Parker's direction. "Come with me, Mr. Monroe," ordered Heller.

The door shut automatically behind them.

Parker couldn't help but to smile as she turned to the young woman who now sat at the desk of power. "Principal Mendez, is it? I must apologize, I thought Heller was the principal."

"I prefer that Heller be the public face of our school," explained Mendez as she thumbed through her phone, as if searching for a number. "She's been here forever, and we share this office, so

39

naturally parents assume she's the one in charge. I don't mind. I'm busy enough trying to fix our budget and – other things."

"Of course," said Parker. "And thank you for bailing me out there."

"Don't thank me," chided Mendez. "Just make sure there's no more gunplay, pretend or otherwise. You know as well as I that guns are a hot button issue, especially pertaining to children and schools. The last thing we need is some hysterical parent misunderstanding something they saw and suing the district for negligence. We live in a world where common sense is a scarce commodity."

Parker nodded, impressed with the young woman's answer. "Well put." She gathered her purse and was halfway out the door when she turned back to Mendez in the middle of dialing a number. "Sorry, before I go, may I ask why Heller isn't principal? You said so yourself, she's been here forever."

"Digging for dirt on a new story, Ms. Monroe?" asked Mendez, offering a sly grin.

"You're familiar with my work."

"I'd always assumed you were a man with a name like Parker until I saw your picture all over cable news," Mendez chuckled. "If you want to know Vice Principal Heller's story just ask her."

Yes, thought Parker. *Maybe I should ask Heller for a ride to the car pound too.*

"Now if you'll excuse me." Mendez flicked her wrist toward the door.

Did you just dismiss me?

Parker felt her neck strain from the smile she forced. "Of course," she apologized. The last thing she needed was to get on this principal's bad side too.

Parker softly shut the door behind her and stepped into the empty hallways of Oak Creek Elementary. All children were safely nestled away in their classrooms, leaving an eerie silence to linger in the toner-scented air. It was the first moment of calm Parker had experienced in months. The stillness reminded her of walking into the morgue that fateful day. The phone rang at four in the morning. Before she answered the unfamiliar number, she knew it would be the police. She knew they'd found Kurt. She knew she would be asked to come in and identify his body.

When Parker finally stood in that cold morgue, and the doctor pulled back the cloth, and Parker viewed what was left of her husband, it was as though all the sound in the world was sucked out of existence at that precise moment. A moment, that lasted for a dreadful eternity.

Suddenly, a man's voice broke the silence.

Kurt?

Parker blinked as her mind raced back to the present day. She once again stood in the school halls. Parker wiped a tear from her cheek as her ears perked. A man's voice exploded out of the silence again. Sharp. Angry. An argument was ensuing close by.

Curious, Parker stepped forward, catching flashes of children working at their desks through the window slivers of doors she passed by.

The man's voice lowered to a harsh whisper now, and it came from a darkened room near the end of the long hallway.

"That is unacceptable!" the man spat in a breathy voice. "Unprofessional! And you know it!"

Parker crept slowly to the room's entryway, where the door was barely ajar. She could see a few desks and music stands and make out brass instruments hanging on the far wall. The room was no doubt a music room – but why was class not in session?

"This wasn't my decision," a hushed old woman's voice answered.

Parker knew that voice — it was Heller's. She leaned forward to confirm with a closer peek. Just around the edge of the doorway, Parker spotted Old Yeller Heller frowning at the man who argued with her — just out of sight.

Heller went on. "Don't be angry with me. She insisted it happen today. It's all her doing." The old woman's words dripped with disdain.

Who is she talking about? Principal Mendez?

Parker blinked to clear her head. This is none of my business. I should walk away right now before I'm discovered and even in more trouble.

Suddenly, the man's hands firmly grabbed Heller by her arms, startling her. "That's a load of shit." He growled.

Parker's heart raced. She clenched her fist, ready to spring into action. She had no love for Heller, but if the old hag was being threatened, Parker would have to step in.

Heller's eyes remained calmed and focused on the man who gripped her so tightly. "You will kindly remove your hands," she demanded.

The hands eased their grip, as if suddenly realizing what they were doing, then slowly dropped to pull away.

"I didn't mean to—" one of the man's hands clenched into a fist. "This is on you, Heller. However this goes down? You own it."

Heller's eyes darted to the doorway, prompting Parker to step back. After a moment, Heller's eyes returned to the man and stayed glued to him as she slowly reached for the door handle to shut it. The door latched shut, muffling the rest of their conversation.

Parker released a long exhale. *That was tense. I'll give it to Heller, though, she can handle herself.*

Jon Bon Jovi parsed Parker's thoughts as he announced to the world he was once again, living on a prayer from her phone.

I really need to turn that down.

Parker quickly plucked her phone from her purse and put it to her cheek. "Hello?" she asked. She exited the empty school hallway – unaware of the vice principal's eyes that trained on her like a hawk from the sliver of a reopened doorway.

9.

"Where in the name of Julie Andrews are you?"

blasted Valerie over Parker's phone. "You were supposed to be home thirty minutes ago so I could head to lunch with Daisy and the girls."

"I'm just leaving the school now," answered Parker as she stepped onto the school parking lot. "I served hard time in the principal's office for brandishing a weapon on school grounds."

"What?"

"I'll fill you in later. Listen, Mom, can you come and pick me up? I need to get to the car pound."

"I can't tell if you're joking."

"I wish I was. My car has been towed."

"What do you mean? Is something wrong with the car? It's a brand-new car!"

"No, nothing is wrong with the—" Parker pinched the bridge of her nose. She felt a massive headache coming on. "Mom, please, just grab Ally and get over to the school."

"I can't do that, Parker, the only car seat for Ally was in your Highlander."

Oh, that damn car seat. Parker lived for the day Ally wouldn't need it anymore. "Can't we just skip it this one time? I'm literally stranded here."

"Do you know what the fine is in Southern California if you're caught carting a toddler around without a car seat?"

"No."

"I don't either, but I presume it's astronomical."

Parker wanted to reach through her cell phone and shake her mother. "Are you seriously not going to come and pick me up?"

"Listen, Parker, I'll call Daisy and reschedule so I can watch Ally. But I'm not going to tote her around town without a car seat when you can just as easily call a ride share or a cab."

"Yeah, yeah, I got it, thanks for the help, Mom." Parker stabbed her finger at her phone, abruptly ending the call. She didn't need to be so short with her mother, but she was tired and exhausted and needed this god forsaken morning to end.

Parker's thumb flipped through her apps on her phone. *Does Oak Creek even have a cab service?* The town hardly seemed big enough. She decided to try for a ride share.

A driver is three minutes away, the app informed.

After a few lonely minutes of standing on the corner sidewalk, Parker's ears caught the roaring engine of a black, 1982 Pontiac Firebird Trans Am as it screeched around the corner. With its tan trimming, the Trans Am could've doubled for the car in the old David Hasselhoff TV show called Knight Rider. It merely lacked the pulsing red LED on the front hood.

The Trans Am skidded to a halt before Parker, revealing another distinct difference from its television doppelganger. The side door carried a large white label that read: "Wonder Plumbing."

Plumbing. Plumbing? What? No – it couldn't be!

The passenger window lowered to reveal the moustache framed smile of the Tom Selleck - wannabe Parker had encountered only an hour earlier – Glory the Plumber. "Evening!" greeted Glory.

Parker sighed. *Fuck no.* "It's still the morning."

"Yeah it is," agreed Glory. "But you need a ride, right?"

45

"Me? No," Parker subtly cancelled her car ride on her phone. She glanced at the back seat of the Trans Am to make sure there were no women tied up in it. All she saw was a messy pile of plumber's equipment, pipes and wrenches. "No, it must have been that *other* guy," she lied. "He's gone now."

"Really?" Glory puckered his lips. "Darn. Who picked him up? Was it a guy in an A-Team van? Or a guy in a DeLorean?"

Parker grimaced. *What's with all the 80's vehicles?* "I wasn't paying that close attention."

Glory shook his head. "Son of a bitch, those guys are always taking my fares," he grumbled. "You sure you don't need a ride?"

Parker folded her arms. "I thought you were a plumber?"

"I am a plumber," said Glory, almost offended by the statement. "But when I fix stuff, it stays fixed, you know? So, on slow days, I drive for a ride share. Or deliver pizza. Or hang Christmas lights. But you know, that's around Christmas time. I got skills!"

"I have no doubt," Parker bit her lip. Glory might be creepy as all hell, but he was honestly no worse than half of Parker's contacts in Chicago. And with as much as he drove around town and serviced people he might have some useful knowledge. "Listen, Glory, how well do you know Oak Creek?"

"Born and raised," he answered. "I know her inside and out."

Yuck. "A friend of mine had her car towed this morning. Any idea where she might find it?"

Glory's eyes widened. "Was she the one who parked at Heller's house?"

"Maybe?" Parker scratched her head. "I didn't ask. Did someone park at Heller's house?"

"It's all over social media. The PTA is up in arms about it. Nobody recognized the car, but if they ever find out--"

"Yeah, yeah, yeah, so where is the car pound again?"

"The Sheriff's office," answered Glory. He pointed just ahead through the windshield. "On main street, about five miles South. Go up Chalmers Avenue, then take a left on Main."

Five miles? She looked at her black Jimmy Choo pumps. *In these things?* Parker had a hard choice to make.

10.

"You sure you don't want a ride?"

Glory's smile was all but gone now.

Parker bit her lip so hard her teeth nearly broke the skin. Riding with Glory would save her a ton of time, but she wanted more out of the deal. An idea hit her. "I will take that ride, Glory, but can you do me a favor first?"

"Sure."

Parker stepped a few paces back and raised her phone. "Just smile for the camera."

Glory gave his best smile and even pointed a gun finger at Parker for extra flare.

"Thank you," said Parker as she snapped the picture. She immediately texted the picture to her mother along with the message: *You left me no choice. If I am not home before noon, call the police.* "Alright, Glory, get me to that car pound."

"Alright!" Glory's triumphant smile widened. He revved his engine. "Hop in!"

There would be no hopping. Parker did her best to climb into the low riding car without splitting her skirt or popping any more shirt buttons. The car smelled of leather, old pizza, metal and something she could only guess was "plumber's butt." She hadn't even completely closed the door before Glory peeled out.

Valerie replied with her own text: *Oh, that's Glory! He's a hoot! Say hello!*

Parker cringed upon reading it. *Of course, my mother would know him.*

As Glory sped to the first stop sign, Parker couldn't help but to notice Huey Lewis and the News' *Power of Love* blasting from the stereo. "You know, you've got the wrong song playing for this car," she stated.

"Say what?" Glory's tone betrayed a legitimate concern, but his eyes stayed glued to the road with his hands firmly in the ten and two positions on the wheel.

"This song is from the movie *Back to the Future*," explained Parker. "If you're going for the whole Knight Rider thing with this car, you need the theme song from that show. Or at least something by Hasselhoff."

"Oh shit, really?" asked Glory. "Was Hasselhoff like some kind of famous composer?"

"*What?*"

"You know, like that Mozart guy?"

"How would you not know who Hasselhoff is?"

"I think he was before my time."

Parker winced. "You're not an 80's child?"

Glory laughed and checked himself out in the rearview mirror. "It's the moustache, right? Makes me look way older! I wasn't even alive in the 80's!" Glory took another corner. "I only graduated like ten years ago."

The statement blew Parker's mind. Suddenly, she felt very old, and Glory's youth became overly obvious. His skin was that of a man in his twenties, and his soft hands were now a dead giveaway. Parker must have missed it all before because she refused to look at him. Her mind now raced to make sense of the anomaly chauffeuring her. "And you're also a parent?"

"My boy's a second grader – Gavin. I try to work as much as I can while he's in school."

49

Parker studied Glory more closely now. The moustache, the Hawaiian shirt, none of it made sense. "What about Mrs. Glory?"

Glory smiled. "Oh, there is no missus. Glory runs a free market, know what I mean?"

God help me. "So why are you driving a car that is older than you?"

"Oh, this thing?" laughed Glory. "My ride share buddies and I get together every year and decide on a theme, right? We buy old beaters, spruce 'em up, and it's like, fun for the older passengers. *You* know. This year, we went with 80's action cars!"

Parker couldn't help but to shake her head in disbelief. Now everything was starting to make some kind of deranged sense. "With the shirt and the moustache, I figured you'd be driving a red Ferrari like Magnum, PI."

"Yeah, Magnum. That's who I am, right? I'm Magnum! Like the condom!"

"No, like the Private Investigator. You've got the wrong car. This is the KITT car."

"No shit? What's KITT look like? She hot?"

"KITT *is* the car," Parker threw her hands up. "Oh wow, I thought kids your age were obsessed with the 80's! You've got so much to learn!"

Glory smiled. "I'm willing to learn."

"*Careful,* Glory," Parker flashed him a stern look, but hid her own smile. *Maybe Glory wasn't so bad?* She wanted to test him further. "What do you know about Vice Principal Heller?"

"Who?"

Clearly, if a woman wasn't on Glory's bedroom radar, she didn't exist. "Scratch that. What do you know about Principal Mendez?"

50

Glory smiled. "She's *super* hot. And new. And *hot.* This is her first year at Oak Creek, I think. But there was no announcement or anything. To be honest, it feels like she just kind of came out of nowhere."

Parker allowed herself an approving smile. "Interesting."

Glory slammed on the breaks, pulling up alongside the brick building that served as the Sheriff's office. "Alright, alright, here we are!"

Parker nodded. "Thanks for the ride." She awkwardly climbed out of the car, once again trying not to flash her driver one way or the other.

"My pleasure," answered Glory. "Any time you need a ride, you just let 'Ol Glory know."

"I will."

"And not just for a ride share, I mean sex too, okay?" Glory tried to shout out his clarification as fast as he could before Parker slammed the door shut.

Parker waved goodbye, pretending not to have heard the invitation. Glory's Trans Am disappeared around the corner.

11.

Parker had never been to the Oak Creek Sheriff's department before and wasn't sure what to expect –

other than it might be occupied by living, breathing people wearing unflattering tan and brown uniforms. There was none of that. When Parker first walked through the tinted glass door, there was no one sitting behind the bulletproof shielding at the front desk. No deputies were in sight. Only an elderly, petite Latina woman sat in the corner of the lobby with a half-finished needlepoint of a rose in her lap. Her wrinkled hands never moved, her beady eyes never blinked, and her breathing remained so shallow that Parker briefly wondered if she had died of old age in that exact spot.

"Hello?" asked Parker to the room. She stepped up to the speaker on the bulletproof glass and pressed the intercom button. "Is anyone here?"

There was no response.

Parker trained her eyes on the old woman. "Do you know where everyone is?"

The old woman remained stalwart, never raising her head. She simply stared at her needlepoint.

Parker slowly approached the woman and bent low to bring their faces within inches of each other. "I'm sorry to disturb you," Parker greeted in fluent Spanish. "I'm hoping you've seen someone that might be able to help me."

The old woman's eyes widened, as she raised them to meet with Parker's. "Your Spanish is good," she said in a weathered voice.

"Gracias. Can you help me?"

"I don't know where they are. I'm looking for my great grandson," the woman gently touched Parker on the arm, then abruptly tugged at her sleeve. "His name is Pedro. Do you know him?"

Leave it to a grandmother to think everyone in the world might know her grandkids. "No," answered Parker. She offered a hopeful smile, despite knowing the odds of finding a missing child grew direr with each passing hour. Still, the elderly woman didn't seem to be overly upset. "When did Pedro go missing?"

The question prompted the old woman to frown, when suddenly, a heavy door near the bulletproof glass opened to reveal a tall, lanky man in a tan hat and matching uniform. He spoke with a young, bubble gum chewing girl who looked barely old enough to have graduated high school. "Try Ramirez again and get him to come in," said the man.

"He doesn't speak Spanish," the girl noted in a slight valley-girl accent, the kind where every declarative sentence sounds like a question that masquerades as an insult.

The man grimaced. "What? Isn't he from Mexico?"

"Minnesota."

"Really?" The man stopped in his tracks. He turned to challenge the girl. "I'm pretty sure on his application he said he speaks Spanish."

"He's fluent in Mandarin."

"Mandarin?"

"It's Chinese."

"I know—" The man's thoughts were derailed again as he spotted Parker standing next to the old woman. "Oh, I'm sorry. I didn't see you there. Hello, Ms.—"

"Monroe," greeted Parker. She stood up to extend her hand. "Parker Monroe."

The man smiled. "Bill. I'm Bill. The Sheriff. Sheriff Bill." He eagerly reached to shake Parker's hand. "Have we met before? You look awfully familiar."

Parker tried smiling back politely to Bill who kept shaking her hand as though it might jog the memory of him loose. His tanned face wasn't particularly handsome or ugly, in fact, if there was an exact middle point between the two extremes he would be its poster child. "I don't believe so."

"You sure?" asked the Sheriff. "My mind is like a steel trap. I never forget a face!"

Parker shrugged. *Maybe you've seen my face plastered all over cable news after being fired?*

"She doesn't remember you," said Bubble Gum chewer. "Awkward."

Bill let out a nervous chuckle. "Ha! Yeah, okay." He snapped his fingers. "Powers! Get Ivan Powers on the phone," he said excitedly. "I remember now, he's the one who speaks Spanish! See? Steel trap!"

Bubble Gum popped an impressive bubble in the face of her boss and turned to march back to the heavy door.

Bill nodded to the old woman doing needlepoint. "She's been here for over an hour and doesn't speak a lick of English."

"She's looking for her great grandson, Pedro," informed Parker. "He's missing."

Bill blinked. "How do you know that?"

"She told me."

"You speak Spanish?"

"I grew up in this town," answered Parker. "We're thirty miles from the border. I figured taking Spanish might come in handy."

54

"Huh. I took French."

Parker impatiently looked at her watch. "Sheriff--Bill, is it? I hate to press you, but I'm running way behind today. I'm here to claim my car from the pound. Would you like me to ask this woman anything for you before I pay my fee and be on my merry way?"

Bill nodded appreciatively. "Yes, of course. If you could, tell her that we have a translator on the way."

Parker was about to recount the Sheriff's words in Spanish when Bill added an addendum. "And tell her, we'll assist her with a missing person's report. And ask her if she has any family who might speak English that we can connect with. And ask her if she lives nearby. And then ask her when she saw Pedro last."

Parker took a deep breath. "Anything *else*?"

Bill smiled. "No, it's good to see you."

"What?"

"No, it's good. That's good, I mean. Just tell her all of that stuff, please?"

Before Parker could turn and open her mouth to speak, the tinted street door to the lobby opened with a digital chirp. A younger, handsome Latino, dressed sharply in a grey silk suit, walked in. His eyes lit up with a smile upon seeing the elderly woman. "Abuelita!" he greeted with open arms. The old woman turned up her nose at the man, who spoke quickly to her in Spanish. Parker could only catch so much of it, but determined the man was asking his mother where she'd been.

"Excuse me," Sheriff Bill interrupted. "Who are you, and do you know this woman?"

"Who am I?" asked the young man, nearly offended by the statement. He shook his head. "Yes, of course, I have been so rude," he apologized. "Her name is Cecilia. She is my

55

grandmother." He firmly shook Bill's hand. "I am Victor. Victor Cortez." Victor then nodded to Parker with a gracious smile.

Commanding the room's attention, Victor knelt to speak with his mother on an eye to eye level. "Abuelita, you had us all worried," he said in English. "You were not at the bus stop where you said you'd be. We've been looking all over town for you."

Parker watched Cecilia's expressions carefully. She looked at her grandson with a mixture of anger and confusion. Bill said Cecilia didn't know any English—so why was her grandson not addressing her in Spanish? Something didn't feel right. Parker stepped forward to interrupt Victor's tender display. "Do you know this man?" asked Parker to the old woman in Spanish.

"Yes," Cecilia answered slowly in her native tongue. Her eyes did not stray from Victor's. "Victor is my-- grandson."

Victor pulled his steely gaze away from Cecilia and cast it upon Parker. "You know Spanish?"

"A little," Parker lied.

Victor slowly rose to his feet to face Parker.

Parker could see Victor tensing up, despite the charming smile that remained plastered on his face. She decided to press Victor with a friendly but ignorant question that she already knew the answer to. "Your grandmother mentioned someone name Pedro. Do you know who she's talking about?"

Victor's smile eased into a mask of concern. "Pedro is my nephew," he answered. Victor turned his attention back to Cecilia and spoke to her in Spanish once again. "Abuelita, Pedro is at home. Please, please, won't you come with me? We can go see him together."

Cecilia's eyes narrowed. She turned to look at Parker, then to Sheriff Bill, then back to Victor. Slowly, she held her hand out to her grandson, who in turn, gently helped her to her feet.

Bill, not understanding any of the conversation that had transpired before him, stepped in. "Now, hold on here, I'm not exactly sure what is going on, but this lady came in looking for Pedro." He turned to Parker for confirmation. "Right? Pedro is missing?"

"Pedro is safe at home," assured Victor. He turned so that his back was turned to Cecilia. "I must apologize, but my grandmother. She gets—confused, now and then. She's old, and she is the one who has been missing. She's had us worried. That is why I came here."

Bill screwed up his face into an idiot grimace. "How do I know you are who you say you are? Do you have an ID?"

"Of course," said Victor. For a moment he looked puzzled by the request. But Victor complied, pulling his California driver's license from his wallet to show the Sheriff.

Bill nodded to Cecilia. "Does *she*?"

Victor smiled. "Sheriff, if I were not her grandson, surely, she would not feel comfortable enough to come with me. I appreciate your concern for her safety. And I'm sure it has nothing to do with you wondering about her legal status in this country."

Bill's eyes hardened. "Safety, Mr. Cortez, is my *only* concern right now."

Sensing the temperature of the room rising, Parker stepped in to diffuse the situation. "Perhaps if you left your contact information for the Sheriff, Victor, he could reach out later if he has any more questions."

Victor took a moment to look Parker over, then nodded in sudden agreement. "Of course!"

Parker watched Victor and the Sheriff as the appropriate contact information was exchanged. She wasn't entirely sure what she had just stumbled onto, but the silent alarm in the back of her head was practically screaming right now. Something just wasn't right.

Stop being so paranoid, Parker told herself. *Sniffing out stories isn't your job anymore.*

Cecilia slowly walked toward the door with Victor. The old woman glanced back at Parker one last time, then to Sheriff Bill before muttering something in Spanish to him and disappearing out the door.

Parker and Bill watched through glass doors as Victor helped the old woman into the back of a black Cadillac Escalade with tinted windows. "Fancy car," Bill commented. "*Expensive* car."

"Is that a crime?" asked Parker.

"Of course, not." Bill rubbed his chin. "Say, what did the old woman say to me before she left?"

Parker frowned. "She called you an *Idiota.*"

"Cool," said Bill. He scratched his forehead. "What does that mean?"

12.

"I'm home!"

announced Parker stumbling through the front door. "Three hundred dollars later, and the Highlander is free to terrorize the streets of Oak Creek once again!"

"Mom!" squealed Ally as she clomped out of the kitchen. She raced across the hardwood floor into Parker's open arms.

Parker squeezed her youngest tightly – she needed a good Ally hug. "Hello, little one!"

Valerie emerged from the kitchen in an apron. "We were just making cookies together," she informed. "Ally is quite the little helper. How was your old classmate, Bill?"

"Bill?" Parker grimaced. "You mean, the Sheriff?"

"Yes, Parker you went to high school together."

Parker threw her purse and keys onto the chair. "Really? I think I would have remembered that, Mom."

"If you say so. Have you eaten lunch?"

Parker set Ally back down and kicked off her stiletto heels. The rims of her feet throbbed like never before. "No time," she answered. "I'm exhausted, I can barely breathe in this skirt, and I just want to put my head down and close my eyes for ten minutes."

"Why don't you go upstairs and take a nap?"

Parker waved her hands as she stumbled toward the living room couch across from Valerie's grand piano. "No, no, if I do that, I'm not going to wake up. I've got exactly an hour and a half before I need to leave for school."

"Parker, *I* can pick up the kids!" Valerie offered.

"No, Mom, it's gotta be me! I've got to see this through!" Parker held her head. She felt drunk with exhaustion. In a desperate attempt to find comfort, she unzipped the back of her skirt and shoved it to the floor to let her belly expand back to its natural state. "Oh, hell yes, that's soooooo much better." Parker lumbered to the couch and sank into it, grabbing a blanket off the arm and pulling it over her.

"Parker, you need to rest." Valerie insisted.

"Hello? That's what I'm doing! Ten minutes!" Parker stretched her legs out and pulled the blanket close. Her eyes shut. "Wake me up in ten minutes."

"Ten minutes?"

"Ten minutes."

Ten minutes later, Valerie gave her daughter a gentle nudge.

Parker smacked her lips. "Huh? What?" She didn't even bother to open her eyes. "Give me another ten minutes."

Ten minutes after that, Valerie was back at the couch, promptly nudging her daughter.

"Five more minutes!" Parker whined.

The process repeated until forty minutes later, Parker didn't wake up at all.

13.

Deep in sleep, Parker's head filled with recent memories.

Images of Kurt swirled about the dreamscape as he played with a younger, happier Maddy. They sat side by side at the upright piano of their old apartment in Chicago. Kurt corrected her fingering on scales, scribbled notes onto her sheet music, and sometimes, just sat and marveled at his prodigy daughter.

Kurt never complained about putting his own music career on hold, but Parker knew he missed it, and teaching Maddy was just the outlet he needed from being a stay-at-home dad. It helped that Maddy was a natural with the ivory keys. Her playing never bothered Drew and could lull Ally to sleep with the right song selection. The graceful arpeggios of Beethoven's Moonlight Sonata proved to be such a song. The notes raced through Parker's dream as she continued to sleep on Valerie's couch.

Moonlight Sonata -- the last song Kurt would ever teach his daughter. The song Maddy practiced when Parker informed her of Kurt's death.

Parker watched Maddy in her dream gracefully play the notes. Her fingers landed perfectly and with a nuanced touch beyond her years. Then the dream world around Maddy suddenly grew cold and dark. Maddy's fingers stumbled as she approached the end of the song. Instead of single notes, she crushed the keys angrily, pounding them with her fists into utter discord. She pounded, harder, and harder, screaming as she did so until—

Parker startled awake on the couch, her shirt soaked in her own sweat. Her chest heaved up and down, as she realized the living room was completely dark except for a single music lamp at the grand piano. Maddy sat there quietly in her night gown.

"Maddy!" Parker gasped, still trying to get her bearings as she woke from her dream. "Wh--what time is it?"

Maddy didn't respond. She sat perfectly still at her grandmother's piano.

"How long was I out?"

Maddy remained quiet and still.

Parker checked her phone. It was 10:17pm.

Fuck. I slept the entire afternoon? Through dinner?

Parker slapped her forehead. "Shit, I missed pick up, didn't I?" she grumbled. "Obviously, I missed it. I'm sorry."

Maddy bowed her head.

Parker tried smiling innocently. "And I just swore, so I owe you another five dollars – right?"

Maddy curled her hands into fists. The fists began to shake.

Valerie swept into the room, tying her robe at the waist. "What was all that racket on the piano?" she asked, then noticing Maddy. "Maddy, was that you? Why are you playing at this hour? You'll wake your brother and sister!"

Maddy turned her head toward her grandmother but didn't utter a word.

Parker sighed, finally getting her bearings. She frowned at her daughter. She finally knew what was going on. "That was your plan, right, Maddy? Make a huge scene? Make a big racket on the piano?"

"What?" asked Valerie, astonished at the accusation. "Why would Maddy do that?"

"To let me know I screwed up," answered Parker. "She's pissed I didn't pick her up from school."

"But *I* picked you up, Maddy," said a confused Valerie. "I don't understand, was I not on time?"

"This isn't about you," Parker corrected.

Maddy finally broke her silence. "You said you'd be there," she said in a quivering voice.

"Maddy, your mother was exhausted!" Valerie defended. "She'd been up for hours just—"

"Mom," Parker interjected. She locked eyes with Valerie. "I got this." Parker rose from the couch and dusted herself off to slowly approach her daughter.

"You *got* this?" Maddy scowled at her mother. "You can't show up on time. Ever. You don't even have any pants," she sneered.

"I don't need any goddamn pants," Parker shot back, kicking her skirt across the floor and out of the way. "You got a problem with me, Maddy, you take it up with *me*. You sure as hell don't wake up the whole house by banging on a piano in the middle of the night!"

"You said you would be there, Mom!" Maddy shouted, pounding her fist on the piano keys.

"That's Mom, the Almighty!" Parker shouted back.

"You're a terrible mom and I'm not playing your stupid game anymore!" Maddy exploded out of her seat and stood toe to toe with her mother. "It's stupid! I hate that game! And I hate *you*!"

"Maddy!" Valerie gasped.

Parker threw up her hand at Valerie to stop her from interfering any further. Maddy's words lingered in the night air. Parker wanted Maddy to own the moment, for better or worse. After an uncomfortable silence, Parker swallowed the lump in her throat and stared into Maddy's trembling rage filled eyes. "I don't want to see you or hear you until you wake up for school tomorrow morning," she commanded. "Go to your room."

Maddy's breathing increased. Her entire body shook. But she did not take a step.

"Go to your room!" Parker screamed at the top of her lungs. She pointed the way to the stairs.

Maddy stormed off and proceeded to clomp up the stairs. Each step seemed to contort every muscle in Parker's body tighter and tighter until her ears caught the slam of a bedroom door. It was a miracle Drew or Ally hadn't woken up.

Parker finally exhaled, and noticed Valerie standing at her side with her jaw dropped open and eyes as wide as golf balls.

"Parker," Valerie started in a whisper. "For the love of Condoleezza Rice—"

Parker slowly shook her head. "Why didn't you wake me up, Mom? You were supposed to wake me up!"

Valerie frowned. "I tried, Parker. You were out. Cold. And I don't blame you. So, I took your keys, packed up Ally and went to pick up Drew and Maddy. You're *welcome*."

"Thank you, it's just—" Parker found her own fists clenching like Maddy's did. *Is that where she gets it from?* "I told her I would be there."

"You need to stop being cryptic with me, Parker. You never told me what happened between you two in Chicago. I've been patient, but you're living in my house now. And I've got a granddaughter mad with rage banging on the piano in the middle of the night."

"I know," said Parker. She held her throbbing forehead. She always got headaches when she was starving, and her stomach growled viciously to remind her she'd slept through dinner. "You're right. You deserve to know. I'm just--hungry."

"Leftovers are in the fridge. Grab a plate, and two glasses."

"Two?"

"I think we could both use some wine," answered Valerie as she headed to the door to the cellar.

14.

As the midnight hour approached...

Valerie poured a 2012 bottle of Saint-Emilion Grand Cru with great care, filling Parker's glass first. "Here," she said. "This should take the edge off."

Parker practically robbed her mother of the glass, then gulped the red liquid in its entirety before Valerie had even finished pouring her own. "Yup," Parker belched. "Sure does. Hit me again."

"Sweet Eva Marie Saint," Valerie grumbled. "You're supposed to sip and savor." She elected to pour half of what she did before.

"Come on, Mom," said Parker, waving her in for more. "Don't be shy. Filler up."

Valerie poured a single drop more. "You can have more after you explain Chicago."

Parker stuck her tongue out and plopped herself onto the couch. Despite having changed into her favorite *Slippery When Wet* classic Bon Jovi t-shirt and sweat pants she felt uncomfortable and anxious. Valerie sat across in the armchair, watching her daughter closely as she toyed with her glass, rolling the wine around within it.

"Tonight," Valerie prompted.

"Hold on, I'm getting there." Parker raised her glass of wine, this time taking a long deliberate sip.

"Parker!"

Parker held out her finger to signal her mother to wait as she finished her sip. "There. Lips are suitably loose now." She coughed, having downed the wine too fast. "Excuse me. Chicago. Chicago—"

her voice trailed off. "So, you know how, on occasion, I can be late to events and things?"

Valerie tried not to roll her eyes. The more accurate statement might have been that on rare occasion Parker showed up on time. "I'm aware."

Parker let out a nervous laugh. "After Kurt died, my tardiness kind of went into a death spiral. Juggling work, three kids, it was a lot, even with the new nanny."

"I would think so."

"I tried everything. I got the kids into a carpool, which worked pretty well at first, but then I'd often be running late on my pick-up days and it just kind of became this – thing."

"Thing?"

"Carpool kids are mean and evidently they don't like waiting around at school for thirty minutes while I fought cross town traffic. Their mothers didn't like it either. By the way, their mothers are also mean, I guess, that's where these kids got it."

Valerie arched a brow as she savored another sip. "I'm surprised you weren't kicked out of the carpool."

"Ah, see, they threatened to kick me out, but through some clever accounting on my part, I was able to stay in."

"You paid them off."

"And, I made the nanny takeover all carpool responsibilities." Parker held her empty glass in the air to accept a phantom toast.

Valerie shook her head. "That's – one way of handling it."

Parker shrugged. "It worked. But Maddy found the whole thing embarrassing. 'Why can't you be like the other moms? Why can't you ever show up on time?' But none of the other moms were busting their ass every day trying to track down leads to expose the corruption of our favorite shit-head Senator. I kept telling myself, once I break the story, once I finally nail Hammers, I'll take a vacation and make it up to Maddy, and Drew and Ally. I just needed to get the story done and out. I needed that win, so I could -- move on, you know?"

Valerie held the wine bottle up to signal she was ready to reward her daughter with another pour. Parker eagerly accepted. "None of this sounds so bad, Parker," Valerie assured her.

"It wasn't bad. *I* didn't think it was bad. Things seemed to be working just fine. But then Maddy insisted on starting up piano lessons again. Which was a big deal because—" Parker let the sentence linger, searching for strength to finish it.

"Maddy only ever learned piano from Kurt." Valerie finished the sentence for her. Valerie's heart sank as she watched her daughter's eyes well up.

"Right," Parker paused, allowing the emotion to wash over her. When the wave passed, she took another sip and pressed on. "So, I found a local teacher, someone nearby, and we met with her, a Mrs. Johnson, I think. It didn't matter, because Maddy hated her. And she hated, Mrs. Weatherby, the next one I found. And, Mr. Schmidt. And Mr. Mish." Parker began to count the names on her fingers. "Then there was, Klingsborn, Sandquist and Mauler, all more expensive than the previous, all further and further away from home." Parker held her forehead, reliving the trials in her mind. "Finally, *finally*, we found Mrs. Lidstrom. An older lady. A former concert pianist who owned a piano store in downtown Chicago and gave lessons in the back room. It was far from home, but close to work, and watching her and Maddy work together you'd think they were musical soulmates or something. They really hit it off. Forty bucks an hour for each lesson, which seemed a little steep but whatever. Later on, Maddy told me she wanted to go an extra half hour so Lidstrom raised her price to fifty an hour and wanted it in cash, and I was all – really? But you know, Maddy was happy playing again, and learning again. So, I paid it."

"None of this sounds bad."

"The problem was, the nanny could drop Maddy off, but picking her up was too much. For drop off, she already had to pack up Drew and Ally to drag them into the city and then back again, but the nanny was also taking courses at a community college and needed to be finished with everything by 7pm. And since the piano store was on the way home from my work, it made the most sense for me to pick Maddy up."

Valerie nodded. "Okay."

"I was never, ever on time, Mom. Maddy would be furious when I finally pulled up to the curb. Usually, thirty minutes later."

"How many piano teachers did you say you went through?"

Parker recounted on her fingers. "Seven. Eight including Lidstrom."

Valerie poured herself some more wine. "My dear, Parker, did it ever occur to you that Maddy settled on Lidstrom precisely, so you would be *forced* to pick her up?"

Parker frowned. "Please don't tell me that."

"Why?"

"Because it makes what I'm about to tell you far worse."

15.

Parker downed the last of her wine glass.

"Now, for the record, I won't let Maddy have a cell phone until middle school. So whenever I was late to pick up Maddy, I'd call Lidstrom to let her know. Meanwhile, my deadline for the Hammers expose was fast approaching. My source was getting cold feet about turning over his evidence, and I needed to keep him engaged. So, when it came to picking up Maddy, thirty minutes late would turn into forty minutes, and so on and so on. Sometimes I even took Maddy back to the office with me just to sneak in a few more hours of work. I was so close, and so tired, and then—" Parker snapped her fingers. "Just like that, my source grew some balls and finally delivered! He told me he's got access to records that would prove Senator Hammers was illegally funneling campaign money to buy off a mafia boss, who would then hire thugs to start fights at immigration protests. One of those protests exploded into a full-blown riot that led to seventy-five million in store front damages and the death of five people."

"Including two cops," Valerie bowed her head. "I remember. It made national news."

"Fucking Hammers," Parker clenched her free hand into a fist. "My problem was, I didn't have the files in my possession. The mafia accountant did everything old school, wrote everything down by hand so there was no chance of a computer hack. I was going off what my source was telling me. He claimed to have snapped pictures of the records, but now informed me he was holding out for a better offer. One of my competitors from the New York Times caught wind of the story and that undercutting bitch was willing to deal in twice the cash. Fuck that. I was not about to let five months of my hard work get upended in the eleventh hour. I wanted the win. I wanted to prove to myself, my family, the whole goddamn

70

world that Parker Monroe was still a force to be reckoned with."
Parker sighed. "So, I made the biggest mistake of my career. I lied
to my editor, told him I had the files when I didn't, and I convinced
him to run the story."

Valerie's jaw dropped open. "That doesn't sound like you at all."

"It was a gamble." Parker swallowed. "That I lost. The day I got
fired started with Jerry calling me into his office at ten o'clock that
morning, demanding to know who my source was for the Hammers
piece. He said Hammers was furious, demanded proof and that he
was going to sue for libel, slander and everything in between. I told
Jerry to cool it, to trust me, and that I'd get the docs. But when I
went through my usual channels to contact my source, it was like --
he never existed. The guy had just vanished. Disappeared. He never
even went with the New York Times for more money, which I was
counting on to validate my headline. I spent the day kicking over
every rock I could to find my source. Jerry and I argued on and off
for hours. My phone was blowing up left and right with everyone in
the world – rival journalists, threats from Hammers' lawyers,
talking heads on cable, everyone but my source.

"Jerry finally called me back into his office for the final time around
six. I shut my phone off to plead my case without interruption.
Three hours later, I turn it back on, and its full of messages from
the nanny."

Valerie's eyes widened. "Oh my."

"Yup. I was so wrapped up with the chaos of the day, I'd forgotten
to pick up my own daughter from piano lessons. Only this time, I
wasn't thirty minutes late, or forty, I was *two and a half hours*
late."

"Parker,"

"No, Mom, it gets worse. To her credit, the nanny was way ahead
of me sensing something was wrong. Normally, Maddy and I would
have shown up at home hours ago. So, the nanny starts calling

around. She tries the piano store but finds out it's been closed for two hours. Then she tracks down Lidstrom's personal number – but Lidstrom says Maddy told her that her *mother* had arrived, way late as usual, to pick her up! But the nanny can't confirm that with me, because she can't get a hold of me, and meanwhile I'm thinking, who the fuck picked up my daughter from piano lessons? Because it sure as hell wasn't me!

"So, I start freaking out, leave Jerry in the dust and I drive like a madwoman downtown to the piano store, all the while dialing everyone I can think of who is involved in Maddy's life. Friends. Mothers of friends. Teachers. No one has seen her and I'm starting to get hysterical. I call the police. They want me to come down to the station, fill out a report. Finally, I get to the piano store, and spend the next few hours going into full reporter mode and interviewing every smelly bum on the street and passerby to see if anyone has seen my beautiful, missing eleven-year-old daughter. Nothing. And I am losing it!" Parker took another deep breath, trying to hold back her tears and anger. "Finally, one bum who lives in a cardboard box in an alley three blocks away tells me he watched a girl Maddy's age get into a cab at the taxi stand across the street a few hours ago. He found it noteworthy because she was so young and alone. Then, the nanny calls me back, and tells me Maddy just called the house."

Valerie was about to breathe a sigh of relief but held onto it. Parker clearly wasn't finished.

"Maddy only called to relay a message. She wanted to 'say goodbye to Drew and Ally.' Then she hung up!"

"Oh, Parker."

Parker wiped the tears away from her cheeks. "So, I call in another favor at the station, and get Maddy's call traced. It came from a payphone at a Greyhound station across the river. I rush over there, and by now its nearly 11pm. The station is getting ready to close. And there she is, my little Maddy, curled up on the bench, completely passed out with her coat as a blanket and her music folder as a pillow."

Valerie finally exhaled.

Parker tapped her fingers incessantly on her glass. "I was so relieved to see her. And so *pissed*. I didn't wake her. A security guard approached me, asked me if I was her mother. I said yes, and he told me he'd been keeping an eye on her on and off all night and was getting ready to call the police. And then I notice it clutched in Maddy's hand – a one-way bus ticket."

Valerie ruffled her brow. "Where on Earth was she planning to go?"

"To San Diego. Which puts her in spitting distance of *you*."

Valerie smiled and clutched at her heart as if flattered. "Oh," she said softly. Then stiffened her posture. "Oh!"

Parker frowned. "Yeah. At least, she likes one of us."

"Where did she get the money to do that?"

"Ha!" Parker snorted. "This is how super-villain brilliant my daughter is. Remember when she told me Lidstrom raised her price? It was a lie. Maddy had been skimming off the top for months. I guess she was preparing for the day I really fucked up. And wow, did I ever fuck up."

Valerie bowed her head. "You did." She looked up with a glimmer of hope in her eyes. "But Maddy isn't innocent in all of this. Her actions were premeditated. She lied about you picking her up. She stole money. She wanted to punish you."

"It worked."

"But she endangered her own life in the process!"

"I know, but she's eleven, she's angry and she just lost her father!"

73

"For the love of Julie Andrews, that doesn't make it better! She's lucky you *are* a good investigator and found her at all! Honestly, I think both of you need some serious counseling."

"I know, I know," Parker shifted uncomfortably. "I just want to establish a new baseline, first, okay?" Parker set down her glass of wine on the coffee table and began to rub her temples. "We moved out here to start over. I kind of want to give that a chance."

"Family counseling is nothing to be ashamed of."

"Baby steps, Mom." Parker took a deep breath. "Step one, school. Step two, a new piano teacher. That's the next thing I need to work on."

"You're the mother," Valerie conceded. She stood up from her seat and retied her robe. It was a time-honored gesture to signal she was finished with whatever conversation she had been having late into the night. "I might suggest, however, the very first thing you work on is getting to school on time. Without having your car towed."

Parker aimed her fingers as a gun to her mother. "Good plan."

16.

Today is a new fucking day, and I'm going to 'mom' the shit out of it.

Parker awoke with a renewed energy and jumped into the shower. She slipped into the outfit she'd chosen the night before, a white blouse and navy pants combination that wouldn't earn an eye roll from Maddy, nor any leering if she happened upon Glory. Most importantly, it fit her current body comfortably. She glided across the upstairs to find Drew in a desperate search for matching tube socks. Parker wadded a pair of Pokémon socks into a ball and threw it at his head.

Boom. Mommed that.

Ally woke up crying in her room across the hall. In a flash, Parker swept in with a fresh diaper and changed Ally before Valerie even knew what was going on.

Diaper bomb – defused. Fucking mommed that too.

With twenty-two minutes until lift-off for school, the Monroe family was running on all cylinders – save for one.

Parker took a deep breath before knocking on Maddy's door and entering her dark room. "Maddy?" she called to the huddled mass of sheets on the bed. "It's time to get up. You don't want to be late for school."

The mass shifted, revealing a foot and an arm.

Parker tried to keep her voice light. "Maddy, come on, it's time to get up. New day. New start. Let's do this, huh? *I'm* dressed. I'm ready – see?"

Maddy's head popped up. Her squinty eyes examined her mother's outfit.

"I was planning on talking with your music teacher today after I drop you off. See if she had any recommendations for a piano teacher. What is your music teacher's name?"

"I don't know." Maddy answered with a yawn.

Parker grimaced. "What do you mean you don't know?"

"We didn't have music class yesterday."

"Huh," Parker bit her lip. Her mind flashed back to the arguing voices she'd heard in the music room. Was it related? She shook the question from her head. "Maybe you don't have music class every day. I'll ask around."

"Sure."

Parker tried not to frown at Maddy's delivery of the word. Her heart yearned for it to contain a quantum of gratitude or excitement to acknowledge the prospect of starting up piano lessons again. But her head knew that would be too much to ask from a sleepy eleven-year-old coming off the screaming match from the night before. "Alright then," Parker nodded. "See you downstairs."

No tears, no foul – right?

Twenty minutes later, Parker had both kids loaded up in the Highlander and was pulling out of the driveway. Valerie and Ally waved goodbye from the porch window. Parker took a moment to enjoy the fact she'd left on time.

Tuesday is my bitch.

Parker's hopes for a timely arrival at school would soon be threatened by a blue Ford Explorer seven cars ahead and paralyzed with fear. Afraid to challenge oncoming traffic and complete its left turn into the school parking lot, it simply straddled the middle of the road and blocked the entire intersection, earning a litany of angry honks. The ordeal went on for five minutes, prompting several cars to deposit their children directly into the streets to walk the rest of the way to school, congesting traffic even more.

Parker's patience wore thin. "Blue Ford needs to grow some fucking balls," she muttered under her breath.

"Mom," Drew perked up at hearing the statement from the back seat. "I thought you weren't supposed to swear."

"Maddy backed out of the game," explained Parker, earning an eye roll from her daughter. "What? You did."

"You could still *try* not swearing," challenged Maddy. "For the sake of decency."

"You're right," Parker agreed. She cleared her throat and turned away to mutter a quieter version. "Blue Ford needs to grow some *gosh-darn* fucking balls."

"Look!" Drew pointed to the Sheriff's car pulling alongside them with its flashing lights.

The Sheriff's loud speaker squawked to life. "Clear the intersection." Stated the voice. "Clear the intersection."

The measured display of authority seemed to be just enough to snap everyone's common sense back into place. Oncoming traffic halted to let Blue Ford in and the drop off lane was rolling once again.

"Do you know the Sheriff?" asked Drew. "He's looking at you."

Parker squinted to see Bill waving to her car as he continued on. "Kind of." *Wonder what he's doing here?* "Whatever, he cleared a path."

Upon her turn, Parker pulled into the parking lot just as another car was leaving a "guest" space. *Perfect timing!* Parker slid into it with relative ease. She couldn't believe her luck.

"You sure you can park here?" asked Maddy.

"Ha, ha," Parker shot back sarcastically. "I've got to hunt down your music teacher, remember?"

Parker said goodbye to her kids and sent them off to their class lines on the playground. She eyed each teacher as they came out to collect their children, wondering which one might be the music teacher. Then, it occurred to her the music teacher would likely teach several classes and might not collect any kids right away. Before she could inquire about it, a familiar voice broke her concentration.

"Something's different about you," said Julie Kimball as she approached with Glory at her side.

Parker hunched her shoulders. "I'm on time and wearing clothes that fit."

Glory tilted his head, as if he wondered if Parker's modest wardrobe was somehow a ploy to make him uninterested. "Well, you're still kind of hot."

"Thanks," said Parker, unsure whether to be offended or flattered. Eager to stay on task, her eyes lit up with a new question. "Say, you two know most of the teachers at this school, right?"

Julie offered a rather mischievous smile. "Um, we know every teacher, every student and every parent who isn't a No-See-Um at this school."

"A No-See-Um?"

"Yeah," said Glory. "By definition, they're not hot. Or ugly. They're just, you know -- there."

"They blend in to the background," Julie added. Her eyes lit up with her open smile. "OMG, Parker, this is the perfect time to get you up to speed on who is who and what is what around here!"

"Well, I don't really have time for—"

"Perfect," Julie cut her off. "Now listen closely."

Julie and Glory went on to describe the categories of parents whose children attended Oak Creek Elementary, all through the lens of Julie's eye for fashion and Glory's sliding scale of hotness.

There were the *Sports Clubbers* -- easily identified by their expensive athletic wear designed to give off the impression they were going to the gym immediately after drop-off. But these were "false goddesses" in Julie's estimation, as she spent an inordinate amount of time at the gym every day and kept close tabs as to who actually followed through.

Then there were the *International Trophy Wives* – a small contingent of foreigners, usually from Russia, China or some Eastern country who Julia and Glory guessed found their American husbands online through a ninety-day program. These were among Glory's favorites, as they ranged from mildly hot, to super-hot and wore shocking colors of lipstick. The thicker the accent the better.

A more elite group, never to be denied were the *Professionals*. Dressed in suits or scrubs, these mothers and fathers loathed venturing onto school grounds and worked hard to blow through the drop-off lane as quickly as possible. In the rare instance they found themselves stepping onto school property, they associated with only their cellphones, loudly broadcasting their conversations so others could understand how important they were. Julie and Glory were split on this group, with Glory more forgiving of women in expensive dress suits. Parker wondered if she might have qualified for such a category at one time.

Then there were the *PTA'ers*, full time mothers who ran the gambit in attractiveness and likeability. They could often be found loitering around school grounds, generally appearing helpful and cheerful. "But it's all an act," Julie explained. "All these bitches are after is your money. Money, money, money. As if public schools are in some kind of perpetual financial crisis or something."

Parker tilted her head, confused by the statement. "Aren't they?"

"Whatever. I hate them."

Glory argued against all PTA'ers being she-devils, happily naming off five he flirted with regularly. He then went on to detail several parent subsets.

The Helicopter Moms – generally newer mothers who constantly hovered over their children and pulled their roller bags to school for them (rarely hot.) These were not to be confused with the *Yellers* – veteran mothers who continually barked orders at their children from a long distance (never hot.) In direct contrast were the *Vanishing Mothers* – notorious for dropping their kids off at the curb for birthday parties and never on hand to discipline their hyper-active Ritalin-laced child when he or she set fire to a piece of furniture, placed a kitten in a microwave, or punched another kid in the crotch.

There were the *Over-Achievers* – usually well-tailored and manicured but afraid to sully their hands. The *Parent Paparazzi* – always adorned with cameras taking a thousand pictures of their spawn. The *Pocho Cartel* – those of Mexican descent who couldn't speak Spanish. The *Telemundos* – those of Mexican descent who couldn't speak English. And finally, as noted before, the mysterious *No-See-Ums* – the blandest of souls whose children had attended Oak Creek for years, but thanks to their preference for neutral color schemes, home-styled haircuts, and an inability to standout or speak up, were completely lost in the daily shuffle. Glory and Julie agreed that the parent body was mostly composed of No-See-Ums, but due to their very nature, it was impossible to directly prove they existed.

"Like black holes," concluded Julie.

"In space," added Glory. "Not the kind in your butt."

"Wow," said a wide-eyed Parker. She took a moment to digest the unexpected dissertation. "You make it sound like everyone here is a total asshole."

"Well, what did you think of Glory and me when you first met us?" asked Julie.

"I thought you were total assholes." Parker folded her arms. "I kind of still do."

"Exactly. Which makes you the same."

"Come again?"

Julie smiled. "You just gave us a brutally honest answer. You didn't sugar coat it. You told it like it is. Like we do. We may be total assholes, but you'll always know where we stand."

Glory gave an enthusiastic thumbs up.

Julie frowned. "And trust me, the same can't be said for any of these *other* assholes." She wagged her finger to encompass all the remaining parents, students and teachers who began to disperse with the ring of the final bell—including the Baby-Face mother from yesterday who Parker suddenly noticed stood at her side and likely had heard the entire conversation.

Baby Face's face carried the same disapproving scowl she had before.

Julie's eyes narrowed as if she were taking aim. "Whatever, Cheryl, move along! None of this concerns you!"

Baby Face quietly pushed her baby stroller away, crooking her head to continue her scowl at Julie.

Parker caught herself nodding. "Holy shit!" She shook her own head and fought off a shiver. "I'm disturbed by the fact that you're almost making sense. And I nearly forgot what I was going to ask you in the first place!"

"Oh yeah!" Julie smiled and rubbed her hands together. "Was it about the gossip surrounding whoever parked in Heller's driveway yesterday?"

"The perpetrator remains a mystery," added Glory, putting his thumb to the side trying to be helpful.

"Uh--no." said Parker, looking away as she casually scratched the back of her head.

"Was it about the hunky new gym teacher who is also a war veteran and an *eligible bachelor*?"

"If you're into that," Glory's thumb teetered toward the "down" position. "He's alright."

Parker waved her hands as she tried to recapture her own thoughts. "What? No, no, no." She snapped her fingers, finally landing on it. "The school's music teacher! I wanted to speak with the school's music teacher!"

Julie smiled. "Oh yes, Mr. Bernstein! He's very good."

"Nice guy. Knows music." Added Glory.

"Mr. Bernstein," Parker took a mental note. She turned her focus on the scattering body of kids and teachers as they filed into the school's doors. "Great, can you point him out? What does he look like?"

"He's short. Caucasian. Grey hair." Julie answered. "Glasses."

"He answers to Mr. Bernstein." Glory added.

Parker tried not to roll her eyes. "Yes, do you see him? I want to ask him about piano lessons."

Julie sucked air in through her teeth as if suddenly in pain. "Oooooh, yeah, that might be a problem."

"And why is that?"

"Because I think he was fired yesterday."

17.

"What?!?"

Parker's heart sank. She dropped her head and looked at the floor to absorb this heavy nugget of news that had somehow been buried deep in the gossip column of the last several minutes. "Julie – I feel like you could have led with that."

Julie shrugged and looked at her watch. "Oh! I'm going to miss my spin class if I don't get moving! We'll see you later, okay?"

Glory's phone buzzed. He checked it and pumped his fist in the air. "Yes! I've got a new fare. Later, Parker!"

Parker hardly noticed Glory's exit. Her mind scrambled to make sense of a music teacher she'd never even met being fired from a school her daughter hardly even knew. Was it true? How had she missed this news? Why was he fired? What did it mean for the music program? How was Maddy going to react to another setback?

Parker instinctively walked toward the school's front office and soon found herself confronting the sharply dressed silver-haired receptionist with ruby red lips.

"May I help you?" asked the receptionist.

"I'd like to see Principal Mendez," demanded Parker.

"She's not available," answered the receptionist. "However, Principal Heller's schedule is clear."

Parker's eyes narrowed at the mere mention of the name. *"Vice* Principal Heller?" she asked in a reflexive effort to correct the receptionist's oversight.

"Yes," answered the receptionist. Her voice dripped with disdain. *"Vice* Principal Heller."

Parker eyed the receptionist carefully, noting her rim-rod posture and perfectly pressed dress. *Oh, you're a Heller Loyalist, aren't you, Silver Fox?* "Yeah, I would prefer to speak with Mendez."

Silver Fox turned her nose up. "What does this concern?"

"I've questions regarding the school's music teacher, Mr. Bernstein."

"Mr. Bernstein is no longer employed by Oak Creek Elementary," explained a new voice. A familiar voice. A voice that made Parker's blood run cold.

Parker turned to see Vice Principal Heller stepping around the corner. *Shit, are you constantly eavesdropping on people, Heller?* Parker forced a smile. "Yes, I just heard."

"That's concerning," Heller challenged. Her beady eyes carefully scanned Parker over. "Considering we have not formally announced his exit."

"Can I ask why he was fired?"

Heller put her hands behind her back. "Mr. Bernstein is no longer employed by Oak Creek Elementary."

"Right," Parker took a deep breath. "I don't suppose you could give me his contact information."

"No."

Parker rolled her eyes back to Silver Fox. "You see — this?" She pointed to the space between her and Heller. "This, is why I would have preferred to speak with Mendez."

"Ms. Monroe," Heller stepped forward. "Employers are not legally permitted to discuss the termination of an employee in the State of California. Nor are we allowed to divulge any personal contact information of employees."

"He's not an employee anymore."

"*Former* employees."

Parker took a step closer to Heller. "Well, can you tell me about the music program? What's going to happen with that?"

Heller blinked. She swallowed. "There is no music program currently being offered at Oak Creek Elementary."

"For how long?"

"I cannot say."

"Are you going to hire a new teacher?"

"I cannot say."

"You can't, or you won't?"

"Ms. Monroe," Heller pulled her suit jacket tight. "Do you have any other business to conduct on school grounds?"

"I cannot say."

Heller's face turned red. "If you have no other business to conduct on school grounds, and are not a volunteer or an employee, then I suggest you get on with your day."

"Great," said Parker, folding her arms. "Then I'd like to volunteer."

"Excellent," Heller forced a smile. "Come back after you've had the proper background check from the Sheriff's department. It usually takes two weeks to get cleared. Unless, of course, they find unusual *gun* violations."

Holy fuck, Heller, was that a joke or are you throwing down with me?

Parker's eyes narrowed. "What is that supposed to mean?"

"Nothing. Other than despite being cleared by the Sheriff, as Principal—"

"*Vice* Principal." Parker corrected.

"-- I can refuse volunteer status to any parent I deem disruptive to the school environment."

"You're saying I'm disruptive?"

"I'm saying if you *are* disruptive I will have you escorted from school grounds. Considering yesterday's display of gunplay and poor choice of clothing you might want to tone things down."

Parker's blood boiled. "My poor choice of clothing?"

"Showing that much cleavage is never a good idea, especially around young boys. As a mother, I would think you'd understand that. Today, at least, you've chosen something more school appropriate."

"Are you—*fucking--kidding me*?" Parker took another step closer to stand literally toe to toe with Heller. Her blood was boiling now. She clenched her right fist.

"Alright, Heller, everything checks out," said Sheriff Bill as he suddenly appeared from the adjoining hallway. Bill stopped in his tracks as he noticed Parker and Heller facing off with one another. "Um – is everything okay?"

18.

Parker blinked, then slowly turned her head to look at Bill the Sheriff.

She forced a smile. "Bill?" she asked, surprised by his sudden appearance. "Bill!" she tried again, more as a statement this time as if seeing an old friend. "What – are – you – doing here?" Parker's mind raced so quickly through the slot machine of possible answers she had to practically squeeze her words out of her mouth.

Bill put his hands on his belt buckle. "Well, there was a break—"

"The Sheriff doesn't need to explain anything," Heller jumped in on Bill's answer as she stepped between Parker and him to serve as a physical barrier. "It's school business, and none of yours."

Parker's smile turned from fake to genuine. *Hiding something, Heller?* "I would argue it is my business. My children attend this school. If there is something amiss that could endanger them, I have a right to know. In fact, all the Oak Creek parents have a right to know. I bet, Bill would agree with me on that. Wouldn't you, Bill?" Parker leaned to the side to see around Heller's small frame.

Bill raised his hands to signal a "don't shoot." He laughed nervously. "Yes, of course, but the school has a right to craft an appropriate communication to parents. We don't want to cause any panic."

"Panic?" Heller snapped.

Bill's hands instinctively raised higher. "Not, that there is any reason to panic!" he corrected himself. He let off a nervous chuckle and looked at Parker. "Parker, really, your children aren't in danger. I can assure you of that. I'd just wait for the official communication from the school district."

Heller winced as she looked back and forth from Parker to Bill. "Do you two – know each other?" She practically choked on her question.

Bill tilted his head, as if unsure how to answer.

Though Parker still couldn't place Bill in her memory, she trusted her mother was right about them attending school together and wanted to press the idea to see if Heller or Bill might break. "Bill and I are old classmates," explained Parker. "You know, high school buddies. Class of '92, right Bill?"

Bill blushed. "Actually, I was a year behind you."

"Go Hawks!" Parker pumped her fist in the air to cover her blunder. "The point is, once a Hawk, always a Hawk. Birds of a feather do shit together, isn't that right Bill?"

"Why do you keep saying my name?"

"Because that's what old classmates do, Bill."

"I see." Confused, Bill raised his index finger as he looked back and forth from Heller to Parker. "I don't see, actually, what is happening right now?"

Parker smiled at Heller. "Vice Principal Heller was just about to tell me all about Mr. Bernstein's music program here at the school."

Bill screwed his face up into an idiot grimace. "Really? Because I thought—"

"I *just* informed Ms. Monroe that Mr. Bernstein is no longer an employee of Oak Creek Elementary, and that we no longer have a music program." Interrupted Heller.

Nice try, Heller. Now I know that Sheriff Bill knew about Bernstein's job situation. But why would he be involved? Parker stepped forward to go toe to toe with Heller again. "What I don't know, is that if I reach out to Mr. Bernstein for a recommendation for a private piano teacher for my daughter that I'm not, in fact, engaging with some crazy lunatic who was fired because he was caught fantasizing about dressing up in skin suits of the children he murders."

Both Heller's and Bill's faces contorted into a portrait of disgust. "Oh, wow," said Bill.

Heller waved her hand to clear the air of the dismal suggestion. "Ms. Monroe – *really!*"

Parker stood her ground. "As an uninformed parent, how am I to know that isn't the case?"

Bill shook his head. "Really, Parker, yuck. I can assure you that is not true. And you can't go spreading rumors about stuff like that. You'll ruin a person's life."

"I would never do that," Parker argued. Her mind flashed back to the headline she ran about Senator Hammers. She would never make that mistake again. "I just want you to understand my concern."

Heller adjusted her suit jacket. "If you wish for a recommendation of a good piano teacher, I can supply you with that, Ms. Monroe. However, I would advise you not to involve Mr. Bernstein. He has much to process."

Parker looked down at the beady eyed devil. "No, that's alright. I'll find one on my own."

Bill nodded and slapped his hands together. "Alright then! Problem solved! I guess we all can move on with our day now."

"Of course! Good day, Bill. *Heller.*" Parker forced one last smile and moved toward the office's front door. But just as she reached it, Bill snapped his fingers.

"Oh," said Bill forgetfully. "I meant to ask, is everything okay with your truck? The Highlander, I mean?"

Parker paused. *Fuck. Why would you ask me that now?* She could feel Heller's eyes burning through her back.

"Highlander?" Heller repeated. "What would be wrong with her *Highlander?*"

"The towing guy is new, and we've received a number of complaints about scratches and—" Bill's sentence sputtered as he saw the white of Parker's enraged eyes. "And uh, never mind. It's not important."

"Your car was towed?" asked Heller. Her nostrils flared. "Generally, cars are towed if they are not functioning, or parked somewhere they shouldn't be. I had a Highlander towed from my driveway just yesterday."

"Huh," Bill shrugged apologetically, signaling he never knew why Parker's car was towed in the first place.

Parker drew in a deep breath through her teeth. *How do I play this?* "Are you accusing me of parking my Highlander in your driveway?" She feigned indignance.

Heller folded her arms. "Did you?"

Shit. She called my bluff.

Parker held her head high. "I'm not going to lie to you, Mrs. Heller," she stated. "So -- I'm leaving." Parker dashed out of the front office without another word.

19.

"For the love of Vera Wang, why didn't you just own up to it?"

asked Valerie as she poured a fresh glass of wine in the living room. She handed it to Parker but held on for an extra beat to grab her attention. "Try sipping it this time, hmm?"

Parker replied with a snide smile. "I will savor every drop," she assured her mother. Parker took the glass and kicked her feet up onto the nearby chair of the dining room table. It was the evening now after another full day. Ally was in bed early after an extended adventure with Valerie at a park down the street. Drew was finishing up his common core math homework that seemed to make simple problems more complicated than they should be. And Maddy was playing piano in the next room, running through her scales and arpeggios like a champ. She wanted to stay sharp for whoever her next teacher might be and insisted on practicing every night.

Parker sipped her wine as promised and looked at her mother. "I should have owned up to it," she admitted, then stuck out her tongue. "If it was anyone else I would have. Maybe. But man, does Heller rub me the wrong way. She had no right to talk to me the way she did. I could probably have her fired for that."

"Oh, Parker, leave it alone. She's not worth your time."

"She's a bully," decided Parker after she took another sip. "With a secret. She's hiding something."

"Is she now?" Valerie looked away as she poured her own glass.

Parker frowned. She was all too familiar with her mother's tone when she tried to politely disagree. "What? You don't think so?"

"I think a big part of you misses investigative reporting," said Valerie.

"I've always had a nose for trouble."

"Smelling it, or stirring it?"

Parker winced. "How the hell would I *stir* trouble with my nose?"

Valerie shrugged tiredly. "It made more sense in my head," she relented. "My point is, this is Oak Creek, not Chicago. The biggest scandal here was your father dying in my bed with a huge smile on his face forty years ago. *Huge* smile." Valerie took a longer sip. "You have other things to do now than chasing down leads and sniffing out stories."

"I know that, Mother."

As if on cue, Maddy entered the room. "I'm done practicing." She announced.

"We heard," encouraged Valerie. "It sounded lovely."

"So," Maddy kicked at the floor. "I sure could use some new *music*. And, you know, a teacher. Where are we at with that?"

Parker turned to her daughter to make a bold pronouncement. "I've made several calls to piano teachers this afternoon. We just need to settle on one."

Both Maddy and Valerie's eyes widened in shock. Neither of them had expected Parker to have made any progress. "So, how do we do choose?" asked Maddy.

"Maybe we just try the first available and see how you like her," Parker paused, looking at her wine glass as if trying to divine the future from its color. "Though I wouldn't *mind* some kind of recommendation."

Valerie forced another smile as she rolled her eyes. "Maddy, why don't you help Drew get ready for bed?"

"Okay," Maddy's eyes narrowed, unsure of what just had happened. She quietly exited the room.

Parker ruffled her brows at her mother. "What was the eye roll for?"

"Oh, Sweet Mary Magdalene," whispered Valerie in a harsh voice. "You're looking for an excuse to talk to Mr. Bernstein, aren't you?"

"He's a qualified music professional."

"He's a stranger who was just mysteriously fired from his job!"

"We don't know the whole story," Parker corrected. "And that is partly why—"

Just then, there was a quiet knock at the front door. Valerie and Parker looked at each other in wonderment. Parker checked her phone – 8:42pm. A borderline time to be considered rude for solicitors. Well past time for any Amazon delivery. "Are you expecting someone?" asked Parker.

Valerie innocently shook her head. "Should I grab my shotgun?"

"Or," Parker interjected as she rose from her seat. "We could look through the peephole."

Parker sauntered toward the front door and leaned in to look through the peephole. "Oh, you've got to be shitting me."

20.

"Sheriff Bill," Parker greeted as she opened the front door.

"And to what do we owe the pleasure?"

Bill offered a confused smile. "Parker?" he asked in surprise. He lifted his phone to double check his notes. "You live here? I have this home registered to a Valerie Parker."

"My mother," answered Parker.

"Right."

"Who is it?" asked Valerie from the background.

"The Sheriff!" Parker shouted back.

"What does he want?"

"He's come for your guns!" Parker shot back.

"He's come for my gams?"

Parker shook her head and looked to Bill. "You have a habit of popping up unexpectedly. What can we do for you, Sheriff?"

"We're going door to door in the neighborhood," Bill aimed his thumb over his shoulder to the deputy at the house across the street. "Letting folks know to keep their cars locked at night. There's been an uptick on car thefts and break-ins, some of it may be gang related."

"Gangs? In Oak Creek?"

"We're not that far from San Diego or the border. Towns like Oak Creek make an easy target because no one expects it. And I see a Highlander is parked in your driveway."

"Too much shit to park it in the garage."

"Just be sure to keep it locked." Bill tilted his head sheepishly. "I'm sorry about that, by the way. I didn't mean to stir up trouble with Principal Heller earlier about your car. I didn't know."

"*Vice* Principal," Parker corrected. "And yes, for the record, I parked in her driveway. Not my finest moment. But it won't happen again." *Why did I confess that to him and not Heller?*

Bill nodded, then simply stared at Parker with his mouth slightly open.

"Is there anything else, Sheriff?"

"You – don't really remember me from high school, do you?"

Parker sighed. "Not really," she confessed again. "I'm sorry."

"Wow," Bill turned red. "You know, we were like, physics partners."

"Are you sure?"

"For a week," answered Bill. "Your usual partner, Neil Carter, got sick that one time with the stomach flu, and then my partner, Trisha Johnson got sick with it too, and so the teacher, Mr. Keiser, had us work together in the lab."

Parker recalled the Great Stomach Flu of '92 but still drew a blank as to the identity of her lab partners. "You remember all of that?"

"You don't'?"

"High school is a big blur for me. To be honest, I couldn't wait to get out of it. How do you remember so much about me?"

Bill's face turned more red. "You're the only girl I've ever met named Parker," he answered. "Parker Jane Parker. That's hard to forget."

Parker allowed herself a smile. Her name was an unusual legacy her mother had bestowed upon her. Because Parker was an only child, and a girl, Valerie wanted to honor her husband's last name and ensure it carried on. Valerie made her daughter's first name her husband's last name, so that if she ever married and took a new name, "Parker" would live on no matter what. Until she married Kurt, Parker's name was technically Parker Parker. "I never liked my middle name," she admitted. "But I suppose my mom had to break it up somehow."

"Well, Parker is a fine name."

"It is," Parker's eyes suddenly widened. She was hit with a memory in physics class. "Omigod, you're that kid who liked to do magic tricks! Bill! Bill Johnson!"

Bill raised his right hand. "Guilty. So – you do remember!"

"Yeah," Parker's voice cracked. As her memories flooded back, she recalled Bill getting beat up a lot by bullies and his tricks never quite landing. He may even have been laughed out of a talent show gone horribly wrong. "You – uh, keep up with all – that?"

"Oh, I love magic," said Bill. "You want to see a trick?"

"I'm good," answered Parker. *Yup, he was definitely laughed off the stage of the talent show.* "Maybe some other time? It's getting rather late."

"Right. I should be going. Keep those doors locked, okay?"

"Of course."

Bill turned to walk down the porch steps. He stopped just as Parker was about to close the front door. "And Parker?"

"Yes?"

"Bernstein is okay in my book."

Parker's eyes widened. "Come again?"

Bill turned to face Parker again. "Mr. Bernstein. You were asking about him at the school. You wondered if he was a child murderer or something crazy like that? He's not. He's a good guy. He's taught music in this town for a long time. I just – thought you should know."

Parker stepped onto the porch. If Bill was willing to talk more she was willing to listen. "Why *were* you at the school today?"

Bill snorted. "Parker," he shook his head, then looked up to the night sky. "I suppose there's no harm in telling you. The district will send out a notification tomorrow. There was a break in last night."

"What kind of break in?"

"The music room. Instruments were stolen, probably a few thousand dollars' worth."

"And you don't think that's odd with Bernstein getting the boot the day before?"

"His alibi checks." Bill hunched his shoulders. "Sure, it's an unfortunate coincidence, but he's not the type, Parker. I have his contact info if you'd like. He's a good man who could probably use a little more music in his life right now."

Couldn't we all?

21.

After a relatively painless drop off the next morning with Maddy and Drew...

Parker made her way south just outside of town to a run-down diner called *The Bottomless Cup*. It didn't take long for Parker to regret her choice of coffee shop with which to meet Mr. Bernstein. The Bottomless Cup made good on its promise of unlimited refills, but the bonus of chunky grounds in one's cup of steaming hot sewage water did little to encourage any but the most die-hard of caffeine addicts. In Chicago, Parker couldn't walk two blocks without tripping over a Starbucks -- an eyesore her eyes sorely missed.

Parker cringed as she put the foam cup to her lips again to choke down another sip, burning the last of her taste buds. She fantasized about throwing the scalding liquid into the face of her squinty eyed tattooed octogenarian barista, then following it with a lecture about the crime against nature foam cups commit simply by existing. But she worried "Popeye" might throw her out with no coffee – and somehow that seemed worse.

Finally, the front glass door swung open with a jingle of its bell as a grey haired, middle aged man wearing a brown sweater vest and round gold spectacles stepped inside. Parker instantly recognized Mr. Bernstein from the picture he had texted her. "Mr. Bernstein!" she waved.

Bernstein straightened his bow tie and glided across the floor with a gentle grace. "Ms. Parker, I presume?" he greeted her with a soft handshake.

"Ms. Monroe," corrected Parker. She offered him the seat across from her. A fresh cup of swill waited for him. "I'm going to apologize right away for the coffee."

Bernstein chortled nervously. "I must say, I was a little surprised by your choice of meeting place. Normally, I get my coffee at *The Bean* near the school."

"You said you lived on a ranch south of town. I thought this might be closer for you."

"I appreciate your thoughtfulness," said Bernstein as he sat down. "Though I'd argue patrons who come here believe coffee is something to be endured, not enjoyed. As if our beverage needs to remind us how trying life can be."

Parker grimaced. She could see Bernstein's eyes moistening. "I'm sorry, Mr. Bernstein. I know this is a tough time for you right now." Having lost her own job a few months ago, she spoke from the heart.

"Fifteen years," Bernstein had to whisper. He cleared his throat and straightened his posture. "Fifteen years I gave to that school. And now — just —" Unable to say the word, he gestured to mimic an explosion with his hands.

"Why do you think you lost your job, Mr. Bernstein?"

"Money," He answered with a rapid certainty. "It's always about money. The music program has been on the chopping block for years. Year after year Heller fought tooth and nail to keep it going. I guess, this year proved too much for her to overcome."

"Heller?" Parker asked in surprise.

Bernstein took a sip of his coffee and frowned. "Oh, god, that is awful." He carefully set the cup down as though it might explode. "I'm sorry, yes, Heller has always been a champion for music. She started the music program with me."

"*Karen* Heller?"

"You sound surprised."

"I just assumed she was the one who cut the program." *Because she's awful. And I hate her.*

Bernstein shook his head. "No, not Heller. This new Principal, *Mendez*, she's the culprit. She takes her cue from the district, I'm afraid. It's why she was hired. Always concerned about the budget. Never the children. Music and the arts are always the first casualty." Bernstein stared at his coffee cup as if debating another sip was worth the risk to quench his thirst. He looked up at Parker. "You sure ask a lot of questions."

Parker grimaced, unsure how to answer. "I used to be a reporter," she decided. *Huh, that sounds weird. 'Used' to be.*

"Oh," answered Bernstein. He shifted in his seat. "Am I being investigated?"

Parker smiled. "Sorry, no -- occupational hazard. No, no, of course not."

Bernstein pushed his glasses firmly back up the bridge of his nose. "I don't mean to be obtuse, Ms. Monroe, but what exactly are we doing here?"

"I need to find a good piano teacher for my daughter, Maddy."

"I can put you in touch with some people." Bernstein nodded. "But honestly, I could have suggested some over the phone."

Parker hunched her shoulders innocently. "I wanted to meet you in person."

Bernstein nervously pushed his glasses back up his nose. "Whatever for?"

"A friend of yours mentioned you could use some more music in your life, Mr. Bernstein. I'd like *you* to instruct my daughter on piano."

Bernstein smiled and coughed out a chuckle. "Oh no, I think I need to take some time to figure things out. I need to look for a new job."

"I'd pay you, of course."

"I couldn't, really."

"Please hear me out," said Parker. She leaned forward, warming her hands on the Styrofoam cup. "My Maddy is a brilliant player – a natural. And for most of her life she's only had one teacher. Her father, Kurt. Kurt played professionally. He loved music. I think you two would have a lot to talk about. I loved going to his shows in the jazz clubs. It's how we met. We got married and decided to start a family. But, Kurt put his career on hold to stay at home and raise our three kids. I don't think he ever regretted doing that, but I do know he missed performing. He'd try to hide it from me, was always polite, but that twinkle in his eye, you know, it wasn't there as much anymore. He needed more music in his life."

Parker paused, reflecting on the moment. Her chest became warm. "When Maddy was around five years old, Kurt caught her fiddling on our piano – and something sparked inside him. The fire returned to his eyes. He started teaching her, and she picked it up really quick. The two of them were thick as thieves. Working with Maddy for years scratched a pretty big itch for Kurt, but he needed more. He missed that thrill of performing in front of a roomful of jazz lovers in a smoky downtown Chicago club. So, we talked about it and agreed that he should start playing professionally again – do a show now and then on the weekends. He was so excited, he started practicing with his old trio on the weeknights after I got home from work. He was in love with music all over again. He was alive, really alive, for the first time in years."

Bernstein smiled. "So why did your husband stop teaching Maddy?"

Parker sighed. "His first night back at performing was at a club called the Blue Note. He'd been practicing for weeks to be ready for it. God, he was so nervous. He wondered if he still had what it took. A part of me wondered if he was going to back out. He said he would be more nervous in the beginning if I was there, watching. So, he asked me to come later. That way his nerves could settle. Funny. He wasn't worried about impressing a club full of people – just me. So, I agreed to show up late. Which, honestly, isn't too big of a stretch for me."

Parker exhaled out of her mouth. "So, I sent him off to go play the set. Took my time getting all dolled up. Waited for the sitter to arrive. Even stopped by work to check on things. I got to the club around midnight and caught the last hour of the set. From where I was sitting, I could only see three players. A bassist. A guitarist. A singer. And there, in the way back, was the upright piano. But I couldn't see Kurt. He wasn't there.

"I texted him. And texted him. Annnnnd texted him. But there was no reply. And I thought, maybe, his nerves did get the best of him. Maybe he was hiding in the back somewhere, I didn't know. When the set finished, I approached his band. *They* asked *me* where Kurt was. He never showed up to the gig."

"Cold feet?"

Parker's mind flashed to the morgue. "No." Her eyes welled up. "He was hit by a drunk driver on the interstate hours before. He never made it to the club. I'd get the call hours later."

Bernstein swallowed. "I'm so – sorry."

Parker took another deep breath. "Yeah."

The two of them sat across each other in silence for a good minute, oblivious to the action of the diner around them.

Parker cleared her throat. "My point is this – Kurt felt incomplete without performing. It was his life's blood. It's what made him whole. My daughter, Maddy, shares this with him. And I think, maybe you share it too, Mr. Bernstein. I think teaching and music are your life's blood. I'm offering you an opportunity to keep it pumping."

Bernstein sighed. "Well, maybe it's not such a bad idea after all," he said as he tapped his coffee cup. "Maybe we could try it until I found another teaching position."

Parker's eyes flashed. She was struck with a brilliant idea. "Another one? What if I got you your old one back?"

Bernstein slowly sat up. "Excuse me?"

"You say it's all about money, right? Budget concerns?"

"I'm most certain about it."

"What if I could raise the money to cover your salary? Save the whole music program?" Parker sat back in her seat. *Oh, fuck, I am good!* "How much money are we talking about? What's your annual salary?"

Bernstein sheepishly gave her the number.

Parker's eyes bulged. She couldn't believe teachers lived off such a number. "Are you butt-fucking me?" she blurted out, grabbing the attention of all the diner's patrons. Parker waved them off. "Don't get excited people! I say that kind of shit all the time!"

"No," Bernstein answered. "I'm not—" he blushed. "Doing the thing you were implying."

"Well, shit!" said Parker anxiously. She clapped her hands together. "This is going to be easier than I thought!"

Bernstein looked hopeful. "You really think you can raise that kind of money?"

Parker found herself nodding. "I'm sure as hell gonna try. I mean, come on. How hard can it be?"

22.

"I'm here to see Principal Mendez,"

Parker demanded later that morning to the Oak Creek Elementary receptionist.

The Silver Fox, as Parker had named the receptionist upon their first meeting, slowly swiveled on her chair to perfectly direct her eye daggers at Parker.

"No," answered Parker pre-emptively. "I do not have an appointment. Yes, I did just watch Principal Mendez enter the building, so I know she is present. No, that's technically not stalking. And hell no, I do not want to speak with the vice principal instead. I want the top banana."

Silver Fox swallowed before answering – a strategy Parker recognized when people wanted to buy time to formulate an answer that sounded helpful but would ultimately prove not to be. "And what is the purpose of this meeting?" asked Fox.

Parker had only one shot to get Mendez's attention. "Tell her I found a way to bridge the negative gap in Oak Creek Elementary's operating income for the coming fiscal year without having to sacrifice headcount." *Yup. I know financial terms, bitch.*

Silver Fox took a moment to process what she'd just heard, then slowly reached for the phone on her desk.

Parker leaned in. "Please be sure to use those exact words."

Much to the Silver Fox's dismay, Parker's gambit worked. Parker was soon granted permission to enter Mendez's office.

Principal Mendez sat at her desk, hammering ferociously at her laptop's keypad. Her head turned back and forth from hand written notes to her screen. She didn't bother to look up as Parker entered.

"Ms. Monroe," greeted Mendez with the minimal amount of inflection one could put into vocalizing a sentence. "I found your attempt at financial jargon most amusing."

"I like your top," replied Parker. "Did you raid my closet?"

Mendez's fingers suddenly froze along with the clatter of her keyboard. She looked up with a confused expression, just as Parker had hoped.

"We're wearing the same top," Parker explained with a chuckle. *Again. And you look way hotter in it than I do, but whatever, Mendez. Youth fades.*

"I see," Mendez tried smiling. "Why are you here, Ms. Monroe?"

"I want to put together a fundraiser for the school and bring back the music program."

Mendez closed her laptop. She tapped on it with her perfectly manicured nails. "No," she answered.

"No?" Parker scrunched her face. *Seriously?* "No? And why not?"

"Say you succeeded."

"Yeah, that would be the plan."

"Say you raised the funds for this year."

"Still the plan."

"What about *next* year?"

Parker resisted the urge to throw up her hands. Instead she calmly answered, "We make the fundraiser an annual thing."

Mendez leaned forward and kneaded her hands together. "That's quite a commitment. We already have fundraisers in the Fall and the Spring. We can only hold out our hands so many times before parents get annoyed, Ms. Monroe."

"Then we engage sponsors. And besides, parents and students won't get annoyed. They'll want the music back. They'll want Bernstein back." assured Parker.

"Bernstein?" asked Mendez. "You spoke with him?"

"I happen to know he's available." Parker nearly shot at Mendez with a wink and a finger gun, but considering her prior offense decided against it.

"Uh huh," answered Mendez. She buzzed the Silver Fox. "Pam, can you get me Vice Principal Heller, please?"

Fuck. "Why are you bringing her into this?"

"She needs to make this decision."

Parker's blood began to boil. "But *you* are the principal. You're her boss."

Mendez leaned back in her chair. "It was on Heller's recommendation that I terminate the music program."

Parker's eyes narrowed. *Bernstein told me that Heller was a supporter of the arts. Why would she choose to end the program?* Parker wanted to poke at Mendez more on the issue, but the office door suddenly swung open. Vice Principal Heller stood in the doorway, alarmed to see Parker in the office.

Heller straightened the cuffs of her suit. "You called for me?" asked Heller.

"Yes," Mendez extended her hand to invite Heller in. "You are, of course, familiar with Ms. Monroe."

"Of course," Heller's answer dripped with utter disdain.

"Parker has offered to create a fundraiser to bring back the school's music program," explained Mendez. She eyed Heller carefully. "Along with Mr. Bernstein."

Heller swallowed. "That's very -- *thoughtful* of Ms. Monroe."

Parker folded her arms. *What the hell is going on right now?*

Mendez went on. "I explained to Ms. Monroe that you were the one who decided to end the music program." The comment almost sounded like an accusation and invited a lengthy stare from Heller. "I think it's only fitting that you decide whether we should proceed with the effort to bring it back."

Sensing blood, Parker jumped in with an innocent smile. "Mrs. Heller, Mr. Bernstein mentioned you started the music program. He praised you as a great supporter of the arts."

Heller's eyes flashed. "You – spoke, with Mr. Bernstein? After I explicitly told you to stay out of the matter?"

Mendez turned to Parker.

Parker stood her ground. *Nice try.* "I didn't mean to offend you." *I also don't give a flying fuck if I did.* "I'm simply trying to help this school get its music program back. I'll do all the work. I'll raise all the money. You won't have to lift a finger. It's important to me. I thought music was important to you too." *Unless there is something going on here that you're not telling me. Or you hate me as much as I hate you. Come on, Heller. Dance with me.*

"Of course, it is important to me," said Heller breathlessly.

"Then help me bring it back."

Heller's jaw dropped. She shot Mendez an incredulous look but was unable to formulate any words. After an awkward silence, she finally pushed some out. "Putting on a fundraiser is far more complicated than you think, Ms. Monroe. There are permits, school and district by-laws to consider, parental approvals, petitions and of course –" Heller finally smiled as the idea came to her. "the PTA."

"Sure. The PTA. Of course."

Heller was practically smacking her lips now. "You'll need to get approval from them first. They'll want assurance you aren't competing with their other fundraisers."

You're going to throw as many barriers at me as you possibly can aren't you, Heller? Parker kept her eye on the prize. "So, you're essentially saying, if I get the PTA to sign off on this fundraiser that you'll give me your full support?"

Heller's smiled widened. "Of course, I will support you."

"Your *full* support." Parker wanted to clarify.

Heller held her head high. "Oh, Ms. Monroe. When I commit to something. I give it my absolute full attention."

"Fantastic."

It's on, Heller. I'm bringing music back. And whatever you're hiding? I'm exposing it. You're about to get "Parker-ed."

Yup. I made myself a verb.

23.

To get ahead of the PTA issue...

Parker opted to engage members immediately and assess the battlefield. For days, during pick-up, she'd noted women sitting at a folding table outside the school's front office armed with a barrage of home-made signs that shouted "Support your school! Support your PTA!" in neon letters. Despite the bold colors, most parents simply ignored the pleas, while others took the time to explain they "didn't bring their checkbook," they "gave last year," or they "already pay taxes."

Those working at the table varied day to day. When Parker showed up early to pick up her kids, she found a young diminutive blonde woman working the table who greeted her with a smile that devoured nearly her entire face. Remembering what Julie had said about the PTA always wanting money, Parker pulled the forty dollars in cash she'd earmarked for this first meeting from her wallet.

"Hello! I'd like to donate to the PTA," hailed Parker.

"Oh, wonderful!" the woman gleefully clapped her hands together. "The PTA thanks you! Are you donating at the twenty-five, fifty or one-hundred-dollar level?"

Parker paused. "Um, I've got forty," she answered displaying her thin roll of twenties. "So, I guess, the twenty-five level. Can you make change?"

The woman's enormous smile shrunk as her eyes searched for meaning. "Change?"

Not wanting to lose any momentum, Parker thrust the cash at the woman. "Just take it all. I'm sure you'll figure it out."

"Oh, the PTA thanks you!" The woman grabbed the cash and carefully placed it in a money box. "And the *children* thank you!"

"Yes, the children," echoed Parker. *If children ever thanked anyone for anything, I'd believe that.* Parker rubbed her hands together. "Say, I'm hoping you can help me out. I need to meet with the PTA to get a fundraiser going to bring the music program back to school. How exactly would one do that?"

The woman's smile all but disappeared as she processed the question. "You want to do – *what*?"

"Meet with the PTA to raise funds and bring the music back!"

The woman's left eye began to twitch, as if the very idea were stabbing at it somehow. "*Another* fundraiser?"

"Yes. Vice Principal Heller said I need PTA approval."

"Oh," said the woman nervously. She tried to maintain her smile as her eye twitching grew in strength. "Interesting. Heller never mentioned anything to *me* about it. Who are you?"

Parker extended her hand. "Parker. Parker Monroe."

The PTA woman gently shook Parker's hand. "Holly Hopesmith. I'm PTA President."

"You're President? Great! You're exactly who I need to talk to about the fundraiser!"

Holly coughed out a laugh. "Yes! Wow. Another fundraiser! Ha! And yet we have so many already!"

Parker got the sense Holly was strung so tightly she might snap like a rubber band at any second. "Oh, I would handle everything," Parker tried to assure the woman. "It wouldn't be any trouble for you, I promise, I just need PTA approval. Remember the *children*? This school is full of those little bastards. Let's do it for them." Parker lifted her fists. "Children! Yay!"

"Ha!" Holly released a melodic string of awkward laughter. "Yes, the children!"

As a former world-class journalist, Parker had interviewed murderers, corrupt politicians, gang leaders, tyrants and warlords, and yet something in Holly's laughter made her appear more dangerous and unbalanced than any of them. "Is this a bad time?" asked Parker. "Shall I come back?"

Holly wiped the moisture from the edge of her twitching eye. "I'm so sorry, Ms. Monroe, there's just a lot to consider. Things are never simple around here. There are rules. Procedures! To get approval you'd have to join the PTA, make an official motion at our next meeting and then get a majority vote of the present members for it to pass."

Parker hunched her shoulders. "That *sounds* rather simple."

Holly paused, as if astounded by the revelation. "It – does, doesn't it?"

"When's the next PTA meeting?"

"Next Thursday night."

"Then sign me up! I'd like to volunteer for the PTA." Parker's mind began to race with the amazing power point presentation she'd put together to sway the PTA into approving her motion.

Holly's enormous smile returned as her twitching suddenly lessened. "Lovely," she pushed forward a ledger and a pen across the table. "Just fill out your name, address and phone number, sign and date, and pay your one hundred dollars."

"Excuse me?"

"You need to pay a hundred dollars to join the PTA."

Parker looked inside her empty wallet. "Um, isn't the PTA a volunteer organization?"

"Of course!"

"So, I'm paying a hundred dollars to volunteer?"

"No, silly, you're paying a hundred dollars to join the PTA. You volunteer for free. It's all for—"

"—the children." Parker's enthusiasm was fading rapidly as she pulled her checkbook from her purse, hoping it still had blank checks in it. "Will you count the forty I already paid toward the—" Parker watched as Holly's left eye begin to twitch again. "Never mind." Parker scribbled her check and was about to hand it over when a large set of hands and muscular forearms slammed a box onto the table in front of her.

Startled, Parker took a step back. She traced the forearms to the bulging biceps attached to the V-shaped torso of a man with a chiseled jaw and coach's whistle draped around his thick neck. "Here are the member packets you asked for, Holly," said the man with a smile.

Holly gleefully clapped. "Oh, thank you! Thank you, Joe, you're just in time!" Holly reached into the box, pulled out a thick red folder and handed it to Parker. "Here is your orientation packet, Ms. Monroe! Welcome to the PTA!"

Parker had barely heard Holly. Her attention was entirely transfixed on the handsomely rugged man before her. Parker couldn't get over how familiar he looked, and yet, was certain they'd never met.

Holly took it upon herself to make introductions. "Joe is our new physical education teacher," she explained to Parker. "Joe, meet our newest PTA member -- Parker Monroe!"

"Parker Monroe," Joe's eyes narrowed as he offered a half smile. "The journalist?"

Parker's jaw dropped. *Holy fuck! Someone actually knows who I am because of my work!* "Yes," she answered in shock. "Yes, that's me! How did you know that?"

"I can read," answered Joe. He shook his head as if realizing how stupid that made him sound. "I mean, I've *read* some of your work."

Parker's heart fluttered. *My heart flutters?* "Well, it's always nice to meet a fan." She extended her hand.

Joe hesitated, then finally put forth his hand. "Yeah, uh, whatever."

Parker kicked herself inside her own head. *Never assume they are fans just because they've read your work.* Parker lost count of how many people she'd offended with her articles over the years. Still, she was excited that someone in this god forsaken town had heard of her. Her excitement turned into shock as she shook Joe's hand. His firm grip was like a steel vise. Parker was relieved when the hand shake was over.

"Anyway, nice to meet you. I've got a—thing," Joe awkwardly pointed over his shoulder. "—to finish. So, if you ladies will excuse me."

Are you--? Is he--? Creating an excuse to blow me off? Parker grimaced. "Of course," she nodded politely. As Joe turned to leave, Parker started to massage her throbbing hand. She watched him carefully as he disappeared through the front entrance of the school. "That guy has a hell of a handshake."

"Oh, yes," agreed Holly. "Probably a holdover from his Army days."

"Wait," Parker smiled back at Holly. "Army days. You're telling me he was a GI? Named Joe?"

Holly titled her head like a confused puppy. "His name is Joe, yes."

"With a firm handshake that one might liken to a *'kung-fu grip?'*" Desperately wanting Holly to pick up on her 80's action figure reference, Parker outstretched her hands as if offering a present.

Holly still wasn't following. "Are you referring to his short temper?"

Now it was Parker's turn to look confused. "Temper?"

"My son says he shouts at all the kids in gym class. I suppose he tries to run it like the Army."

As the final bell went off to dismiss the students, Parker was struck with a new clarity by Holly's statement. Her mind flashed back to the first day of school when she watched two powerful arms angrily grab Heller in the darkened music room. Parker hadn't recognized Joe's face just now, but some part of her mind must have recognized his hands, forearms and voice. She'd be willing to bet hard cash that GI Joe was the man who had threatened Heller. Parker could remember his words as clear as day.

"Whatever happens next, Heller--it's on you."

What happened next was Mr. Bernstein was fired from his job and the music program was cancelled. Then shortly after that, the school was broken into and music instruments were stolen. How did a gym teacher fit into the picture? And why would Heller, after years of supporting the music program, decide to cancel it?

24.

"I admit, it's all rather strange,"

confessed Valerie when Parker filled her in on the latest in the kitchen. "But these questions are only going to distract you from what's really important."

Parker's mouth dropped open. "Are you saying I'm easily distracted?"

Valerie cradled her own forehead in her palm. "Sweet Martha Stewart, I can't tell if you're joking anymore."

Parker folded her arms in protest. "Mother. I'm a highly trained and experienced world class journalist. I can't simply turn off my powers of perception. I can't help the fact that I'm hyper-aware of every detail in my environment."

Just then, Ally pulled at Parker's pant leg. "Yes, dear," answered Parker looking down and noticing her two and a half-year-old for what seemed like the first time. "What is – holy mother of fuck! What the hell happened to you?"

Ally smiled back innocently through a face completely covered in bold colors made to look like she was either an alien clown or Tammy Fae Bakker in a goth phase. Parker looked around the kitchen to discover thirty or so colored markers littering the table and floor with their caps off. As best as Parker could determine, Ally had just attempted to put on her own make-up Crayola style.

"A bold look, Ally," complimented Valerie with a smirk. She patted Ally on the head.

"Were you just watching her do this the whole time?" Parker blasted at her mother.

"My perceptive powers aren't anywhere nearly developed as yours, so who can be sure?"

Parker grabbed a wash cloth and dampened it in the sink. "I'm assuming this shit washes off." She rubbed Ally's face, who giggled in response. After a few scrubs, all Parker seemed to have accomplished was to add a rosy blush base. "It's not coming off." Parker scrubbed some more. "Mom, it's not coming off!"

Valerie tried to contain her snickering as the doorbell rang.

"Door!" yelled Drew from upstairs.

Parker threw the washcloth at Valerie. "I'm so glad you're amused by this."

Valerie began to scrub as Parker headed toward the entry way. Parker swore she could hear Valerie mutter a "Well, I'll be, it's not coming off, is it?" as she left the kitchen.

"Someone's at the door!" Drew yelled again from upstairs.

"We've established that!" Parker barked back. Then, as if playing the part of a mother in complete control of her children and life, she plastered a smile on her face and opened the door with the calm grace of a dancer. "Hello, Mr. Bernstein."

Mr. Bernstein smiled and pushed his glasses up the bridge of his nose. "Hello. Is now still a good time?"

"Yes," answered Parker. "Please come in. Maddy, your new piano teacher is here!" Parker did her best to raise her voice without shouting up the stairs. "Maddy? Maddy, are you there?"

"Maddy!" shouted Drew from upstairs. "Mom wants you!"

A door could be heard opening. "What?" Maddy's voice shouted back. "Why are you screaming?"

"Mom wants you!"

"Why?"

"Because some guy is here!"

"What guy?"

"It's time for your piano lesson, just get your ass down here!" Parker finally shouted at the top of her lungs. Parker did her best to offer a calm smile when she refocused her attention on Mr. Bernstein. "Do you have kids?"

Bernstein meekly shook his head. "Um, no, the wife and I were never blessed with children." Bernstein looked to the floor, almost as if ashamed by the statement. "Say, Ms. Monroe. I appreciate what you're trying to do with this and the fundraiser and all but," he looked up. "They're a lot of work and I certainly don't want to cause any trouble for you."

Parker studied Bernstein's eyes, curious of his choice of words. "What kind of trouble?"

Bernstein let out a nervous laugh. "Oh, the complications that such an undertaking is bound to create. You're a busy person, I'm sure. I don't want to make my problems yours."

"Mr. Bernstein, is there something you're not telling me?" Parker continued to search his eyes. *He's holding back. Why?* Parker tried another tact. "Is there something you'd like to tell me?"

Bernstein swallowed. "Only that I love to teach children about the wonders of music. And I'm grateful for what you're trying to do."

Parker invited Bernstein into the dining room where the piano was. "How about we make a deal? You focus on my prodigious daughter over there." Parker nodded to Maddy who suddenly appeared in the family room's entry way. She held her copy of Moonlight Sonata closely to her chest. "I'll focus on saving the music. I don't mind a little trouble, here and there Mr. Bernstein. Without it, I'd have nothing to write about."

Mr. Bernstein smiled in agreement, then turned to the young girl. "Hello Maddy," he said as he outstretched his hand. "Your mother says you're quite the player. I'm looking forward to working with you."

Maddy carefully looked Bernstein up and down. After a brief pause, she reached out to shake his hand. "Hello," she said softly.

"Is that Moonlight Sonata you've got there? Is that a favorite of yours?"

Maddy nodded quietly as she clutched the music more tightly. "I have a little trouble with the ending."

"Oh, I see. The ending of which movement?"

Maddy's eyes widened. "There's more than one?"

"Three to be precise. The final movement is incredibly intense. In fact, when Beethoven first debuted this piece he damaged the piano he performed on by playing it so hard."

Maddy finally smiled. "Huh."

Parker took a deep breath, relieved at Maddy's surprise. She leaned in to kiss her daughter on the forehead, doubly surprised that Maddy allowed it. "Alrighty then, you two do the learning thing. I'm going to help out Grandma."

As Bernstein and Maddy began to work together and pick away at the Sonata's chords, Parker noticed Valerie in the kitchen's doorway chronicling the first moments of the lesson with her cell phone. "You're recording this?" asked Parker.

"Precious memories." Valerie whispered back, a little choked up at the scene.

Parker reached for her laptop off the counter. "Send me a copy. Maybe I can use it in my presentation to the PTA. I want those bitches eating out of the palm of my hand when I'm done."

Valerie stopped recording. "You ever been to a PTA meeting before?"

"No. But how hard can it be?"

Valerie sat down across from her daughter. "There's more P's than T's, and those P's are predominantly strong-willed mothers."

"So? I'm a strong-willed mother. I fucking rock."

"Precisely. As strong-willed mothers, we also insist our children are the brightest and most beautiful creatures God ever created. We are the absolute authorities on what is best for our prodigious children and will fight to our dying breath to uphold and defend them."

"What is the problem?"

Valerie leaned in. "We can't *all* be right *all* the time." Valerie nodded to Ally whose face was a portrait of smeared colors. "Now, imagine a roomful of women who believe they are."

Parker grimaced. "I'm going to need reinforcements." She picked up her cell phone and dialed. "Julie? It's me, Parker. Yeah, crazy right? Listen, I'm hoping I can ask a favor from you. What? Nope. The beauty is it will only cost you a hundred dollars."

25.

Parker was used to hitting tight deadlines...

but Thursday night's PTA meeting arrived fast even by journalism standards. She worked late into several nights gathering her data, fretting over the right stock photos to use and rewriting each slide of her presentation to pull at every last heart string and achieve maximum impact. Now it was time to deliver. Continuing her theme of over preparedness, Parker pulled her Highlander into the school's parking lot at precisely 6:30pm the night of the PTA meeting, a full thirty minutes early. Her plan was to stake out attendees as they filed in. But all she found was a vacant lot until 6:47 when a tanned woman's hand sporting a large amount of diamond jewelry knocked on her driver's side window.

"Sorry I'm late," apologized Julie with a wide smile. She raised her red solo cup and took another sip. "But I didn't really want to show up when you asked me to. Or at all."

"You showed up, that's what counts." Parker rolled down her window. Her nose immediately scrunched up from the strong waft of booze that hit her. "Holy hell, Julie how much have you been drinking?"

"Glory and I have been at the bar for the past hour," she jammed her thumb like a hitchhiker to direct Parker's attention to Glory, who stepped into view, Hawaiian shirt and all. "Maybe longer."

"'Sup! I'm the designated driver!" Glory gave an enthusiastic two thumbs up.

"I promised myself a long time ago I'd never attend a PTA meeting sober," Julie hiccupped. "Mission accomplished."

Parker frowned. She knew it was a risk inviting Julie, but she figured she'd only have to contend with her big mouth. The alcohol might enlarge that same mouth to unacceptable proportions. "Fine. Just remember to vote my way when the time comes."

"What can I do?" asked Glory innocently.

Parker wasn't sure how the PTA might receive Glory's porn-star moustache, but his unbridled enthusiasm made it hard to turn him away. "Are you a PTA member?"

"No, but I can sign up."

"Perfect," answered Parker. "Just be sure to vote for my motion when the time comes. Also, it's gonna cost you a hundred dollars."

Glory nodded. "No problem." He winced. "Can I borrow a hundred dollars?"

"I gotcha, Glory," said Julie as she patted him on the back of the head. "You can pay me back – *later.*" Julie started to giggle.

"Cool." Glory caught Julie as she stumbled backward.

As Parker eyed her would-be allies she regretted the decision to leave Valerie home with the kids. *All I need is a simple majority. If I can sway half the room, Glory and Julie will put me over the top.*

"Oh shit, it's the cops!" shouted Julie in a slurred voice. She stumbled to avoid the bright headlights aimed at her by the Sheriff's car that pulled into the parking lot. Glory struggled to hold Julie upright as she skated in place. "Shit, did he see me? Did he see me?"

Parker climbed out of her Highlander as the Sheriff's car eased to a halt next to her.

Sheriff Bill climbed out of the patrol car. "Evening, Parker." He turned to examine Glory holding a skating Julie. He sniffed. "Wow - - is she drunk?"

"Is she in trouble if she is?" asked Parker.

"Not if she isn't driving and it's after school hours," answered Bill.

"Then, yeah, she's piss drunk." Parker grabbed her laptop from her car. "What are you doing here, Sheriff?"

Bill pulled up on his belt buckle as other cars began to file into the parking lot. "Heller wanted me to show up to the PTA meeting tonight." He winked. "You know, in case things get out of hand."

"Seriously?"

Bill smiled. "Oh, she's been on a pins and needles since the break-in. I told her I'd stop by and look around since the school is going to be open after hours."

"I see," Parker smiled back. "Then don't be surprised if I ask you to do some magic tricks to warm up the crowd."

"Yeah right," Bill laughed the comment off, then scratched the back of his head as if entertaining the thought. "Well, I mean, I've got some cool card tricks if you're in a bind."

"Card tricks?" Parker tried to sound impressed.

Bill's face lit up. "Oh yeah, it's all about the art of misdirection, you know?" He waved his hands like an expert prestidigitator. "Where is your eye looking, and what am I hiding while you're looking right at me?" With a snap of a finger, an ace of spades seemed to appear in his hand as if out of thin air. "Presto!" He offered the card to Parker.

"Amazing." Parker politely refused the card and clutched her laptop. "But I wasn't being serious about warming up the crowd."

"Oh, yeah, I knew that." Bill pretended to wave Parker off.

"I gotta trick for yah, occifer!" hiccupped Julie. She grabbed her crotch as Glory dragged her by.

Parker grimaced. "Let's hope they've got some strong coffee inside."

26.

Oak Creek Elementary's "Great Hall" proved to be nothing of the sort.

Despite being the largest room in the entire school it still somehow managed to feel small and claustrophobic, crammed with a small stage at the front that featured a portable screen lit up by a projector in the back of the room. Folding chairs were sporadically spread across the floor. Parker counted twenty-some people in the room, including President Holly teetering across the worn carpet floor as she carried a podium that looked as though it were two inches taller than her. As Holly plopped the podium down and retrieved a plastic milk carton crate to stand on, Parker made her way to the back of the room to the two women working the video projector.

"Hi, I'm Parker Monroe," greeted Parker. "I'm going to be presenting tonight. How do I plug in my laptop to your projector?"

The first woman offered a thick cable with a frayed connector that looked as though it dated back to the Speak 'N' Spell era. Parker balked, knowing her state of the art laptop would reject such a relic. "Do you have an adapter for that or--?" She looked to the other woman, who she immediately recognized as the Baby-Faced mother from the playground on the first day of school. "Oh, shit – hi!" Parker tried smiling. "Wow, it's *you*. You're – everywhere."

Baby Face arched an eyebrow without a word.

I may be down one vote already.

Parker decided to focus on the first woman. "Perhaps I could quickly email you the presentation?" Luckily, the first woman agreed to the emailing, and plugged in a heavy school laptop that proudly displayed the name "Google" spelled with two "g's" and a "u." Parker imagined the school purchasing their computers in a dark alley out of the back of some Jersey accented guy's van.

"Alright, everyone, if you're just coming in, please take a seat. We're about to get started," announced Holly. The PTA president stood on her tip toes to speak into the microphone. "Welcome, welcome all! I see the Sheriff is here! Wow! A celebrity!" Holly pointed to the back of the room, where Bill leaned against the wall. "And we have some new, um--faces." Her smile weakened as she looked at Glory who sat comfortably in the front row with his legs spread open as far they could possibly go. Julie slouched in the chair next to him and wore sunglasses which made it impossible to know if she was conscious, sleeping or dead. "And I see, Joe Ward, our gym teacher walking in! That's super! We rarely have teachers show up to these things, so that is a real treat!"

Parker looked up from the projector table. *GI JOE?* Sure enough, Joe the gym teacher walked in through the back entrance and reluctantly waved to Holly. His eyes caught Parker's for a moment. She smiled and waved. He sat down without so much as a glance. *Did he see me?*

"And of course, Vice Principal Heller is joining us tonight. How wonderful to see you, Karen!"

Parker watched Heller like a hawk as she entered the room, wearing a proud smirk as an accessory to her stiff navy-blue pantsuit. Heller's eyes locked with Parker's. Unlike Joe's instance, there was no mistaking the contact.

"I'll begin with an announcement from Heller," Holly continued. "We should all be aware that as a result of the 'Riley Incident' on the playground last week the act of throwing dodgeballs will no longer be allowed during the game of dodgeball." Holly's declaration garnered a few polite claps. "Yes, I know, it's about time. I'm relieved Heller has taken such decisive and brave action to reduce the risk of concussions to our children."

Parker resisted the urge to slap her forehead. *Did Heller deliberately start the meeting with such a dumbass announcement to throw me off?* Parker felt obligated to test the waters and shot her hand high up into the air. "Ummmmm—question!"

"Oh yes, of course!" a delighted Holly replied. "Everyone, this is Parker Monroe, one of our newest PTA members! She will be presenting to us shortly. What is your question?"

Parker tried to choose her words carefully. "How are kids supposed to *play* dodgeball if they can't *throw* the ball?"

Holly blinked, perhaps to stave off a twitch. "Oh, well, children are quite creative. I'm sure they'll find a way to make it fun."

"Of course," answered Parker. She was about to sit down when a nasty itch of common sense overcame her. Parker stood back up. "I'm sorry, I don't want to spend any more time on this then we have to, but I just want to offer the simple observation that someone throwing a ball is a key component to someone being able to dodge that same ball. I mean, that's just physics. Am I making sense?"

Holly licked her lips. "Ms. Monroe, I really don't profess to be an expert in the game of dodgeball. I didn't create the rules. I'm only explaining for what the rules allow for *now*. As PTA President, it is my duty to ensure I spread the word appropriately to parents and help keep our children safe."

Parker pinched the bridge of her nose. *Just – stop. Stop talking, Parker. Don't engage this any further. Save it.* "I'm sorry, Holly, you're right. Neither of us are dodgeball experts." *Nice. Let this die.* "Luckily, we *do* have an expert among us tonight who could fill us in on the finer points of the game." *Fuck, what are you doing?* Parker pointed to GI Joe. "Joe, you're the physical education teacher. Educate us. How is dodgeball supposed to work without being able to throw balls?"

Joe sat in the middle of the room. His face blushed a hot red as all eyes turned on him.

Heller put her hands on her hips and stepped forward from the back, so Joe was sure to notice her. "Yes, Joe, *please* enlighten us." Her tone somehow proved threatening and encouraging at the same time.

Joe sucked air in through his nostrils and exhaled. "If I must," he said as he stood up. "In a normal game of dodgeball, there are two opposing teams divided by an imaginary line that throw balls at one another. If a player is hit by the opposing team's ball, they are out. If a player catches the other team's ball, the thrower is out. Both teams play until all the opposing players are eliminated. So, yes, without the act of throwing, the game of dodgeball doesn't really work. Though, I suppose there might be a version where students rolled the ball to each other – but that would be horribly – *lame.*"

With wide eyes, Parker delicately placed her right hand over her heart to feign shock. "Wait. So, I'm right?"

Heller put her hands together as if praying. "Oh, you're more than right, Ms. Monroe," she eagerly agreed. "Thank you for helping me see the error of my decision."

Parker's eyes narrowed. "You're—welcome?"

"The only real solution," Heller continued. "Is to ban dodgeball altogether from the playground. Like we did with Tag and Kickball."

Heller's statement earned several groans and statements from the PTA audience.

"What? No, don't take away dodgeball too!"

"She must! The children! The concussions!"

"Why does Parker hate children?"

"No, Parker clearly hates fun! And dodgeball!"

"Is Parker her first name or her last?"

Parker stared Heller down and offered a silent sarcastic clap in recognition. *Well played, but the night isn't over.*

Holly's eye twitch was on full display as she leaned closer to the microphone. "Okay, order! Order please! We still have lots of things to go through tonight! Please settle down!" The cacophony of complaints finally simmered. Holly took a deep breath to tame her one eye. "Thank you. Now, a few more announcements before we move on. The Back to School dance is next Friday night in this very room from 5pm to 7pm. The theme is 'Safety Dance.'"

Yes! I love that 80's song! Wait...

"We'll need some volunteers to demonstrate proper boundaries and the dangers of invading one's personal space on the dance floor. Any takers? Jill? Great. Any others?"

Yup. It's not the cool Safety Dance. It's literally a dance about safety.

"And let's remember that twerking of any kind is prohibited."

It was all Parker could do not to raise her hand and ask: "Do you need volunteers to demonstrate twerking?" Fortunately, Glory sprung to life and did it for her. "Because I'm happy to help!" He added enthusiastically.

"Um, no," answered Holly, clearly disturbed by the question. "I think we're good."

Glory raised his hand again.

"Yes?"

"What about Popping? Locking? Krumping? Breaking? Turfing? Jerkin'? Or Tutting?"

Holly had to cover her twitching eye with her hand. Lost, she turned to Vice Principal Heller. "Um, do you have any information on those, Vice Principal Heller?"

Heller's smile finally broke down into a scowl. "Use your better judgment, Mr. Wonder."

Glory offered two thumbs up. "You bet!"

"Alright, then," Holly spoke quickly, anxious to get off the podium. "If no one else has any other business to bring up, then I will yield the floor to Mrs. Parker who seeks permission to start another fundraiser."

The statement prompted strong murmurs from the crowd as Holly dashed away.

"Another fundraiser?"

"It better not interfere with my fundraiser."

"Why do we need another fundraiser?"

Glory clapped loudly as Parker made her way to the podium and adjusted the microphone. "Hi. Hello," she greeted. "My name is actually Parker Monroe. And for the record, I don't hate children." She squinted to see in the far back and made contact with Baby Face. "Can we? Can you -- start my power point presentation?"

Baby Face clicked a button on the laptop, but only an empty square of blue appeared on the viewing screen next to Parker. Confused, Baby Face started pressing more buttons, trying to fix the connection.

Parker sighed. *I'm going to have to wing it.* "Okay, well, it looks like we're having some technical difficulties back there. So, while that's getting fixed, let me just dive in." The microphone squeaked loudly suddenly from feedback. "Shit," Parker readjusted the mic. "I mean, fuck. Sorry! This mic looks like something from the Price is Right."

"Why do we need another fundraiser?" shouted a voice from the back.

"Is this going to take money away from our other fundraisers?" shouted another voice.

"What do you have against the Price is Right?"

Parker chuckled. "Alright! Great, wow, you're engaged already. That's good," she said. "That means I've got your attention. And if you save your questions until the end, I promise I'll explain everything. You see, the truth is, I don't want to start another fundraiser."

Parker's statement immediately quieted the room. She felt that all eyes were suitably glued to her. *Wait for it.*

Finally, a hand shot up in the back. "Then why are you here?" asked a mother.

Parker smiled. "I'm glad you asked."

27.

Invoking the great Bob Barker...

Parker pulled the microphone off its stand and walked away from the podium to better engage her crowd. "I don't want to start another fundraiser," she repeated. "And I know neither do any of you. I get it. I might be new, but I get it. PTA already pays for everything. Right? You pay for the new computers in the science lab. You pay for all the balls on the playground, though it sounds like we won't need as many after the whole dodgeball thing. You pay for the playground equipment. You pay for the art supplies in the classroom." Parker made an effort to connect with every mother in that room — except for Julie whose jaw was agape as though she were sleeping. "You pay for those fifth graders who can't afford to go to science camp in the spring, so no child is left out of the experience. You pay for field trips. You pay for special awards to acknowledge students. You pay for every new book that gets added to our library. You fund every special event that teaches our children to steer clear of drugs, make healthy eating choices, and build self-esteem. After the last school bell rings, you pay for the education that continues outside of the classroom and inspires us. You, the PTA pays for all of that and more." Parker stopped her pacing. "Why?" Parker looked directly at Vice Principal Heller. "Why doesn't the school pay for these things? Or the district? We pay our taxes. We get grants from state and federal programs. Where does all that money go?"

Heller's nostrils flared.

Parker answered her own question before Heller could butt in. "Teachers. Oak Creek Elementary puts every cent it can toward paying its hard-working teachers. But, let's be honest. Even with all that focus our teachers live on pathetic salaries. I credit our school for putting teachers first. They are the backbone of our kids' education. But we all know it's not enough. It's never been enough to push our school's education to the first class, award winning experience that Oak Creek Elementary prides itself on giving.

"You know this. Which is why you bust your asses volunteering. Which is why you work hard to raise the funds that you do. To provide your kids with the best. Because they deserve the best. I admire you for that." Parker took a moment to study the crowd, noting several nods by the mothers before her. "All of you have given everything you've got to this school and yet somehow you still find ways to give more. Honestly, I don't know how you all do it. I can barely get my kids to school on time. I don't want to do another fundraiser. It's too much. I cringe about the commitment I'm signing up for. But in the presence of such great women, who've given so much, I can't in good conscience sit idly by and watch Oak Creek's music program fade away simply because the money isn't there. I don't need to remind everyone how critical and life changing music education can be to a young mind. You've read the articles. You know the statistics -- that kids who learn to excel in music score better in math and science. You know that music provides a healthy emotional outlet. You know the benefits of good practice habits and the discipline it takes in learning to master an instrument or play a piece of music. I don't want to do another fundraiser. I don't want to have to save the music program. But I have no choice."

The room remained quiet. Parker allowed herself a modest smile. *I think I may have gotten through to them. Maybe.* Parker looked over to where Vice Principal Heller stood -- only to find her missing. Parker scanned the room. Heller was nowhere to be found. *Did Heller bail just as I was hitting my stride?*

Parker cleared her throat and refocused on her audience. "I'll do all the work," she assured them. "None of you will have to lift a finger. All I'm asking for is your permission to move forward. That's all. It won't cost any of you any more time, money or blood sweat and tears. It's just a matter of saying 'yes.' So, I'm asking you, please, will you allow me to start a fundraiser to—" A bright light flashed in

Parker's face as the video projector in the back of the room suddenly came alive. "Oh!" Parker threw up a hand to shield her eyes. "Wow! It looks as though we finally got my power point presentation going! Nice timing!"

The audience appeared confused by what they saw.

Curious, Parker turned to look at the projection screen behind her. But instead of the first slide of the presentation she had emailed to the PTA, she stared at a photograph of her silver Toyota Highlander.

"That's my car," stated a confused Parker. "What is my car doing--?" She paused. Her heart sank. She finally recognized where her car was parked. It was a photograph of her car in Heller's driveway from the first day of school.

"Wait! That's your car?" a mother shouted from the back of the room.

Oh, sweet mother of shit. Parker hung her head, realizing she'd just made a blatant confession in front of a roomful of mothers. *This might be a game changer.*

28.

"That's your car!"

another mother blasted from somewhere in the room.

Parker looked up at the video screen that displayed the front page of Oak Creek's social media page. The most recent post headlined: *"Oak Creek's Most Wanted! Be on the lookout for these traffic offenders and remind them that safety and courtesy come first!"* Posted by Helcat1913. The post went on to showcase other horrible parking jobs by various parents. A BMW parked in the handicapped space near the front of the school. A picture of a Dodge Ram parked in front of a fire hydrant. And so on, and so on.

"Did you park in the Vice Principal's driveway?" asked another mother.

Fuck it. Face the music and change the conversation. "Yes," answered Parker. "I did. I'm not proud of it."

The room erupted into judgment and chaos.

"What kind of person does that?"

"Doesn't she know Mr. Heller is a very ill man?"

"And she wants us to trust her?"

Parker raised her hands to quell the growing wave of dissent. "If it makes you feel any better, my car was towed! I paid a ridiculous fine! Please, *please* don't let this detract from what we're trying to accomplish tonight!"

"Heller was right!"

"I'm not helping her!"

"She only thinks of herself!"

Then it happened.

Julie, who had remained dead quiet on Glory's shoulder during the entire meeting, suddenly sprung out of her chair and turned to face the crowd. "All of you shut up! Shut up!" she screamed at the top of her lungs. "I said shut the fuck up!"

The crowd simmered in silence, stunned as Julie held her throbbing head.

"I've got a monumental headache," Julie yelled again. "And you horrid bitches aren't helping!" Julie bent over and put her hands on her knees. For a moment it looked as though she might throw up. The mere threat of it kept everyone quietly on the edge of their seats. "Now, you're all well within your right to judge this woman." Julie pointed blindly in the general direction of Parker. "She is an asshole. And like all assholes, she shits everywhere and on everything. That's what assholes do."

Parker winced. *Not sure if this is helping or hurting, but no one is currently yelling at me so I'm going to let it play out.*

"What I'm saying is -- shit happens," Julie clarified. "Especially where assholes are concerned. But don't any of you pretend that *your* shit doesn't stink. It does. I've known most of you phonies for a long time. Mary, in the back there, you cheat on your workouts in the gym. That's right! Your push-ups are a joke. Blanche? We all know about your botched lip job. I mean, look at those things. Your mouth is a fucking flotation device. Jane? Your husband left you for a twinkie two months ago. Not your fault, but stop pretending, okay? We've all seen him and his boyfriend making out at the gay bar downtown. Carrie? Your oldest boy is cruel to animals, constantly plays with his dick in church and will likely grow up to be a serial killer. I'd consider sending him to military school."

The horde of insulted mothers was about to erupt into righteous indignation, but Julie's next yell stopped it dead in its tracks. "Shut your god damn pie holes!" she screamed. "I could go on and on! Like about how Natalia over there likes the taste of her gardener's filthy cock when her husband is away on business. Yup! Word gets around, Natalia! The fact is none of you ho-bags are perfect! All of you have made mistakes from time to time. Parker may have fucked up with the whole parking thing, but let's be honest, Heller acts like a Nazi-bitch sometimes and she probably had it coming. And don't even pretend that you like Heller, either, because I've heard you all complain about her. Now, Parker is trying to do something good, *really* good. I guess. Not just for her dumb ass kids, but for your dumb ass kids. She'll do all the work. God knows I don't want to help her. I'm busy. But for some god forsaken reason she's volunteering to do it! She paid a hundred dollars just to show up and talk to you Stepford wives! So, shit, just let her do the fundraiser, alright? I mean -- damn! Enough, already! Now, are we gonna vote on this, or shall I go down the list about every shitty little secret I know about each of you?"

"Let's vote!" Holly clapped her hands together enthusiastically.

"Smart choice, Holly!" said Julie, pointing to the PTA president. "Because you were next."

Holly joined Parker on the stage. "I hereby motion to allow Ms. Monroe to do a fundraiser to save Oak Creek's music program. All in favor say 'aye' and raise your hand!"

An assortment of hands with "aye's" shot up in the audience, prompting Holly to count them one by one. "That's eleven who are in favor," she declared. "All who are opposed, say 'nay' and please raise your hand." Another assortment of hands shot up, and Holly counted them in turn. She frowned. "That's, um, also eleven who are opposed. Huh."

Are you fucking kidding me? Parker couldn't help but to wonder what the vote would have been had her photograph not suddenly appeared out of nowhere.

"Make that twelve who are opposed," announced Vice Principal Heller as she re-entered the room. "I'm sorry, Ms. Monroe, I know I told you I would support this, but I'm convinced now more than ever that another fundraiser would detract too much money from our current ones. We simply won't raise enough to continue with our established programs. I have no choice but to vote no."

Parker's cheeks and forehead rushed red with blood. *You -- bitch.*

"Then it's eleven to twelve, and the motion is—"

"Wait!" Parker shouted. She grabbed Holly by the shoulders. "Holly, you didn't vote! Are you in favor, or not in favor?"

Holly hunched her shoulders. "As President, I'm not allowed to vote. I can only put forth the motions."

"Fuck." Parker's hand slowly lowered like a balloon rapidly losing air. She spotted Sheriff Bill who had successfully kept his face buried in his phone during the entire meeting so as not to engage at all. "Sheriff! I didn't see your hand go up! Where do you stand on this issue?"

Bill let out as nervous chortle. "Oh, Parker, I'm not a parent. Or a teacher. I don't think I'm allowed to vote either."

"You cannot vote," Heller insisted.

Holly took a deep breath. "So, with a final tally of eleven to twelve—"

"Wait!" Parker shouted again, her hand shooting back up into the air. "I didn't vote! Can I vote? I can vote right? Even though it's my fundraiser? Because I'm definitely in favor of my fundraiser!"

Holly nodded. "Of course! That makes it twelve to twelve." She sighed. "But I'm afraid the motion still won't pass as you need a simple majority of the members present."

Parker's hand and hopes dropped once again.

Julie sprung up from her seat. "Are you fucking kidding me?" she shouted. "You nasty, horrid twats are just begging me to go public with the rest of your smutty secrets! I demand a revote!"

"Ms. Julie!" scolded Heller. "I will not tolerate your drunken rants any more than I will allow you to blackmail any member of this committee into changing their vote! Now, please, sit down and shut your filthy pie hole or I will ask the Sheriff to escort you outside in handcuffs!"

Bill grimaced, looking back to Heller as if saying "really?"

Julie used her middle finger to push her sunglasses back up the bridge of her nose. Then she smiled at Sheriff Bill. "Promise to be gentle with me, Sheriff." Glory quickly tugged at Julie's arm to pull her down into her chair.

Holly's eyes continued to search the room. "Did I miss anyone? Did anyone not vote?" she asked. "For or against?"

Heller became impatient and tapped her foot. "Please just call it, Holly, the motion obviously didn't pass."

Joe the Gym teacher stood up. "I didn't vote." He declared as he stared back at Heller. "I'm assuming I still can."

Heller's jaw dropped open. After a moment's respite, she tugged at her suit jacket to smooth it of any creases. "Alright then, Joe," she swallowed her words. "What is your vote? Are you for or against the fundraiser?"

Joe's eyes narrowed.

29.

Joe turned back to Holly.

"I don't even know why there is a debate about this. I'm new, but as I understand it this school had an amazing music program. If Parker thinks she can raise the money to bring it back, then let her try. I'm in favor of the motion."

Parker let out a sigh of relief.

Holly clapped. "Let the record show that the motion passed at a vote of thirteen to twelve. Ms. Monroe, you may proceed with your fundraiser."

"Thank you," said Parker.

"Woohoo! Fuck you, you PTA twats!" cheered Julie before leaning over and throwing up all over the floor. Victory smelled like vomit.

"Lovely," Holly rubbed her twitching eye. "Can someone go find a janitor? Thank you. Also, I think we've all had a good amount of excitement this evening, so as PTA president I'm adjourning this meeting early. Good night!" Holly dashed off the stage and out of the room. The PTA members began to disband, some with smiles, others as models of rage and disgust.

Glory waved goodbye as he tugged at Julie to follow him to the exit. "Congratulations, Parker! We'll see you around!"

Parker didn't care about her victory right now. Hot with rage, she looked at the photo of her Highlander on the screen behind her, and then to Baby Face, who had manned the video projector. Baby Face was a deer in the headlights as Parker bolted across the room to confront her. "Would you mind explaining to me how the hell a picture of my Highlander is the first image that popped onto that screen as opposed to the presentation I emailed you?" blasted

Parker. "Because if I didn't know better, I'd say you were trying to sabotage me!"

Baby Face's mouth opened, but no sound came out.

Parker looked back at the social media posting. According to its time stamp, the photo was posted by Helcat1913 within the last hour, an incredibly suspicious coincidence. "Helcat1913? Is that your tag?" Parker blasted again.

"You don't need to answer any of that," Heller assured Baby Face as she approached the table. "Ms. Parker is simply a sore *winner* trying to draw attention away from the fact that *she* parked in my driveway the first day of school."

Parker clenched her fist. "So, was it *you* who posted the photo, Heller? Is that why you left in the middle of my presentation? To exact your revenge?"

Heller titled her head. "Are you finally admitting it was you who parked in my driveway?"

"Yes!" spat Parker, owning up to it.

"I knew it!" Heller jabbed her pointer finger into Parker's chest.

"Don't turn this around!" Parker yelled. "Are you Helcat1913?"

"I am *not*," answered Heller coolly.

"Really?" Parker wasn't buying it for a second. "Helcat? *Heller?* What is 1913, the year you were born?"

Heller shook her head. "That would mean I'm over a hundred years old. Do your math!"

"I *did*!"

Frightened by the display before her, Baby Face quietly grabbed her purse and made for a hasty exit. The remaining mothers, Sheriff Bill and Joe stood paralyzed as they watched the catfight unfold before them.

139

"Just fucking admit it!" Parker seethed. "You tried to sabotage my presentation!"

"I did nothing of the sort!" insisted Heller. "When the school's laptop boots up, it loads the PTA's social media page! I can't help the fact that a photo of your flagrant misdeed turned out to be the headline!"

"Bullshit!" Parker was full on livid by now. "You've had it in for me since day one! You've thrown every ridiculous rule in the book at me!"

"Oh, yes, it's all about you, Ms. Monroe. You can't ever see beyond yourself!" Heller took another step forward and wagged her finger. "Is it ridiculous to expect students and their parents to refrain from *shooting* at each other on school grounds?"

"You know damn well that was meant to be a show of affection. You blew it up!"

"Poor choice of words. Is it ridiculous to expect parents to refrain from meddling with school affairs on a daily basis? To do as instructed and not contact fired employees days after their dismissal? Is it ridiculous to expect one's private driveway to be free of trespassers? Is it ridiculous to ask parents to wear appropriate clothing on school grounds?"

"Appropriate clothing?" Parker paused, remembering Heller's brief lecture over her tight clothing. "Oh, I see, was I showing too much of these the other day? Were they threatening you?" Parker cupped her own breasts to push them at Heller. "How many buttons are acceptable, Mrs. Heller, please, *please* tell me! This many?" Parker popped open the top button of her white blouse. "How about *this* many?" She popped another few buttons. "Shall I go on?"

Heller rolled her eyes as Parker continued to expose her cleavage.

Parker threw her arms up in the air. "I don't get it Heller. Maybe it's because you've got the body of a wrinkled eleven-year-old boy, but do you really despise me so much that even my boobs offend you? Are you so desperate to win that you must resort to body shaming? I can't help the fact that after giving birth these things kept getting bigger and dare I say more spectacular!" Parker caught herself full on screaming at the old woman before her. She forced a deep breath in an attempt to calm down, but her adrenaline was pumping way too high. "But you wouldn't know about any of that crap! You haven't experienced the hormonal shit show that childbirth imposes on a woman because you've been so focused on your god damn career you never bothered to have any children of your own! And what did all that hard work get you? You're still just a Vice Principal reporting to a woman a third your age!"

Heller swallowed. She stood in silence as her eyes began to well up. Parker had finally struck a major nerve, and the vice principal was paralyzed.

Bill stepped forward. "Alright now, Parker. Maybe we should all cool off."

"What are you, Heller's bodyguard? Why did she even ask you here?" Parker scoffed as she brushed Bill away and got back into Heller's face. "Maybe it's because payback's a bigger bitch than even her!" Parker leaned forward, so she was nose to nose with Heller. "You're lucky I'm holding back. Because next time, *next time* you decide to pass judgment on me or my family in anything but a purely academic context? I'll come at you with *both* barrels!" Parker cupped her breasts and aimed them at Heller like a shotgun. "How is *that* for gun control?"

Heller's nostrils flared. She remained uncharacteristically silent as she stared straight into Parker's eyes. The moment felt like an eternity.

Satisfied, or exhausted, she couldn't decide which, Parker turned to scan the remaining PTA mothers who gawked at her in abject silence. Her eyes found Joe, who was the only person in the room who appeared remotely comfortable. For the first time, he looked at Parker with a half a smile, smug though it was. "You got something to say, GIJOE?" Parker challenged.

"No, Ma'am." He answered softly.

"Smart." Parker buttoned her shirt back up and grabbed her laptop off the desk. "Now, if you'll all excuse me, I've got a mother fucking fundraiser to plan."

Parker took her leave.

30.

"How did it go?"

Parker repeated Valerie's question on her cellphone as she marched toward her Highlander in the school parking lot. "I may or may not have lost my shit in there." Parker over-pronounced her words to remain in control of the adrenaline high that continued to surge through her. Her heart pounded at her chest like a trip hammer.

"Can you move forward with the fundraiser?" asked Valerie.

Parker stopped at her car, closed her eyes and drew in a deep breath of the dry evening air. She exhaled. "Yes. The measure passed by one vote."

"One vote? That's amazing!"

Parker opened her eyes in time to spy Joe walking to his car. "Yeah, it is," she answered. Out of the periphery she saw Heller emerge from the school's windowed doors, carrying a black leather briefcase. Her boney little legs carried her at a brisk pace. Parker's eyes narrowed as she watched Joe look at Heller, who didn't so much as bother to glance his way. The vice principal ignored him as she unlocked her car, climbed in, and drove away, taking a sharp left. "That's odd."

"What's odd?"

"Heller just left," Parker answered, looking at her watch. 8:04pm. "And she's driving away from her house."

"How do you know?"

"Are you kidding?" Having parked in Heller's driveway, she was all too familiar with the location just up the road in the opposite

143

direction. In fact, it was a short walk away. *Why would Heller feel the need to drive to the PTA meeting at all?*

"Maybe she's hitting the bar. You've turned several people to the bottle over the course of your career."

Parker grimaced. She shifted her attention back to Joe who also watched Heller drive off. *Is he wondering the same thing?* "Listen, Mom, I've got to go. I'll see you when I get home, okay?" Parker didn't wait for her mother's goodbye. There was a new zip in her step as she approached Joe. "Joe! Hold on!"

Joe was just about to open his car door when his head turned toward Parker. He looked up and frowned.

Out of breath, Parker waved hello. "I didn't mean to bite your head off in there," she panted. "And I wanted to thank you."

"For what?"

Parker chuckled. "You know, for helping me pass the measure. And sticking it to Heller. But mostly for passing the measure."

Joe scowled. "Ms. Monroe, I didn't vote the way I did to stick it Heller. And I didn't do it to help you."

Parker eased off the pedal of her enthusiasm. "Okay."

"I did it, because it was the right thing to do."

"Oh hell, you're one of those?" joked Parker. Joe wasn't having it. "Fine, whatever, I'm just trying to say thank you."

Joe opened his car door. "Have a good night."

"Now, wait a minute," Parker stepped in front of Joe's car. "Did I offend you or something? Ever since we met—" Parker couldn't finish the sentence.

Joe tapped his finger on the roof of his car. "What?"

"I don't know, you've been really cold and stand-offish. Normally people only do that *after* they've gotten to know me. So, what gives?"

"Why do you always think everything is about you?"

Parker brushed a strand of hair away from her forehead. "I don't think that."

"Then why are we still talking?"

Because you know something about Heller. And I want to know what it is. "You didn't have to show up tonight," retorted Parker. "You're the only teacher who did. That says something."

"What does it say?"

Parker threw her hands up in the air. "You tell me!"

Joe sighed exhaustedly. "Why--are you so interested in me?"

Parker threw her hands on her hips. "Why do you think everything is about *you*?"

"Good night."

Parker decided to play her ace. "I heard you and Heller arguing in the music room," she blurted.

Joe froze.

"It was the first day of school."

Something in Joe's eyes changed as he glared at Parker. Parker could practically feel the heat radiating off him. "You were--spying on us?"

"I didn't mean to. You were arguing. I could hear it down the hall. It sounded—intense."

Joe shook his head. "We were simply having a disagreement."

"I saw you grab Heller forcefully by the arms."

Joe's eyes began to glisten. His lips drew tight as he stared at the pavement. "Shit," he muttered. He turned back to Parker. "You saw that? I didn't mean to -- I apologized. It's just – sometimes," he choked on his words as he clenched his fists. "I don't need to explain this to you. And I *don't* have a problem with Heller."

"I just want to understand."

"You want to understand?" Joe let out a noise that somehow combined an angry grunt with a laugh. "Let's just say I have hard time taking orders from desk jockeys who care more about the rules of engagement than the safety of their troops."

Interesting. Is he talking about Heller? Or Mendez?

Joe looked to the night's starry sky in an effort to calm himself. "Listen," he gulped, trying to hold his emotion back. "I didn't want to hurt Heller. And I don't want to be rude. I just don't trust reporters, okay?"

"Good thing I'm retired."

The comment invited another scornful glare from Joe. "No, Ms. Monroe, you were fired." He corrected.

The words shot through Parker's heart like a hot jagged blade. *Shit, are you kidding me? The one guy in this god forsaken town who's familiar with my work read the one thing I got wrong?*

Parker swallowed. "You're referring to my story on Senator Hammers."

"Come on, that was hardly a story," Joe scoffed. "You wrote a hit piece that slandered a good man."

Joe's last sentence twisted that same jagged blade deeper into her heart. Parker felt every muscle in her body clench. "A good man? Do you know the senator personally? Are you a close friend of his?"

"No," answered Joe. "But he's a former ranger. And he's always supported us troops. That's enough for me."

Big mistake. "Well, I *do* know him," Parker clenched her fists. "I've met him. I spent a year researching him. He's a liar, a cheat and fraud."

"That's funny coming from someone who lost her job over writing a fake headline."

Oh—no—you—didn't. Parker felt her cheeks glowing hot red. "You know what? I don't want your stupid vote. Take it back."

"No way." Joe slowly shook his head. He allowed himself a small grin, as if finding a satisfaction having turned the tables on Parker. "Are you telling me you would throw away all of tonight's work – just out of spite?"

Parker remained silent, stewing in her anger.

"I'm not changing my vote." Joe declared. "It's the right thing to do. I guess you're just going to have to live with that, Ms. Monroe. Good night."

Without another word, Joe climbed into his car and drove off.

Parker closed her eyes.

Damnit, Joe. I was just starting to like you.

31.

"I don't understand what the big deal is,"

said Valerie in the chaos of breakfast the next morning. Maddy and Drew maneuvered around their grandmother to pack their lunches as Ally painted her face with scrambled eggs. "Nothing he told you was wrong."

"Senator Hammers is a good man?" quoted Parker.

"Other than that." Valerie shrugged innocently. "Forget about him. You got the win. Maybe you should focus more on how you're going to actually pull this fundraiser off."

"Yeah, yeah, yeah," Parker shooed her mother away. It was hard to argue with Valerie when she was all dolled up like a movie star in her favorite blue sundress for a morning brunch. Valerie simply refused to get riled up about anything before seeing her girlfriends. She had completely revamped her social schedule to take care of Ally every day since school started. Valerie deserved a morning off.

"I might also suggest making nice with Heller," added Valerie. "It sounds like you gave her a big black eye last night."

Parker's eyes widened with a smile. "Omigod, I haven't told you! Heller *called* me last night!"

"Last night?" Valerie sounded skeptical.

Parker pointed to the living room. "I get home, everybody's asleep, so I take my skirt off and curl up on the couch to pass out."

"Of course."

"Then, at about 10pm, I wake up to my phone going off, but as soon as I pick up, the caller hangs up!" Parker's breathing picked up, excited at dispensing her own gossip. "I check the number, I don't recognize it, but I see it's local, so I call *back*."

"And?"

"Goes straight to voicemail. 'Hi, this is Karen Heller, I'm currently away from my desk butt-fucking parents every chance I get, please leave a message and I'll get back to you.'"

Valerie gnawed on the rim of her blue horn-rimmed sunglasses. "That's not what her voicemail said."

"The point is, she felt compelled to call me. Maybe, I got through to her!"

"All the more reason to reach out." Valerie checked her watch, a clear sign she was anxious to meet her friends.

Parker grimaced, knowing she'd lost her mother's attention. "Go. Do your brunch thing with the girls and talk about me behind my back."

Valerie pretended to pout. "You sure you don't want me to bring Ally? The girls would love seeing her."

Parker smiled at her mother's empty gesture. She knew Ally's car seat wouldn't fit into Valerie's two seat convertible Jaguar. The correct answer would be: "No, of course not! Go have fun!" Which is precisely what Parker offered.

"Excellent," said Valerie. "I'm going to grab a different purse. Please make sure your car isn't blocking mine."

"Of course," answered Parker. Valerie's Jaguar hadn't seen the light of day since school started, stuck in the garage like a dusty trophy.

Parker watched her mother disappear around the bend only to find Maddy, leaning against the corner, arms folded, scowl at maximum power as she relentlessly tapped her foot. Parker pasted a smile on her face. "Yes?"

32.

"Were you going to ever tell me?"

asked Maddy. She arched her left brow.

Parker squinted. "Tell you--*what?*"

Maddy rolled her eyes in the typical *Duhhh, how is it not obvious?* fashion and stomped her foot. "You know! About how the whole—"

Parker suddenly felt her phone buzz in her back pocket. She raised her index finger to shush Maddy. If this was Heller calling back she wanted to take it. "Hold on, I gotta get this." Parker pressed the phone to her ear as her daughter tossed her hands into the air. "Hello! Mr. Bernstein?" *Shit, false alarm.* "How are you?"

"I hope I'm not interrupting," answered Bernstein. "I'm just, well—" His voice trailed off.

He sounds nervous. "Are you okay?"

"I'm—feeling a little sick, actually. Flu, I think."

"I'm sorry to hear that." Parker waited for a response. "Did you need something?"

"I—just can't help but be curious, I guess. How did the meeting go?"

"Oh, right!" Parker slapped her forehead. "Yes, the PTA approved the fundraiser, Mr. Bernstein."

Bernstein let out a sigh of relief. "That's—wonderful news."

"We're not out of the woods yet, though, we still need to raise the money."

"Of course."

150

"Will we see you tonight for Maddy's lesson?"

"About that," Bernstein coughed. "The spirit is willing, but the body—not so much. Please apologize to Maddy for me and have her repeat this week's practice schedule."

"I will. I hope you feel better."

"Yes, thank you. Good bye."

Mr. Bernstein's line clicked off before Parker could even respond. She blinked to get her train of thought back. "Maddy, what were you--?" Parker blinked again, realizing her daughter no longer stood in front of her. "Maddy?"

"Never mind," whined Maddy as she darted past with her backpack in tow.

"Wait!" Parker chased her daughter into the living room. "Come on, Maddy, talk to me! What were you going to say?"

Maddy stopped in front of the large living room picture window. She slowly turned to her mother with another roll of her eyes.

Don't your eyes get tired of doing that?

Maddy gulped. "What I was *trying* to say was—"

"Shit!" Parker muttered under her breath. Her eyes suddenly tracked Valerie driving away on the street in the window behind Maddy. "I was supposed to move my car!"

Maddy grimaced. "*What?*"

Parker waved the thought off. "No worries, your grandmother obviously made it out okay. I'm sorry, *what* were you going to say?"

"We're going to be late!" announced Drew as he teetered into the living room holding Ally in front of him like an oversized doll. Ally chewed the last of her eggs like a cow, dribbling bits onto the floor.

"Drew, I was speaking with your sister, so please don't—" Parker checked her phone. "We've got two minutes! Plenty of time to get ready." Parker turned back to her eldest daughter. "Maddy, forgive me. You were saying?"

Maddy sighed and pointed to Parker's bare legs. "You need pants."

Parker looked down and realized she still wore her outfit from the PTA meeting last night. "Fine, but we're not done talking, okay, young lady? I'm super, super, super interested in whatever thing you were going to tell me!" Parker dashed up the stairs. "Somebody wipe your sister's face!"

If it were the first day of school, Parker might have panicked. But she found a fresh pair of jeans on the first try and threw on her Bon Jovi Bad Medicine t-shirt in record time to fly back down the stairs. "Out the door, people!"

Parker grabbed Ally and the keys to her Highlander as Maddy and Drew raced out the front door. "Into the car!" Parker pressed the unlock button on her remote about ten times as she secured the front door behind her.

"Mom?" asked Drew from the front steps.

"What? What are you waiting for? Why aren't you in the car already?"

"Where *is* the car?"

"What are you talking about?" blasted Parker. She paused at the edge of her driveway. Her *empty* driveway. "What--? Did your grandmother move it?" Parker scanned the nearby streets of the neighborhood.

There was no Highlander to be found.

Furious, Parker dialed her mother. Valerie was quick to pick up. "Mom?!Where did you put my car?"

"Your car?" Valerie answered. "I didn't move your car. You moved it for me, remember?"

"I *didn't* move my car for you!"

Valerie sighed. "Really? Honestly, Parker, I don't ask for much—"

"Mom!" Parker screamed. "Neither of us moved my car, and it's gone! It's fucking gone!"

"*What?*"

"I think someone stole my car!"

33.

"I don't understand, Parker,"

Valerie stated matter-of-factly. "Are you saying someone stole your car?"

"Yes, that's *literally* what I just said," Parker answered tersely.

"But why—would--?" Valerie's signal cut in and out. "—come and get—"

"Mom, you're breaking up."

"I'm – up—you --? Parker?"

Fuck this. Parker ended the call. Questions swirled in her mind with the raw force of a twister. She could feel the shocked stares of her children who stood paralyzed in the driveway. *Focus, Parker.* She drew in a deep breath to center herself. *What needs to happen?* Her thumbs stabbed at her phone screen.

Maddy's eyes welled up. "Someone stole our car?"

"Yup." Parker continued to work her thumbs.

"Don't we need to call the police?" Maddy cried.

"Be quiet," Parker hit the send button on her phone, then turned her attention to the crime scene. She surveyed every inch of the empty driveway, the street curb, the neighbor's houses. Nothing more seemed out of place, and yet -- "Something isn't right."

"Our car is gone!" reminded Drew.

"Something *else!*" Parker growled. She aimed her phone at the driveway and clicked a few pictures, hoping to capture the fleeting clue that eluded her.

"*What* isn't right?" asked Maddy.

"I don't *know*, Maddy, and I can't think when you guys keep interrupting!" Parker clicked a few more pictures of the surrounding area, when she noticed her eldest sniffling uncontrollably. *Damnit.* Parker could normally focus like a hawk when investigating a crime scene but the added ingredient of her own children served to completely misfire her instincts. Parker softened her posture and her voice. "Listen, I didn't mean to yell. I *will* call the police." *Even though there is jack shit they can do about it right now.* "But first, we gotta get you guys to school, okay?" *And then, I might be able to hear myself think!*

Ally clapped spontaneously.

"Are we going to walk?" asked Drew.

Just then, a large black van with a red racing stripe and spoiler on its back rounded the neighborhood corner. Parker's mind filled with the A-Team's theme music as she watched the van race up the street and cross to her driveway. As it eased to a halt, she realized the van's stereo was playing the actual theme music, she hadn't imagined it at all. *This van must be part of Glory's network of friends who theme their cars from the 80's.*

Drew's eyes bulged. He fell instantly in love with the iconic van. "What – is – *that?*"

A young Hispanic man rolled down the passenger window and smiled at them. "You sent for a ride share?"

"You must be Julio," greeted Parker.

"Yes, ma'am!" Julio smiled and waved. "You guys need a lift to school, huh? What happened?"

"Our car was stolen!" Drew shouted excitedly as his mother rolled open the side door and ushered her kids inside. Maddy was the last to board, trying to hide her tears with a quick wipe of her hand.

"*Wow*, really? That's no good!" said Julio. He looked to Parker. "Is he kidding?"

"He's not kidding," answered Parker. She threw Ally on her lap. "Can you drive like they did on the TV show? We're running late."

Julio's smile widened. "Just make sure you're all buckled in, okay?"

Maddy looked more worried than ever. "Is this thing safe?"

Julio answered by peeling away from the driveway as fast as the van would take them.

34.

The A-Team car chase over to the school...

provided the exact distraction Parker needed to snap her kids back into reality and give her time to text Valerie and call Sheriff Bill. Maddy, Drew and Ally tailed their mother as they marched into the Oak Creek's front office fifteen minutes after the last school bell rang.

"I swear, Parker, you've got the worst luck," Sheriff Bill stated over Parker's cell phone. "I'll get this filed right away and start running your plates. I want to stop by your house and have a look around. Ask the neighbors if they saw or heard anything. Probably this afternoon as my morning's pretty busy."

"I appreciate it," Parker's eyes locked with those of the Silver Fox at the reception desk. Fox immediately frowned as she paused her typing. "I'll call you later."

Bill clicked off.

Parker appreciated Bill not giving her a hard time for laying into him the night before. He kept it professional, which was probably more than she could expect from Fox. Parker didn't bother with any pleasantries as she propped Ally up to sit on the desk edge and grabbed the first pen in a mug full of them. "My kids are late. I need to sign them in."

The Silver Fox slowly pulled a large blue binder from under her desk and presented it to Parker. "And the reason for this tardiness?"

"My car was stolen." Parker scribbled her name into the binder. Parker's tone was deadly serious, so as not to invoke anything close to 'my dog ate my homework.'

Fox turned back to her computer as if hiding a slight grin. "Huh. Some might call that *karma.*"

"Others call it grand theft auto," Parker turned to Drew and Maddy. "Get to your classes. *Now.*"

Drew and Maddy nodded before running down their respective hallways. Their speed prompted Silver Fox to explode out of her chair. "No running!" she shouted.

Parker stepped into Fox's view. "Karma? You know something I don't?"

Fox planted her fists on her hips. "Considering your parking history, I find it ironic—*that's all.*"

Parker clamped her lips tight, and clenched her fist, desperately trying to keep her blood from boiling over again. A part of her wanted nothing more than to reduce Silver Fox to a pile of ashes. But with Ally watching, smiling innocently as she played with two pens on the table top as if they were dolls—Parker knew she had to be better than that. "Know what? I'm sorry," she apologized. "I'm just a little on edge this morning. I didn't come here to--" Parker's words drifted as she looked past Fox to Heller and Mendez's shared office door. She half expected Heller to come bursting out and throw the Monroe kids' tardiness in her face. But the scene never developed.

Fox slowly let her hands drop to her sides, as if disarmed by Parker's apology. She followed Parker's eyes to the office. "She's not here," Fox informed. Her voice still carried a crisp edge with which to defend her boss. "Heller, I mean."

"Really?" *That doesn't sound like Heller.* "Taking a sick day?"

Silver Fox turned up her nose. "I'm sure she's just running late. I don't know when she'll be in. I wouldn't advise waiting."

A tardy Heller? "Sure, I've got—stuff. But can you—?" Parker couldn't finish her sentence, distracted by the trembling wetness of

Fox's eyes. "Can you tell her I—" *Is she about to cry?* Parker yanked a pen out of Ally's nose and helped her down to the floor. "Can you tell Heller I stopped by? Have her give me a call. I'd like to speak with her." In truth, Parker dreaded the idea of it, but her mother was right. She'd need Heller's help if this fundraiser was going to work. Maybe Heller's call last night was a sign she recognized the same truth.

Silver Fox tugged at the rims of her suit jacket. "I will let her know." Fox sat back down in her seat and began to type away, throwing herself in her work.

"Great." Parker studied the receptionist closely. This wasn't the usual rudeness she'd come to expect from Silver Fox. *What the hell is going on this morning?* "And—"

"Yes?" Fox snarled.

"Coffee." *I always think better after coffee.* Parker hadn't had a decent cup since moving to Oak Creek. "Is there a respectable place nearby? Preferably in walking distance."

Fox never once looked up from her keyboard to answer. "The Bean," she answered, pointing to the front door. "Two blocks South."

"Thanks," Parker grabbed Ally's hand to make their exit.

Just as Parker opened the door, Silver Fox felt obligated to fire one last shot across the bow. "I heard what you said to Heller last night," grumbled Fox, still staring at her keyboard. Her lip trembled. "She deserves better than that."

Parker left without another word.

35.

Heller deserves better than that?

By the time Ally and Parker made it to the quaint little coffee shop with a hand painted sign that proudly announced The Bean in bright pastel colors, Parker's ire was at full strength again.

Heller got half of what she fucking deserved.

Parker didn't let the Silver Fox have it this morning, sensing it would've been more like beating a sick puppy. But the reality of her car being stolen, combined with all the questions that stirred in her mind, topped off with Fox's dumb-ass parting shot made Parker itching hard for a fight. Parker stormed up to the barista bar with fire stoking her empty belly.

"I'd like a tall white mocha over ice with whipped cream," demanded Parker.

The plump bearded man-child with streaks of grey in his finely coiffed hair and his name tag scribbled illegibly in rainbow letters nodded with a smile. He eagerly grabbed a cup to write on. "Got it," he said. Then paused. "What size was that?"

"Tall," answered Parker.

"Hot?"

"Cold."

The man-child replaced his white cup with one made of clear plastic and scribbled. He paused again. "Mocha?"

"White Mocha," Parker corrected.

"You want whip on that?"

"Yes!" Parker growled. "Did you hear anything I first said?"

Parker's tone prompted a glare from the man-child, who clearly didn't understand the morning she was having. "I'm—simply—being--thorough."

"Sure, you are."

Man-child nodded to the more pleasant Ally, who clapped happily. "She want anything?"

Parker tilted her head. "A venti triple macchiato with soy milk."

"Seriously?"

"No—she's two!"

Man-child took a deep breath and firmly placed the empty cup on the counter. "Just because I'm young and hip doesn't mean I'm into your brand of sarcasm."

Parker leaned forward, smelling blood. "I'll remember that. See, I remember things, because I listen when people talk to me. I don't need to be lectured by some millennial studying—humanities?"

Man-child gulped. "Political science."

"*Just* as useless—who colors his hair grey to be taken more seriously while he probably still lives at home with his mother!"

Just then, the bell of the coffee shop's front door rang to announce the arrival of Valerie Parker. The vision of glamor greeted her only daughter with the pure drama of outstretched arms. "There you are! I got your text! Are you alright? Are you ready for me to take you home?"

Man-child nodded to Valerie as she rushed up to Parker. He grinned. "That your mom?"

Parker sighed and dropped her head. *Shit.* "Yes."

"Moved back in with her, did you?"

161

Parker's head dropped lower as Valerie lovingly wrapped her arms around her. Somehow it melted the anger within her, leaving only raw shame. "Yes."

"So, to be clear, you want one tall white mocha over ice with bitter cream, two pumps of look in the mirror and a side of deep regret, is that about right?"

Parker took a moment to appreciate the epic counter-punch. "That would be perfect."

The man-child smiled confidently as he ran Parker's card and set about to create the drink.

Valerie's jaw dropped. "What was that all about?"

"He gets me," said Parker. She tugged Ally's hand and headed with Valerie over to a small circular table. "How was brunch with the girls?"

Ally climbed into Valerie's lap, happy to see her Grandma. "Oh, I canceled that. Did you call the Sheriff? What did he say?"

Parker shrugged. "That my car is probably in Tijuana by now."

"I don't understand. Didn't you lock it last night?"

Parker glared at her mother. "Yes, Mother, I always lock it!" Parker blurted the statement out as fact, but quickly checked the back of her mind to be sure. "I know I locked it."

"I'm just saying, your juggling a lot of balls," said Valerie. She smiled at Man-child who served Parker's iced white mocha in a tall open glass with a straw. Intrigued by the drink, Ally clapped her hands.

"No, Ally, that's for Mommy," explained Parker.

Ally pouted, the first time all morning, followed by a persistent whining.

162

"Here, play with my phone," Parker cued it to Candy Crush and handed it over.

Valerie winced. "Wow."

"Are you kidding? She's a Candy Crush savant!" Parker took a sip of her mocha milkshake. "Beats my score all the time. I just—can't handle the whining right now. I need a moment to think."

"Cars get stolen. The Sheriff even warned us that car theft was on the rise."

Parker took another sip. "There ever been a car stolen in your neighborhood since you've lived here?"

Valerie looked off to the side, dipping into her memory. "Packages, yes. Mail, sometimes. No cars that I can remember."

"Don't you think it's weird that my car was the first? The very night after my PTA presentation was sabotaged and I had a major blowout with Karen Heller?"

Valerie chuckled. "Why do you think everything is always about you, Parker?"

Parker frowned. *That's just what Joe said.* "I don't think that."

"Don't invent a conspiracy," suggested Valerie. She turned to Ally, who smiled back – then promptly dumped Parker's phone into the tall white mocha.

36.

After a short drive home...

Parker tossed her mocha soaked phone into a can of dry uncooked rice. "I feel like I should have seen that coming," she grumbled. The rice was Parker's go-to Hail Mary for drowned phones. With a little luck, after a day or so the rice will have absorbed all the moisture out of the phone allowing for it to recharge.

Ally stood on a chair next to the counter, watching her mother bury it with rice. "Awwww, phone hurt?" she asked.

"Phone hurt." Parker sighed as she caught herself staring blankly at the rice can. There was a sudden stillness in the air that seemed to stem the flow of time. Parker noticed she held her next breath, as if some part of her worried what exhaling might bring.

"Are you okay?" asked Valerie.

Parker blinked. "Kurt taught me the rice can trick." Her lungs became heavy. "I'm ashamed to admit I had to think for a moment to remember that."

Valerie offered a warm smile as she put her hand on her daughter's shoulder.

Parker looked to the ceiling, holding back her tears. "He made this parenting thing look so easy, you know? He was a natural."

Valerie chuckled. "Are you kidding? He called me in a panic all the time."

"What?"

"Kurt was a very nice man, and a great father, but after Maddy was born, he felt like he was drowning in diapers and baby vomit. I'd have to talk him off a ledge about once a week."

Parker' stomach turned. "Kurt never told me about that."

"I'd always assumed you knew." Valerie shook her head, sensing this news was not the comfort she'd meant it be. "Maybe he didn't want you to worry."

"But I'm his *wife.*"

"You were also a star reporter on the rise. Maybe he thought you had enough on your plate."

You're missing the point. Parker clenched her lips, struggling to make sense of this news. "Why call *you*? Why wouldn't he call his own mom if he wasn't going to call me?"

Valerie tossed her head back into mock laughter. "Oh, please – *her?* You know how that conversation would go."

Valerie's dislike for Kurt's mother was no secret. She was a hard woman for even Kurt to love, and competitive as Valerie was, she relished the fact that her son-in-law sought her advice over that of his own mother. Still, this revelation, for reasons she didn't fully understand yet, seemed to shake Parker to her core. *All this time I had no idea. What else did Kurt never tell me?*

"I didn't mean to upset you, Parker," assured Valerie. "I just thought you'd like to know it wasn't easy for Kurt either. Every parent struggles."

"I'm not—upset," Parker lied. *At least, I can't think of a good reason to be upset.* "I'm just surprised, that's all. It's been a long week and—" The doorbell rang granting Parker a welcome pardon from the conversation. "I need to get that."

Parker caught a glimpse of Sheriff Bill's car parked at the curb through her front window and rushed to the door.

"Hello, Bill," she greeted, opening the door.

"You *are* here," said Bill with a smile. "I tried to call before coming over."

"My phone died."

Bill whistled. "Ouch! Your car and your phone in the same day?"

"Yup. Sucks."

"Good afternoon, Sheriff." Valerie greeted, walking into the entry way. "I presume you're here about my daughter's stolen car?"

"I'm just following up."

Valerie smiled. "You two carry on," She jingled her car keys. "I'll run and pick up the kids from school." Valerie gave Parker a quick squeeze on her way out the door.

"Thanks, Mom." said Parker.

"Is this a bad time?" asked Bill, sensing the frailty of the moment.

Parker waved her hands. "No, no, it's fine. Ally? Why don't you come out front with me and the Sheriff, okay?"

Ally ran to her mother from the kitchen and followed her out the front door to the driveway with Bill.

Bill frowned as he watched Valerie race down the street in her Jaguar. "Your mom has a hell of a lead foot," he observed.

"Always has." Parker wasn't interested in small talk. "What did you find out?"

"We canvased the neighborhood. Nobody heard or saw anything," answered Bill, scanning the area once again. "And you said you didn't hear a car alarm go off. So, this clearly wasn't any smash and grab or some kid finding a joyride. This was a pro."

Parker presumed as much. She was hoping for more. "Why my car?"

Bill lifted his shoulders. "Why not? I told you there was an uptick in car thefts. You park outside. It's easy bait."

Parker wagged her finger. "No, no, no." What bothered her so much in the morning, the thought she couldn't articulate with her kids making her crazy, finally surfaced. "Look around. This is SoCal. Hardly anyone parks in their garage because they're so full of shit."

"Shit!" Ally repeated jumping up and down.

Fuck. "I'm mean, *stuff*, Ally," she corrected her toddler. "Stuff."

"Shit!"

Parker huffed. "My point is, why not choose that BMW parked over there?" Parker pointed to the silver Beamer parked in the driveway across the street. "Or that Camry up the road? Why did a pro go after my Highlander?"

Bill shrugged again. "I don't know. Maybe the perp liked the color of your car, or was drawn to the roses in your mom's flower bed, or maybe he was sideswiped by a Highlander one time and wanted revenge or—"

"Maybe she was a member of the Oak Creek PTA," Parker blurted.

"That's not funny."

"It's a little funny." Parker noticed Bill's face was dead serious. "Oh come, on, you don't think it's a little odd that the morning after Heller reveals me as her parking gremlin that my car is stolen?"

"Parker," Bill bit his lip. "Have you spoken to Heller since last night? Communicated with her in any way?"

"No," Parker snapped her fingers. "That's a lie, actually, she did try calling me last night."

"What time?"

"I'd have to check my phone to be sure, but I can't as it's taking a rice bath. I'd say around 11pm or so. She didn't leave a message, and when I called her back, she didn't pick up." Parker watched as Bill jotted the note down in his note pad. "Why?"

167

"We got a call from Mr. Heller late this morning," said Bill.

"So?"

"Karen Heller never made it home last night."

37.

A chill crawled up Parker's spine.

"Last night?" she asked. "What about this morning?"

"She hasn't come home at all." Bill clarified.

Parker's jaw dropped open. *This can't be coincidence. Can it?* Parker's portrait of shock was quickly replaced with a puzzled expression. "I'm confused."

"Karen Heller is missing." Bill spoke very slowly as if talking to a child.

"Yeah, I got that," Parker scorned. "You said Mr. Heller called this morning, but his wife never made it home last night. If that's true, why would he wait so long to contact you?"

"Mr. Heller is a very ill man who needs his rest. It's not unusual for him to be in bed before his wife returns home on a night she's working late. When he woke up this morning and saw that her car was gone, he assumed she'd already left for school. It wasn't until the school called asking if Heller was coming in to work, that he knew something was wrong. No one has been able to reach her since."

That might explain why Silver Fox was acting so uppity. Parker rubbed her chin. "But, really, the husband doesn't know for certain if his wife came home at all."

Bill squinted. "Yes, he does. She wasn't there this morning."

Come on, Bill, work with me. The devil is in always in the details. "Yes, but if he's a heavy sleeper, she could have returned home and left in the morning and he never would have known. Which is why he didn't call. We can't be sure as to exactly when Heller disappeared."

"She's missing," Bill repeated. His voice carried a hint of frustration. "Regardless as to when she came home or not, no one knows where she is *right now.*"

"Right." Parker put her hands behind her back and rocked back and forth on her toes. She didn't want to scare Bill off from giving her any more information. *The second a cop's ego thinks you're trying to edge in on his or her investigation, they shut you out.* "Do you have any leads?"

"Only the one you just gave me. You're the only person after the PTA meeting to have received a call from Karen Heller." Bill screwed up his face. "Wait, why would she call you?"

To apologize for acting like a world class bitch? "Your guess is as good as mine. I presume she got my number off the PTA list of parents, so we know it wasn't some random butt-dial. But then why would she not answer when I called her back?"

"Maybe she couldn't answer," Bill postulated. "Maybe she was in trouble. Maybe she needed your help."

"Really? She needed *my* help?" Parker challenged. "If she was in trouble, I'd be the last person she'd call."

"You're right. She hates you."

"Well—hate, is a pretty strong word." For some reason Parker found it uncomfortable accepting the fact that Heller might hate her as much as she hated Heller. "I mean, I'm pretty awesome. Who hates awesome?"

Bill looked at Parker out of the corner of his eye. "Alright, so why did she call you?"

"I don't know." Parker searched her memory for any clue. A theory was forming inside her brain that sounded preposterous—*maybe it wasn't Heller who called? Maybe it was someone with Heller's phone?* It sounded incredibly paranoid. *It's not always about you,*

Parker, she reminded herself. Then it hit her. "After the PTA meeting, I happened to notice Heller didn't go home."

Bill scratched his head. "Um, yeah, I think we established that as the problem."

"No, I mean she deliberately drove away from the direction of her house up the street. There was no hesitation. This wasn't some random thing, she drove like she knew precisely where she was going next." *God, do I miss investigative reporting!*

"Interesting." Bill jotted down the note in his pad. "You got anything else?"

Parker frowned. Her high on discovery had already faded. "No." Her eyes lit up. "But I can ask around!"

Bill smiled. "That's alright, Parker. I've already got a full team working on this." Bill finished writing and clamped shut his pad. "Thanks for your time."

Parker's heart raced. "Wait. That's it?" *You drop all this juicy gossip about the woman I hate and just leave me?*

Bill stared at Parker blankly. He sniffed. "Well, if you remember anything else that you think would be useful, please call me." Bill started for his car.

Why did he sniff? "I can help, you know. I'm a hell of an investigative reporter."

Bill smiled and opened his car door. "I know. And if I need any help, I'll call you. And be assured we're still working on your stolen car, okay? We haven't forgotten about that." Bill shut the door and started his car.

Fuck, Bill, don't just drive away! Parker found herself pouting. Then, her heart skipped a beat as she saw Bill roll down his window. He smiled smugly.

"Yes?" asked Parker.

"By the way," Bill pointed to Ally. "I think your daughter needs a change."

Shit, is he teasing me? Parker sniffed at the sudden odor wafting in from beneath her. She looked down to see Ally pulling at her pant leg.

"Poopy," said Ally.

"Have a nice day!" Bill rolled up his window and drove away, overly pleased with himself.

"Ha, ha," said Parker dryly. She brazenly flipped Bill's car the bird.

"Ha ha," Ally repeated. She lifted her pointer finger to emulate her mother's obscene gesture.

Parker's eyes nearly popped out of her head. "Shit!" She quickly but gently reached for her daughter's hand to put down her finger.

"Shit!" Ally repeated.

Parker shuffled her stinky daughter off the driveway. "Let's get you changed. And no telling Grandma about this, alright?"

38.

Parker stared anxiously at the glowing blue lights of the digital oven clock in her mother's kitchen.

"It's 3:32," she announced. Her head swiveled to Ally, who doodled with crayons at the kitchen table, completely lost in her work. "Mom and the kids should have been back by now. What the hell are they doing?"

Ally continued to scribble away.

"Yeah, you're right," agreed Parker. "Probably ice cream or something. Take the edge off a long day." She turned to the counter and looked at her phone in the rice can. It had only been a few hours since the mocha dunk, but Parker felt naked without her phone. "I suppose, there's no point in trying to charge that yet. I'll have to use a landline like some Neanderthal."

Ally looked up and giggled at the word.

Parker nodded. "You said it. This whole thing is a mess. No car. No phone. Every fiber of my being is screaming at me to get out there and sniff around for clues about Heller."

Ally flashed her mother a concerned look, mirroring precisely what she saw.

"I know, I know, Bill said his team had it covered. But come on, those hacks probably couldn't find their way out of a paper bag. And let's be honest. Bill's not exactly Sherlock. He needs my help." Parker turned back to the clock. "Damnit, it's still 3:32?"

Ally slapped her hands to her cheeks. "Oh no!"

"Then it's settled," Parker decided. "We can't wait any longer. You and I need to rent some wheels. And if it so happens we fly by the school and Heller's home then all the better."

Ally clapped.

"I knew you'd be game. You're the adventurous one."

Ally cheered as Parker grabbed the bulky cordless phone off its cradle on the kitchen wall and listened for a dial tone before punching the number on an 80's ride share. After describing her mother's address to the dispatcher, she rifled through a cluttered drawer to find something to write on. Buried deep in the back behind the AA batteries, masking tape, thumbtacks, yarn, crayons and paper clips was an unopened box of index cards. Parker tore the box open, quickly penned a note in crayon and taped it to the fridge:

"Ally and I are off to find a rental car. We'll bring home dinner!"

Parker cupped the remaining cards in her right hand, testing their weight. They reminded her of the post-it notes she'd sometimes use to sort through ideas when waded through a tough investigation. "Huh. We've got about fifteen minutes before the ride share arrives. I'm sure Grandma wouldn't mind if we used a few more of these." She turned back to Ally. The two and a half-year-old eagerly stretched for the cards. "You want to draw on some? Can you draw me an evil witch? With lots of warts?"

Ally scribbled a dark angry mess of black, green and purple onto an index card and handed it back to her mother.

"Perfect!" Parker labeled the card "Heller" and taped it to the center of the kitchen bulletin board. "Now, can you draw me a music teacher?"

It was highly likely Ally had no clue what a music teacher was, but it didn't deter her from scribbling another angry mess, this time of blue and orange. She appeared to enjoy the profiling task.

"Very good." Parker labeled the card "Bernstein" and placed it next to Heller. She rubbed her chin. "Ally, I'm going to need quite a few more of these."

39.

After sufficiently wall papering Valerie's kitchen with index cards...

Parker and Ally enjoyed a short trip to the edge of town to Sergio's Used Car Lot. There, a large, brown and tan 4x4 truck with circular lights on its top eased to a halt in front of Sergio's office. Parker considered herself an 80's expert having spent so much of her childhood in it, but even she had to ask the truck driver as she helped Ally out.

"Really?" said the driver. "You never watched The Fall Guy as a kid?"

Parker shook her head, ashamed she'd forgotten the TV action comedy detailing the adventures of Hollywood stuntman, Colt Seavers. "I should've known that."

"It was probably before your time." The driver winked and smiled.

"Aw. God bless you, Colt."

The 4x4 drove off, leaving Parker and Ally at the mercy of Sergio himself, a portly middle-aged Russian man with a kind smile that greeted them in the lot. As it were, Parker and Ally were the only customers at the only game in town that could rent her some wheels. It was either this, or an hour's drive to San Diego, which Parker figured wouldn't have given adequate snooping time before returning home with a promised dinner. Parker's mandate of a family sized vehicle that could tow three kids, plus two adults and whatever crap they'd buy during a weekend Target-run that got out of hand reduced Sergio's inventory to two possible options.

The first was a Honda Pilot SUV formerly owned by a Mary Kay consultant which would have been perfect if not for its shockingly hot pink paint job and the long, plastic eye-lashes that were glued and bolted around its headlights. "Not exactly subtle," deemed Parker. "I could use subtle these days."

The second option sported a modest grey paint job, could seat up to seven passengers with room in the back for a Target, supermarket or Toys R Us run during Christmas time. But Parker couldn't help but cringe at the idea of it.

"What's wrong? Is no good?" asked Sergio.

"It's—" Parker swallowed. "It's a minivan."

"Yeah. Chrysler. Town and Country. Good minivan."

Parker hemmed and hawed. "Yeah, it's just—" *I fucking hate minivans. I hate everything about them. They are boring. They are bland. They don't accelerate worth a damn. They look funny. They tell the world that you've given up on anything remotely exciting in life and that you have literally sacrificed your last shred of dignity to the gods of practical solutions, conventional wisdom, and cottage cheese thighs.* "There's nothing else?"

"There's San Diego." Sergio smiled. "Unless you want to buy car. You want to buy car today? I give deal. Great deal on car."

Parker frowned. She wasn't ready to buy before seeing what her insurance company was going to offer. *It's only temporary*, Parker told herself. "Fine, I'll rent the minivan."

After a credit card deposit and a mere ten signatures, Parker found herself sitting in the front seat of the Town and Country with Ally strapped into the supplied car seat behind her. Parker squirmed in the leather, trying to get comfortable more with the idea. "Let's get this straight," she told the car. "I don't like you. I'll never like you. It's just how it is. Just get me to where I need to go and not break down or get stolen or some crazy shit like that and we'll get along the next few days just fine. Got it?"

Parker pushed the ignition button, and the engine and stereo roared to life. Bon Jovi's dramatic guitar opening to "Wanted Dead or Alive" hummed through the speakers on the FM radio – a clear favorite of Parker's. *Coincidence?* "Huh." She fought off the urge to grin. "If you think playing one of the most awesome songs ever written is going to win me over, it's going to take more than that."

But it's a good start.

Parker put the minivan into drive and took off from the lot. Like the song went, she was determined to find any clue of Heller – dead or alive.

40.

The Town and Country glided across the asphalt...

not nearly as smoothly as Parker's Highlander and turned a hair wider on corners. It didn't sit as high, but admittedly high enough for a decent view of the road. Parker found her best excuse for hating the car when the front right speaker started rattling during Bon Jovi's chorus. *Yup, my car is way better*, she told herself.

After about twenty minutes of getting the feel for the car, Parker found herself pulling up to Oak Creek Elementary. The lot was empty, as was to be expected so late in the day, and the school was most likely locked. What piqued Parker's curiosity was the direction that Heller had turned the previous night after the PTA meeting— when she didn't go home. Parker circled in the empty lot, pulled up to the exit, and turned left just as Heller had done.

The road wound through a neighborhood of parks and houses for several miles. Did Heller stop at any of them? Finding that would be a needle in a haystack. Finally, the road cleared to a stoplight at the Highway 50 intersection on the south edge of town. Parker recognized it—she had crossed it on the way to the Bottomless Cup the day she met with Bernstein. And somewhere, an hour's drive down that road closer to the border, was Bernstein's home.

Parker gripped the steering wheel tightly. Did Heller go and see Bernstein after the PTA meeting? She shuttered to think what it might mean if it were true. Bernstein presented himself as a gentle man, but the coincidences with Heller's disappearance were adding up in all the wrong ways. Was he really sick when he called this morning? Or just pretending to cover for – what? Parker was tempted to make the drive, when another option hit her.

Another person who might be able to shed some light on it is Mr. Heller. Perhaps it's time to introduce myself?

Parker turned the car around and headed back toward the school. She zoomed past the empty lot and up the street toward Heller's home. To her surprise, two Sheriff's cars were parked before the small grey stucco home – one in the driveway, one at the street curb.

Shit.

Parker slowly pulled her minivan along the side of the street, just past the Sheriff's car to get a clear view of Heller's door.

I don't suppose Bill would be thrilled to find me lurking around. But if he's not in there, I could pretend to be a good friend of Heller's checking in on the husband.

Parker stopped her car and threw it in neutral. "What do you think? Think it's a good time to say hello?" Parker looked back to Ally for permission. But Ally was fast asleep from all the driving.

Just then Parker saw the front door open, and a smiling Sheriff Bill emerge.

"Fuck!" Parker turned away and quickly put the minivan into gear. She eased up the street, but not so fast to draw attention.

The ruse didn't matter. Parker spied Bill in her rear-view mirror. He shuttled to his car and flung open his door. Red and blue gumball lights flashed on with a quick whoop of the siren, followed by an announcement on the loudspeaker. "Would the nosey woman in the minivan please stop her vehicle?"

"Double fuck!" Parker eased to a halt on the street. Bill slowly walked up to the driver's side. Despite Parker's anger over being caught, she plastered a huge smile on her face when she rolled down the window. "Is there something wrong, officer?" Parker batted her eyes.

Bill smiled. "You just can't help yourself, can you?"

"I was in the neighborhood, I thought I'd drop by."

"Parker."

"Okay, fine, I'm curious. Is that a crime?"

"*Parker.*"

Desperate to be heard, Parker raised her finger. "Bernstein! Have you questioned Bernstein? He says he was sick, but he lives in the general direction of—"

"Parker!" Bill shouted. He took a deep breath and smiled. "It's okay."

"Ha! I knew you'd come around. You won't regret this, Bill. I live for investigating shit like this."

Bill chuckled. "No, no, I mean the search is over."

Parker gulped. "Over?"

"We found her. We found Heller."

41.

Parker casually titled her head, trying not to hint at her absolute shock.

"You found her?" she blurted. "So, where is she?"

Bill looked away. "Well," he stammered. "we don't know."

Parker sat up in her seat. "You *don't* know?"

"She won't tell us."

"She won't tell you." Parker tried to hold back a smug grin. "So, really, you didn't find Heller at all."

"Heller sent a text to her husband about an hour ago."

Parker gave her best heavy sarcastic nod. "A text?"

"Yes."

"She didn't even call."

"No."

"She didn't stop by. Pop in. She sent the most emotionally detached communication one can send in the twenty-first century to a spouse worried sick about her not coming home."

Bill swallowed. "Correct."

"That doesn't sound strange to you?"

"Of course, it does," Bill admitted. "Why do you think I'm here?"

Parker nodded to the other Sheriff's car. "I see you brought back up."

"Deputy Michaels was first on the scene when we got the call from Mr. Heller. I joined him shortly after."

Parker took a mental note of the name. "None of this sounds right. What exactly did Mrs. Heller text her husband?"

Bill flipped open his notepad. "You know I'm simply humoring you, right? I don't have to do this."

"Just read the damn text."

Bill cleared his throat. "'Ken, I didn't mean to worry you. There is something I have to take care of. I will be home soon.'"

"Soon?" Parker drew a deep breath in an effort to clear her mind of the insults it was hurtling at Bill. She couldn't believe his amateur assessment. "That's it? You're ending a missing person's case based on that? How do you even know it's Heller texting and not someone else?"

"Mr. Heller and Mrs. Heller went back and forth a couple times. We had him ask her a question only the two of them would know."

"And?"

The Sheriff shrugged. "It checked out."

"What was the question?"

Bill clapped his notepad shut. "It's private, Parker. Mr. Heller seems satisfied. And frankly, I've told you more than you need to know."

Parker reached for her door handle. "I want to speak with Mr. Heller."

Bill pushed on Parker's door, preventing her from opening it. "Oh no," he insisted. "That poor man's been through enough today. He doesn't need to play twenty questions with you. This is police business. Case closed. Let's all move on with our lives."

Parker glared at Bill but left it at that. There was no point in making a scene. She turned to look at Heller's house, and noted the small, dark shadowy figure that peaked through the blinders. *Mr. Heller, you and I will speak – soon.* Parker put her minivan into gear. She forced a smile at Bill. "I guess we'll see."

"See what?" asked Bill.

"If this case *stays* closed."

"Why wouldn't it?"

"Karen Heller has yet to come home." Parker rolled up her window and drove off.

42.

"What in the doting Doris Day did you do to my kitchen?"

asked a stunned Valerie as she took in the sight before her. Post-it notes, and index cards lined every inch of the bulletin board and spilled over onto the wall, connecting ideas and names with strings of red yarn. Valerie muttered some of the topics: Old Yeller Heller, Mr. Bernstein, Stolen Instruments, Stolen Car, Bad Coffee, PTA Bitches, but squinted at the ones that seemed to confuse her -- Silver Fox, Baby Face, Bottomless Cup. "And why are there random doodles with each name? Did you pull Ally into all of this?"

Parker slammed her plastic bag full of Chuck's Chicken Chunks fried chicken onto the kitchen counter. "Food!" she yelled at the top of her lungs. Maddy and Drew's footsteps could be heard scampering across the ceiling before they clomped down the stairs like a pair of Clydesdales.

Ally happily pointed to her crayon profile drawings for her grandmother. "Mine!"

Parker started to pull out the boxes of fried chicken. "Mom, this is how I sort through my thoughts sometimes," she grumbled. Parker found herself slamming each subsequent box of chicken onto the counter harder than the previous. "For all the *good* it did."

Valerie opened her cupboard full of plates to assist her daughter's efforts. "Why do you say that?"

"They found Heller."

Valerie's eyes widened. "They did? Is she okay? Where has she been?"

Parker pried open a box of chicken and bit into a large drumstick, tearing the meat off the bone like a savage. She stared at her mother as she chewed. "She won't say."

Valerie frowned. "I don't understand."

Parker shook her head. "I don't either. She texted her husband. Said she'd be back soon. None of this shit makes sense." Parker threw her hands in the air. "But everybody seems to think it's okay!"

Drew rushed into the kitchen and eagerly attacked the boxes of Chuck's Chicken. Maddy took her time, watching her mother and grandmother closely.

Valerie prepared a plate for Ally. "What did the Sheriff say about it?"

Parker took another sizeable bite. "That its none of my business." She growled with a mouthful. "Can you believe that?"

"He's right."

Parker stopped chewing. At first, she thought the statement had come from Valerie, but her mother's eyes were as wide with surprise as Parker's. Parker turned to find Maddy standing next to her with her arms folded. "Excuse me?" asked Parker.

"He's right," Maddy repeated. "It's none of your business."

Parker's jaw dropped. She had to wipe her face suddenly to keep from chicken falling out. "You want to explain yourself, young lady?"

"Are you going to listen?" Maddy scoffed. "Like you said you would this morning?"

Parker firmly slammed down her drumstick onto the counter. "You want my full attention? You *have* it."

Maddy gulped, given pause by her mother's measured calm – a clear sign of the volcano of anger bubbling beneath the surface. Yet the eldest child would not back down. "It's Chicago all over again."

Parker blinked. "What?"

"All you care about is the story. You don't care about anything else."

"That's not true."

Maddy pointed to the kitchen wall. "Then what is that?"

Parker clenched her fists. "Maddy, I don't expect you to understand. But there's something very wrong going on here."

"I know! I thought, for once, you were going to act like my mom!"

"I don't need to act!" Parker founder herself seething. She took another bite of chicken to calm herself. "I'm a great mom!"

"No!" Maddy shouted. She trembled as she searched for her words. "Other moms--they make dinner! From scratch! And they pick their kids up from school on time! And help their kids with their homework! They don't get into trouble with the principal! They don't get their cars stolen! They don't sneak around trying to solve mysteries all day long!"

"I need to figure out what is going on at your school, Maddy!"

"That's not your job!"

"To protect my children? Yes, yes, it is my job!" Parker barked. "I need to know you are safe in your school! I need some assurance your principal, or your gym teacher or your piano teacher aren't crazed lunatics making trouble!"

"My school isn't safe?" Maddy's eyes glistened. "Is Mr. Bernstein— a crazed--lunatic?" The idea seemed to break her brain.

Oh fuck. Parker scratched her head, realizing her huge mistake. "No, Maddy." *Shit.* "I'm sorry. Get that out of your head, okay? I was just making a point."

Maddy's face wrinkled into a portrait of anguish. Her lips trembled. "Why would you say that?" She cried.

"I'm sorry! I'm sorry, Maddy, listen—"

"You ruin everything! Why do you have to ruin everything?" Maddy screamed and ran out of the kitchen. Her feet clomped up the stairs until she slammed her bedroom door shut.

Valerie finally exhaled as though she had held her breath for the duration of the fight. "*That* could've gone better."

Parker hung her head in shame. She was used to arguing with adults. Sometimes Maddy fooled her into thinking she could be spoken to like one.

Drew took a bite out of his chicken. "Well," he said chewing. "If what you say is true, school might want to rethink their no gun rules."

"Drew!" Parker snapped. "There is nothing wrong with your school, okay?"

"But you just said--!"

Parker flashed her son an angry glare. "I know what I said."

"Parker," Valerie put her hand on her daughter's shoulder. "Drew has a point. If Heller is okay. If you're saying the school is safe. Then what is all this about?" She waved her hand over the index card covered wall.

I don't know. Fuck—I don't know!

Without a word, Parker grabbed her phone out of the can of rice and exited the room.

43.

Hours later, Parker sat in the front room in total darkness...

staring at the smooth brick on the end table. Her phone had been plugged in hours ago but had yet to come back to life.

Please work. I need a win. I need something to go my way tonight. Just – work for me okay?

The phone did not respond to Parker's quiet pleas. Only the faint hum of the refrigerator circulated through the main floor of the house.

Please? Pretty, pretty please?

Bed time with the kids had proved to be as miserable as ever. Maddy wouldn't speak or say goodnight. Ally passed out. Drew wanted to go to bed early. Even Valerie looked too tired to pass judgment on any of Parker's antics.

I'm not crazy. Something weird is going on at that school. And it's not good.

A bright white light suddenly beamed from the phone, prompting Parker to sit up and take notice. Parker watched anxiously as her phone went through a long arduous booting sequence, until it finally displayed the home screen she so sorely missed. "Yes!" Parker pumped her fist into the air. "Hell yes!"

After regaining a signal, the phone vibrated to life with a litany of text messages she'd missed throughout the day that rolled in all at once. Parker held her phone, scanning and scrolling through the alerts. Sheriff Bill tried to call her several times, followed by more texts asking if she was there and why she wasn't responding. There were a few from Julie asking if she'd heard about Heller. Even a

188

message from her old editor, Jerry, insisting that Parker get over herself and call him back sometime.

"Oh, how I've missed you," said Parker, kissing and hugging her phone. Parker noticed the battery was only charged at 2% and didn't dare unplug it. Having checked the last of her email accounts, Parker gently laid her phone back down. "You get some rest, old friend. I'm going to go make us some tea. Then, we'll play a nice game of Emoji Blitz together."

Parker turned to walk into the kitchen, when her phone buzzed again. Another text had just come through.

Parker tilted her head and stared at her phone out of the corner of her eye. It was nearly midnight. Who would be texting? Parker picked her phone up and found the following message.

Do you feel guilty yet?

Parker blinked. The name at the top of the screen read as Old Yeller Heller – the label Parker had given to Karen Heller when she had saved her number in her phone the night before.

"Fuck me." Parker snatched her phone off the table and typed a response.

Everyone was looking for you today. Where have you been?

Parker's heart thumped as she waited for Heller's answer.

Finally, her phone buzzed again.

Don't pretend you are concerned.

Parker winced. Something was off about the response. She typed again.

Why did you call me last night?

The phone buzzed.

I'll explain everything tomorrow.

189

Parker frowned. Karen Heller was a conniving witch, but cryptic texting seemed to be a stretch even for her. Either this was a completely new side of Karen Heller, or it wasn't Karen Heller at all.

The phone buzzed a final time.

`Sleep tight.`

44.

Parker kept her mouth shut the following morning...

for fear she might involuntarily blurt out details of her late-night text-a-pade with Heller. Parker glided through her morning routines with an eerie calm, affording her children extra space to ready themselves for school. The experiment appeared to confound both Drew and Maddy, who dressed and packed their bags with unusual care as though they feared they might have entered some sort of twisted parent trap. Was Drew's hair perfect? No. Did Maddy's outfit match? Hardly. Was anyone's homework even finished? Parker wasn't even going to tempt fate by asking this particular morning. Only one question raced over and over through her mind: How would Karen Heller explain her absence when she finally returned to school?

But when Parker reached for the car keys on the kitchen counter, only to have Valerie step in front of her, she knew there was no fooling her mother. "What's going on with you?" asked Valerie.

Parker batted her eyes and forced a smile. "Why, whatever do you mean, mother?"

"You're never this quiet. And I know you just saw Ally pour cereal in her pants."

Shit. How did I miss that? Parker played coy as she looked over at Ally swinging her legs at the table with a bowl of cereal resting upside down on her crotch. "There are some clean pants in the dryer."

"You want *me* to clean it up?"

"I've got a meeting at school. I was hoping you could watch Ally today."

Valerie folded her arms. "*All* day?"

"It's a long meeting."

"Uh huh," Valerie didn't bother pretending to sound convinced. "What's really going on?"

"Nothing," Parker lied. She angled slightly to shout past her mother. "Drew! Maddy! Let's go!"

Valerie followed her daughter and two grandchildren out the front door. "I know you all too well, Parker, and you've got that look in your eye like you're up to—" Valerie stopped dead in her tracks at the top of the driveway. "Is that?" She gasped with a smile. "Is that a *minivan?*"

Parker hung her head, having forgotten about her rental wheels. She pressed her key fob to unlock the car. "It's a temporary arrangement."

"But you hate minivans!" Drew chuckled as he slid open the side door.

"It's a rental. We're not keeping it. Just get in the damn car."

Valerie patted Parker on the back, relieved she felt she'd discovered Parker's big morning secret. "Well, I applaud your sensible choice."

"I didn't have a choice, Mom, it's all the car place had." Parker hopped into the driver's seat as Maddy climbed into the passenger side. "We'll chat later. Off to school, now! Ta ta!" Parker waved goodbye as she revved the minivan in reverse.

For the first time since school had started, dropping the kids off proved to be a perfectly average portrait of nothing in particular. Either no crazy parents tried to cut in the car line, jump the curb, park in the handicapped spaces when they shouldn't, or Parker simply didn't notice them. Maddy offered her mother the usual soft but detached preteen "bye" that could be interpreted as anything from "I'm still mad at you" to "my life sucks" or on rare occasion -- "goodbye." Drew gave his mom a happy squeeze and

192

bolted out of the car after his sister. That left Parker to find a parking space on the street just outside of school, and march straight to the front office of the school as the final bell rang for class.

As Parker entered the lobby, there was no sign of Heller or Mendez. Their office door was closed. The Silver Fox typed madly away at her computer, pretending not to notice Parker as she approached her desk.

Why is she always typing? "I'd like to speak with Vice Principal Heller," announced Parker.

Silver Fox continued to type away without so much a glance at Parker. "Principal Heller is not in right now," the Fox declared.

Parker squinted to better examine Fox's poker face. "But Vice Principal Heller's coming in today, right?" Parker tapped her fingers on the top of Fox's computer monitor.

"I'm not at liberty to say."

"Well, she sent *me* a text last night saying she'd be in."

Fox's fingers froze over her keyboard. She slowly looked up at Parker. "She—*texted* you?"

Parker nodded quietly in an attempt to prolong Fox's discomfort. "I'm going to be around working on PTA stuff. Can you have her contact me when she gets in?" Parker lifted her phone displaying the text she'd gotten from Heller. "She has my number. Because, you know, she texted me."

Fox drew a frosty breath. "Then why don't you just text her yourself?"

Parker's nodding eased to a halt. "Good point," she said. Parker had never succeeded in getting a hold of Heller when she initiated the contact, but she found the Silver Fox's reaction most interesting. Either Fox was jealous of Parker's communication with

Heller or baffled by it. Parker's thumbs stabbed at her phone's display. "Look at me, I'm texting her right now."

What time will you be at school today? We need to chat.

Parker hit the send button.

The Silver Fox rested her chin on her palms. "Hmm. No reply?"

Parker's lips parted into a forced smile. *Something tells me you might know the reason why.* Parker was about to ask Fox another question when her phone suddenly buzzed. Fox and Parker looked at each other in surprise. Parker turned her phone over to read the response from Heller's number.

Soon.

"Was that – her?" asked Fox.

You seem genuinely surprised by this. "Yes," answered Parker. "She says, she'll be here soon."

Fox smiled. "Well then, there's nothing to worry about, is there?" As if catching herself expressing some form of forbidden emotion, the Silver Fox straightened her posture, erased her smile and began to type again.

Parker leaned forward. "Were you worried?"

Fox's typing slowed as she formulated her response. "She was missing, Ms. Monroe. I'm just glad to hear Principal Heller's okay."

Vice Principal. "Of course." Parker sighed. "I'm going to wait here since she's on her way."

"Mmm, hmm."

Parker took a seat in one of the chairs along the office wall. But after thirty minutes of Candy Crush, Heller still was a no show.

45.

Are you still coming?

Where are you?

Hello?

Parker sighed as she sent another barrage of texts to Heller that failed to earn any response. She'd wasted an hour of her time waiting in that front lobby.

Either she's fucking with me, or someone's fucking with her.

Even the Silver Fox appeared curious enough to check in with Parker every ten minutes. "This isn't like Heller to do this," informed Fox.

Parker bit her lip as the Principal's office door finally swung open. Out stepped Mendez, carrying a slim document folder. Parker couldn't help but frown in bitter awe at how Mendez managed to make a boring colored beige suit look amazing on her athletic body. *Just once I'd like to see her slum it in sweat pants and some ratty t-shirt from a really crappy band -- like Foo Fighters.* The young Latino woman paused as she caught Parker's gaze. "Ms. Monroe," she greeted coolly with an arch of one brow. "You're here. In my lobby. Again."

"I'm waiting for Heller," explained Parker. "She said she would meet with me today."

"Oh," Mendez grimaced. "I wasn't aware she was coming in." Mendez handed her folder to Fox. "Did she say when she would be in?"

Just then, Parker's phone buzzed to life.

Soon.

Parker looked around the lobby. Fox's hands were off her own keyboard as if Parker's phone buzzing had mesmerized her. "Was that her?" asked Fox.

"She says she'll be here soon." *Again.* Either the timing of the text was a coincidence or Parker was being watched. Parker scanned Mendez's hands, neither of which carried a phone.

Mendez sighed. "Then you should come back when Heller arrives."

Tired of the runaround, Parker threw up her arms. "Come on, you're not at all curious that your vice principal has been missing?"

"Missing?" Mendez pointed to Parker's phone. "You mean the woman who just texted you saying she was coming in?"

"I just think it odd, that no one knows where she's been."

"Do you know where *I* was last night, Ms. Monroe?" Mendez challenged.

"No. Where *were* you last night?"

Mendez folded her arms. "I'm not telling you, because it's none of your business."

I walked right into that one.

"Now, as a former journalist I know you have an uncontrollable need to ask lots of questions, but I can't have parents waiting around in my lobby all day. It's a distraction and a liability. So, please, leave and come back. I'm sure Heller will text you when she arrives."

I wouldn't bet on that.

Parker's mind raced for a counter punch to the landmine of common sense Mendez threw down. Parker didn't want to admit that if she left, she feared she would miss an opportunity to catch Heller in the act – of what she wasn't sure. That was, of course, if Heller bothered to show at all. Something was completely wrong with how all of this was unfolding, and it ate at Parker's soul.

Finally, the front glass door to the lobby opened, giving Parker the save she needed.

46.

"Holly!" Parker greeted the PTA President so enthusiastically it frightened her.

"You showed! Finally!"

A wide-eyed Holly nearly stumbled with the stack of boxes she carried into the school's lobby. "Oh, hello! Ms. Monroe?"

"Don't tell me you forgot our meeting too!" Parker scurried to relieve Holly of one of her boxes.

Holly smiled, glad that Parker had taken some of the weight off her arms, but greatly confused. "I'm sorry, were – *were* we meeting today?"

"Uh, *yeah!*"

Mendez turned up her nose. "I thought you were meeting with Heller."

"Heller, Holly and I were going to put our heads together about the fundraiser," Parker lied.

"Wow, I'm so sorry, I'd entirely forgotten about that!" Holly apologized. Her eye began to twitch.

"So, see, there's a good reason for me to stick around!" stated Parker. "Because PTA. Because fundraiser. Because stuff!"

Mendez's eyes narrowed like a hawk. "Fine. Then please confine your activities to the PTA office."

"You've got an office?" Parker feigned excitement. "Of course, you've got an office, you're the President!"

"It's really more of a storage room," Holly sheepishly explained.

"I'm sure it's fine. Why don't I help you with all this shit?" Parker used the box she carried to nudge Holly out the hallway before Mendez could insist she leave again.

The women travelled several halls deep into the labyrinth of the elementary school. Their journey ended at a single door that opened to a small windowless box of a room, making the PTA office more of a storage closet than a storage room. After depositing the boxes onto a pile of yet more boxes, Parker and Holly found themselves sitting across from each other at a small, square folding card table under the dim single light bulb that hung from the ceiling on a string. They were surrounded by piles of art supplies, papers, forms and a patchwork of various kiosks, one of which would rattle occasionally on its suggesting some small critter might be nesting there.

Over the next forty minutes, Parker did her best to feign interest while listening to Holly's laundry list of concerns over having so many different fundraisers. But Parker's incessant toe tapping and habitual phone checking finally broke Holly's concentration.

"Should we meet some other time, Ms. Monroe?" Holly asked politely. "You appear rather distracted."

Parker immediately ceased her tapping. "I'm sorry. I'm just wondering when Heller is actually going to show up." Parker noticed Holly's eye twitch start up again. "I mean, we can't get very far without her, you know, *blessing*."

"Of course, of course," Holly agreed. She drew a deep breath and became very silent. Her eye twitch stopped. Then, in the next breath, her lips tightened into a trembling pout. Her body shook.

"Holly?"

Holly shuttered as she broke down into an uncontrollable sob.

"Oh, *wow*. Feelings." Parker's stomach twisted into knots. Anger, hubris and pride were the feelings she was used to dealing with in her co-workers. But strange crying adults who weren't part of an article she was writing made her uncomfortable as all hell. "Um, Holly, are you alright?" *Stupid question.* "I mean, you're here. Crying. I'm – also here. Is there something I can help you with?" *To make you stop crying? Because it's freaking me out.*

"I'm sorry," Holly blubbered. She reached for a tissue in her purse. "I'm sorry, I'm just so – the pressure – there's a lot to do, you know? There's a lot to figure out, and no offense, but this new fundraiser—I'm just not sure how we're going to get it all done!"

Parker nodded. "Oh, Holly, don't worry! I told you, I can handle the music fundraiser. It's why I joined the PTA in the first place."

Holly blew her nose into a tissue. "That may be, Ms. Monroe, but I'm afraid it may detract from our other fundraisers. The more money people give to yours, the less they give to others. There's only so much money in this town. Parents get really sore when you keep asking them for so many donations all year around."

Parker's phone buzzed again. She glanced at her screen out of the corner of her eye, trying not to bring Holly's attention to it.

Soon.

Parker hated the fact each time her phone buzzed it put her on edge. *What the hell am I doing? Heller's being an ass-hat with her texting game while Holly is all broken up just trying to do the right thing for the school. She's got the real problems and needs real help.*

"Was that – Heller?" asked Holly, trying to hold back another bout of sobbing.

Parker turned her phone over. "It's not important," she said. "Holly, I want to apologize. I didn't mean for the music fundraiser to complicate things so much. Especially for you. No one seems to care more about this school than you do."

Holly looked up from her tissue. She smiled. "Thank you."

"How many other fundraisers do you have?"

"We have a paint-a-thon for our art programs, a raffle ticket drawing for new playground equipment," Holly's voice drifted off as she counted a total of eight different fundraisers over the course of the year. "And now we have yours."

"That sounds like a real cluster."

"Cluster?"

"A cluster fuck." Parker shook her head at Holly's empty wide eyes, forcing her to translate. "It's *bad*."

Holly's eyes welled up again.

"But!" Parker raised her index finger in an attempt to break Holly's emotional roller coaster ride. "*What* if we put some of them together? Into one, super big fundraiser?"

Holly shook her head. "No, we've tried that before. You're just asking parents to spend more money in a shorter amount of time. They don't like to do that. It's better to spread it out."

"Even if you built it around some crazy cool event?"

"Like what?"

Parker was shooting from her hip right now. "Like a rock concert. Or a carnival. Or a casino night. Or a carnival rock concert casino night. You get some cool rides, some fun entertainment for people, throw in your raffles, auctions, whatever, sell tickets in advance – if it's a big enough event you can find sponsors. Local businesses would want to advertise in it. I know you guys do this on a smaller scale, but I'm saying scale it up. Like, on a Bezos or Elon Musk scale."

Holly winced. "I don't know."

Parker leaned forward to fold her hands on the table. "It's worth running the numbers. If you have some more time this morning, we can work together to find out if we're even in the ballpark."

Holly dropped her shoulders. "I suppose it's worth a shot."

47.

To Parker's own amazement...

the next several hours flew by as Parker and Holly brainstormed ideas, reviewed ledgers from years past, and researched vendor web pages. Tackling such a tangible problem that could actually make a difference in her kids' lives, let alone the community, energized Parker with a euphoria she hadn't felt in years. Soon, a framework plan of a Halloween themed carnival event that incorporated all of the school's fundraisers took shape. When she tallied up the initial budget numbers, Holly's smile wasn't the forced toothy face devouring Joker's grin she'd first greeted Parker with, it was a genuine expression of joy and hope.

"This might actually work," Holly gasped in astonishment.

The school bell rang and snapped both Holly and Parker out of their daze.

School bell?

Parker looked at the time on her phone. "Holy shit, we've been at this all day."

"I guess so," answered Holly. "I'm suddenly hungry. We didn't even have lunch! And no word from Heller?"

Parker doubled checked her phone. No new texts had come in. "No." *Fuck Heller.* "But you know what? If we move fast, we could probably run this by Mendez to see what she thought."

Holly agreed, and the two them gathered their things to race out of the PTA storage closet to the hallway. Outside, the bustle of kids dismissed from their lines could be heard as the pair made their way to the front office, catching Mendez just as she was shutting her office door.

"Principal Mendez, could we show you something? Quickly?" asked Holly.

Mendez let out a heavy sigh, clearly anxious to get on with her weekend. "This really can't wait until Monday?"

Holly looked to the floor. "Well, I suppose it could—"

Parker jumped in. "Sure, if you're not interested at all in how we can triple your school's fundraising power in one night. We only skipped lunch to volunteer to work on the thing the *entire day*." Parker thrust a mess of papers at Mendez. "But, if your school's budget isn't important to you, that's okay."

Mendez frowned. "Really? Triple?" She took the handful of papers and began to examine them. "A carnival?" she hemmed. "Sounds like an insurance nightmare waiting to happen."

"I checked, the school's insurance will cover it," informed Parker. "We just need to up the liability coverage for that particular day, which Holly has already budgeted for in our expenses." *Suck it.*

Mendez looked harder at the numbers. She folded the top page back and forth to check more figures. "I'm going to need to look at this more closely." At first Parker wondered if Mendez meant on Monday, but Mendez swiftly reached for her office door knob to open it. "Do either of you mind waiting another fifteen minutes or so?"

Both Parker's and Holly's eyes popped. "Oh, you mean *now*? Great! Yeah, sure!" Parker spoke for the both of them.

"It's not a problem," added Holly. "Ginger knows if she doesn't see me on the playground to come to the front office."

"Ginger?"

"My third grader."

204

Shit. "Right, my kids don't have that protocol." *Or the wherewithal,* thought Parker. "Lemme go find them while you two look things over."

It didn't take long for Parker to find Drew and Maddy on the emptying playground. When Parker explained the situation, Maddy met it with her usual display of disdain.

"Can we just wait in the minivan?" groaned Maddy. She held out her hand to accept the keys.

"Sure." Parker dug in her purse to find the car keys and slapped them onto Maddy's hand. "I promise I won't be long."

"Whatever."

As Parker parted ways with her kids to make her way back to the front office, her phone buzzed again.

I'm here.

Parker rolled her eyes. "Well, will wonders never cease?"

48.

Heller's going to think the tongue lashing I gave her at PTA was a bubble bath.

Parker marched into Mendez's office with a fresh spring in her step. To Parker's surprise, only Holly sat across the desk from Mendez, with a young blonde girl sitting in a chair near the wall that Parker could only assume was Ginger. The rest of the room was empty, as was the lobby. Fox must have left for the day.

Holly and Mendez looked up from their papers. "You're back," stated Mendez. "Great, I have some questions about some of these numbers."

"Where is she?" blasted Parker.

"Who?"

"Heller." Parker held out her phone. "She said she was here."

Both Holly and Mendez looked to each other in bewilderment. "We haven't seen her."

Just then, Drew waltzed into the office behind Parker, his backpack in tow. "Mom, can I have the keys?" he asked.

Parker spun around to look past her son to the empty lobby. Still no sign of Heller. "I *gave* you the keys."

"We need the *right* keys."

Parker frowned at her own mistake. *I must have given them the Highlander keys by accident.* Parker dug into her purse to give Drew the minivan rental keys. She handed the new keys to Drew. "Sorry. Now go. I'll be there in a few minutes."

Drew ran off as Parker's phone buzzed again.

Where are you?

"Is that Heller?" asked Mendez. She stood up from her desk.

Parker frowned. "Yes," she growled as she angrily typed her response.

In the front office. Where the hell are YOU?

The phone buzzed with an answer.

Waiting.

"What the fuck is this woman's problem?" Parker stormed out into the lobby and looked down each empty corridor. There was no sign of anyone, other than Drew who walked back into the lobby.

"So, we just want to make sure that you want us to use the minivan," greeted Drew.

"What?" Parker snapped. "Of course, I want you to use the minivan! What is going on out there? How is this so complicated?"

"We thought you might want us to use the Highlander."

"The Highlander is gone, Drew!" Parker found herself almost yelling now.

Drew hunched. "No, it's not. It's in the parking lot."

Parker shook her head. "There are a gazillion Highlanders in the world. It probably just *looks* like ours."

"Okay," Drew sighed as he turned to walk out the door. "She says use the minivan!" he shouted to Maddy across the parking lot.

Parker's phone buzzed again. Only this time, the words scraped at Parker's heart.

Still waiting.

Mendez looked over Parker's shoulder to read the same text. "What does she mean by that?"

The texting all day and night. The Highlander getting stolen. All of this was connected in a very, very bad way. Parker pushed out the front door into the parking lot. She caught Drew walking toward Maddy who stood in the center of the lot between two cars parked opposite of each other – the rental minivan, and a filthy silver Highlander that looked hauntingly familiar. Maddy played with one set of keys to unlock the minivan, as signified by its blinking hazard lights.

Drew shouted to his sister. "Mom said, just go to the minivan!"

"No, but see, the keys work!" Maddy shouted back. She pressed the keys to the Highlander, and sure enough the hazard lights flickered on and off. "It's our car! I knew it! I found our car!"

"Maddy, stay where you are!" Parker yelled.

Maddy rolled her eyes. "It's fine, Mom, it's our car!" She walked toward the Highlander.

"Maddy!" Parker screamed as she sprinted toward her daughter. "I said stop!"

Maddy squinted as she neared the Highlander, ignoring her mother's command. "It smells kinda bad. There's something in the back."

"What is it?" asked Drew.

"Drew!" Parker pointed at her son. "Go back to the school! Now!" Drew quickly obeyed as Parker reached Maddy ten feet from the car. "Maddy, god damnit, I said stop! You need to listen!" She yanked Maddy by the arm to pull her away, but it was too late. Maddy had already pressed the remote button to open the Highlander's back gate.

"Stop yelling at me!" Maddy cried.

The Highlander emitted a series of loud beeps as its hydraulics whirred to open the back gate, letting a foul cloud of stench to hit Maddy and Parker. Parker watched helplessly as her daughter's face contorted into an expression of abject horror. Maddy screamed. Parker pulled her daughter's face to her chest to shield her from the sight, but it was too late. Maddy had already seen the contorted body of an old woman stuffed into a plastic trash bag, her feet high above her own head as if some mannequin folded in half. The dead woman's face that peeked just above the bag's line was gaunt, discolored and sporting an infested hole where the left eye socket should be, and a dried eye rolled back in the other.

Karen Heller had returned to the school after all.

49.

An hour later...

red and blue gumball lights flashed in every corner of the school's parking lot that wasn't already cordoned off with yellow "crime scene" tape. A sizeable crowd of onlookers stood in the park and on sidewalks nearby, whispering to each other as they pointed to Parker's Highlander and the first responders and deputies that surrounded it. Sheriff Bill watched closely as his CSI team carefully inspected every inch of the SUV, checking for prints on the door handles and steering wheel. Occasionally they would look to one another, then to Bill for an instruction as to what to do next. "Take pictures," Bill would remind them. "Take lots of pictures. I want every inch of that vehicle documented!"

Good thing I'd already taken my own pictures before you got here, thought Parker. She sighed as she watched a deputy nearly trip over his colleague. *These guys have obviously never covered a murder scene before.* In fact, Parker couldn't recall if a murder had ever happened in the city of Oak Creek when she was growing up. In Chicago one seemed to happen every other day. Regardless, Oak Creek's finest did their best to project an air of security and professionalism as two of them lifted the trash bag that contained Heller and put it on a gurney.

One of the deputies looked back to Bill again. "Uh, Sheriff? We don't need a body bag, do we? I mean, she kind of came with her own." The deputy poked at one of Heller's feet next to her forehead. "And she's been stuck in this position for so long. It might take some doing to flatten her out, you know?"

Bill scratched his head, hyper aware that Parker watched him in smug judgment. He cleared his throat. "The bag is evidence," pronounced Bill. He couldn't help but wince at his own statement. "Just cover her with a blanket. We'll let the morgue sort it out, okay? Now get going." Bill shooed his deputies onward, then looked back to Parker. "What?"

"Nothing," said Parker. She tugged at the warm but itchy blanket that the first responders had thrown around her earlier. No matter what the crisis, a first responder's first response always seemed to provide warm blankets. She and Bill watched as his deputies rolled the gurney away.

Bill turned back to the Highlander. "We're going to have impound your car – *again*. It's evidence too."

"Keep it," said Parker. "There is no way my kids are going to want to climb into that thing now."

"Riiiiiight," Bill grimaced. "How *is* your daughter doing?"

Parker glanced over to the school entrance, where Maddy sat on a folding chair with a similar heavy blanket wrapped around her. The school counselor, a middle-aged woman named Rebecca Buck whose large lips reminded Parker of a duck, patted Maddy's arm as though she were some kind of injured animal. "Maddy's going to need some time to process this." *Along with a shit ton of therapy.*

Drew sat in a chair next to his sister, also wearing a blanket as first responders continued to look him over. Parker hated to leave her kids in the care of strangers, but Mendez insisted that they and Holly's daughter be evaluated right away. Holly had done a better job of shielding her child from the scene and insisted she take her home immediately. Parker had to stick around to make her statement to the police. Parker couldn't help but note that Mendez appeared to have little interest in working with the kids herself, yet she always stood within the earshot of the crime scene. Even now, she planted herself about ten feet away from where the sheriff stood, talking on the phone with someone Parker guessed was an insurance agent. *Always worried about the liability, aren't you, Mendez?*

Parker kept close to her Highlander. She wanted to absorb every detail about the crime scene in case Bill's team screwed something up.

Bill reviewed his notepad. "So, um," he couldn't look Parker in the eyes. "I'm also going to need your phone."

Parker didn't even bother looking at Bill. "Nope."

Bill pulled up on his belt buckle. "The texts you received from Heller's phone. You know, the ones you didn't bother to tell me about until *after* a dead body showed up in your car? That's evidence, Parker. You know that."

"Oh, but Sheriff, just yesterday you were convinced that it was Heller, herself, who was innocently sending those texts."

"Well, clearly it was not!"

"I don't want to say I told you so--" Parker poked her finger into Bill's chest. "But-I-told-you-so! Maybe now you'll listen to me when I say there's weird shit going on in this town. I'll supply you a copy of the texts. With time stamps. But you're not taking my phone."

Bill pulled Parker away from the Highlander and the prying eyes of his deputies. He spoke in a hushed voice. "Listen, you gotta at least *look* like you're playing ball, here. Do you read me? People are already talking--"

"It's been an hour!"

Bill raised his hands to hint for Parker to keep her voice down. "I don't control the internet! Word is spreading!"

"Yeah? What are they saying? What are *you* saying?" Parker frowned. "Are you saying – I'm a *suspect*?"

Bill coughed. "Not officially. Maybe. Kind of? The public expects me to look at this from all angles—"

"Are you fucking kidding me?"

Bill pointed to the Highlander. "Heller's dead body was found in the back of your Highlander!"

"My *stolen* Highlander! And I was the one who found Heller and reported it!"

"A roomful of PTA moms heard you threaten her with both barrels the other night!"

"I was talking about my *boobs*!" Parker glared at Bill, who despite his height, never appeared so small as he did right then. "Bill, do you really think I killed Karen Heller?"

"No, of course not, it's just—these are facts, okay? And people are going to distort these facts and they are going to run with them! I've seen it before."

Parker closed her eyes. "Yes, I know, it looks bad, but you've got other leads, right?"

Bill's silence was deafening.

Parker looked to Bill. "You don't have any other leads, do you?"

"I've got a working theory." Bill fumbled his notepad open. "It needs some tweaking. But I think this might be related to some kind of gang initiation. There's been an uptick in Los Zetas activity, and we're only an hour from the border."

Parker felt her jaw straining. "Uh huh. That's not — entirely horrible. Go on."

"To gain admittance to the gang, members have to prove themselves. Steal a car, for instance. Execute a rival. You get the picture. Sometimes victims are randomly selected. Heller could have been one of them."

Parker nodded slowly. "Nice work, Sheriff."

"Thank you."

"That would explain just about everything that's happened."

"Not bad, huh?"

"Except that's not what happened."

50.

"You don't know that," Bill folded his arms.

He paused and swiveled his head around to see if his deputies were still watching. They weren't. "Okay, how do you know that?"

Parker spoke in a moaning voice. "I don't know, can you trust the word of an alleged murderer?"

"Cut that out."

"I might be trying to lead you astray."

"You're hilarious."

Parker's eyes widened. She tapped Bill in the chest. "Oh shit, you know what I should do? To really mess with you? I'll apply for a private detective license!"

"Please don't do that."

"I can see it now, a single mother, wrongfully accused of murder—"

"You're not wrongfully accused."

"So, I'm rightfully accused?"

"Just stop."

"--wrongfully accused of murder, she becomes a private detective and then hires herself to clear her own name!"

The Sheriff stomped his foot. "Are you going to tell me or what?"

Parker dropped her theatrics and stared at Bill intensely. "Come on, it's so obvious. Heller is wearing the same outfit she did the night of the PTA meeting, which confirms she never went home. Remember, I saw her drive in the opposite direction of her house. She was clearly going to meet someone that night, someone she knew, and I think that person is the person who shot her. Heller knew her killer."

"That's quite a jump."

"Not at all." Parker pulled up her phone with a picture she took of the bloody hole in Heller's left eye socket. "Heller was shot in the face at close range."

Bill looked around as he pushed Parker's phone down. "You took pictures?"

"I'm a reporter!"

"*Were* a reporter."

"Listen, this means Heller was facing her attacker when she was shot. I found no obvious signs of struggle, if you don't count being stuffed into a trash bag, but that would have happened after she died. So, whoever she met with wouldn't have given her any cause for alarm. She knew her killer, or at least recognized her killer." Parker raised her phone and swiped over to her text messaging app. "Then there is the little matter of all these texts. I never gave Heller my number, but when I joined the PTA, I had to give all my contact information. Anyone with access to that ledger would have been able to find my info."

Bill rubbed his chin. "Then all the killer would have to do is unlock Heller's phone with the fingerprint from her dead hand. But why text you?"

"Why steal my car? Why tease me all day with texts? Whoever it was knew enough about my relationship with Heller to know how to exploit me as a suspect. And then, of course, the big reveal this afternoon. It was deliberately theatric. The killer wanted to put on a show."

"That's a lot of work," Bill shook his head. "Why? What's so special about you?"

Other than my incredible investigative powers? "I don't know. But I think whoever killed Heller was in that PTA meeting."

Bill grimaced. "Maybe, but you weren't the only one getting texts from Heller's phone. So did Mr. Heller. Whoever texted him knew enough about their relationship to fool him into thinking they were his wife."

"Then, clearly, it's someone who knew Karen Heller very well, like –" Parker caught herself.

"Who?"

Parker hated confessing the name. "Mr. Bernstein. He had his own troubles with Heller. She fired him, after all."

"I looked into Bernstein. His alibi checks. Bernstein was sick with the flu that night. Trust me, I've known Bernstein for a long time. That guy is no killer."

"I'd like to believe that." *Seeing how he's my kid's piano teacher and all.*

"You were on your way to winning his job back. Why would Bernstein risk screwing that up by shooting her? It doesn't make sense. There's no motive."

Parker felt relieved to hear Bill's opinion on it. Her gut told her Bernstein wasn't the shooter, but she wanted to be sure. "That leaves just one other possibility outside of the PTA." Parker nodded up the street to where Heller's house would be.

Bill coughed. "*Mr.* Heller?"

Parker shrugged. "Granted, I've never met the man, but maybe he has some crazy insurance policy on his wife and wanted to cash out? It's been done. We can't rule him out."

"I can," said Bill. "That man can barely get out of bed most days."

Parker marveled at Bill's childlike certainty. *Oh Bill, you've been so wrong about so many things so far, you can't take any suspects off the table.* "Have you informed Mr. Heller of his wife's condition?"

"You mean, her death?" Bill sucked air in through his teeth. "No. We tried calling but he hasn't picked up. As soon as I'm done here I'm walking up there to see if he's home. I don't look forward to giving him the news."

"I could go with you."

"What? No, Parker, you're already in the thick of this. You need to lay low and let things cool off."

"Yeah, I *am* in the thick of this, and everyone is going to think I had something to do with Heller's death!"

Bill grabbed Parker's shoulders to look her straight in the eye. "I promise, *for real*, if anything pops up I will share it with you. But only if you promise to do the same. You get any more weird texts or phone calls you need to tell me – immediately."

Parker pouted. "Fine."

"In the meantime, try to keep from having any more dead bodies show up in your car, okay?" Bill gently turned Parker back toward the front of the school. "You've got more important things to tend to."

Parker's heart sank when Maddy looked in her direction. Only they didn't connect to her like they usually did. Not even to roll them annoyingly at her mother's antics. No, Maddy's eyes were vacant of any energy – a sight her mother had never seen before.

51.

Parker approached Rebecca Buck, who still hadn't stopped patting Maddy's arm.

She nodded to the counselor as if to say – I'll take over now. The counselor nodded in return and stepped away to afford Parker space with her kids. "Maddy? You ready to go home?" asked Parker in a soft voice.

Maddy continued to stare straight forward as if hypnotized by the flashing police lights.

Parker deliberately stepped in front of her daughter's line of sight. *Come on, kid, give me something.* "Maddy? Did you hear me?"

Maddy swallowed. "I heard you."

Parker knelt down to meet her eldest at eye level. She brushed a strand of Maddy's brown hair away from her eyes. "How are you doing?"

As if a switch had suddenly been flipped, Maddy's eyes suddenly turned to lock with her mother's. "I'm fine."

I doubt that. "You want to talk about what you saw? Do you have any questions about it? It's kind of a lot to process—even for me."

"I'm fine."

Parker nodded, not wanting to push the issue. "Okay," She turned to Drew. "What about you, young man?"

Drew shrugged. "I'm bored." He patted his tummy. "And hungry."

"That's a bad combination." *But a good sign.* "Let's go home." Parker rose to her feet, a simple maneuver that seemed to strain her tired legs. She held out her hand to Drew. "Keys, please?"

"Are we taking the death car?" asked Drew.

Parker grimaced. "I think we're done with that one. Like – *forever*."

"Good." Drew reached into his pocket and handed Parker the minivan keys. "I don't want Heller's ghost following us home."

I wouldn't put it past her.

Mendez stepped forward just as the kids got to their feet. "Ms. Monroe," she greeted solemnly. "If either of your kids needs extra time before coming back to school on Monday, just let me know. We will see to it they get their homework."

"Thank you," said Parker. She eyed Mendez carefully as she turned to walk back into the school. *What's your deal, Mendez? You're hot, you're cold, I can't figure you out – yet.*

Parker's phone buzzed as she led her kids across the parking lot. Without thinking, she habitually answered it. "Hello?"

"Parker!" Julie shouted through the phone. "Omigod, Parker! Are you okay? Are the kids okay? I just heard!"

Shit, you heard already? "We're fine, Julie," assured Parker, clasping her hand around the edge of her phone so as to mute the noise. She could feel the eyeballs of the crowd burrowing into her. "Now's not a good time to chat."

"Okay, okay, of course, of course! I just gotta know! Just quick tell me!"

"Tell you what?"

"Did you do it?"

"*What?*"

"Did you plug Heller?"

"No!"

Julie breathed a sigh of relief. "Thank God, because, you know, I wouldn't blame you if you did, honestly, she treated you like shit, and you can trust me, okay? I would take your secret to the grave, okay?"

"Julie, I gotta go!" Parker quickly hung up the phone. "Jesus, Julie, what the fuck?"

Parker herded her kids into the minivan as quickly as she could.

"Why are they staring?" He pressed his face against the side window, staring back at the crowd of people on the other side of the yellow tape.

"They're just nosey," answered Parker. "They want to know what happened." *They're not the only ones.*

Parker pulled out of the parking lot, forcing the crowd to part ways for her. She drove up the street toward Heller's house, and found Sheriff Bill and Deputy Michaels walking toward it. Parker couldn't help but wonder how Mr. Heller would react to the news of his wife's death. That was, if he didn't already know about it.

As Parker drove by, she noticed that dark, shadowy figure in Heller's window again. Mr. Heller appeared to be taking note of her, just as she was him.

One way or another, Mr. Heller, I'm going to learn your story.

52.

"We're home!"

Parker announced as she opened the front door.

Right on cue, Ally came running from the kitchen with her smile as wide as her face. She raced into the arms of her mother, with Valerie hot on her heels.

"Thank Bette Davis's bedroom eyes you're back," proclaimed Valerie. "I got your message, I just can't believe it! Heller? Dead? In your car?"

"I hope you've got a good Malbec picked out for tonight."

"I think you're going to need something stronger than wine." Valerie quickly grabbed Drew by the shoulders to inspect him, then did the same to Maddy. "You poor dears, it must have been awful to see all of that. Are you alright?"

"I didn't get to see anything," said Drew, with a hint of morbid disappointment. "Maddy is the one who found her."

"Maddy?" Valerie gasped. "My, oh my, are you alright?"

"I'm fine." answered Maddy quietly.

Valerie glanced at Parker, who subtly shook her head as a warning not to press her daughter too hard.

After an uncomfortable silence, Maddy faked a yawn. "I'm going to go to bed."

"You don't want dinner?" asked Valerie. "I'm making enchiladas."

"I'm not hungry," Maddy insisted. "I'm just really -- tired." Maddy slowly sauntered up the stairs.

"Oh, okay," Valerie clenched her fists closely to her breast. "I'll save some in case you change your mind, alright?"

"Good night." Maddy disappeared around the bend at the top of the stairs.

Valerie once again checked with Parker, who held her hands up as if to say, "let's give her some space." Valerie frowned. Space never fit her M.O. as a grandparent.

Drew waved his hands in front of Valerie. "Well, *I'm* hungry!" It was rare to hear such a grumpy demand from the first grader.

Parker and Valerie tried to keep the rest of the evening light for Ally and Drew, as if respecting some unspoken rule not to discuss murder in front of children. It was only after Parker had put them to bed that she would even dare to broach the subject. She checked on Maddy, who was sound asleep on top of her covers and still wearing her day clothes. Convinced there was nothing more she could do for her that night, Parker tip-toed back downstairs to join Valerie in the front room.

Valerie had just opened a bottle of Glenfiddich 21 and poured generous helpings into two shot glasses.

"You're not screwing around," noted Parker, taking a seat next to her mother on the couch.

"It felt like a whiskey night," said Val. "Down the hatch."

The two women clinked their glasses together and downed the liquid gold.

"Oh hell," said Parker, feeling the burn. She pounded her chest. "That's rich."

"At two hundred bucks a bottle, it better be." Valerie poured another round. "You're allowed to sip it this time. Now, tell me what happened."

Parker shook the remaining burn off before detailing the events of the past twenty-four hours, weighing her theory of the killer likely being a PTA member against the Sheriff's theory of gang related violence.

"Interesting," said Valerie. "Your theory can rationally explain everything that happened."

Parker raised her glass. "Thank you."

"Except that's not what happened."

Parker nearly choked on her whiskey. "Excuse me?"

"Really, Parker, I'm surprised at you," chided Valerie. "Granted, I'm not some awarding winning investigator, but you seem to have forgotten some very important facts."

"Enlighten me." Parker tossed back her head as she downed another shot.

"Your car was stolen. And I told you to sip."

Parker clenched her teeth, enjoying the new burn in her chest. "I haven't forgotten either of those things."

"Your car was stolen right out from under our noses. No alarm was set off. You said the Sheriff estimated it to be the job of a professional."

"And?"

"How many PTA mothers are professional car thieves?"

"Fair point," Parker put down her shot glass onto the coffee table with a solid knock. "How many PTA mothers are award winning journalists? Yet, here I am."

"Whoever stole your car has a very specific set of skills."

Parker took a moment to reflect on the idea. The only set of skills she could clearly identify was that of GI Joe, the former professional soldier. His skills were lethal, but car thieving was far

224

from the required curriculum of basic training or Ranger school. "I'll keep that in mind," said Parker as she noticed a shock of blue color on the side of the couch. She leaned over to find a pile of blue plastic shopping bags. The kind one might find in an electronics retailer. "What's all this?"

"Security."

Parker pulled out a cubed box with the picture of a wireless security camera on it. She turned the box over to examine it. "Seems pretty high tech for you."

"The young man at the store said it uses my Wi-Fi. Movement triggers an alarm that rings your phone and takes a video."

Parker sighed. "You're worried about our security?"

"You're not?"

"Yeah, but I figured you'd just buy another gun."

"I did that too." Valerie smiled at the idea of blasting an intruder, even though she'd never had the opportunity. "She's a beaut. You wanna see her?"

Parker shook her head. "No! And whatever it is, keep it locked up and away from my kids." Parker presented the box to her mother. "I'm not installing these on my own, you know. You're going to help."

"No need, I've got a man coming over tomorrow." Valerie noted Parker's sore posture. "You don't approve?"

"It's just—" Parker blew out her lips. "—I don't want the kids freaking out. You know, like they see these cameras everywhere and wondering if we're in danger all the time."

Valerie tilted her head. "We *are* in danger."

Parker couldn't offer a rebuttal. She simply watched her mother out of the periphery of her eye.

"Parker, I know a part of you tries to look at this as a detached journalist, so you can 'get the scoop' or whatever you call it, but the fact is, it was *your* car that was stolen. From *my* house. The killer, whoever it is, targeted *our* family. Who is to say he or she is finished with us?"

Parker poured another shot. She hated when her mother made so much sense. "Why us?"

Valerie accepted a pour from her daughter. "I hate to say it, but maybe you were right from the beginning." She swallowed. "Maybe this has less to do with Heller, and more to do with you."

53.

The next morning, the Parker household woke up to a prompt 7 am doorbell chime.

"That'll be him!" Valerie hollered over the hairdryer whirring in her bedroom. "Can you get it?"

Still groggy from her late-night whiskey shots, Parker lumbered down the stairs in her oversized *Have a Nice Day* Bon Jovi t-shirt she slept in as the doorbell continued to chime and chime again. "I'm coming!" she growled to the door. "No need to wear the button out!" Parker threw open the door only to find— "Glory?"

Glory Wonder's moustache framed a smile that gleamed so brightly it nearly gave Parker a headache. "Yup, yup, good morning, Ms. Monroe!" Glory pulled down his sunglasses a smidge to look Parker up and down. "You look positively glowing! You know, for um, finding – a dead body in your car yesterday."

Parker pulled down on her oversized shirt, suddenly realizing she wasn't wearing pants. *Good thing, I shaved my legs yesterday.* "So, you heard about that too?"

"Oh yeah, yeah, it's all over town."

"Fantastic."

"You've even got your own catchphrases. Like, uhh," Glory snapped his fingers. "Mrs. Murder! Killer Mom. Don't ever park with Parker. Double barrel boob shooter. Of course, I set 'em all straight. I tell 'em you're a Man Killer. But, you know, in the good way. You want to see the MEME's that are going around?"

Parker exhaled loudly. "What—are you doing here, exactly?"

"I'm installing security cameras," Glory pouted. "I think. I'm pretty sure that's what your mom said when she called me yesterday."

Parker leaned to the left to see Glory's plumbing / Knight Rider inspired Trans Am. "So, you're a plumber, an 80's ride share driver, and a handyman?"

"I like to think of myself as an entrepreneur." Glory lifted his toolbox. "Can I come in?"

Parker weighed her options. "That depends. How do I know you're not the one who murdered Karen Heller and are setting these cameras up to secretly monitor and sabotage me?"

Glory gulped. "Wow, um, I wasn't expecting *that*. Okay," he took a deep breath. "Um, your mom called me. So, there's that. And I've never killed anyone. That I remember. So, there's thaaaaat—"

Parker found Glory's confusion all too sincere. "Alright, shut up. Come in."

"Wait!" Glory raised his index finger. He stammered. "How do *I* know, that *you* didn't kill Heller, and are inviting me over to kill *me* and stuff me in the back of *your* van to dispose of the evidence?"

Because none of that makes any sense and it would make me the dumbest murderer to have ever murdered anyone. But instead of chastising Glory, Parker decided to flash an evil grin. "You don't." Parker left the door open as she turned away and walked further into her house.

Glory gulped again.

"Oh, she's just messing with you, Glory," said Valerie as she descended the stairs, a picture of elegance in a bright blue dress with her hair immaculately crafted. Valerie never greeted visitors without being fully composed for the day. "How are you?"

"I'm good," Glory couldn't hide his smile. "It's always a good day when *you* call."

Parker's ear burned at the tone of Glory's voice. *Are you flirting with my mom?*

Valerie handed Glory the blue plastic bags full of cameras and accepted a gentle kiss on the cheek.

Parker's jaw dropped.

"Where would you like these installed?" asked Glory.

"What would you recommend?" Valerie replied with a subtle toss of her hair.

"*I've* got a few ideas," Parker interjected. She snatched the bag of cameras from Glory as if to snap him out of her mother's spell.

Glory blinked. "Oh! Right!"

"Follow me," Parker ordered, before flashing her mother a look.

54.

An hour later...

four security cameras were installed and positioned to cover each side of the house, along with a new front doorbell with a concealed fish eye camera. "Anytime anyone comes to the front door, you and Valerie's phones will be notified." Glory explained as he went through the final setup of Parker's phone app in the kitchen.

"What about the other cameras?" asked Parker. She took her phone from Glory to play with the live views of each camera. Never one for instructions, Parker preferred to just start pressing buttons to see what happened. Parker cycled through each camera. Glory had perfectly framed the front driveway, both side alleys and the backyard. No one could occupy any space surrounding the house without the cameras picking them up. Even now, Parker watched a live video feed of Drew and Ally kicking a ball to each other in the grassy area next to the pool.

"All cameras will behave the same way," said Glory. "But you might want to play with the schedule and sensitivity settings. Otherwise, your kids will be setting them off all the time."

Parker's phone buzzed. A notification popped up.

Motion detected in the backyard.

"Like that," added Glory. "But honestly, the ones I'd pay most attention to is your front door and your garage side alley."

"Why the garage alley?"

Glory clicked Parker's phone app to view the alley full of three garbage cans and the side door leading to Valerie's garage. "Your fence is high and private enough on that side that your neighbors can't see anyone coming in and out of the side door. Somebody who wants to break into your place can work on that door without drawing too much attention. Once they're in the garage, they have access to your whole house. These cameras will keep the riff raff away. But if a pro really wants in, they're going to get in. At least you'll catch them on video and hopefully help the Sheriff track him down."

Parker couldn't help but to notice Glory looked a little different in the kitchen's light. *More mature?* "How do you know so much about all this?"

"My house used to get broken into all the time," Glory shrugged. "I got tired of it." His eyes dropped to the floor as if feeling the weight of an old memory. After a moment, he looked up, and the light in his eyes returned when he noticed the web of yarn connecting Ally's drawings on Parker's suspects wall. "Oh, wow, what is all that?"

"Oh—that? It's nothing." *Just the manifestation of my obsessive need to find a killer.* "I need to reorganize it."

Glory's eyes scanned every inch of the wall. He squinted to try and make sense of the names and the scribbles. "The Twitchy-Eye Lady? The Hapless Sheriff? The Silver Fox? Are these cartoon characters?"

"It's just how I organize my thoughts."

"What is a Creep-a-zoid?"

Parker blushed. *That was my code name for you, Glory, before I got to know you a little better.* "Nothing important." Parker became anxious to change the subject. "Say, Glory, since you know so much about security stuff, do you have any ideas how someone might've stolen my Highlander without setting off the alarm?"

Glory couldn't take his eyes off the wall. "How new was your car? Did it have keyless entry? Or was it an old beater?"

"Only a few years old. Keyless entry."

"Well, you used to be able to buy these things called 'amplifiers' online. They're banned now. Harder to find. But they'd unlock a car, no problem."

"How?"

"Any car with a keyless entry has a sensor that calls out to the keys. If the keys are in range of the sensor, say a few feet, they call back, the car will unlock when you put your hand on the door handle. What amplifiers do, is magnify that signal, so your car keys don't have to be right next to the car. They can be like, fifty feet away or so, and the door will trigger."

Parker's stomach sank. "Fifty feet would include most of this house!"

"Right. So, while you're sleeping at night, some kid with an amplifier can be trying all the cars parked on the street or driveways to see what opens up. Most people don't keep their keys in places that would block the signal, like a refrigerator, or a microwave. It's crazy easy to break into a car if you have something like that."

Parker shook her head. "But my car wasn't just broken into, it was taken. Wouldn't the minute someone drove it out of the fifty-foot radius, the car would sense the key was missing and shut down?"

Glory scratched behind his ear. "Errrrr, right. So, there must be a way around that. I don't know. Everything electronic can be hacked if you have enough time to work on it. You know – computers. Nerds. Zeroes. Ones."

"Got it, thanks." Obviously, Parker had found the limit to Glory's knowledge on the subject.

Just then, Valerie glided into the kitchen with a check in hand. "Sorry I had to step away, Glory! I hope this covers everything!"

Glory's eyes brightened as he received the check from Valerie. He smiled when he looked at it. "Wow, Valerie, you're always so generous. This is too much! You know you qualify for my *special discount*, right?"

"Don't worry about that," Valerie patted Glory's hand. "Just keep taking good care of us, okay?"

"You know I will."

Parker suddenly felt last night's dinner in the back of her throat.

"Bye now!" Glory disappeared out the front door and headed toward his Trans Am.

"Holy fuck, Mom! Flirt much?" Parker scoffed at her mother.

Valerie grinned at her daughter. "Says the woman with no pants."

Parker pulled down on her over-sized t-shirt again. "I rolled out of bed to answer the door while you were still getting ready!" Parker's eyes widened. "You were getting ready, because you *knew* he was coming!"

"Of course, I did. I'm the one who called him."

"And you look fabulous!"

"I *always* look fabulous." Valerie turned up her nose. "Parker, are you implying I have some romantic interest in Glory?"

"Do you?"

Valerie smiled. "Now, Parker, you know full well that I've enjoyed many gifted lovers of the years."

"Oh hell," Parker closed her eyes. Valerie always had an incredible knack for making her daughter regret asking certain questions.

"I'm a woman, still very much in her sexual prime."

"Stop."

"And I won't apologize for any of my previous conquests."

"God no--Mom!"

233

"So be careful not to venture into the land of 'None of Your Business."

"Message received!" Parker saluted her mother while staring at the floor. "Just stop talking about it!"

Valerie patted her daughter's cheek. "You have a much greater mystery to solve."

55.

"I'm fine."

Maddy grumbled again from under her bed's comforter.

Parker crossed the maze of dirty clothes strewn about her daughter's bedroom wooden floor to reach the window. She yanked a string that pulled up the blinders with a loud flapping noise. The bright Saturday sun blasted into the room and seemed to cause Maddy to writhe in pain as though she were either hungover or was transforming into a vampire.

I would take either of those possibilities over the current truth.

"It's noon," said Parker. "You need to get up and eat something."

"I'm not hungry."

"Get up," Parker snapped her fingers. "You can sulk downstairs if you want, but you're not going to hide in here all day. We need to talk about what happened."

"Why?" Maddy moaned.

"Because—" Parker balked. *Good question.* She mashed her tongue against the back of her teeth as she went through every School House Rock episode in memory to see if they had ever covered anything close to this. They had not. "Because, that was some messed up shit you saw yesterday. And when you see messed shit like that it helps to talk about it." *I'm pretty sure that's a direct quote from Blossom.*

Maddy threw her comforter off her head and sat up straight in her bed. "Fine," she snapped. "Let's talk about it!"

"Great!" Parker threw open her arms and outstretched them to Maddy. *I wasn't expecting her to give in so quickly.* "Okay!" Parked swallowed. "Do—you have any questions?"

Maddy squirmed in her seat.

Parker tried softening her tone. "You can ask me anything, Maddy."

"Anything?" Maddy folded her arms.

"Anything."

"And you're not going to give me some stupid watered down 'kid answer' to try and make me feel better? You'll tell me the truth?"

"As ugly as it gets."

Maddy took a deep breath. "Did you do it?"

Parker glowered at her daughter. "You had better know that answer already."

"I'm just making sure!"

"Don't squander this opportunity."

"Alright," Maddy stiffened her posture. Her eyes darted off to the side to contemplate her next move. They slowly rolled back to her mother. "Are you *glad* she's dead?"

"Of course not!" Parker instinctively shot back.

It was Maddy's turn to glare at her mother and challenge the quickness of her answer.

Parker sighed. "Alright, the truth is I don't know how I feel about it. It's no secret that Heller and I didn't get along. A part of me, the bad part of me, is relieved I don't have to deal with her anymore. But I wouldn't wish what happened to her on anyone."

Maddy swallowed. "What *did* happen to her?"

It hadn't occurred to Parker that Maddy didn't have a chance to process the crime scene with any clarity. "It appears Vice Principal Heller was shot in the head at close range."

"No, I mean, *why* did it happen to her?"

"That's a great question." Parker bowed her head. "I don't know."

Maddy's eyes welled up. "But you want to find out, don't you?"

Parker raised her head to lock eyes with her daughter. "It's not a matter of wanting, Maddy."

"Why can't you just leave it alone? Let the police investigate!"

"Heller was found dead in the back of my car."

"I know, I was *there*!" Maddy burst into tears and buried her hands in her face.

"Maddy, look at me," Parker grabbed her blubbering daughter by the arms. "Look at me! Maddy? Look- -at-ME."

Maddy took a deep, erratic breath in an effort to calm down. She stared at her mother through bloodshot eyes.

When Parker stared back, she found her own mind laser focused. "Listen to me. Murders are either crimes of passion, committed in the heat of the moment, or they are methodically thought out to achieve a result. I believe whoever did this had a plan. They're after something. Maybe Heller was simply in the way." Parker blinked, astonished at her own words. *Was Heller in the way?*

Maddy used the inside of her palm to rub the tears from her cheeks. "How do we know if the killer got what he was after?"

Parker eased her grip on her daughter's arms and began to massage them up and down. "Another great question – except never assume it's a 'he' unless you have evidence that suggests it."

Maddy rolled her eyes. "How do we *know*, Mom?"

"We don't. All we can do is wait, investigate, observe and look for some kind of break in patterns."

"Patterns?"

"We are creatures of habit, Maddy. Everyone has some kind of daily routine that gets disrupted now and then by major events in their life. Murder certainly ranks up there, but there are more common ones like getting married or—" Parker felt her stomach tighten as Kurt's face flashed at the forefront of her memory. His mangled corpse from the car accident followed. "—a death in the family. Getting fired. Packing up everything you own to move across country and live with your mom. Starting a new job or—" she looked a Maddy. Her lips quivered. *Shit.* "—a new school." Parker held her forehead, trying to hold back a crushing wave of emptiness. She couldn't help but to tremble at the taste of her own despair.

Parker suddenly felt Maddy's thin arms wrap around her, pulling her close for a hug. The two of them cried together, sharing their grief and loss for perhaps the first time since Kurt had died. Parker marveled at the whirlwind of emotions stirring inside her. Heller's murder had somehow brought them back together, at least for this moment.

As the tension slowly began to fade, Maddy chose to ask one last question of her mother. "This isn't over, is it?"

Parker sighed. She knew what Maddy was really asking. The killer was still out there. And something told them both that he or she wasn't finished. Parker swallowed. "Not by a long shot, kiddo."

56.

Dear Oak Creek Parents,

Last Friday, a terrible tragedy befell our school with the death of our beloved Vice Principal, Karen Heller. Highly respected among both staff and students, Karen was seen as a relentless champion for Oak Creek Elementary. The absence of her tireless energy, consummate professionalism, and undying dedication will be felt throughout the school and community for years to come. On Monday, we will be flying the American Flag at half-staff in her honor and starting the day by observing a moment of silence to reflect on our loss. I encourage you to speak with your children, so they understand the gravity of what is happening and are respectful. Details of Karen's funeral will be forthcoming for those who wish to attend. Kenneth Heller, who is understandably devastated by the loss of his wife, has asked that any flowers, memorials and tributes be sent to the school's front office so as not to be overwhelmed. We will collect everything and deliver them to Mr. Heller.

Finally, many of you have reached out to our front office with questions regarding the circumstances of Karen's sudden passing. The local Sheriff's department has issued the following statement:

"Karen Heller was found deceased on school grounds last Friday by a local family. The death is being investigated as a matter of due course, and additional details will

239

follow. We ask that the public refrain from any wild speculation or judgment while evidence and facts are collected. We also ask that the privacy of the family who discovered Heller be respected, as it is important to afford them space during this very confusing and difficult time. Remember that our community remains among the safest in the nation and there is no reason to panic. But should you see any suspicious activity report it immediately."

In closing, I want to echo the Sheriff's sentiments and assure you that your children are safe and secure at Oak Creek. If you have any questions or want to speak with me directly, feel free to schedule an appointment.

Principal Mendez

Oak Creek Elementary

Parker winced when she reread Mendez's email on her phone. "That's a huge collection of words that say practically nothing," she declared.

"Here," said Julie as she set two freshly Man-Child brewed drinks down on the small circular table at The Bean. "The barista says he added two shots of intrigue to your white mocha, whatever that means."

Parker looked over her shoulder to the Man-Child, whose man bun seemed larger today. Man-Child nodded to her with a smile. "It means he still gets me." Parker looked back to the email on her phone. Mendez's note read more like a public relations memo than anything else. "At least Mendez didn't throw my family under the bus and call us out by name."

"She didn't have to," replied Julie stirring some sugar and cream into her mug. "Everybody in town knows Heller's body was stuffed in the back of your car." The comment earned a few uneasy stares from nearby patrons, to which Julie boldly added "Well, it's *true!*" as if to pre-empt any questions or comments from them.

"Yes, I can't *imagine* how word is spreading so fast," Parker sighed. "I'm just going to keep pretending like asking for your help was a good idea." Though Parker had to admit, she needed the distraction.

Monday school drop-off had proven to be more awkward than usual. Maddy wasn't her usual flavor of pre-teen angst, having reverted back to her more recent somber "I'm fine" routine. Drew obsessively asked as to whether the new security cameras had caught Heller's ghost lurking about their house and Parker couldn't figure out if she was actually hearing people whisper "#MurderMom" as she walked her kids to school. Parker had decided to invite Julie to coffee at the last minute to vent. Luckily, Julie was all too eager to help a friend in need, even if it meant skipping pre-lunch yoga, and especially if it meant getting the inside scoop.

"So!" Julie smiled as she took a long, gleeful sip. "What could you possibly want to talk to me about?"

Parker retrieved a thin set of stapled pages from her purse and pushed them over to Julie. "I copied this in the PTA office this morning. It's a roster of all current members. I think whoever was involved with Heller's murder was at our meeting. I'd like you to look at that list and see if any names jump out."

"They *all* jump out as a bunch of self-absorbed bitches," Julie groaned as she glanced the papers over. "What exactly are you looking for?"

Parker tilted her head, confused by Julie's sudden lack of enthusiasm. "People who might have something to gain from Heller's death."

"Hmm. Gonna have to get more specific. *Everyone* hated her."

Parker tapped her finger on the list. "Come on, Julie, you've got the 'in' on everyone. Are any of these people struggling with massive debt? Are any of their kids failing class? Do any of them have access to a gun? Do any know how to break into a car from their wild college days?" Parker lost her train of thought as she watched Julie's eyes glaze over. "What is going on with you?"

"It's nothing. Go on."

"No, you seem distracted. What's wrong?"

"Well," Julie took a slow sip, which erupted into a mini-lecture. "Parker, you're being so thorough and everything. You're looking at *everyone*, big, small, dumb, fat, and hell, you even asked *Glory* point blank if *he* was the murderer!"

Parker's eyes widened. "Are you--? Are you offended that I don't think you killed Heller?"

"Maybe," Julie rolled her eyes to the side. "I mean, what, you don't think I could do it? I could do it! I work out every damn day, Parker, I'm strong as a fucking bull, and I'm fierce and I am *dangerous*!"

"All true," agreed Parker. *How do I salvage this?* "But to be honest, anyone with your killer abs and a butt like that couldn't possibly have found time to commit murder between their regimented work outs, yoga classes and juicing schedule."

Julie softened a bit. "It just would've been nice to have been considered, that's all."

Parker took a deep breath. "Okay. Did you murder Karen Heller?"

"No," Julie smiled as she settled more comfortably into her chair. "But thank you for asking."

Parker tapped the list again. "So, can you help? I'm looking for things out of the norm. Unless you're a professional killer or a sociopath, murder is a major pattern breaker for people."

Julie snatched the list off the table to bring it in for a closer look. "They're *all* psychos for joining the PTA." Her eyes darted up and down, absorbing the first few names. "No one is jumping out to me in a 'first degree' way just yet. I mean, Heather's a bitch. Jane always parks in the handicap space in front of school. Lorna's having an affair with her pool cleaner. Debbie's kids act like entitled dicks. Molly's nice, actually, but boring as all hell. Tabitha's breath always smells like eggs—I guess she likes eggs. There are so many, this is going to take some time."

"What about Holly?"

"The President?" Julie arched a brow. "You've met her. She's one French twist shy of snapping like a rubber hair tie. But she's always been like that. I'm surprised you haven't mentioned the one name on this list who was actually paid to kill people."

The statement gave Parker pause. "Oh, you mean, Joe." As a former Ranger, Oak Creek's gym teacher was trained in several highly lethal forms of combat and would have considerable experience with guns. Still, something felt "off" about him committing such a high-profile murder and making a big show about it. "Somehow that seems too obvious."

Julie hunched her shoulders. "Hey, I appreciate an American beefcake as much as the next girl but--"

Parker rolled her eyes. "Please, he's not *that* good looking."

"Sure, if you discount the perfect pecs, chiseled jaw and cocky Eastwood smile thing." Julie smiled deviously as she took another sip of her coffee. "I'd saddle up for a night with him even if he *was* the killer."

Parker frowned. Ever since she'd learned of Joe's political allegiance to the man who ended her career she considered him damaged goods. "Yuck. That's gross. About as gross as my mom flirting with Glory." Parker started gulping down her mocha to drown out the recent memory.

Julie smirked. "Oh, I wouldn't worry about that. They were only a one-time thing."

A white mist of mocha exploded out of Parker's mouth like a geyser.

Covered in spit, Julie's smile vanished. She slowly blinked and then reached for a napkin on the table to begin dabbing her face.

Parker's stomach twisted into knots. *Holy hell, what just happened?* "Julie, I am sooooooooo sorry!" *Mom and Glory?*

Julie forced a smile as she shook the spit off of the PTA list. "I'm going to go and clean up, now." She stated in a strained voice.

"Don't hate me!"

"It's--*fine.*"

There was that word again. *Fine*, meant anything *but* these days. "We're you serious about my Mom and Glory?"

Julie's lips twisted into an impish grin. Her silence was clearly payback. "I'll keep going over the list. But if I were you? I'd talk with Joe. If for no other reason than to check him off *your* list."

57.

Parker hated to admit Julie was right about Joe.

To not question him would be a gross act of negligence, despite Parker's mocha-filled gut telling her Joe made little to no sense as a suspect. Yes, Joe had appeared to threaten Heller, but he had already apologized for it and admitted his actions were born out of frustration. Joe was a new teacher at Oak Creek, what could he possibly have to gain from Heller's death?

Let's just get this over with.

Toward the end of the school day, Parker moved some sympathy flower arrangements that adorned the front office to slip under the Silver Fox's radar and make her way to the school's playground. There she found Joe instructing an unruly class of fourth graders in the finer points of a kick ball game. She sat on a small bench under some shade, waiting for the bell to herald the end of class. Joe routinely blew his whistle and barked out instructions, quizzing the kids on the rules of the game. If they got a question wrong, he'd make them do push-ups telling them "you will be smart, or you will be strong!" The kids ate it all up, giggling at his military clichés as they struggled to do even one push up off their knees. All in all, the class looked kind of fun, that was until Parker noticed the young boy with freckles off to her immediate side who had been freakishly staring at her the entire time.

"Jesus!" Parker's entire body seemed to spasm all at once.

"Hi," greeted the boy.

"Hi."

"Do you need a buddy?" asked the boy.

Parker blinked, still recovering from the startle. "Do I need a *what*?"

"A buddy."

"Ummm," Parker looked the freckled kid over. "Do I look like I need a buddy?"

"You're sitting on the Buddy Bench." Explained Freckles. "When you sit on the Buddy Bench, it means you're looking for a buddy."

"Oh. Wow. That actually works?"

Freckles shrugged. "I'm here, aren't I?"

"It's just, you know, if I were a kid, and I saw somebody sitting on this bench, I would wonder why that kid doesn't have any buddies. Like, maybe there's something wrong with him."

"Is there something wrong with *you*?"

"That depends on who you ask."

Freckles sighed as he looked up to the sky. "Listen, Lady, do you need a buddy or not?"

"I'm good, thank you."

"Then stop sitting on the bench!" Freckles yelled.

Parker was so surprised by the outburst, she immediately stood up. The yelling had also grabbed the attention of GI Joe who looked over in her direction. Luckily, the bell rang, and the children's homeroom teacher emerged from the side door to collect them. As the kids exited the playground, Joe walked toward Parker with a smug grin on his face. He playfully tossed the big red kick ball up and down.

"Making new friends, Ms. Monroe?" asked Joe.

Parker nodded to the bench. "I think this bench might be broken."

"I'll have someone look into that." Joe stopped directly in front of Parker to look her square in the eyes. "Can I ask what you're doing here? Parents aren't exactly supposed to be wandering the grounds during school hours. Especially considering what happened."

"I wanted to speak with you."

"That's funny. Last time we tried that it didn't go so well."

"Well, that was before Heller's dead body showed up in the back of my car."

Joe's smile faded. "Yeah--I'm sorry." He pushed on the red ball between his palms, testing its pressure. "That must have been quite a shock. How are your kids?"

"They're – *fine*." Parker quietly chastised herself for using the very word she was on her daughter's case about. "That's not true. I think Maddy is taking it pretty hard. Drew is overly concerned about Heller's ghost. You had both of them in your class today. I'm wondering how they looked to you."

"I haven't noticed anything unusual. I'll certainly keep an eye on them." Joe searched Parker's eyes. "That's not really why you're here, is it?"

Parker swallowed. "No."

Joe let out a nervous laugh. "You're wondering if I had something to do with it, aren't you?"

"You were a Ranger; how would *you* assess the situation?"

Joe nodded. "Listen, I want to help, but I already told your boyfriend everything I know."

"My *boyfriend*?" Parker scoffed.

"Yeah, the Sheriff," Joe's eyes widened upon noting Parker's stunned silence. "Oh, hell, I just figured. I see the way you two chat, and he's always looking at —"

"Gah! Stop! He's not my—" Parker's face turned red hot. "I'm trying to help solve Heller's murder!"

"Hold on, now," Joe held up his hands, letting the ball drop. "I meant no offense. But I've cooperated with the police, and I'm done answering questions, okay? And you and I, we just don't seem to--"

"—mix?" Parker tried to finish Joe's sentence.

"—like each other." Joe said at the same time, making the moment even more awkward.

I'm losing him, and I can't imagine my stupid 'boyfriend' asked all the questions that I would want to ask. "Joe, I think maybe you and I need a fresh start."

"I've got to go," Joe pulled away and headed toward the school's side door. "Besides, *she* looks like she needs to talk to you a lot more than I do." Joe pointed to behind Parker.

She?

Parker spun around to find Principal Mendez standing uncomfortably close. "Gah!" *And why does she smell so good all the time?*

Mendez carefully folded her arms and turned up her nose to look down at Parker. "Ms. Monroe, if you would please come with me."

Shit!

58.

This is the second time I've been summoned to the principal's office and the school year has barely started!

As Parker trailed Mendez into her office, she began to plea bargain. "Principal Mendez, I know I'm not supposed to just wander around the school, but, honestly, I was just checking up on the well-being of my children," she started as Mendez sat down in her leather office chair. "I'm concerned as to how they're adjusting."

"Stop insulting my intelligence, Ms. Monroe." Mendez extended her hand to offer Parker the chair across from her desk. "I'm cutting you some slack because of what happened, but if I catch you poking around again, I'm going to have to get the Sheriff involved."

Wow! So, I guess we're back to the Cold-Hearted Bitchy Mendez! "Understood."

"Good lord, I sounded just like Heller." Mendez shimmied as if to free her body of Heller's spirit. "And it's not why I asked you here."

Parker shifted in her seat and pointed to herself. "I'm—*not* in trouble?"

Mendez kneaded her hands together and placed them on her desk. "As you know, the front office has been helping to manage Mr. Heller's affairs since Karen's death. Ken Heller is a very sick man and needs our support."

"What does that have to do with me?"

"Last night, Mr. Heller contacted me. The funeral is set for this Friday night at the Presbyterian Church. Ken has asked that you attend."

Parker's eyes narrowed. "Random, but--okay."

"He'd also very much like you to read the eulogy."

"Oh, um," Parker's chair seat suddenly felt very small. "Why?"

"He didn't say."

"Is he aware that his wife and I pretty much hated each other?"

"I don't know."

"Is he aware that I'm technically a suspect in his wife's murder?"

"I don't know."

"Well, I don't know about doing this," admitted Parker. "It seems really unorthodox. Can I talk to him about this?"

"He asked not to be disturbed before the funeral. He was very insistent."

Parker let out an exhausted sigh. "Is he expecting I write the eulogy or?"

"He said he would write it."

"Why can't Karen's family read it?"

"The Hellers have no family. Any siblings they had are long passed. And they have no children of their own. There is only Ken now, and for whatever reason, he's asking for you. It seems like a rather simple request. Can I tell him you'll do it?"

Holy hell, what kind of set-up is this?

"On one condition." Parker sat back in her chair. "I want to speak with him, alone, after the funeral is over."

Mendez breathed a small sigh of relief. "I'll let him know."

59.

"Why in the name of Jane Powell's pipes did you agree to do that?"

asked Valerie after hearing her daughter's pronouncement when she returned home from school with Maddy and Drew.

"Agree to do what?" asked Drew, tugging at Valerie's pant legs.

Valerie bent over to gently squeezed the cheek of her grandson. "Your mother is going to draw lots of unwanted attention to herself in a public forum, Dear," she explained in a singing voice.

Drew squished his face. "I don't know what that means."

"Go play with Ally," ordered Parker, flashing her mother a glare.

Drew happily dashed off to play with his little sister using watercolors in the kitchen. Maddy sighed and headed for the stairs.

"And where are you going?" asked Parker.

"Homework," Maddy shot back as if to say 'duh.'

"Then will you practice the piano after dinner?"

"What's the point? My teacher's been sick forever and may be a murderer." Maddy's voice trailed off as she disappeared up the stairs. The door slammed shut.

Parker looked back to her mother. "I know it's wrong, but I'll take this attitude over 'Mopey-Maddy' any day."

"You never answered my question," said Valerie.

Parker threw her hands to her hips. "That makes us even, I think. You and Glory had a *fling?*" Parker almost choked on her words.

"Who told you that?"

"It doesn't matter, Mom, you're old enough to be his grandmother!"

Valerie flashed her trademark smile that wasn't so much a genuine expression of happiness as it was an attempt to keep herself from pouncing with the savageness of a lioness. "That's ridiculous. The math doesn't add up. I was twenty when I had you, which means you would had to have been around ten or twelve to have given birth to Glory."

"*Gahhhhhh*, damnit, Mom!" Parker closed her eyes, trying to wipe the images from her brain. "Why did you have to go there?"

"That's practically Maddy's age. What kind of loose-legged daughter did I raise?"

"*Bleck!* Stop! I get it!" Parker raised her right hand as if to surrender.

"What you *don't* seem to get is that reading this eulogy is probably another Heller set-up!"

"Mother, *of course* it's a set-up." Parker's words carried a hint of frost. "I'm not an idiot. But the request has placed me in a lose – lose situation. If I don't do it, I'm sure to be branded as the 'heartless bitch' who couldn't get over herself to help an ailing widower. By agreeing to do it, I'm walking into whatever Mr. Heller's got in store. At least I'm walking in with my eyes open and I get something out of it – an exclusive with Ken Heller, himself. I've been dying to speak with that guy."

Valerie frowned at the statement.

"Poor choice of words, I know," conceded Parker. Anxious to move on she threaded her fingers together and stretched them backwards. "So, what do we know about Ken Heller?"

Valerie shook her head. "No one knows anything about Ken Heller. He's kept to himself, especially these last few years. I've lived in this town for all my life, and I've probably seen him only a handful of times."

I wonder if Julie can dig up any dirt on him? Parker rubbed her chin. "What kind of man would marry the likes of Karen Heller?" Before she could give the question any serious thought, her phone buzzed. "Oh hell," she grumbled after checking the ID and putting her phone to her ear. *He's the last person I want to talk with right now.* "What?"

"I thought you said were going to keep a low profile?" asked Sheriff Bill.

"I *never* say that," Parker shot back.

"Giving the eulogy about the woman found murdered in the back seat of your car seems like a bad idea."

How did he hear about the eulogy so quickly? "Thanks. I'm not one of your deputies and I'm certainly not your *girlfriend* or anything, so I'll do what I want."

"My girl--?" Sheriff Bill fell silent for what felt like a micro eternity. "What's gotten into you?"

"Nothing," lied Parker. She couldn't help but replay Joe's boyfriend comment back in her mind over and over, which only fueled her current frustration. "I'm trying to find a killer. Are *you* trying to find a killer? Or are you still following all the wrong leads?"

"Wow."

"Indeed." Parker swallowed and took a deep breath. She knew she was being unreasonable, but her heart was pounding with fight in it. "Listen, I'm sorry. I'm just a little –"

"No need to apologize," Bill tersely interrupted. "Good night, Parker."

"Wait! Bill—" The phone call went dead. Parker hit herself in the forehead with her cell phone. "Stupid, stupid, stupid!"

"Which part?" asked Valerie. "Insulting your one ally in law enforcement or are we still talking about you reading the eulogy?"

Parker put down her phone to look her mother squarely in the eyes. "Oh, I'm going to read the fuck out of that thing. And this time, I'm bringing in the big gun to back me up."

"And who would that be?"

Parker grinned. "You."

60.

When Friday night's funeral arrived...

there was still no sign of Ken Heller's eulogy. No emails had graced Parker's inbox, no letter in the mail, not so much as even a sloppily hand-written note on the back of a napkin. Any time Parker had pressed Mendez about it, she simply responded with some muted variation of a soulless apology followed by "he's still working on it."

I'll bet he is. "You tell Mr. Heller to take his sweet ass time." Parker would cheerfully respond. "I'm sure he wants to get it just right."

As predicted, word had spread like wildfire throughout town that Parker would be reading Ken's words to those who attended his murdered wife's funeral. It fueled a wide range of reckless speculation—would Parker break down and confess to killing Heller in the middle of it? Would Ken Heller drop some kind of truth bomb to reveal any family secrets and crack the case wide open? Was Parker trying to ingratiate herself with Mr. Heller to convince him to drop possible charges against her? Were they having an affair, and did Parker off Karen Heller to have Ken all to herself? Never mind the fact that the two of them had never met—those kinds of details didn't seem to matter.

If nothing else, the gossip served as free advertising for Karen Heller's memorial service. Parker's jaw dropped upon turning the corner in her hated minivan to arrive at Thompson's Funeral Home next to the Presbyterian Church a full thirty minutes early. The parking lot was crammed with cars, along with every street curb for as far as the eye could see.

"It's like the whole fucking town is here!" Parker grumbled.

"Parker, your children are present," reminded Valerie. She nodded to Maddy, Drew and Ally in the seats behind them.

"It's like the whole gosh-darn fucking town is here!" Parker corrected herself.

"Does she talk like this around you all the time?" Valerie asked her grandchildren.

"Yup," agreed Maddy, shifting in her seat.

"Oh no!" Ally gasped.

"Don't sweat it, Grandma, we know not to say those things." said Drew.

Parker wasn't even listening, her eyes constantly scanning for a parking space. "Was Heller really this popular? I thought everyone hated her!"

Valerie smirked. "Oh Parker. They're not here for Heller. They're here for *you*."

"Well, let's give 'em something to talk about." Parker gunned the gas of her minivan, jerking its occupants back only to immediately slam on the breaks when the Prius ahead of her took one of the few open parking spaces. "Shit! Sorry. I just felt like that moment needed a punctuation."

Valerie calmly patted her daughter's arm. "Of course, dear."

Exactly twenty-seven minutes and eight blocks of walking later, Parker and her family entered a packed Funeral Home with their heads held high -- except for Maddy who pulled awkwardly at the loose fit of her outfit. "I feel like everyone's watching us!" she whispered.

"That's because they are," Valerie calmly whispered back with a smile as she nodded to the few familiar faces out of the sea of eyeballs that tracked her. Always composed, Valerie seemed to thrive on the attention. Having accidently killed her own husband with fantastic sex the night of their honeymoon meant she was no stranger to controversy in the town of Oak Creek.

"Let 'em watch," said Parker, smoothing out the crease of her new dress. If she was going to step on a hornet's nest tonight she was going to do it looking and feeling like a million bucks. "I'm just going to say it, but I look smoking hot in black. I need to wear black more often."

"Mom!" Drew anxiously pulled at his mother's skirt.

"Don't pull on my dress, Drew. What do you need?" Parker looked down at her son, whose face had turned an ashen grey. "Drew?"

"G-g-ghost!" Drew pointed to a dark adjoining corridor, where a small, hunched figure stood alone watching him.

Maddy smacked her brother in the chest with the back of her hand. "That's no ghost, dummy. Ghosts don't wear glasses."

Parker traced the outline of Drew's "apparition" with her eyes. In the muted light, the old man projected an unearthly vibe. *Is that Ken Heller?* Parker started for the man when the Silver Fox stepped into her path.

"Good!" greeted Fox sternly. "You made it. We were beginning to wonder."

Parker peeked over Fox's broad shoulders to watch as the dark figure was ushered into an adjoining room by a grey-haired woman in church robes. The door shut behind them. "Yeah, parking was a bitch. Was that Ken? I need to speak with him." said Parker.

Fox looked back over her own shoulder. "After the service," assured Fox. She presented a small white envelope. "Mr. Heller asked me to give this to you."

Parker carefully took the envelope from Fox's bony fingers. She breathed a sigh of relief as she felt the weight of it. "So, it *does* exist," she said to Fox. "Good. I'll give it the once over before going on stage."

"Stage?"

"Sorry, you know what I mean." Parker cringed at her own Freudian slip. She couldn't help but to think of this entire funeral as some macabre sideshow.

The soft, vibrato of an electric organ suddenly began to fill the room.

"The service is going to start soon," said Fox. "You and your family have reserved seats in the front row."

"Reserved?" *Of course, sitting me in the back wouldn't nearly be the same spectacle, would it? Now I'm certain this is all for show.* Parker did her best to feign gratitude. "Thank you."

Parker led her family into the parlor up a narrow aisle separating two overcrowded sections of folding chairs that seated all walks of Oak Creek citizenry. With the number of people who stood shoulder to shoulder along the walls, Parker wondered if Heller's casket might be more comfortable. Just as Fox had said, five seats remained open in the front row, with an additional open seat on the opposite aisle. Parker and her family quietly sat down.

A door on the wall behind the casket opened up to reveal the old man Drew had pointed out earlier, who followed the grey-haired woman in robes. The old man glanced at Parker for a brief moment and then stared at the floor as he slowly shuffled to the last remaining empty chair up front.

So, that is Ken Heller, she thought, leaning forward for a better look at him. After sitting, Ken's eyes never left the floor.

The robed woman stepped up to the podium and adjusted the microphone.

"Good evening," she started. "We are gathered here in this time of great sorrow—"

Yup, yup, keep talking, lady.

Parker quietly opened the white envelope Fox had given to her. If she could read through all of it before the pastor was finished,

258

she'd be able to edit out any landmines in her head before having to 'go live.'

Parker slipped the paper out of the envelope without looking, but something felt weird about it. It felt smooth and glossy, like a "—goddamn greeting card?" she whispered to herself angrily. Parker looked down at the folded Hallmark card in her hand that featured a picture of a kitten dangling from a string of yarn. Parker's face flushed red as she opened the card to read the large printed words exclaim "Hang in there!"

Parker shot a look over to Ken Heller, who continued to only stare at the ground. *Are you fucking kidding me right now, Ken Heller?*

"What's wrong?" whispered Valerie, leaning in to her daughter.

Parker handed her mother the card, who grimaced in confusion.

"—and we all know Karen would have liked that very much," said the pastor. She outstretched her arm to Parker. "Now, I'm told we have some very special words prepared in Karen's honor. Ms. Monroe?"

Parker froze.

61.

I knew it! This whole thing was a goddamn setup!

Parker clenched her fist and took a deep breath.

I knew it was, Mom knew it was, even Bill knew it was, and yet I was hoping Ken Heller had some fucking class unlike his bitch of a dead wife!

Parker tried to hide her own grin as she reached for her purse.

Luckily—

Parker pulled out a folded piece of paper.

--I planned ahead with my own prepared speech. And Ken? This one is going to be the talk of the town for generations to come!

Parker proudly stood up and nodded to the pastor. Before she could take a step toward the podium, Ken Heller also rose from his chair. Parker froze – again.

Without a word, Ken slowly shuffled across the aisle toward Parker, never once taking his eyes off the floor. Parker stared in awe at the man, whose head barely reached her shoulder. He lifted his hand, which held two pieces of paper with typing on them, folded cleanly in half. Ken lifted his glistening red eyes and tried smiling at Parker. He gingerly grabbed her wrist to guide her hand to accept the paper, and then clasped it as if to shake it with a strange gratitude.

Parker's anger flushed away, not sure of what to make of the man before her. She wanted to believe the hope she saw in Ken's eyes was genuine.

Lips trembling, Ken nodded to Parker and then slowly turned to shuffle back to his seat.

Parker's heart raced as she opened the folded papers and scanned the few first sentences. It was definitely a eulogy absent any overly cute cat photographs. She weighed her own speech in her left hand which she'd written the previous night after several glasses of wine and knew it to be fucking gold. She weighed Ken's speech in her right hand.

Parker took a deep breath and approached the podium. She quickly looked over the audience, noting any faces she recognized. Silver Fox sat in the first row next to Ken. Julie and Glory sat near the back on the edge of their seats. GI Joe stood in the back, near President Holly and a few other PTA moms and Baby Face. Even Man-Child showed, sitting near the middle aisle. Parker found it strange that Principal Mendez was nowhere to be found, nor her supposed boyfriend, Sheriff Bill, or the music teacher who had been Karen's music partner for so long.

"Ms. Monroe?" the pastor cleared her throat, as if to cue Parker to move on.

Parker nodded to the pastor with a smile. "Yes, of course." She delicately placed Ken's speech on the podium and pressed down with her fingers to flatten out the crease.

Okay, Ken. Game on.

"Hello. My name is Parker Monroe, and I am reading on behalf of Ken Heller," she explained. Parker nodded toward the widower, who continued to stare at the floor.

The air suddenly felt heavy, as Parker looked down at Ken's words. She began.

"Many of you knew Karen Marjorie Heller as the vice principal of Oak Creek Elementary. She carried this title for over a third of her life, and nothing made her prouder. Karen took her job very seriously, as she knew the profound impact it had in shaping the young minds of our town, our great State of California, and ultimately, our future. It is no secret that Karen's passion for education instilled in her a stubborn confidence. Because of this, some might have found Karen difficult to work with or relate to."

Parker paused. *Most people found it difficult to work with or relate to*, she corrected silently in her mind. *Stop it, Parker! Just read the damn thing.*

"I knew a different Karen. A loving, gentle and very private woman I would call my wife for nearly fifty years. I knew the diligent student I would date as a teenager. I knew the precocious piano player I fell in love with at my first recital at the Methodist Church when I was ten.

I remember waiting my turn to go on stage at that recital. My eyes were transfixed on this beautiful girl in a periwinkle dress playing Chopin. Her long and soft brown hair was twisted into a perfect French braid with a red bow to accent it. Butterflies fluttered in my stomach. Karen tickled those ivories like no one I had ever seen before. Like I only could dream of doing. Any girl who could play like that, and was so pretty, well, I just had to meet her. But as fate should have it, when my turn came to go on stage, my nerves got the best of me. My fingers trembled, then fumbled, and I butchered Mozart's Sonata in a most spectacular fashion. I rushed off the stage in tears. I was nothing short of – humiliated."

Parker nearly choked on her last word. She took a moment to stare at Ken, whose eyes were closed now. He breathed shallowly, as if any effort beyond that might cause him to crumble.

Parker swallowed and continued.

"To my surprise, after the recital was over, I was approached by this young, bright, blue-eyed girl with a smile bright as the sun. A smile that instantly faded upon seeing my red eyes and nose. This angel before me introduced herself as Karen and put her hand on my shoulder.

'Don't worry' she told me. 'You weren't that good, but you weren't that bad, either.' I can—" Parker paused again. The words on the page appeared to blur for a second. She refocused. "I can work with that."

Parker swallowed her breath before continuing.

"Karen took me on as her pet project and gave me pointers about performing. She helped me to visualize myself playing confidently before every recital from then on. We became fast friends, and eventually attended the same middle school, where I found myself struggling and falling behind in math. Once again, Karen came to the rescue. She'd look at my homework and no matter how atrocious my logic and arithmetic would be, she would always tell me the same thing: 'I can work with that.'

The phrase would become a code that Karen would adhere to all her life. No matter who you were, where you came from or how good or bad at something you were, Karen was eager to help you become better. She'd work with whatever you gave her and help you improve upon it. But to do that, Karen would refuse anything but your best effort. She would challenge you. Push you. She'd drive you crazy sometimes. But in the end, after all the fights, the tears and whatever followed, you would have learned something about yourself. Sometimes it was something about yourself that you never knew was there, or even thought was possible. And you'd be better for it. A better person.

It is only fitting, that after years of dating my one true love, when I finally presented her a modest diamond ring during a sunset walk on Redondo Beach, that she gave me a most familiar answer: 'I can work with that.'"

Parker had to squint again. *Why are the words so blurry?*

"Karen went on to work in education. First, as a teacher, but it was soon clear to the district that she had potential for more. She was put on the fast track to become vice principal at Oak Creek, a track that was derailed for a time when she was diagnosed with breast cancer."

Oh hell.

"Even after losing both breasts and all of her hair from the radiation and chemotherapy, she never once complained. Not once. After discovering her treatments made it impossible for her to bear children, she refused to blame anyone. She simply chose to deal with whatever hand life had dealt her. 'God never gives you anything you can't handle' she'd say. 'I can work with that.'"

I'm a terrible person.

"Karen took several years off from being vice principal to come to terms with her cancer and the fallout of never starting a family of our own. Karen considered adopting, and even taking early retirement and not returning to education. But in the end, her calling to help children reach their potential won her heart back. I had my concerns regarding the stress returning to work would have on her. But it was my turn to be supportive and tell her: 'I can work with that.' So, she returned to the very same job as vice principal to the very same school she'd loved for so long."

The things I said to her!

"So," Parker tried to choke back her tears. "So, —if Karen were here today, she'd want us all to remember one thing: that we are all capable of more. We are all capable of becoming better. But to become better, whether it's a better pianist, a better teacher, a better athlete, or a better person – we must all strive to do and be our best – right now. Remember that, live that, and you will have honored Karen's memory." Parker's voice trailed off. She held her forehead and trembled.

The paper that contained Ken's speech was now sopping wet, the printer ink running and blotting up. Parker looked up. Her eyes met with Ken's again. His quivering lips parted to mouth the words: "Thank you."

Then Parker felt the warm hands of Valerie gently grab her shoulders and lead her away from the podium. Parker found her seat again as the organ music began to play.

62.

After the service, as attendees gathered in various rooms to share stories of remembrance...

Parker was asked by the pastor to follow her to a private study. Parker found herself sitting alone on a couch before a fireplace, trying to decipher the muffled roar of the clamor outside. After fifteen minutes or so, a small door behind a wooden desk opened with a soft creek. The small frame of Ken Heller shuffled through, his beady eyes smiling at Parker in a peculiar way. It took him a long stretch to reach the armchair across from her, where he rested his bones with a weary sigh.

"Long day," he said in a tiny voice. He cleared his throat, as if to shake the dust off vocal cords that hadn't been used in ages. "Longer week."

Parker sized Mr. Heller up from his winged tipped shoes to his balding white head. He didn't strike her as a particularly rigid man, comfortably slumped in the cushions of his seat, nor did his eyes carry any hint that could rival the fire that often raged in his late wife. He exuded an air of calm about him, the kind that took a lifetime to cultivate. *Perhaps from dealing with Karen on a daily basis.* Regardless, Parker thought it best to begin their meeting with the expected pleasantries before diving into a game of a thousand questions. "I'm sorry for your loss, Mr. Heller."

"Please, call me Ken," the old man let out a half-hearted chuckle. "I'm sorry too. I didn't mean to take so long on the eulogy. I wanted it to be just right. You're a famous writer, after all."

Parker couldn't help but to smile. She found Ken's natural charm disarming. "You wrote a fine speech."

"Thank you." The old man smiled back as if to ask: 'That's it? That's all you have to say?' He seemed to marvel at Parker's quiet restraint. "I imagine, you're wondering what this is all about."

"I've a theory."

Ken nodded. "Please. Test it."

Parker raised her eye brows in surprise. Ken's mind appeared sharp and playful as ever. "I think you wanted to fill every seat in that parlor today."

Ken's smile turned into an impish grin. "Go on."

"You wanted as much of the town as possible to see Karen the way you did. To shatter any misconception they might have had about her. I can't think of a more dramatic draw for such an audience than to ask your wife's antithesis to read her eulogy."

"Ha!" Ken allowed himself a weak chuckle followed by a series of coughs. "I do enjoy a good show. But you are hardly Karen's opposite. You are both stubborn. Driven. Opinionated. More alike than either of you realized."

"To be fair, you don't really know me."

"I know enough. Karen and I followed your news career for years. It's not often one of her students wins a Pulitzer."

Parker leaned forward. "You're telling me, all this time, Karen Heller was a fan?"

"Heavens no," Ken chuckled and coughed again. "She never forgave you for coming up with Old Yeller Heller. Said you wouldn't know common sense if it came up and sat on your face. Then again, Karen was always hardest on those she thought weren't living up to their potential."

"So, she saw me as a disappointment."

"A work in progress," Ken corrected. It was his turn to lean forward. "Something you need to understand about Karen, is that she found it very hard to let go of anything or anyone she thought was worth saving."

Parker blinked, taking a mental note of Ken's words. "Do you think that is why she was killed?" she asked bluntly. "Because she couldn't let go of something?"

Ken's face turned an ashen white. The light in his eyes dimmed as his smile dissolved away. "I wish I knew," he looked down to the floor in an effort to compose himself. After a short pause, he raised his head to meet Parker's gaze again. "I can't make any sense of what happened. I know Karen wasn't popular. She ruffled feathers. Some even hated her. But to —" Ken choked on his words. "for someone to do — what they *did*?"

Parker reached across to touch Ken's wrinkled hand. "Anything you can remember, no matter how trivial, might be helpful in finding your wife's killer."

Ken took a deep breath and clasped his free hand on top of Parker's. "I'm glad," he whispered. "to hear you say that. It tells me you've already begun."

"Begun what?"

"Looking for Karen's killer."

Parker slowly pulled back. "I have every intention of *helping*," she stated. "But the Sheriff is running the investigation and--"

Ken frowned. "Have you met the Sheriff?"

"Of course."

"That man couldn't find his way out of a paper bag."

Ouch. Parker tried to offer a reassuring smile. "Mr. Heller — Ken. Sheriff Bill is," *not the sharpest tool in the shed?* Parker found it difficult not to agree with Ken's assessment. "--*actively* investigating the matter." She grimaced at her own phrasing.

"He's an idiot," Ken stated as a matter of fact. He let the words sink in before continuing. "I am very sick, Ms. Monroe. I don't know how much time I have left on this world. I don't want to leave it without knowing my wife's killer has been brought to justice."

Parker suddenly became very aware of her own breathing as a silence fell upon the room. She stared into Ken's trembling eyes.

"This is why I've asked you here." The widower spelled it out. "I want to hire you."

"Hire me?" Parker pressed her lips tight. Her heart pounded. She was surprised, flattered, confused and conflicted all at once. If word got out that she'd been hired to investigate Karen Heller's death due to the perceived inadequacy of local law enforcement, Bill's pride would serve as an even greater albatross. Add to that Parker's lack of an investigator's license and the fact that she was still technically considered a suspect in the very murder she'd be investigating and the whole thing made for a legal minefield sure to explode in her face. Still, there was now an opportunity to gain access to information Ken might have been reluctant to have shared with Bill.

"Well?" asked Ken. "You're quiet."

"I can't take your money," said Parker. "And I can't make any promises."

Ken swallowed. "But you'll try, won't you?"

Parker nodded. "I'll try. But only if you're willing to work with me and answer any and all of my questions."

Ken let out a sigh of relief. "I can work with that."

Parker lifted up the 'Hang in there!' cat greeting card. "You can start with explaining *this*."

Ken's face lit up once again. "Heh," he chuckled. "You don't like kittens?"

"I don't—not like kittens."

Ken's impish smile returned. "I thought it might help break the tension today." He chuckled and coughed as if a child caught having pulled a prank. "And to be honest—I thought it was funny."

63.

"How did it go?"

Valerie wasted no time in accosting her daughter when she joined the main parlor room. Most of the crowd had dwindled, and only a few stragglers remained.

"Ken Heller has managed to retain his sense of humor." Parker handed her mother the cat greeting card. "He will also be joining us for dinner next Tuesday to answer more of my questions."

Valerie arched a brow. "Oh? The two of you hit it off, did you?"

Parker shrugged. "I can't help that I'm such a people person."

"Uh huh. And what are you making for this dinner?"

Parker gently bit the tip of her index finger. "Yeah, see, I was hoping *you* could handle that. Maddy could maybe play a few songs on the piano, and—" Parker spun around to examine the room. She noticed Ally endlessly tugging at the hem of Valerie's dress. Drew was standing before Heller's closed casket, slowly approaching it like Indiana Jones might an ancient booby-trapped tomb. But Parker's brooding eldest was nowhere to be found. "Where is Maddy?"

Valerie scrunched her face up. "I thought," she turned around. "I swear, she was standing right next to me a minute ago."

Just then, the pastor approached Parker and her mother with an apologetic smile. "We're going to be closing up soon. You're more than welcome to continue your discussion in the courtyard out front."

"My daughter is missing," rebutted Parker. Her eyes narrowed. She thought she saw a flash of Maddy's brown hair pass by the parlor's front entryway. "Hold on."

Parker marched to the entrance. There, she found Maddy quietly trailing a tall, sturdy-framed man in a deep navy suit reaching for the handle of the funeral home's front door. Maddy reached out her hand. "Mr. Ward?" she asked in a cracked voice.

Joe the gym teacher slowly turned to address Parker's daughter.

"Maddy?" he said. His eyes displayed a mix of surprise and confusion. "Did you need something?"

Parker edged herself to the side of the entry way so as not to be seen. She wanted to see where this was going.

Maddy kicked her foot into the floor. "You were a soldier, right?"

"Affirmative," answered Joe.

Maddy swallowed. "Have you been to war?"

"Iraq and Afghanistan." Joe nodded without hesitation.

"So—you've seen a lot of--*death*?"

Joe paused before answering. "More than my share."

Parker waved her mother and kids off as they approached. *Where are you going with this, Maddy?*

Maddy looked up from the floor. "You ever kill anyone?"

It was Joe's turn to swallow. His mouth opened, but no words came out.

Shit. Parker's eyes popped. She stormed into the entryway with her hands held out. "Woah, woah, too far, Maddy, this is not okay!"

Maddy turned to her mother with glistening eyes. "Mom!"

"We don't ask such personal questions!"

"Are you kidding?" Maddy cried. "You do it all the time!"

"It's my job!" Parker caught herself. "*Was* my job!" She turned to Joe. "Mr. Ward, I am so sorry. That was entirely inappropriate. Maddy, say you're sorry to your teacher!"

Joe held up his hand. "It's okay." He nodded. "It's okay. Maddy's been through a lot."

"I just," Maddy stammered. "I just want to understand! Why--?" She choked.

Parker put her arm around her daughter, just as Valerie had done for her earlier that evening.

Joe took a deep breath. He looked directly at Maddy. "You want to know how one human being could bring himself to take the life of another."

"Yes!" Maddy pleaded.

Joe looked to Parker. "I can offer my—" Joe took a moment to choose his word. "*perspective*. That is, if I can trust you're mature enough to handle it and keep it between us. And if it's okay with your mother."

Maddy turned to Parker with pleading eyes.

Parker gave a slow nod of approval.

Joe leaned forward toward Maddy. "Now, I could stand here and give you all the recruitment spiel about how it's a soldier's job to protect our great nation. How there is no greater calling than to serve and fight for those who can't fight for themselves. But that isn't what you want to hear. It *is* what they tell you. At the beginning. So, when it comes time to meet the enemy it's easier to pull that trigger. You feel as though you're fulfilling a greater purpose." Joe became quiet, as if his mind seemed to replay the memory of his own first time.

"Did it—help?"

Joe's eyes trained on Maddy again. "Not really. The sad truth is, you don't need it. When you're in combat for the first time, and you're being shot at, and half your platoon is dead because a Humvee drove over some improvised explosive, well, your adrenaline is pumping like crazy, you're trapped, you can't run and all you want to do is survive. So, you fall back on your training, your mission and your buddy next to you. In that moment, you're tapping into something deep within you. Something —primal. Something we all have."

Maddy's eyes widened in horror.

"The dirty secret is, you push anyone to their breaking point, you threaten their life or their loved ones, you threaten all they hold dear, well, I don't care who you are—hell hath no fury like it. People will fight to the death to protect what's most important to them. Every time. If you don't believe me, just ask your mother." Joe turned to look at Parker.

Parker's heart rate spiked.

"Ask your mother," Joe reiterated. "Just how far she would go to protect *you*." Joe looked back at Maddy.

Maddy slowly pivoted to catch her mother's gaze, waiting for the answer to the question that lingered in the air.

Parker solemnly nodded, finally understanding the point Joe was trying to make. "He's right. There is nothing I wouldn't do." *Or any mother, for that matter.*

Satisfied, Joe's eyes softened. He offered a comforting smile to Maddy. "Now, it sucks that an eleven-year-old is thinking so much about death and killing. And I get it, you're curious. You're trying to make sense of it. But we've a saying in the Army. Don't dwell on how a soldier died -- remember how he lived."

Maddy frowned. "Mrs. Heller was no soldier."

"Oh, that woman was as tough as any soldier I've ever known. But you're missing the point. We're all born one day, we'll all die another day. It's all those days in between that count. I went to war to protect those days. Your days. So, you could grow up and do all the great things you're going to do in life without having to worry about stuff like this."

Maddy cleared her throat. "How do you know I'm going to do great things?"

"I don't," Joe patted Maddy on the arm. "So, don't let me down." Joe straightened his posture and turned for the door. "You ladies try to enjoy the rest of your weekend. And Parker?"

Parker folded her arms in an attempt not to be impressed. "Yes?"

"Good speech, tonight."

Without another word, Joe opened the door to the funeral home. To his great surprise, the door swung open to reveal Sheriff Bill, who, the for the first time, carried an expression on his face that meant "all business."

64.

Joe and Bill locked eyes with one another in the doorway.

Neither seemed to offer so much as an inch to the other as they sized each other up. Parker and her daughter watched the awkward standoff in stunned silence.

"Sheriff," Joe greeted coolly.

"Mr. Ward," Bill responded in kind.

"The funeral is over. It's a little late to be paying your respects."

Bill nodded past Joe to acknowledge Parker. "I'm here on business."

Parker's eyes narrowed as she did some sizing up of her own. Bill had a clear height advantage, but she couldn't imagine him lasting thirty seconds against Joe's solid frame and years of combat experience if the two ever mixed it up. *What is with the dick parade?*

Joe finally stepped aside and extended his hand to offer a clear path inside. "Don't let me stop you."

Bill stepped into the entrance and walked toward Parker. He paused, when he noticed Joe still waited at the doorway, watching him in earnest. "Business, that's none of *yours*," he explained to Joe.

Parker tried to defuse the tension with a kind smile to Joe. *Does he think he's protecting me?* "Joe, thank you, for speaking with Maddy. We'll see you at school on Monday."

Joe nodded gratefully. "I'm happy to help." He gave Bill once last glance before exiting.

Parker turned to her daughter. "Can you go find grandma and tell her to wait in the parlor a few minutes? I need to speak with the Sheriff."

"Sure." Maddy frowned, disappointed she wouldn't be privy to whatever the Sheriff had to say.

As soon as Maddy returned to the parlor, the Sheriff led Parker to the far opposite corner.

"What the fuck was all that?" Parker blasted Bill with a harsh whisper.

"What was *what?*" asked Bill innocently.

"You were a total dick to Joe!"

"Yeah? Well, I don't trust that guy."

"Really? I couldn't tell with the whole Toretto / Hobbs reenactment."

Bill frowned, anxious to move on. "Is your phone on?"

"No. I shut it off. It's called funeral etiquette."

"Turn it back on."

Parker reached into her purse to find her phone. She turned it on, waiting for the boot up sequence to complete. Finally, the home screen blinked on, followed by several new text messages chiming in one after the other. The last few were all from Bill, with variations of: "Call me!" But the first text message was not from Bill. It was from *Evil Incarnate*—Parker's most recent label for Karen Heller. The message jumped out to Parker:

Nice speech tonight. Almost believed it.

All color flushed from Parker's face as she looked at the timestamp. She had received Heller's phone text thirty minutes ago.

"You got a text, didn't you?" poked Bill. "From *her* phone."

277

Parker nodded.

"What does it say?"

Parker showed Bill the screen. "How did you know?"

"I flagged Heller's phone in case it was ever turned on again. The carrier notified me about thirty minutes ago that a text was sent to your number. They triangulated the signal through cell towers to this area. So here I am."

Parker's stomach sank. "So, whoever stole Heller's phone was sitting in the audience tonight." She searched her memory, trying to remember all the faces she'd seen from the podium. All the usual suspects were there, minus Bill, Mendez and Bernstein. "And you think it was *Joe*?"

"I can't be certain. The phone was turned off after the text was sent. I didn't want Joe to know that's why I was here. Heller's phone is a detail we've deliberately kept from the public."

None of this adds up. "I don't think it was Joe."

"And why not?"

"Joe wears his emotions on his sleeve. The text doesn't fit the moment we just shared."

"The moment you just *shared*?" Bill scoffed.

Parker rolled her eyes. "It's not what you think."

"Come on, Parker."

Parker held up her phone. "Whoever sent this text is toying with us—with me."

"Why?"

"I don't know."

Bill shook his head. "Well, I wouldn't get all gushy over Joe and count him out just yet."

278

"I don't get gushy—ever."

"Joe is no American hero, that's for damn sure."

Parker looked up at Bill out of the corner of her eye. "Why would you say that?"

"I pulled his file." Bill wrapped his fingers around his belt buckle to hoist it up. "The guy was court-martialed for attacking his commanding officer. The incident led to a dishonorable discharge from the Army."

Parker released a heavy sigh. "Fantastic."

"If I were you? I'd keep my distance. Joe is a loose cannon."

65.

Parker couldn't sleep a wink that night.

She lied in her bed, tracing familiar patterns in the texture of the off-white popcorn ceiling. The same ceiling she had stared at as a teenager the night before any big mid-term or final. Parker couldn't help but to chuckle at how nervous she got on test day, when nearly thirty years later, she'd be hard pressed to remember any of the material. Recalling how the Pythagorean theorem worked or the details of the French Revolution did little to settle the myriad of questions that raced through her mind this night. And yet, one question, above all, kept surfacing in her stream of consciousness, as if gasping for air to keep from drowning--

Why me?

Heller's death was one thing. But why was Parker's car chosen to stash the body? Why was an alleged killer continually poking at her with cryptic phone texts? What was the purpose of it all?

Parker watched her stream of questions wash away, until only one trickle remained.

Why don't I just ask the killer?

Parker sat up in her bed, staring at the last text message from Evil Incarnate:

Nice speech tonight. Almost believed it.

Parker knew pursuing a text conversation with a murderer was probably not a strategy Sheriff Bill would approve of. Or her mother. Or any sane person. But Parker was convinced whoever was working Heller's phone was practically screaming for her attention. *Why?* Parker's thumbs went to work as she composed a new message:

Dear Killer. You seem desperate for my attention. I'm tired of your games. What the fuck is your problem?

Parker cringed. *Don't invite more trouble than you've already got, especially where murderers are concerned.* She quickly deleted the text and composed a new one.

What do you want?

Parker tapped the send button. She stared blankly at the phone screen, half-expecting a reaction. Five minutes later, she put the phone down in disappointment.

If the killer was smart, he or she would keep the phone off so as not to be tracked. Only when the phone was turned back on would he or she be inclined to respond. And who knew when that would be?

Wide awake, Parker went back to staring at the ceiling.

This person has singled me out. This person continues to engage me. I've met this person. I know this person. Right? Maybe—

Parker looked across the room to a familiar bookshelf. Neatly organized biographies of Jon Bon Jovi were next to a haphazard library of middle school and high school yearbooks.

Could this go back further than the past few weeks?

Parker slipped out of bed to cross the room. She pulled the yearbook from her senior year, and began paging through it, her nostrils filling with ozone emitting off pages unseen for decades. Her eyes scanned the hundreds of pictures of teenagers, some who she recognized, some she'd never met. Parker had graduated with five hundred other students, and the high school was simply too big to know everyone. She smiled as she found Julie's photo. The younger version sported much fuller cheeks, with large round glasses and bangs that curled up toward the sky. Her hair formed a perfect triangle.

Shit, Julie, you really bloomed later in life, didn't you?

Parker turned the page to find photos of herself in Debate Club, Math League, and Future Leaders of America. She rolled her eyes, disgusted at the awkward teenager who stared blankly into the camera so long ago. "Yuck." She flipped another few pages and squinted as she found a boy who looked like a much thinner, stick-pole version of Sheriff Bill dressed in an over-sized tuxedo. Young Bill sported a black satin cape with his arms outstretched dramatically as if casting a spell. The caption read: "Magic Club." No one else appeared in the picture.

Maybe he made all the other members disappear? Poor Bill.

Parker flipped a few more pages. She found the younger version of Baby Face in the sophomore section. *I went to school with her?* Even Holly, the current PTA president, retained her ridiculously large smile when cheering for the varsity football and wrestling teams. But aside from those few faces, the more Parker dug in, the more people she initially thought she remembered, only to become less sure if she truly recognized anyone else at all. *People can change a lot over thirty years.* As exhaustion finally crept in and her eyes grew heavy, Parker began to question everything she'd seen tonight. Could she trust *anyone* she went to high school with?

Parker shook her head and closed the book.

This could spiral out of control pretty quickly.

Parker took a deep breath, welcoming the tiredness like a warm blanket. After tossing the yearbook onto the window seat, she slipped back under her bed's covers. Sleep came quickly. So quickly, that she didn't even notice her phone light up and buzz with an alert:

There is Motion in your Backyard.

66.

"Did you see this?"

Valerie lifted her phone up before the yawning face of her daughter who had finally sauntered into Monday's breakfast.

Parker squinted, reading the motion alert from the backyard last night. "Yeah?" she answered in the tone of a question. "So?" Parker gently pushed her mother's phone aside to notice that Maddy, Drew and Ally were already dressed and munching their cereal at the table. "What's going on here?"

Maddy's spoon clinked in her empty bowl. "You overslept," she answered. Maddy didn't bother to even glance up as she took her bowl to the sink. "So, I stepped in and got the kids ready for school."

Kids? You're still a kid! "Who are you and what have you done with my daughter?" asked Parker.

"Ally doesn't have school," Drew added. "You woke her up for nothing."

"Shut up, Drew."

Parker grinned as Maddy walked past her to exit the kitchen. "*Annnnd,* there she is."

Valerie lifted her phone back up in front of Parker's face. "What do you mean '*so?*'"

Parker frowned as she tried dodging the phone, but Valerie kept matching her head fakes to keep it in her face. "I looked at the video log this morning." She snatched the phone out of her mother's hands. "There was nothing there."

Valerie turned her nose up. "Sweet Susan Hayward, there's a video log?"

The question gave Parker pause. Valerie normally did a good job of keeping pace with advances in technology, certainly much more than her friends who still thought phones were just for making phone calls. But every once in a blue moon her mother would show her age. Parker always found it ironic that the greater the age, the younger the reaction to tech. "Yes, that's the whole point. The app keeps a record of everything the cameras detect." Parker recalled the video clip from the motion in the backyard last night when she fell asleep. She tapped on it and showed Valerie a forty second black and white video of their backyard bathed in infrared light. Other than the subtle sway of a few tree branches in the wind, nothing moved in the yard. "See?"

Valerie let out a sigh of relief. "That's good to know. I have to admit, after the text you received at the funeral, I'm a little on edge."

"Understandable." *Which also tells me I should definitely not mention that I replied to that same text.*

"Then what triggered the motion? Why did the camera go off?"

Parker hunched her shoulders. "Maybe a leaf fell, or a squirrel sneezed, I don't know. But nothing else was triggered, and everything seems to be in order. I think we're good."

Drew's ears perked. He slowly twisted in his chair to catch his mother's attention. "Unless it was Heller's ghost!"

"Oh no!" Ally added, slapping her hands onto her cheeks.

Parker sighed.

"Can I see it?" Drew exploded out of his chair to paw at his grandmother's phone. "Please?"

Parker handed the phone over, allowing Drew to ingest it with wide eyes. "See?" she assured. "Nothing there. Glory said we'd get false alarms now and then."

"Hmmmmm," Drew rubbed his chin. "Ghosts are usually invisible."

"Usually?"

"I'm gonna have to look at this in the lab. Can you send it to me?"

"Do you have an email?" challenged Parker.

"Do I *need* an email?"

Parker plucked the phone from Drew's hands and handed it back to Valerie. "We'll figure something out." She winked. "Go finish getting ready."

"On it!" Drew sprinted out of the kitchen and up the front stairs.

"What about you?" Valerie asked Parker. "Don't you need to get ready?"

"Not without coffee, I don't." Parker poured herself a cup of the machine roasted coffee, took one sip and immediately spat it out. "Gahhhhhhhhh!"

"Maddy took it upon herself to make a pot."

"It tastes like—socks!"

Valerie arched an eyebrow, sensing Parker's performance might be some dramatic ploy to achieve an end. "Do you want *me* to drop off the kids, this morning?"

Parker cringed as she took another sip, then force-gulped down enough caffeine to wake herself up. The sheer horror of the experience was enough to bulge her eyes. "Nope! I got this! Today is the day I go and do the thing!"

"Which thing? You mean creating a successful fundraiser for the music program?"

Parker wiped the coffee moustache off her face with her shirt sleeve. *Shit. Forgot about that.* "Uhhh, yes, that -- too."

"Or do you mean strengthening your maternal bonds with your children?"

"That's a given." Parker tried to wipe the lingering taste of the coffee off her teeth with her tongue. "Let's just cut to the chase and say I'm going to solve this goddamn murder, ghost and all."

"Doing all that today, are you?"

Parker raised her index finger to mark a point. *Any* point. "I've got a plan."

"Well, if you see Heller's ghost, tell her to stop floating around our backyard. Next time she does it, she'll find herself at the wrong end of my twelve gauge."

Parker slammed down her coffee mug, spun on her heel and marched for the stairs. "You can't shoot a ghost, Mom, everybody knows that!"

Valerie tilted her head. "It won't stop me from trying."

67.

Infused with sock-flavored coffee...

Parker dropped Maddy and Drew off at the playground and then proceeded to march directly into the Oak Creek Elementary school front office. Ready to blast any obstacle to smithereens with a dose of over-caffeinated reasoning, Parker's eyes immediately locked onto her first target – Silver Fox. The receptionist sat quietly at her desk, unaware of the verbal smackdown she was about to endure should she so much as bat an eye at Parker's request. "I'd like to meet with Principal Mendez," Parker demanded. "Is she in?"

To Parker's surprise, the Silver Fox kept her nose buried in the soap digest magazine she held. "Sure," she answered in a dull, unimpressed tone. The Fox casually flicked her wrist in the direction of Mendez's office. "Go right in."

Parker nodded with a surprised stutter. "Alright then!"

"Go on, now." The Fox's eyes never left her magazine.

"Thank you, I will!" Parker continued her march toward Mendez's office, suddenly aware of how loud her own voice was. She knocked and pushed open the door, revealing a tall, thin dark-haired woman dressed in a business suit standing before Mendez's desk.

"I don't understand why this keeps happening!" the woman blasted Mendez. "This has got to be the tenth time I've been in your office to go over this!"

"Eleventh," Mendez calmly replied as she kneaded her hands together and rested them on her desk.

Parker was about to apologize for intruding on the conversation, when she realized neither Mendez or her opponent had noticed her. Parker took a half step back out of the doorway. She'd seen this fiery woman before, pointed out by Julie on the playground as a Helicopter Mom affectionately referred to as "Cray-Cray." Nothing was ever good enough for Cray-Cray when it came to the care and safety of her child, as she had personally charged Oak Creek Elementary with making that a priority over everything else. "The point is," Ms. Cray-Cray continued. She lashed an accusatory finger at Mendez. "My child could have *starved*!"

Parker watched closely for Mendez's reaction. The young principal's normally immaculate appearance was, for once, not without flaw. Several of Mendez's hairs were out of place, and slight bags shown just beneath her eyes. Despite that, Mendez stared at the woman across from her with absolute focus and calm.

"I'm sorry that your child missed his morning snack yesterday," Mendez apologized. "But I can assure you, there was no danger of him starving."

"Tenth snack!" Cray-Cray corrected. "He's missed ten of them!"

"Over the course of a year."

"Do you know what that can do to a child's development? His growth? I'm probably going to have to go to the doctor now and get a prescription for growth hormones! And if I do? I'm sending you the bill!"

Mendez slowly nodded. "You are welcome to try."

Cray-Cray clenched her fists. "I don't even understand how this keeps happening! Can you explain to me why this keeps happening? I mean, I delivered the snack to your front office last Friday, with *explicit* instructions to give it to Charles. Explicit instructions! And no one was here!"

Mendez took a deep breath. "So, you didn't speak with my receptionist? Or a teacher? Or anyone?"

"No, but I wrote out explicit instructions—"

"Explicit, yes."

288

"—and I left the snack bag on the front chair like I always do. You would think after ten times your people would figure it out!"

"The front office is very busy," Mendez explained. "And if no one was present, we were probably off dealing with something very important."

"You're saying my child is not important?"

"What I'm trying to say is that if you want to guarantee your child has a morning snack, it is probably best to send it *with* him when he leaves for school."

Cray-Cray blinked. For a moment, it looked as though she might have fully understood Mendez's statement. Then she started to practically foam at the mouth. "I'm a busy woman."

"Of course."

"I work full time. Do you work full time?"

Holy. Fuck. Parker felt her blood boil. *How much of this shit is Mendez going to put up with?*

"I do work full time." Mendez's eyes narrowed. "Here, at this school."

"You're making fun of me!" Cray-Cray blasted. She tossed her arms up in the air. "Where is Vice Principal Heller? At least she would listen to me! At least she would make an effort to correct the problem!"

Mendez slowly stood up and looked Cray-Cray directly into the eye. "She's dead."

Cray-Cray blinked again. "I'm going to be calling the USDA about this."

"Do what you must."

Cray-Cray clutched her purse closely and spun on her stiletto heels to march out of the office. She glared at Parker as she passed by. "Good luck dealing with that one!" growled Cray-Cray.

Parker turned her head to track Cray-Cray as she opened the front office door. "Good luck calling the United States Department of Agriculture!" answered Parker. Cray-Cray didn't hear the statement as she b-lined to her BMW parked in the handicapped space. Within thirty seconds she had peeled out of the school's parking lot. "Because, you know, the USDA is all about child starvation."

Parker pivoted back to Mendez, who sat back down at her desk to begin typing away. Parker nearly felt bad for the young principal – and what she was about to do to her. *Should I stir a boiling pot?* Parker held back a grin. *Of course, I should.* "Good morning, Principal Mendez!"

68.

Mendez kept her eyes glued to her computer screen.

"Now is not a good time, Ms. Monroe."

"Come on, I can't be nearly as bad as Cray-Cray, can I?" asked Parker. She took a decisive step onto Mendez's checkered carpet. "And your receptionist seemed to think this was the perfect time."

Mendez frowned as she stared at the open door behind Parker. "She just let you walk in here?"

"All but drew me a map."

"That would make you the third interruption this morning!" Mendez raised her voice enough for it to carry out the office door, only to be answered by silence. "She's not out there is she?"

Parker looked back through the doorway for any hint of the Silver Fox. All she found was an empty swivel chair. "No." Normally, Fox was a tight-ass, guarding the front office like a Pitbull. What had changed? Heller. *Fox never was protective of the office*, thought Parker. *She was protective of Heller. Now that she's gone--* "Maybe, she's having a hard time," Parker offered. "I imagine she and Heller were very close."

Mendez sighed as she frantically clicked her mouse. "I've a lot of work to do, Ms. Monroe. So, if you could--."

"You must be incredibly busy taking on all of Heller's duties," Parker interrupted. "Is that why you didn't attend Heller's funeral?"

Mendez's mouse hand froze. She glowered at Parker, before carefully, and slowly closing her laptop.

Oh shit, that got your attention didn't it? Parker tried to pass the question off innocently. "You had to have known parents would notice."

Mendez instantly drained her face of any trace of emotion or expression. She became a blank page – entirely unreadable. It was a tactic often used by professional poker players, something that could only be mastered after years of training and practice. "Of course, I knew people would notice," answered Mendez. "I knew people would talk. And gossip. And judge. None of that matters to me. I had my reasons."

Parker stepped further into the office.

"Reasons I don't need to share with you."

Parker stopped dead in her tracks. Mendez was clearly putting up every wall she could. *What are you hiding, Mendez?* "Believe it or not, I happen to care about this school. I'm here to help."

"That's not why you're here," challenged Mendez.

"Of course, it is. I'm in charge of a major fundraiser. And I'm concerned that people aren't going to give money to a school mired in a murder investigation."

"*What* murder investigation?" asked Mendez.

Parker balked. "The one where the body ended up *in the back of my car*."

Mendez kneaded her hands together again on her desk. "There's been no official explanation to the public as to how Heller died. The parent who was just here a minute ago didn't even know Heller *had* died."

"She didn't know a lot of things. Are you telling me, you're going to pretend the murder didn't happen?"

"No, but I'm not going to shine a spotlight on the bullet in Heller's forehead." Mendez leaned back in her chair. "You've taken up a lot of my time, already, Ms. Monroe, so let's cut to the chase."

"I told you—"

"No, you fed me a line." Mendez stood up from her desk. She stepped forward to meet Parker face to face. "I don't like being fed lines. Why are you really here?"

Parker stared Mendez up and down. Gone was any hint of the disheveled woman she'd happened upon mere moments ago. Mendez stood firm, projecting the confidence of an MMA fighter sizing up an opponent, forcing Parker to wonder for the first time – could she take Mendez if it came down to a fight? Despite her manicured nails and stiletto heels, Parker sensed there was a whole other side to Mendez that no one could guess. Former military? Undercover FBI? Former cop? Rugby player? Moonlight Roller Derby skater? Parker's super mom strength and willingness to pull hair and play dirty suddenly felt inadequate. Still, Parker folded her arms, refusing to be intimated. "You seem to have me all figured out," said Parker. "Why don't you just tell me why I'm here?"

Mendez didn't hesitate. "You want to know if I had anything to do with Heller's murder. I didn't. You want to know if this school is still safe for your children. It isn't. Not yet. You want to relive your glory days as an investigative journalist and help capture a killer to make up for an embarrassing end to an otherwise distinguished career. It won't work."

Parker swallowed. *Fuck you.*

Mendez continued. "But the main reason you are here, is doubt. Doubt that is eating away at the pit of your stomach. Doubt about a certain music teacher who used to work in these halls. Because, should you successfully re-install him, and then discover he had anything to do with Heller's death? Then you will have screwed everything up and embarrassed yourself – *again.*"

293

Parker clenched her fist. As much as Parker's ego hated to admit it, Mendez's assessment was nearly dead on. A little too dead on. "You sure don't talk like an elementary school principal."

"You don't talk like a PTA parent." Mendez shot back. "So how did I do?"

"You missed one thing. The most important thing."

"And what was that?"

"I'm here, because I want to know if I can trust you."

Parker's statement gave Mendez pause. "You can't."

Parker shrugged. "Well then. *That's* good to know."

Mendez softened her stance. "Have you spoken with Mr. Bernstein? I'm told he wasn't present at Heller's funeral either."

Parker's eyes narrowed. *You just reamed me. Now you're trying to help?* Confused, she decided to play along. "He's not taking my calls, and I don't know where he lives. I was hoping you could help me out with his address. That is, if you can trust *me*."

"I can't."

"Then I really am wasting both our time." Parker began to turn for the door when Mendez cleared her throat.

"I can't trust any parent," explained Mendez. "Some parents talk too much. Some not enough. And yet, somehow, with as much gossip that transpires in this town, often the most important things are left unsaid. I find that shameful. Wouldn't you agree, Ms. Monroe?"

Now, what the fuck did you mean by all that? Parker turned back to Mendez. "I feel like you're trying to say something to me without actually saying it. If so, I would prefer you just--*say it."*

Mendez visibly rolled her eyes. "I said what I said."

"Great. Because I can't tell if the important thing you said was eluding to how other important things are left unsaid, or if there is still something important that you haven't said."

Mendez crossed the room to meet Parker at the doorway. "I want you to listen very carefully to what I'm about to say *now*, Ms. Monroe. I'm *not* kicking you out of my office." Mendez extended her arm to show Parker the exit.

"You're not?"

"And I'm afraid I can't help you with locating Mr. Bernstein's address." Mendez gently used two fingers to nudge Parker into the front office space. "Since he was a former employee, to do so would be a breach of confidence. That is why Oak Creek Elementary keeps all employee records safely locked away in our blue filing cabinet. Have a nice day."

Before Parker could even blink, Mendez had shut the office door between them.

"What the fuck just happened?" Parker looked around herself. The Silver Fox was nowhere in sight. The front office was completely devoid of any signs of life. Parker finally blinked at the sight across the room. "I'll be damned," she muttered. Just ahead, stuck in the center of a series of black file cabinets, was a single blue one—with the keys hanging in the upper right corner lock.

69.

If Parker hesitated about whether to open the blue filing cabinet, it was only for a second.

Not knowing how much time she had before the Silver Fox would return, or if some random teacher or parent might happen upon the front office, Parker crossed the room as if she belonged there, twisted the keys and dug into the alphabetically organized files. Her fingers and eyes worked diligently together, as if going into some investigative autopilot mode she hadn't turned on for months, all the while a tiny little voice in the back of her head screamed at her-
-

Are you kidding? Mendez might be setting you up!

Parker ignored the warning as she thumbed into Bernstein's file and yanked it. She set the folder down on the top of a smaller neighboring cabinet, flipped to the first page and snapped a picture with her phone.

Mendez might be calling Fox over right now to catch you in the act!

Parker snapped another picture. And another. Until all twelve pages of Bernstein's file were captured. She closed the file and looked to Mendez's door, which remained shut throughout the entire process.

Or maybe she really is trying to help you in her own way?

Parker scanned the room and the nearby hallways. No sign of Fox. All she could hear was the soft whirring of Fox's desk computer. Parker squinted to see out the front glass doors. No one.

You're an idiot, Parker. But since you're here—

Parker's heart raced as she pulled open the drawer to return Bernstein's file. She poked around and found *another name – Joe*

Ward, aka GI Joe the Gym Teacher. His file was significantly lighter, only a page and a half. Two snaps and it was stored in her phone. Parker stole another quick scan of her surroundings. She detected some bustling down the adjoining hallway.

You've got maybe another sixty seconds?

Parker snatched Principal Mendez's file. Click-click! She claimed two more pages, returned the file and eyeballed a pull tab labeled Karen Heller.

Do you need it? Can't you just ask her husband about anything you don't know?

Out of the corner of her eye, Parker caught movement outside the front glass door.

Shit.

Parker took a deep breath. Normally people caught in the act of wrong doing reacted hastily or nervously. Luckily, Parker was well practiced in the art of "belonging somewhere." She calmly folded Mendez's file, replaced it in the cabinet and turned to find PTA President Holly strolling in. Parker smiled at her.

"Ms. Monroe," greeted Holly. "I was just thinking about you!"

Parker casually closed the cabinet door. "Hopefully nothing too awful."

Holly let out a small chuckle. She appeared unusually at ease with no tick to tug at her eye. "No, I wanted to tell you I thought your speech at the funeral was, well—*brave*. But you disappeared."

"I tend to smoke-bomb out of those kinds of things." Parker's eye caught movement down the adjoining hallway. She slowly moved away from the filing cabinet and toward Holly as the Silver Fox made her way back to the front office. Parker nodded. "But I appreciate that, thank you. I need to run to my next appointment, but don't think I haven't forgotten about Boo Fest!"

Holly smiled nervously. "Yes, it'll be here before we know it! I was hoping we could meet soon to go over some more of the details."

"Slippery When Wet," Parker shot back as she circled Holly to position herself for the exit.

Holly winced. "Excuse me?"

"That's the name of a Bon Jovi cover band I read about the other night. They're going to be playing at a bar in town this Thursday. They could be the perfect entertainment for our Boo Fest fundraiser!"

"Oh! Really? Bon Jovi? Aren't they kind of – dated?"

Holy shit, woman, don't make me punch you in the throat! Parker forced a smile. "What? *No!* What's say you, me and some of the other PTA'ers get together, check them out, and we can cram through some Boo Bash stuff over beers? Who knows, you might even have some fun?"

Holly gently fanned herself as though she were experiencing some kind of hot flash. "*Fun?* My, yes, fun sounds like fun!"

"That's pretty much the meaning."

Holly giggled playfully. "Ha! Good one!"

Parker pushed the glass door open, just as Silver Fox returned to her desk. "So, great! It's a date. I'll text you the details. Bye!"

Parker disappeared out the door.

298

70.

"Call Mom,"

Parker ordered to her phone as she raced her detestable minivan down the winding highway road. After a few rings, Valerie picked up. "Parker?" Her voice boomed throughout the minivan's interior. "Where are you? We expected you back over an hour ago!"

"I'm on my way to Bernstein's place," answered Parker as she adjusted the volume. The files she had snapped appeared too small to read comfortably on her phone, so she had decided to print them later, extracted Bernstein's address and hit the road. "It's a bit further south than what I was expecting."

"Bernstein? I thought he wasn't answering your calls? Does he know you are coming?"

"Nope."

"I don't know if this is a good idea."

"Probably not." *Especially since Mendez practically begged me to look into him with her whole 'I'm going to say something but not really say it at all' mysterious, mixed signals kind of way. The principal obviously suspected Bernstein of something. Unless she's trying to throw me off her own trail. Regardless I need to proceed with caution.* "I'm going to text you his address, so you'll know where to find the body."

"That's not funny."

"I'll be fine, Mom, I just want to talk with him." *And I'm only half-kidding about the body thing.* "Can you pick up the kids from school if I run late?"

"Of course! Just call me back as soon as you are done, okay?"

"Deal."

Parker's navigation kicked in as she ended her call. *"In five hundred feet, turn left,"* instructed the computer.

Parker eased her minivan to a halt. She peered down the long dirt road that disappeared under a thick canopy of trees. *Whatever is down there, it's remote and secluded.* Parker wondered if she should have given the Sheriff the heads up. *No, he'd just try to talk me out of it.* She drew in a deep breath and stepped on the accelerator. "Alright, Bernstein. What are you hiding down there?"

The dirt road stretched on for about a half mile before opening up into large ranch style clearing fenced in with long wooden logs. The road ended at a dusty driveway set before a modest two-story wood paneled farm house. Two cars were parked on the sparsely grassed lawn--an older brown station wagon, and a newer Honda accord. To the right of the house was a horse stable and a barn connected by another fence. A massive oak tree stood tall in front of the house and dangled a tire on a rope of twine that swung back and forth due to the efforts of the young Hispanic boy playing on it.

As Parker pulled up to the house, her eyes met with the boy's, prompting him to dismount from the tire and sprint to the front door. The door opened, revealing a small Hispanic woman, probably close to Parker's own age, dressed in blue jeans and a red t-shirt with her long black hair pulled back into a pony tail. The woman ushered the boy inside. She shut the door behind her and approached Parker's van, while wiping her hands on the dishrag she carried.

Parker was sure to smile and wave as she parked and exited her minivan. "Hello!" greeted Parker. She pulled out the bouquet of "Get Well" flowers she'd picked up on the way out of Oak Creek.

The woman eyed Parker suspiciously. "Can I help you?" she asked with a thick accent.

"I'm hoping so. I'm looking for Mr. Bernstein. Does he live here?"

The woman didn't offer so much as a nod, instead tracing over every inch of Parker. "Who are you?"

"My name is Parker Monroe. Mr. Bernstein teaches my daughter piano lessons. I know he's been sick." Parker raised up the flower bouquet. "So, I thought I'd stop by to see if he's okay. Cheer him up."

"He very sick."

"So, he *is* still sick?" asked Parker, wondering how much English the woman had fully understood.

"Very sick. No lessons."

Parker smiled. "No, I'm not here for lessons." She flirted with the idea of speaking to the woman in Spanish but didn't want to tip her hat on that just yet. "Is it okay if I see him?"

The woman shook her head. "No, he too sick."

Parker noted the gold ring on the woman's left hand as she continued to play with her dish towel. "Are you his wife? What's your name?"

"Imelda," a soft and familiar voice called from the door, followed by a heavy cough.

Parker turned to find Mr. Bernstein, wrapped in a bathrobe looking feeble as ever, standing in the doorway with a handkerchief pressed to his red nose.

"My wife's name is Imelda," Bernstein continued in a weak voice. He turned to the woman and spoke his next phrase in perfect Spanish. "This is Señora Monroe. I teach her daughter piano. She's the one trying to get my job back."

The statement finally lit a smile in Imelda's face. "Oh," she nodded approvingly to her husband.

Bernstein coughed up something into his handkerchief. "What on Earth are you doing all the way out here?" he asked Parker.

"I was worried about you," she replied. *And relieved to see you actually are sick.* "I didn't see you at the funeral. You haven't returned my calls. What's a girl supposed to think?"

Bernstein coughed again, with much more effort than before. "I'm sorry, I've just been trying to beat—whatever this thing is."

Guilt?

"We're hosting Imelda's extended family in a few weeks," Bernstein continued. "It's always a rather grand affair. There is so much to do. And then I heard about Karen. I'm afraid it's all been a bit too much." Bernstein stared at the ground, lost in a moment of what appeared to be genuine sadness.

Imelda only stared quietly at her husband, as if unsure if she should touch or comfort him. Seeing the two of them together highlighted their age difference. Bernstein had to have been in his late fifties, at least fifteen years older than Imelda.

"Yes, it was quite a shock for everyone," added Parker.

"I wish I—" Bernstein stopped himself. He wiped a tear away and looked up at Parker. "Do you want to come in? I'm going to need to rest soon, but you're welcome to have some lemonade before you go. I hate to have you come all the way out here and leave with nothing."

I don't intend to. "Lemonade sounds wonderful."

Parker stepped into the farm house's front room, modestly decorated with furniture styled as though it came from the 1970's, save for the white grand piano in the corner. The baby Baldwin was covered with music books and sheets. Toy trucks, cars and action figures were scattered about the worn carpet floors, yet there was no sign of the boy she'd seen playing on the tire swing. Most curious of all, not one picture adorned any wall or shelf, nor any mirror of any size -- only a few small paintings of the southwest landscape.

302

"I can't believe you drove all the way out here," exclaimed Bernstein as he settled into a chair. "How did you even find the place?"

Parker pretended not to hear the question as she studied one of the paintings, a portrait of a Mexican cowboy on his horse, riding toward the sunset. "It's no trouble, really," she said. She bent down for a closer look at one of the action figures based off a popular super hero movie franchise. Parker recalled Bernstein saying he and his wife could never have children. "Who was the boy I saw outside?"

"Oh, him?" Bernstein smiled with pride just as Imelda emerged from the kitchen with two glasses of lemonade. "That's my nephew—*Pedro*."

71.

Parker's memory instantly flashed an image...

of the elderly grandmother she'd met in the Sheriff's office weeks ago on the first day of school. *What was her name?* "Cecilia," Parker said out loud. "Would she be Pedro's great-grandmother?"

Bernstein's lips curled into a confused smile. "Uh, yes, as a matter of fact. Do you know her?"

Imelda emerged from the kitchen with a tray of three lemonade glasses, dripping with condensation.

"I met Cecilia at the Sheriff's office," replied Parker.

The statement froze Imelda in her steps. "Abuela?" she asked with wide eyes, turning to her husband for clarification. "Sheriff?"

Huh. You understand English just fine, thought Parker. "Cecilia was looking for Pedro."

Bernstein carefully grabbed a glass of lemonade off the tray. "Odd. I don't seem to remember Pedro ever missing. He's been staying with us for weeks. And to involve the Sheriff?" He took a sip of lemonade and winced. "Oh, dear." Then in Spanish to Imelda. "Imelda, please, these drinks are much too sour. We can't possibly offer this to our guest. Can you add some sugar?"

Imelda tilted her head as if to mull over the request. "Sí," she replied, then disappeared back into the kitchen.

"Too sour," Bernstein explained to Parker. "I must say, I'm baffled by your meeting with Cecilia. I know she gets confused now and then, but when you said it the way you did you made the whole thing sounds rather suspicious."

It is, thought Parker. "Cecilia's grandson eventually came into the office looking for her, what was his name--?"

"Victor."

"Yes, Victor Cortez." *I remember. Just seeing if you do.*

"Imelda's brother." Bernstein confirmed.

"Right. He assured Cecilia and the Sheriff that Pedro was safe at home. Is this his home, Mr. Bernstein?"

Bernstein smiled again. "It is for as long as Pedro needs it to be. His mother, you see," Bernstein leaned back to see if his wife was listening in the kitchen. "Imelda's sister-- she's having a bit of bad luck, right now, I'm afraid. We're taking care of Pedro until his mother can get her affairs in order."

"What kind of bad luck?"

Bernstein widened his smile as Imelda re-emerged with another tray of lemonade. The couple exchanged an uneasy glance, followed by Bernstein nodding to Parker. "I'd rather not discuss such unpleasantries. It's a family matter. You understand."

Nope. "Of course."

Imelda's eyes narrowed. "Lemonade?" She pushed the tray forward.

Parker caught herself as she reached for the lemonade glass presented to her. She paused, watching the water dripping down the side of the glass. It looked delicious, and yet something felt off to her. *Am I overreacting?* In her experience, it always paid to be paranoid, but if she was wrong, she didn't want to discourage the Bernsteins from helping her in the future. *It's time to force a graceful exit.* Parker smiled politely and continued to reach for the lemonade only to flinch suddenly. "Oh!" She laughed as she reached into her purse for her phone. "Sorry, I've got to take this."

Parker put the phone to her ear. "Hello. Mmmm. Really? Well, shit. Alright, Mom. Yup, just put a wet cloth to it and see if the bleeding doesn't stop." She looked to Imelda, then to Bernstein. "I'll head back right now. I'm at Bernstein's place. Yup, you have the

305

address." Parker was sure to make eye contact with Bernstein and his wife, so they understood a third party knew of her location. "Okay, I'll see you in a bit." Parker put the phone down and smiled apologetically. "Ally did a back flip off the kitchen table."

Bernstein's eyes widened in horror. "Oh my! I hope she's alright!"

"I need to head back. Anyway, thank you for your time, and I hope you're feeling better, Mr. Bernstein!" Parker bolted for the door.

"Hmm?" Mr. Bernstein put his hand to his throat and swallowed as if in pain. "Yes, thank you, I'm getting better with each day."

Bernstein and Imelda watched Parker run to her car from the window of their house.

72.

They're obviously hiding something.

Parker threw her minivan into gear and pealed out of Bernstein's dirt driveway.

Mendez must've suspected that too. She practically pointed me to Bernstein with her leaving the keys to the filing cabinet. Why couldn't she just tell me what it is? Should I even trust her?

Parker watched Bernstein's farmhouse shrink in her rearview mirror. She could see the odd couple watching her from their window. And there, in the window just above, was a hint of the boy's face pressed against the glass – Pedro. Parker turned the corner at the driveway's end and onto the two-lane highway.

Maybe I'm just paranoid. But Imelda creeped the shit out of me. Hopefully she bought the whole fake phone call thing with my mom.

The "Ally Back-Flip" was a variant of a tried and true routine Parker had used several times in the past. She often employed it to get out of dead-end interviews with attention-whores who pretended to be witnesses. Of course, it also came in handy during supremely boring staff meetings.

And what was up with the lemonade? Did she lace it with Rohypnol or GHB or something? That's awful to think. I'm a terrible person. Imelda's probably a lovely woman who I just don't understand. A lovely woman who drugs strangers and then hacks them up to bits. Fuck! What is wrong with me?

Alone on the road, Parker pushed the minivan to a solid seventy-five miles an hour. She shook her head. She knew she wasn't operating at peak performance. This whole motherhood-PTA-fundraising-murder-mystery thing was a delicate dance.

Focus, Parker, get rid of the noise. Everyone keeps saying Bernstein is such a great guy. Why? I need answers.

"Call the Sheriff," Parker commanded Siri.

"Calling the Sheriff now," Siri cheerily replied. The minivan filled with a digital chirping as the phone tried to connect.

"Parker?" Bill answered after a loud click. "Everything okay? Did you get another text message?"

"No," Parker gripped the steering wheel to hug the next curve. "Tell me everything you know about Gerome Bernstein."

"Bernstein?" Bill remained silent for a few seconds. "Why? Where are you? It sounds like you're driving."

"I just paid a visit to Bernstein at his house."

"Of course, you did."

"Do you remember that old woman who came into your office looking for Pedro? Her name was Cecilia. Did you know that same Pedro is living at Bernstein's place?"

"Parker, there are a lot of Pedro's in Southern California."

"Sure, but I confirmed it with Bernstein. These Pedros are one and the same."

"Okay," Bill blew into the phone. "Having a Pedro in the family is not exactly a crime. Where are you going with this?"

Parker grimaced. "You don't think that's weird?"

"I'm a cop who does magic. *That's* weird."

"Come on, Bill, work with me."

"Fine. Did you *see* Pedro?"

"I did."

"Did he *look* alright? Any bruises, cuts, or anything that seemed out of the ordinary?"

Parker frowned. "No. But--"

"Did Pedro seem afraid? Like he wanted to leave? Did anyone try to hide him from you? Pretend that he wasn't there?"

Damnit. No, no, no and no. "I'm telling you, something is off. Maybe it's Bernstein's wife. Or her family. He eluded to her sister being an unfit mother. She was acting funny the whole time."

"Who? Imelda?"

Parker glowered at Bill's name on her phone screen. "Funny, I didn't mention her name." Her pulse spiked. "Bill? How do you know the wife's name?"

"Parker—"

Parker's cheeks flushed red. "Damnit! You know these people? And you didn't tell me? How do you know these people?"

"It's--complicated."

"That's not an answer!"

"Parker, come on!" Bill let out an audible sigh. "Listen, I will explain everything. But not over the phone, okay? It's kind of – sensitive. Just, I, I can assure you, Bernstein isn't a threat."

"Why are you always defending this guy?"

"Tomorrow night. I'll stop by. I'll explain everything. It's not what you think."

Parker's mashed her lips together. "No good. You need to explain this *tonight*."

"I can't. There are other things going on in this town other than just—"

"Solving a murder?" Parker blasted. "Tomorrow morning. The Bean. After school drop-off."

"Fine. Whatever." Bill relented. "You're buying."

Parker rolled her eyes. "You know I'm unemployed, right?"

"Yeah? I'm living off a Sheriff's salary. And I'm doing you a favor. *Again.*"

Parker shook her head. "Just order something cheap." Parker's voice trailed off. Her eyes focused on the blue Chevy Tahoe SUV closing in behind her in the rearview mirror.

"Heh. No promises." Bill clicked off.

"He had better have a good explanation," Parker mumbled to herself. "A fucking brilliant explanation." Her eyes flashed again to the rearview mirror. The Chevy was pulling up fast. Parker noted her speedometer, she was now going about eighty miles per hour. She stared at the Chevy in the mirror. "Alright, jack-ass, you can ease up now."

The Chevy accelerated.

Parker gripped her steering wheel. *Is this guy going to ram me?* She jerked her steering hard left to pull into the empty oncoming lane and avoid being hit. To Parker's surprise, the Chevy also jerked to the left and stayed right on her bumper.

That's not good.

The Chevy eased off a little, riding Parker's bumper. She squinted for a better look at the Tahoe's driver, but its windows were tinted too dark to reveal anything. Parker switched back to the right lane. The Chevy followed suit. It gunned ahead.

Parker's body jerked forward as the Chevy tapped her minivan's bumper. "What? The? Fuck!" Parker stomped her minivan's accelerator. The Chevy's engine roared to life behind her. In no time, Parker was speeding down the road at 92mph and the Tahoe was still closing in.

Parker knew there was no way her minivan was going to outrun this Chevy. "Siri, call the Sheriff!" she yelled. Parker swerved into the opposite lane again to avoid being run over.

"Calling the Sheriff now," Siri calmly replied. The digital chirping started to break up signaling a weak connection.

"Come on, come on!" Parker's speedometer held at 93mph. The RPMs were maxed out. "Come on, you stupid minivan!"

The Chevy's imposing blue hull pulled up alongside Parker.

"Something went wrong with the call," Siri explained. "Shall I try again?"

"Yes, fucking try again!"

The Chevy swerved closer to Parker's minivan, causing her to flinch off the road, but never touching her. Parker's tires squealed as she straightened out.

"Calling the Sheriff now," Siri said again. The phone chirped again in an attempt to connect.

The Chevy swerved at Parker, just barely missing her as she edged away off the road. "Fuck, is this guy playing? Or trying to kill me?"

Parker looked away from the Chevy and glanced up the highway. A small, but sizeable gas truck had rounded the next bend and was heading directly for her. Its foghorn blared out warning, but there was nowhere for Parker to go.

"I know!" she growled. Parker pumped the brakes in an effort to swing behind the Chevy, but it mirrored her move. When she sped up to pass, it matched her speed. "Stop it!" Parker screamed at the Chevy.

Smoke erupted from the gas truck's tires signifying it slammed on the breaks. Parker had no choice but to slam on hers, causing her minivan to shake and shimmy. The Chevy raced ahead, disappearing around the bend, leaving Parker and the gas truck to face each other head on in a game of melting rubber versus shrinking road space. Parker's ears filled with the grind of the anti-lock system. She prayed that both she and the truck driver had tried stopping in time. When she decided they hadn't, she released her brakes and swerved to the right. She accelerated past the truck, scraping the side of her van on the edge of its grill.

Parker's minivan flew onto a small dirt clearing off the side of the road. She slammed on the breaks, kicking up a dust storm as she skidded to a halt. She wiped beads of sweat off her forehead, just as Siri connected.

The phone clicked on. "Parker?" asked an annoyed Bill. "What is it now?"

73.

Parker pushed open the front door to her house with an exhausted sigh.

The post adrenaline rush of her near-crash experience had left her feeling hollow, raw and more confused than ever. Ally scampered in from the kitchen with bright eyes and open arms, but Parker barely had the strength to lift her.

"Mommy!" Ally cheered.

Parker held her youngest as tightly as she could. Her arms trembled. "Oh, you have no idea how much I need this, Ally!" Parker whispered.

Valerie, Drew and Maddy were quick to follow. Drew rushed into his mother's arms. "Mom, I'm so glad you're okay!" he said as he squeezed her tight.

Parker looked to her mother. "You told them?"

Valerie calmly brushed a strand of hair away from Parker's forehead. "Was I not supposed to?" asked Valerie. Her eyes scanned Parker up and down, no doubt, as if examining her for holes.

"I didn't want the kids to worry," answered Parker.

Arms folded, and head tilted toward the floor, Maddy glared at her mother. "Worry about what? You almost getting killed?" she asked snidely.

"Maddy!" Valerie stared down her granddaughter. "Mind your tone. Your mother's been through enough."

"Didn't have to be," Maddy scoffed. "All she had to do was pick us up from school." She turned to Parker. "Where were you? What were you even doing?"

Parker tried clenching her fist, even that felt difficult. "Maddy, I don't need to explain everything I do in a day—"

"We've already lost Dad!" spat Maddy. Tears welled up in her eyes. She turned back to Valerie as if appealing to a judge. "It's like, she won't stop until she joins him! Am I the only one who sees it?"

"This isn't your mother's fault!" Valerie insisted.

"You sure about that?"

Parker was about to step in when Valerie, in a rare moment of concise and direct parenting, put her foot down and pointed to the stairs. "Go to your room."

Parker's jaw dropped agape – almost as wide as Maddy's.

"I didn't do anything!" Maddy shouted.

"I won't say it again."

Tears in her eyes, Maddy sauntered up the stairs without a word.

Valerie turned to Parker and noted her expression of shock. "Don't look at me like that. I'm your mother."

The doorbell rang, snapping Parker out of her stare. "Umm, that would be Bill."

"We'll pick this up later," declared Valerie. She snapped her fingers at the kids. "Drew, Ally, let's head back into the kitchen and finish dinner."

Holy shit-balls, Mom, that was some serious parenting you just threw down!

Still trembling, Parker took a deep breath in an effort clear herself and spun on her heel. She opened the door to reveal Bill's smug smile.

"You okay?" asked Bill.

Parker nodded. "I think I'm still in shock." She looked back to watch her mother disappear into the kitchen. "About a lot of things."

"You know, I'm half tempted to think you concocted this whole car chase story to get me to rearrange my schedule and come over." Bill stepped into the entryway and took off his hat.

"Ha, ha, not funny." Parker gently shut the door.

Bill sighed. "A guy can dream, right?"

Parker looked at Bill awkwardly. *Was he—attempting to flirt? Come on, Bill, let's not do that now.* "What did you find out?"

"Without the license plate number, I can't be sure. There was a report filed about a stolen blue Chevy Tahoe just outside of town a few days ago. Fits the profile of a Los Zetas gang that operates near the border. The same one that I think may have taken your car and returned it with Heller's body. My guess is they were out joyriding when they found you on the open road and decided to have some fun."

Parker shook her head. "Nope. I'm not buying it. It happened just after I left Bernstein's place."

"I will admit the timing is suspicious, but—"

"Oh, right, *Saint Bernstein* is above reproach,'" Parker was sure to use air quotes.

"I never said that."

"You haven't said anything. That's the problem," accused Parker. "Why are you so protective of Bernstein? What does he have on *you*?"

Bill smirked. "It's not like that."

"Then what's it like?"

Bill looked toward the kitchen, as if sensing Valerie might be listening. "Can we go out back? Talk where there's a little more privacy?"

74.

Bill and Parker stepped onto the freshly cut lawn behind Valerie's house.

It was a large sized plot, private just as Bill had hoped, and entirely fenced in. Bill placed his hat back onto his head and stared at the oak trees along the fence's edge. "Before I was Sheriff," he started. "Before I was even a deputy, I was a border patrol agent."

Parker examined the Sheriff closely as he sheepishly dug the tip of his boot into the grass. "Go on," she prompted.

"I didn't last at it for more than a year. My duties mostly revolved around the border checkpoint. Inspecting vehicles. Making sure no contraband was entering the country. Guarding against gang members trying to sneak in. Coyotes. Drug trafficking. Illegal aliens. I inspected a lot of people during that time. Most of them I'd never see again. But there were a few regulars who'd come and go. One of them, was a guy named Gerome Bernstein. I saw him nearly every weekend."

"Why so many trips to Mexico?" asked Parker.

Bill smiled. "He loved the culture. The people. The music. He even volunteered to teach music down there. I don't know how it all started, but every weekend Gerome would drive his car, jam packed with all sorts of musical instruments, and he'd work with kids and adults at various churches in poor towns. He usually travelled alone. Eventually this young woman joined him, Imelda. He told me she was a parishioner at one of the churches. They fell in love. Got married. From that point on, she accompanied him on every trip. I visited with them whenever I inspected their car. They were nice people. Friendly, and a welcome break from those I had to pull aside for a closer look."

Parker tilted her head to the side. "Okay. I don't know why you couldn't just have told me this over the phone."

Bill coughed out a laugh. "Well, see, that's not the whole story." He swallowed. "Gerome and I had a routine when I inspected his car. I knew that station wagon inside and out. I took note of every instrument. I knew his inventory. And every weekend, he pulled into the checkpoint like clockwork. Except for one day—" Bill's voice drifted off. "I'll never forget it. Gerome was tenser than usual. So was Imelda. They were polite as ever, but something felt—"

"Off," Parker finished his sentence. "Yeah, I know the feeling."

Bill nodded. "When I inspected his car, it was full of instruments like it normally was, all the same ones, but they were packed denser somehow. And that's when I saw it — two little wiggling tennis shoes just barely poking out of a blanket underneath all the instruments."

"They were smuggling a child into the country."

Bill nodded again. "And its mother."

"What did you do?"

Bill hung his head. "Nothing."

"You let them go?"

"Yeah," Bill kicked his toe into the grass again. "I cleared Bernstein. And then I went straight to the front office and resigned. That was the day I decided being a border patrol agent wasn't for me."

Growing up so close to the Mexican border, Parker was always of two minds about those who dared to cross it illegally, and those who assisted them. On one hand, she empathized for families desperately fleeing war and poverty to seek a better life in America. But as a reporter, she was also keenly aware of the abuses many of those same people suffered at the hands of human traffickers and drug smugglers. Children suffered the worst of it, often used as pawns to exploit loopholes in a catch and release legal system, or worse yet, traded as a commodity in human trafficking. Parker had always presumed an unspecified amount of Oak Creek's non-English population was "undocumented." But no one ever seemed to talk about immigration – legal, illegal, or otherwise. As long as the peace was kept, no one dared to stir the pot about the status of their neighbor. Parker now had no choice but to stir away. "Why didn't you turn them in?"

Bill shrugged. "You think I should have?"

"I'm not judging. I just want to understand."

Bill wrapped his fingers around his belt buckle. "Keep in mind this was twenty years ago. I was young. I was still trying to find my compass." He stared off into the distance, beyond the yard's fence. "I figured if a guy like Bernstein was willing to risk it all to sneak a mother and child across our border, they must've been decent people. I didn't want the kid and the mother to be separated. I don't know. I guess, in the end, I just didn't have the heart for it."

"If you were faced with that same choice today, what would you do?"

"My job." Bill said adamantly.

"You wouldn't be the first border agent to ever have let someone through," said Parker. "But if this got out, it would end your career."

Bill nodded. "I know."

"Does *Bernstein* know?"

"A year later, when I was just a deputy, I heard Bernstein started teaching at Oak Creek. His car was stolen, so I volunteered to go and take his report. I'd always been curious if I'd made the right decision. I went to his home and checked him out. I spoke with Imelda. They seemed alright. Then before I left, I told him what I had done."

"How did he react?"

"At first, he was scared, but then I assured him that wasn't the reason I was there. I just wanted to know who those people were, and what happened to them. He said they had met him through the church he volunteered at in Mexico. They were desperate to reunite with the husband who had already crossed the border but had fallen sick. Bernstein swore that was the only time he'd done anything like that, and if I had to turn him in, he'd come willingly. I said letting the mother and her child through was as much on me as it was him, and that we should both move on. So, that's what we did. Bernstein was incredibly grateful for that and went on to have a great career teaching music at Oak Creek. I promise you, he's not the one who killed Heller."

Parker folded her arms. "That's a real sweet story, Bill. But something is really off about Bernstein. Maybe he is a good guy, but maybe he's mixed up in something he shouldn't be. He is the common denominator in all of this."

Bill bowed his head. "I know. You're right."

Parker's eyes popped open. "I'm – what?"

"You're right." Bill opened his hands to Parker as an offering. "Everything you're saying makes sense. I don't know how that truck that nearly ran you off the road fits into all of this, but it has to be more than a coincidence. I'm going to check it out. I'll grab a few deputies and head back down to Bernstein's. Press him some more. See what shakes loose."

"Press Imelda," Parker insisted. "Her sister might be involved. And I'll do some digging of my own."

"Dig all you want. But you have to promise me you'll refrain from any more road trips like today's. Somebody's got it in for you."

Parker rolled her eyes. "Bill—"

"I'm serious, Parker. You could've been killed."

75.

Parker did her best to focus in her bedroom that night...

blocking out Bill's warnings, Maddy's tirade and trucks trying to run her off the road. The hazy red numbers of her childhood digital alarm radio clock turned to 12 am as she flipped through printouts of the school files she'd captured on her phone earlier that day. Parker had repeatedly poured over them since Valerie and the kids went to bed. But to her chagrin, nothing stood out as overly suspicious.

Heller's file was by far the thickest, having been at Oak Creek the longest. Heller always received reasonably high marks in her reviews, though the phrase "has a tendency to be overly strict with regard to disciplinary action" showed up more than a few times. Her salary was embarrassingly low for a vice principal, but judging from the other staff salaries, that seemed par for the course.

Gerome Bernstein's file presented as exemplary. *Of course, it does.* He'd received teacher of the year twice in the school, and once in the district. Bernstein's review scores were nothing less than perfect. The file even included several letters collected over the years written by parents who wanted to express their thanks and appreciation for Bernstein's work. "My son loves music because of Mr. Bernstein!" one parent wrote. "My daughter practices piano every day, and we owe it all to Bernstein!" another wrote. "Oak Creek's music program is the best I've seen in any school in the district," yet another proud parent exclaimed. "And that includes the Eagle's high school program!"

Really? Parker quietly balked in her mind. *Nobody has anything bad to say about this guy?*

Parker checked her phone, wondering if Bill had met with Bernstein yet. He hadn't texted her if he had, and there were no new emails other than one from a handsome Saudi Prince requesting Parker's social security number, so he could transfer sixty-nine zillion dollars into her account if she promised to keep it safe. Another new email popped up from PTA President Holly who had forwarded last year's PTA budget at Parker's request. Parker wanted to make sure her projections weren't out of line for those in their Boo Fest fundraiser.

Parker flipped to GI-Joe Ward's file. The shortest by far. He'd earned his online degree taking advantage of a Veteran's program that helped place wounded soldiers into the workforce. Oak Creek even received a tax break for employing him. But there was no mention of a dishonorable discharge from the Army as Bill had suggested a few nights ago, not that it would be in his school file.

Finally, there was Mendez. Other than the usual contact information, only a single paragraph went on to explain she was a Harvard graduate with a Master's in Finance. Parker took the liberty of scribbling in a few extra notes to fill in the blankness of the page including:

"overqualified"

"athletic build"

"painfully cryptic"

"hard to read"

"hot and cold – like the flu!"

"Looks way better in my navy suit than I do (never wear that around Mendez)"

"Shit—girl crush?"

"No--jealous."

"Who is Mendez? Really?? Where did she come from?!?!?!"

Parker's phone suddenly buzzed alive. She snatched it off her desk.

There is motion in your backyard.

Again? Parker spun around to peer out her window. The camera's security light beamed on and bathed the empty backyard in a bright white light. Nothing. She stood at her window, quietly, watching for any hint of the source that might have triggered the alert. No bird flapped away. No squirrel dashed across any branches. The yard was lifeless.

That was, until a long, dark shadow emerged from the shadow of the house.

Parker's heart jumped as she pressed her hand to the window, only to settle down when she recognized the outline of her mother slowly step out onto the lawn. Valerie was wrapped in her usual satin robe, her arms outstretched to support the shotgun that she aimed expertly at the fence line.

"Oh hell, Mom," said Parker to herself. "Go easy on the squirrels."

Parker watched Valerie scan the yard down the barrel of her gun for the next few minutes. In an odd way, Parker found it relaxing that her mother was so on the ball. When Valerie appeared satisfied that no intruders were present, she slowly lowered her shotgun and disappeared back into the house.

Parker yawned, and then rubbed her eyes. Feeling the night would yield no secrets to her, she took a final glance at her phone to skim Holly's email. Going over the ledgers was a sobering reminder of how much the school depended on the PTA raising money for their programs.

I really need to make sure I put more time and effort into this.

Parker couldn't believe all the items listed that the PTA paid for: playground equipment, computers, music instruments, office supplies, after-school programs, before-school programs, they supplemented lunches, breakfasts for kids in need and even—

Parker tilted her head. She reread the last item numerous times to be sure of it.

"Now—what the fuck is *that*?"

76.

The next evening, Parker opened the front door to greet Mr. Heller's twinkling eyes and disarming smile.

He wore dark slacks with a tweed jacket and had neatly combed what remained of this thin white hair. Heller clutched a brown leather document holder under his arm. "Am I too early?" he asked.

Parker smiled, impressed that the man had put some effort into dressing up for his visit to the Monroe estate. "You're right on time." She pointed to the document holder. "Is that for me?"

Mr. Heller's eyes brightened. "Of course! Yes!" He presented Parker the holder. "Though I'm not sure why you asked for them. It took a little doing, but you said they were important."

Parker took hold of the leather bag. "Oh, they *are* important." She resisted opening the bag right away, despite her desire to rip through every last page inside. There would time for that later. Instead she studied Heller's reaction to her receiving it. *He looks more confused than concerned. Either he's a wonderful actor, or he can't possibly suspect what these papers might detail.* "Thank you. Please, come in. Mom's prepared something special tonight."

Mr. Heller filled his nostrils with the scented wafts emanating from the kitchen. "Smells delightful. Chicken?"

"Duck."

"All for me?"

"It's the least we could do for having you come all this way." *And it might help soften the blow later.* "I know it's not easy for you to get out and about."

"It's already worth it." Mr. Heller happily followed his nose and stepped inside.

For the next hour, Mr. Heller sat with the Monroe family at their dining room table, enjoying the succulent pan roasted duck, paired with a bottle of Domain de la Vougeraie Clos de Vouget Grand Cru 2014. The French pinot noir was one of Valerie's most recent acquisitions, and at two hundred dollars a pop, well worth the price. Of course, to keep Maddy, Drew and Ally from grumbling about the entire dinner, an alternate meal of Kraft mac and cheese with extra, *extra* cheese was served with milk. In the end, Parker's gamble over dining with the kids had paid off. Heller delighted in their company, and even Maddy refrained from having any outbursts, something Parker wondered if Valerie might have warned her ahead of time against doing.

After dinner, everyone gathered in the front living room to listen to Maddy play the baby grand piano. While Maddy deftly worked her way through Chopin, Mozart and Rachmaninoff, Parker took the opportunity to scan through some of the documents in Heller's bag. She occasionally glanced at Mr. Heller, who didn't seem at all bothered at her studying the papers. Instead, he nodded in gentle approval to what he heard from Maddy, sometimes even softly tapping his foot.

Maddy finished with Moonlight Sonata, a surprise that instantly grabbed Parker's attention. Parker listened carefully to her daughter's playing. It was technical, almost robotic, but without flaw as she finished. *But she finished*, Parker thought to herself. *That's the first time she's finished the piece in one sitting since Kurt died.*

"Wonderful!" Mr. Heller applauded. "Thank you, young lady. I very much appreciated your playing for me tonight."

Maddy quietly closed her music book and nodded without so much of a glance at her guest.

Parker grinned. Maddy had completely disarmed Ken Heller, which would help make her job easier of asking some tough questions.

But Maddy's silence seemed to intrigue Heller, who shifted forward in his seat. "I do wonder," he said, drifting his voice.

Maddy paused and turned her head. "Wonder what?"

Heller kneaded his hands together with an impish grin. "Moonlight is such a brooding and somber piece. You played it perfectly. But—"

Maddy arched her left brow, a signal that reminded Parker of Valerie, who watched in earnest from across the room with Ally sitting in her lap. "But--?"

Heller looked to Parker as to whether he should proceed.

Parker's stomach tightened. *Maddy, please behave yourself.* She gave the nod.

Heller proceeded. "It also felt rather—hollow."

Oh hell, did I just consent to that?

Maddy's right brow raised up to join her left. "You're saying," Maddy swallowed. "It wasn't good?"

Heller attempted to disarm Maddy with a chuckle. "No, I said it was technically perfect. But music is more than just playing the right notes at the right time. It's about how the musician injects emotion and feeling into the song. Your emotion takes us on a journey. We feel what the musician feels. That is the difference between playing music—"

"—and making music." Said Maddy. She drew in a deep breath.

Heller's grin widened. "You've heard that phrase before."

Maddy's eyes welled up. "My Dad used to tell me that." She wiped a tear from her eye. "It's hard to explain."

"You don't have to explain anything," assured Heller. "The music will do it for you. If you let it." Sensing that Maddy was on the edge of breaking down, Mr. Heller placed his hands together as if in prayer, and bowed solemnly. "Thank you for your bravery tonight, young lady. I truly enjoyed your playing."

Maddy nodded and stood up from the bench. She paused a moment, then turned back to Heller. "If it's okay—I could play for you again. Sometime. If you want."

Parker's eyes widened.

"I would like that," answered Heller.

Fanning herself with her hand, Valerie cut through the warmth of the room. "Alright," she said, lifting Ally to her hip. "That's as good a segue as any. It's starting to get late, and I imagine you two have a lot to talk about."

"We do," said Parker. She broached Maddy and put her arms on her shoulders. "That was wonderful, Maddy. Thank you."

"Sure," said Maddy in her usual monotone voice.

Well, it wasn't an emotional gut punch, so I'll take it. Parker turned to her mother. "Thanks, Mom. The duck was fucking delicious."

"Oh my," said Heller, shocked at the language. He smiled at Valerie. "But I agree. What *she* said."

Valerie disappeared upstairs with the children, leaving Mr. Heller and Parker alone in the living room. Heller tried to hide his yawn. "I'm sorry, I'm not used to being up past seven. But a deal is a deal."

Parker sighed. "I'll try to keep this short."

"Don't worry about that." He pointed to the bank statements in Parker's hands. "Did you find what you were looking for?"

Parker frowned. "I think so."

"You don't seem happy about it."

"I hope I'm wrong. How involved were you with your wife's finances?"

"Not very. Karen had been running everything for years. She took them over when I was diagnosed with pancreatic cancer. My time in the hospital made keeping up with the bills very difficult."

"What stage of cancer are you in now?"

"Oh, Ms. Monroe," Heller chuckled with a dry cough. "I'm afraid, I'm on the encore." Heller shrugged. "I try not to dwell on it. Now is all about managing the pain."

"I imagine the medical bills have piled up."

"Insurance only covers so much."

Parker looked Heller dead to rights in his sad eyes. "Is that why your wife was stealing money from the PTA?"

77.

The light in Ken's eyes faded.

His charming smile all but disappeared.

"Oh, my," he muttered to himself. He pointed to the bank statements in Parker's hands. "Is that what these say?"

Parker took a deep breath and sidled over to Ken to show him the statements. "These only go back a year's worth, but there are deposits of $2500 into your joint account during the Fall, Winter and Spring of last year. These correspond with checks I found cut from the PTA made out to Karen Heller the same day, for the same amount, with a note on them regarding ADMIN-MISC."

"Okay," said Heller, trying to follow.

"The problem is, no one knows what ADMIN-MISC is. Do you?"

"No," Ken's posture slumped. "No one at school knows what that is?"

Parker recalled her efforts to find answers preceding the night's dinner. She had first called Holly, who confirmed she had no idea what ADMIN-MISC was but presumed it must be to supplement the cost of administrative office supplies. As last year was Holly's first year of being president, the PTA budget was handed to her directly by Karen Heller. Holly was told "this budget is how it has always been done." Not wanting to upset the apple cart, Holly never questioned it. Parker tried to follow up in person with Mendez, but the Principal was tied up at a district meeting all day. Mendez did confirm in an email that all administrative office supplies came from the school's budget, not the PTA's. Mendez also did not know of any item that ADMIN-MISC could have accounted for. Nor did the Silver Fox, who when pressed on the matter tersely informed

Parker that "the only person who could possibly know for certain is Karen."

"No one living," answered Parker. She pointed to the statements again. "There's more. Roughly two weeks after each $2500 deposit was made into your account, a corresponding check was written to someone else who cashed it just days later. See? Check 3178, check 3259. In the Fall and the Winter. But the name of the casher isn't listed here."

Ken's eyes narrowed. "There's no third check in the Spring?"

Parker shook her head. "No, but your wife did withdraw $2500 in cash precisely one week before school started this year." *Also, exactly one week before I arrived on my mother's doorstep.*

Ken took off his glasses to rub his eyes. "I had no idea about any of this." He looked at the statements again. "But I don't think those payments had anything to do with my medical expenses."

"You're sure?"

Ken pointed out a few other ledger lines. "These checks here? They were cashed by my insurance company. These other ones were to drug stores and the like. It's a lot of money, but between my social security and Karen's salary we managed it."

"How is your money situation now that Karen's gone?"

"My life insurance issued a modest check," stated Ken. "It's more than I need."

Parker noted Ken's drop in voice. This man was clearly hanging on to the hope of finding his wife's killer before he died. "So, if it wasn't to cover medical expenses, what was it for? Because it wasn't for the school."

Ken rubbed his eyes again. "I don't know."

"Would anyone have any reason to blackmail you or your wife?"

Ken coughed out a laugh. *"Blackmail?"*

331

"Karen wasn't exactly popular," explained Parker. *I, for one, considered her to be a nasty demon-bitch of the highest order.*

"That was never a secret," explained Ken. "Isn't blackmail used to *protect* secrets?" He looked toward the corner of his eye as if to loosen a blurry memory. "Unless--"

Parker's eyes lit up with hope. "Come on, Ken, whatever it is, just to tell me."

"You say she withdrew the last of the money a week before school?"

"That's what your statement says."

Ken rubbed his chin. "That was about the time two men came to our door one night."

Parker straightened her posture. "Two men?"

"It's hazy, I was having a—" Ken paused. "A bad night, if you will. There was a knock at the door. I was in my recliner, when Karen looked through the peephole and decided it was safe to answer. She opened the door and found two men dressed in dark suits."

"They wanted money?"

"No, they were agents of some kind. They were looking for someone. A man had gone missing. They were going door to door."

"Do you remember who? Did they give a name?"

"It was rather unusual," Ken squinted. "Downing. No. *Darling.*"

"Darling?"

"Yes. Karen told them she didn't know a man by that name, so they went on their way."

"Did you believe her?"

Ken gave a tired smile. "She was my wife. Why wouldn't I?"

The response made Parker wonder about her own relationship with Kurt. She was surprised, almost offended to learn he had called Valerie for parenting advice whenever he felt overwhelmed with the kids. Here was Ken, staring at strong evidence his wife may have laundered money from the PTA before she was brutally murdered, yet he appeared oddly unfazed. "You're taking all of this incredibly well."

Ken's smile faded. "No, it bothers me greatly. I won't pretend to understand why Karen took that money, and I don't know who she would have given it to. But I do know, she wouldn't have done something like that unless she felt it was vitally important. A matter of life or death." Ken bowed his head. "I guess, in the end it was a matter of *her* death, wasn't it?"

78.

Long after Ken Heller had left...

and agreed to have the bank pull digital scans of checks 3172 and 3269, Parker once again found herself wide awake at midnight, in her darkened bedroom staring up at the moonlit ceiling, going over every detail in her head. To her surprise, there was a gentle knock at her door. She sat up in her bed to watch the bedroom door creak open. Maddy stood at the threshold, her slender form backlit by the nightlight in the hall.

"Maddy?" asked Parker. "What are you doing up? It's a school night."

"I couldn't sleep," said Maddy. "Can we talk?"

"That depends on your definition of 'talking'," answered Parker. "Lately all I've gotten from you is attitude."

"I know." Maddy stared at the floor. "I'm sorry."

Parker felt a warmth ignite inside her. She knew moments like this with a pre-teen were rare. She scooted over to make room on her mattress and patted the pillow next to her. "Come on up."

Maddy slowly sidled up to her mother and lay next her. They both stared at the ceiling blankly. Maddy couldn't help but to immediately wince. "O-M-G, mother, how much time did you spend on *that*?" She pointed to intricate yarn strings that connected all of Ally's crayon drawings of suspects that Parker had apparently migrated from the kitchen wall onto her ceiling.

"Oh that?" asked Parker innocently. "An hour. Maybe two. It's literally the last thing I see before I go to bed every night."

"Mother, you are *obsessed*!"

"I know." It was Parker's turn to apologize. "I'm sorry." She pinched the bridge of her nose. "I just can't see the big picture yet. And it's driving me nuts."

"Why can't you?"

"There are too many pieces missing." Parker opened her eyes again. "And honestly, my mind is a wreck these days. Between this, the PTA, the fundraiser and trying to be a parent to you guys – it's a lot. I don't know how your dad did it. He managed you kids way better than I ever could."

"Yeah, he did." Maddy agreed. "But that's *all* he did. He gave up everything to be our dad."

Parker smirked. "Kurt gave up a lot, Maddy. But he never gave up music. That was always a part of him. It's a part of you too."

"Maybe. But it's what killed Dad."

Parker sat up in bed. "Why do you say that?"

Maddy sat up to look at her mother. "Well, it's true isn't it? He was trying to start his music career again. He died on the way to the show, right?"

Parker sighed. "Maddy, a drunk driver killed your father. You can't blame music. Or Dad for chasing after something he loved doing." Parker finally put two and two together. "Are you afraid that's going to happen to me?"

Maddy swallowed. "I don't want you to die, Mom."

Parker took her daughter into her arms and hugged her tightly. "Oh, Maddy. That's not going to happen." She hugged Maddy tighter. "I'm going to grow really, *really* old so that I can drive you even more crazy."

Maddy pulled away. "How do you know? What you're doing is really dangerous!"

"Maybe. But I'm not dying any time soon. For starters, if I did, who is going to write the best-selling novel of what's happened in this crazy town and turn it into a Hollywood screenplay?"

Maddy rolled her eyes but couldn't hide her grin. "Whatever."

"I'm serious. Momma needs to make it rain." She brushed a strand of Maddy's hair away from her forehead, just as Valerie had done to her the other day. *The apple doesn't fall far from the tree does it?* "So, are we cool? At least, for the next twenty-four hours until I do something else crazy?"

Maddy shrugged before plopping her head back onto the pillow. "I suppose."

Parker's phone buzzed to life.

There is motion in your backyard.

The security light popped on outside the window.

"What's that?" asked Maddy.

"Oh, something keeps triggering the sensor in the yard."

Maddy sprung up again on full alert. "Shouldn't we check it out?"

"I promise you, your grandmother is all over it."

Maddy turned to look out the window. She grinned mischievously. "Though you should know, in your novel? It would probably sell much better if your main character met some tragic end."

"Ouch!" Parker's heart skipped a beat. "Are you saying you want me to die now?"

"No," Maddy shoved her mother playfully. "I'm just saying, it would probably sell more copies. You remember that summer super-hero movie? Where the bad guy *won*? He destroyed half the universe!"

"Your point?"

Maddy threw her hands up in the air as if surrendering. "Just saying. No one saw it coming. It sold a lot of tickets."

"Maddy! I'm not killing my own character. Nobody's dying," insisted Parker. "Certainly, not anytime soon."

Suddenly, a loud booming noise exploded in the backyard. Parker and Maddy's eyes widened to the size of golf balls. They'd heard that sound before.

Valerie had fired her shotgun.

79.

"I saw a man,"

explained Valerie to Sheriff Bill. She rested her shotgun on her left shoulder, the barrel aimed safely up. "On my property. So, I shot him."

Bill squinted as he aimed his flashlight through the large hole torn open by buckshot in Valerie's wooden fence. "Whatever you saw, it's gone now."

"I saw a man," Valerie insisted. "Dressed in black. With a ski mask. He was hopping over the fence."

Bill turned to Parker. "Did your cameras catch anything?"

Parker shrugged. "It's hard make anything out other than some movement on the fence line."

Valerie frowned. "I know what I saw."

"Maybe it was a ghost!" a small voice yelled from behind.

Parker joined her mother to look up and spot Drew at his opened bedroom window on the second floor. "Drew!" Parker shouted. "Go back to bed! Maddy? See that he goes back to bed!"

Maddy emerged from the darkness behind Drew to tug at his arm. "Come on, cowboy."

Drew saluted his grandmother. "I believe you, Grandma! I hope you shot him good!"

Bill turned to Valerie. "Your neighbors called this in. You freaked them all out. You can't just go shooting at whatever moves out here!"

"I most certainly can," retorted Valerie. "This is my property. I will defend it as I see fit."

Bill waved his hands. "Listen. There's a lot of crazy stuff going on right now. If I'm going to station a deputy outside your home, I need to know that you're not going to accidently shoot one of them."

Parker stepped forward. "You can do that?"

"Accidents happen all the time."

"No, I mean, you can station a deputy at our home?"

"Yeah, well, I'm the Sheriff, right?" Bill pulled up on his buckle. "I don't know what's going on, here, but I don't like it. So, let's just play it safe." He pointed to Valerie's shotgun. "And play it cool, okay? In fact, maybe I should just take that for now."

Valerie clutched her shotgun tightly. "Over my dead body."

"Valerie, I need to know my deputies are safe."

Valerie offered a gentle smile along with the most calm and charming rendition of her voice. "As long as they don't invade my home they will be."

Parker tugged at Bill's arm. "Sheriff, a word?"

The Sheriff grumbled as Parker pulled him to the opposite side of the patio. "Parker, I won't put my men in danger."

Parker lifted her cell phone so that Bill could read its screen. "Look. She's not making it up."

Bill's eyes scanned the text message sent from Heller's phone:

Missed me!

"This was sent shortly before you and your deputies arrived," explained Parker.

Bill rubbed his chin. "I guess there's no point in tracking the phone this time. We obviously know where he or she was." He nodded to Valerie who eyed him like a hawk. "Does she know?"

"Who, *Grambo*? I'm not sure if it would make her more trigger happy or less. To be honest, I'm not sure if more trigger happy is a bad thing."

Bill scratched the back of his head as if weighing all his options. "Okay," he decided, stepping back to Valerie. "Here's how its going to work. For the next few days I'm going to have a patrol car keeping your house and the surrounding area under surveillance. My deputies will not step foot on your property, even if it's to check something out, without your permission. They will always identify themselves. They will always knock first or call first. You will never shoot first – at all. Nor will you meet any of them at the door with a shotgun."

"Handgun?" asked Valerie.

"No guns!"

Valerie playfully waved the Sheriff off. "Oh, I'm only kidding, Bill. Lighten up." She winked at Parker. "Or am I?"

"That's not helpful." Parker turned back to Bill. "If we're done, here, I'll walk you out."

"We're done," said Bill. He followed Parker to the side gate that led to the alley of the house. "I worry about your mother."

"She's the one person I don't worry about," stated Parker. "Did you follow up with Bernstein?"

"I tried calling," answered Bill. "Then I took some guys down there this morning to have a look around. He wasn't there."

Parker flung her finger at Bill. "Ha! See? He's probably digging buckshot out of his ass right now."

"So, I called him again in the afternoon," Bill added. "And he picked up. He said he'd been out. I went down to his place and met him. Imelda made lemonade. They introduced Pedro. Nice kid. I told him about your car incident, and he seemed gravely concerned about your safety."

"Shit!" Parker snapped her fingers in disappointment. "And I suppose you believe him?"

Bill hunched his shoulders. "I'll keep any eye on him. But he wasn't hiding anything about Pedro. That says something."

"I'm telling you," Parker shook her head. "I don't know how, but somehow he's involved in all of this."

"He's involved in *something*."

"Thank you again for such a quick response tonight."

"Well, your neighbors did call 911."

Parker let out a chuckle. "What I'm trying to say, is that you've been really fantastic these past couple days," said Parker. *Especially considering you thought I was being overly paranoid when all of this started.* "I feel like I should buy you a beer. Yes. In fact, that's what I'll do. I'll buy you a beer. Tomorrow night, at The Dive."

"Ms. Monroe are you asking me out on a date?" asked Bill sheepishly.

Parker let out a hearty laugh. "Ha! You're funny! A date!" She wiped away her smile when she noticed Bill wasn't laughing with her. "Oh hell. No! *Sorry.* I thought you were joking!"

"Awkward." Bill tried to take it in stride as he opened the next gate to the front driveway. The red and blue gumballs of his squad car washed the odd couple in their flashing lights.

Parker patted Bill on the back. "No, no, it's a PTA thing! There's a Bon Jovi cover band playing at the bar. I've invited a bunch of PTAer's to check them out. I'm thinking they might be fun for Boo Fest. 8pm. Join us. I'll buy you a beer."

Bill tried to smile. "You think that's a good idea?"

"Bon Jovi and beer are always a good idea."

"No, I mean, things are heating up, Parker. And you've said so yourself, whoever killed Heller was probably at your last PTA meeting."

Parker gently grabbed Bill by the shoulders. "Why do you think I invited *all of them* to come?"

Bill looked up to the night sky as if praying to the god of reason. "Oh, boy. So, this isn't just some PTA gathering. You're going to try and shake things up to see what happens."

"Oh yeah, baby."

"That is such a bad idea." Bill shook his head. "The killer is going to see right through this."

"Yeah, but that's exactly why the killer is going to show up tomorrow night."

Bill ruffled his brow. "I don't follow."

"He won't be able to resist. If it's one thing these dumb-ass texts from Heller's phone are proving, it's that Heller's killer is a narcissist a-hole who thinks he's way smarter than everyone else."

Bill looked directly at Parker with wide eyes. "Yeah, those people are *really* annoying."

"Right?" Parker waved off Bill's sarcasm. "The point is, he won't be able to help himself trying to prove how smart he is by standing right in front of me tomorrow night without me knowing. Which is when he will totally fuck up."

Bill rubbed his chin. "So, the killer's a *he*?"

"Sorry, force of habit. Most a-hole narcissists I've met over the years have been men. Though Karen Heller is a notable exception." Parker shrugged. "I don't know. Though Mom was certain she shot at a man tonight. And if she knows anything – she knows men. But it was dark. I guess, I can't rule out either sex yet."

"As long as you're *sure.*" Bill blew out his lips. "Maybe I should go to this thing. I could do it at the end of my shift. I've a feeling you're going to need back up. You're smart, Parker. But this guy or girl or whatever this killer is – they've been a step ahead of you the whole time."

"You don't need to rub that in." Parker grimaced. "But tomorrow night? That's when I catch up."

80.

A converted warehouse on the outskirts of town, the bar known as The Dive appears precisely as its name would imply.

The Dive boasts only two features, neither of which have anything to do with the quality or taste of its drinks. The first, is a giant neon sign depicting a shapely woman diving into a pool sized beer stein. The second, is the bar's sizeable pit that serves as a dance floor, making it a favorite destination amongst Oak Creek women seeking to escape the pressures of their jobs, husbands and families. A modest stage rises above the front of the pit, keeping whatever band is playing safely out of the reach of screaming mothers. Thursday night, that band was *Slippery When Wet*, and Parker Monroe couldn't have been more excited.

"Holy hell, these guys are really good!" shouted Parker as she navigated the crowd to bring two pitchers of beer to Glory, Julie, and Holly who sat at her circular wooden table left of the stage.

"What?" yelled Holly, who had stuck cotton balls in her ears to protect them from the booming bass of *Living on a Prayer*. Her eye practically twitched with the beat.

Parker sat down next to Holly and leaned toward her. "I said, we should book these guys for Boo Fest!"

After a rousing chorus, *Slippery When Wet* triumphantly finished their song, prompting the lead singer to pump his fist to the heavens and give a hearty "Thank you!" The bar erupted with cheers.

Parker beamed at the sight. "My god, that guy looks just like Jon Bon Jovi. Right down to that cocky dumb-ass adorable smirk."

Julie poured some beer into her mug. "You're dreaming, girl, that's not Jon Bon Jovi."

"I know that, Julie, I just think he *looks* like Jon Bon Jovi," insisted Parker. "I mean, how crazy would it be, if the actual Bon Jovi dressed up as a cover band and covered their own songs in disguise so they could intimately reconnect with their fans without the pressure that comes with their fans! Omigod, I just blew my own fucking mind!"

Julie remained unimpressed. "That's not Jon Bon Jovi."

"Maybe," a man's voice interjected. The new player poured himself some beer from the other pitcher at the table. "It's Jon Bon Jovi's half-brother, *Juan* Bon Jovi, in disguise."

Parker tilted her head, horrified both at the thin, middle aged man in a blue turtle neck that she did not recognize, and the ridiculously offensive joke that he had just made. "Um, we do not mock Bon Jovi here. Who are you?"

Turtle neck smiled and enthusiastically put out his hand to shake Parker's. "Oh, I'm Brad! Brad Jameson! I teach third grade!"

"Are you with the PTA, Brad? Because this is a PTA event, and I don't remember seeing you at the last PTA meeting." *And believe me, I'm keeping track. Especially tonight.*

Brad looked to Holly for an explanation. "I, uh, couldn't make it that night. Am I not supposed to be here? I thought all of PTA was invited."

Holly gingerly patted Brad's arm. "You're fine, Brad. Parker is just—" she looked at Parker, searching for the word.

"Curvy?" tried Glory.

Parker was just intoxicated enough to appreciate Glory's comment. "Bless you, Glory."

"*Intense.*" Decided Holly. She then smiled as if to soften the blow. "Though I don't know what I'd do without her help on Boo Fest. She's been *amazing!* I can hardly believe we're only weeks away!" The thought seemed to trigger more eye twitching. Holly tried to maintain her toothy smile, but it was clear the stress was getting to her. "I'm going to go powder my nose." The PTA President stood up and headed toward the ladies' room near the back of the bar.

Brad bobbed his head to the filler music as he tried smiling at Glory, Julie and Parker. "Yeah, groovy," he said awkwardly. He continued to bob his head to the beat, flustered that no one else seemed to appreciate his rhythm. "Yup. I'm going over *there.*" He pointed without looking and stood up to leave.

"Yup. Brad's the killer," announced Julie as she drew a long sip from her beer.

"No, Brad just kills moods," said Glory. He scanned the crowd around him. "You really think the killer is going to show up tonight?"

"I do," answered Parker. She'd been reading the crowd all night, making sure she'd greeted every PTA and school related person she recognized who paid the cover charge. Silver Fox and Baby Face even showed up, sitting together at a table in the far corner of the bar that was diametrically opposed to Parker's. More noticeable were the absentees. No Mendez, and no GI Joe.

"Well, nobody's died *yet.*" noted Glory.

"I don't think that's how this is supposed to go," explained Julie. She guzzled the rest of her beer and wiped the foam off her upper lip. "*How* is this supposed to go?"

"We observe. Look for anything out of place." said Parker. *Speaking of which* -- Her eyes suddenly spotted the semi-familiar face of a man ordering a drink at the bar. "I'll be back."

Parker approached the young man with brown hair and an athletic build from behind, so he wouldn't see her. Clearly bored, the man fiddled with his cell phone as he waited for the bar tender to finish filling his mug from the tap. "Deputy Michaels," greeted Parker. "I almost didn't recognize you without your uniform." Parker had only seen him a handful of times. He was the first on scene to break the news to Ken Heller that his wife had been murdered. Bill spoke fondly of him as a "dependable right-hand man."

Michaels smiled at Parker and reached up to tilt the brim of a deputy's hat that was absent. He blushed when he couldn't find it and settled for a nod. "Ma'am."

"Are you here off duty because you're a closet Bon Jovi roadie?"

"Bon Jovi—is that who's playing?"

"Oh boy. Then you're here 'undercover'." Parker was sure to use air quotes.

The bar tender slid a full beer mug into Michael's firm grip. The deputy took a sip. "Technically, I'm off duty. But Bill asked me to keep an eye on things until he could show up. He thought the uniform might taint your 'experiment.'" He took another sip. "Any luck?"

"Not yet. You?"

Michaels lifted his free hand to reveal several slips of papers held between his index and middle fingers. "I've had four different phone numbers stuffed into the back of my pants like dollars in a G-string."

"So, a slow night for you too."

Michaels chuckled. "Bill said you were funny." Michaels took another sip of his beer. "Can I get you something?"

Parker kept her flirtatious smile in place as she studied Michaels' eyes. She couldn't help but find the timing of his appearance tonight rather suspicious. Then again, a quick text to Bill would quickly solve it. "I'm good, thank you." Parker pulled out her phone and texted Bill straight away:

You send Michaels?

Michaels nodded to Parker's phone, clearly aware of what she was doing. "Tell Bill, I said hello."

Parker's phone buzzed with Bill's reply:

Yup. He's good.

"If you need anything. If there's any trouble. I'm right here, okay?" assured Michaels.

The crowd erupted into cheering as *Slippery When Wet* once again returned to the stage. "Hello, Oak Creek!" yelled fake Jon Bon Jovi. "We've got a few more to go if we wanna get paid, so let's say we crank this to eleven!"

Parker patted Michaels on the shoulder. "I'm going to check in on Fred and Daphne." As the band started up again with a rousing rendition of *It's My Life*, Parker pushed her way through the crowds to make it back to her table where Glory and Julie sandwiched a newcomer at the table – Joe Ward the Gym Teacher.

"He was an 80's action hero!" Julie protested loudly at Joe. "You've seriously never heard of him?"

Joe greeted Parker with wide eyes and a plastered smile, the universal signal for help. "Parker! Omigod! Please! *Please* join us!"

Parker grinned mischievously. "Glad you could finally make it, Joe!"

Joe blinked as if in pain. "Just trying to support the cause!"

Parker's eyes narrowed at the vacant seat next to Julie. "Where's Holly?"

"I thought she went to the bathroom," dismissed Julie.

"That was, like, fifteen minutes ago."

"Maybe she had the taquitos," added Glory, who eagerly bit into another one of the appetizers.

348

"I'm going to go look for her," stated Parker. "You guys keep Joe entertained!"

Parker pushed her way through the crowd until she hit a long hallway that led to the bathrooms. "Holly?" Parker asked as she pushed the bathroom door in. The women reapplying their lipstick at the sink stared blankly back at her. No feet with Holly's shoes showed at the bottom of any stalls.

Parker returned to the hallway and eyed the men's bathroom door, half tempted to check inside. *It wouldn't be my first journey into one.* Then, she felt the cool breeze coming from further down the hall. She followed it to an exit door, slightly ajar as if to keep it from locking shut. Normally, underage teenagers would resort to such a tactic to sneak inside the bar.

Curious, Parker pushed open the door and stepped onto the cracked tar of the dark rear lot. It sported several large, metal garbage bins overflowing with plastic trash bags. An old beater of a Sprinter RV with the words Slippery When Wet painted on its side was parked off to the side. At the far edge of the lot was an SUV – a powder blue Honda Pilot parked just outside of a street lamp's circle of light.

No sign of Holly.

Parker was about to return to the bar, when she noticed the subtle movement out of the corner of her eye.

The Pilot was rocking from side to side, ever so slightly.

81.

Parker squinted at the rocking Honda Pilot.

Oh hell.

Under normal circumstances, she would simply let the matter be. But on a night like tonight, Parker had to know what was going on. She stormed across the lot up to the Pilot, noting the windows fogging over from the activity inside. She could hear a woman gasp in a high soprano voice.

"Oh god, oh god, oh god—" the woman's voice steadily climbed each note of an octave.

Parker pulled on the latch of the rear's passenger side door. The door was unlocked, and flew right open, revealing the heads of a middle-aged man on top of a woman, pumping away to her obvious delight. The woman looked above her as she climaxed, only to notice Parker's glowering stare.

"Oh god! Oh *shit!*" yelled the woman.

"Hello Holly," greeted Parker.

Brad the turtle-necked third grade teacher looked up and smiled exhaustedly. "Oh, hello!" he said with a proud sigh. "I'm Brad!"

"We've met."

Holly was not so proud and scrambled to push Brad off of her. "Oh, shit, oh shit, oh shit!" she mumbled.

Brad pulled up his pants. "What's the big deal?" he chuckled. "We're both married!"

"Not to each other!" Holly reminded.

"Brad, I need to speak with Holly," said Parker. "Alone."

"But – I" Brad stammered as he fumbled with his belt.

"Beat it, Brad!" Parker barked. She jammed her thumb back over her shoulder to show him the way.

"We're still on for Saturday, right, Holly?" Brad hopped out of the SUV.

"Just *go!*" Holly wined. Brad practically skipped off as Holly buried her head in her hands. "Oh shit. This *isn't* what it looks like!"

"It looks like you're having an affair with Brad to relieve all your eye-twitching crazy stress in life."

Holly dropped her hands to look Parker in the eyes. "Okay, it *is* what it looks like." There wasn't even a hint of her tell-tale eye twitch, a fact the PTA president was eager to point to as if it might justify her actions. "See? No twitch."

"You could have sex with your own husband."

Holly frowned. "What do you think *started* the twitch?"

Parker folded her arms. "I don't care, Holly. You lied to me!"

Holly's jaw dropped open. "I did no such thing!"

"Really?" Parker furrowed her brow, temporarily distracted by the fact that Holly's breasts were still hanging out of her bra and opened blouse. "Can you--? Do something about that?"

Holly blushed and pulled her blouse tight to begin to correct her wardrobe.

Parker continued. "Tell me, Holly, how long have you and Brad been doing this?"

"Since last Fall."

"Mm hmm. And when did *Heller* find out?"

Holly rolled her eyes, realizing Parker had obviously already done the math in her head. "Last Fall."

"She threatened to expose you, didn't she?"

Holly's eyes widened in horror. "I didn't *kill* her, Parker!"

"But I'm right, right? She threatened to expose you!" Parker jabbed her index finger at Holly's heart.

"Yes, but I *didn't* kill her!" Tears began to form in Holly's eyes. "Is that what you think? I would never--!"

"No, that's *not* what I think," Parker clarified. "What I think is, Heller got you to sign off on extra money for the PTA budget in exchange for not telling anyone about your affair. Yes or no?"

Holly looked to the floor of her SUV. "Yes."

"So, when you told me you had no knowledge of what item ADMIN-MISC was in the PTA budget -- you *lied* to me."

Holly began to cry as she held her forehead. "I'm sorry. Yes! I lied! I couldn't exactly risk exposing me and Brad, now could I?"

"Expose—that's funny," Parker chuckled. "Your panties are still wrapped around your ankles."

"Oh god!" Holly slammed her knees together.

Parker pressed her advantage. "What did Heller need the money for?"

"I don't know."

Parker whipped out her phone and lifted it up as if to take a picture. "I feel a selfie coming on. Let's take one together for the school yearbook. What do you say?"

"I don't know!" Holly interrupted. "All Heller told me was that it was for some kind of special investigation. She said it was important for the school, but that no one could know about it. Not the teachers, not even the principal. Heller assured me, she would pay the money back!"

Special investigation? The term conjured memories of political wars between Congresses and Presidents. *Obviously, that can't be what Heller meant.* "Anything else you forget to tell me?" asked Parker.

Holly shook her head. "No," she groaned. "Are you going to tell anyone?"

"About Heller's PTA secret fund? Eventually."

Holly's face turned hot. "I mean about *me and Brad.*"

"*Riiiiight,*" Parker was sure to be over-dramatic in her delivery. "Here's the thing. I don't want other people to know, that I know about Heller knowing about you and Brad, and you knowing about Heller's money."

"Okay—so?"

"For now, let's keep this between you and me."

"And Brad."

Parker rolled her eyes. *Yes, that idiot, too.* "And Brad." Parker's phone suddenly buzzed in her hand.

It was a new text message from Evil Incarnate – aka: Karen Heller.

Where, oh, where, could my dear Parker be?

Holly couldn't help but to notice the color drain from Parker's face as another text buzzed in.

Are you hiding from me?

"Parker?" asked Holly. "Are you okay?"

82.

Parker surveyed her surroundings to make sure she and Holly were still alone.

"I'm fine," said Parker. *But things are finally starting up.* "I think we should head back inside. Together."

"Fine," Holly rolled her eyes. "Can you turn around while I—pull up my undies?"

Parker turned her back toward Holly just enough to keep her in the peripheral but grant some privacy. Parker's thumbs worked madly on her phone while she shot glances around the backlot. Was the killer out there? Or was he or she actively searching for Parker?

Regardless, I think it's safe to cross Holly off the list, thought Parker. Her mind scrambled to make sense of the "special investigation." *It can't be anything official. Bill would've mentioned it. Heller must've meant a "private" investigation.*

On a hunch, Parker punched a search into her phone with three key words:

`darling - private - investigation`

Parker smirked at the headline result at the top of the search page:

Darling Detective Agency - Los Angeles, California

Bingo.

A related headline below it announced an even more chilling coincidence:

Los Angeles Detective Gone Missing While Working Unknown Case...

"I'm ready," informed Holly. She smoothed out the rest of her dress. "You're not texting anyone about this, are you?"

"I told you, it's between us," Parker assured Holly. Her phone buzzed again from another text – again from Heller.

There you are!

Parker's stomach turned. She looked up to notice the dark silhouette appear at the bar's exit door. Concerned for Holly's safety, she pushed the PTA president back into her SUV and slammed the passenger door shut.

"Hey!" Holly growled.

Parker climbed into the front seat and locked the car. "You have your key fob?" she asked bluntly.

"Yes, but what is going on?" Holly yelled.

Without a word, Parker punched the ignition button on the Honda Pilot, and threw the SUV in reverse, thrusting Holly forward into her seat. Parker sped out of the lot backwards, never taking her eyes of the bar's back door. She watched the shadow move back inside.

"Parker!" Holly screamed angrily.

Parker revved the Pilot forward now, speeding around the side of the bar into the front parking lot where she skidded to a halt before the entrance. "Holly!" Parker yelled back. She locked onto Holly's eyes with a steely gaze. "Listen to me. No questions. I need you to drive home and lock your doors. *Now.*"

Holly's eye twitch returned. She knew Parker was dead serious. "Okay," she whispered. "Okay, I can do that."

Parker jumped out of the driver's seat, allowing Holly to climb in from the back. "Go!" She smacked the side of Holly's Pilot as if spurring on a horse. Holly stomped the accelerator to leave the parking lot.

Parker stormed toward the entrance of the bar.

Oh, it's on now, you murdering bastard.

Parker's thumbs worked her phone again, this time texting Sheriff Bill:

Killer is at the bar. Alert Michaels.

Parker's phone buzzed in response. To her disappointment, it wasn't a reply from Bill, but another reply from Heller's number.

You're not chickening out, are you, Parker?

Parker angrily punched in a response. It was a guess at best, an empty bluff at worst, but she had to try and go on the offensive.

I *know* about Detective Darling. You killed him too.

Heller's phone replied.

I'm not finished.

Parker flashed her hand stamp to the bouncer at the entrance and entered the main floor once again. Her eyes found Glory and Julie at their table on the other side of the room. They might have as well been a world away. *Option B*, she thought. Parker turned to search the bar stool where she'd last seen Deputy Michaels, Option A – only he wasn't there. *Shit!*

Parker took another step in the room, only to be cut off by the large, imposing body of Joe Ward.

"Hey, Parker," greeted Joe with a smug smile. "I've been looking for you."

83.

Parker's heart raced as she stared Joe down to gauge his intentions.

"You have?" she asked innocently.

Joe's eyes narrowed as he, in turn, tried to read Parker. "Yeah. I think, you and I have *a lot* to discuss."

Parker's stomach twisted. Was there something more in Joe's tone? Or was she simply imagining it? Could he have been the one sending Parker cryptic texts off Heller's phone all along? "We do?" Parker asked, trying to buy more time.

Joe stepped closer until he was inches away from Parker. She could feel his hot, beer laced breath on her face. "Is there somewhere we can go to talk? Just the two of us?"

Parker curled her fingers around her phone and lifted it to her chest. *If he is the killer, and he mistakenly left Heller's phone on, all I need to do is call it.*

Joe's smile dissolved into a frown. "What -- you need to call for back up or something?"

Parker looked Joe straight in the eyes. "I *really* need to make this call."

"And I *really* need to talk to you," Joe insisted. As though realizing he might be coming off as overbearing, or perhaps pretending to realize it, he forced a smile. Joe gently put his hand on Parker's phone wrist, encouraging her to put the phone down. "Come on, let me buy you a beer."

"Is this guy bothering you?" asked a new voice.

Parker watched Michaels step in and press against Joe. Michaels winked at Parker, apparently having gotten the message from Bill to be on the lookout.

Joe spun on his heal and puffed his chest to confront Michaels. "Hey man. We're just trying to have a conversation. The lady doesn't need any help."

Michaels stepped closer to Joe. "I wasn't asking you. I was asking the lady."

Parker used the distraction to access Heller's phone number and call it. As it dialed, she watched Joe for any hint of a reaction if his cell phone rang or vibrated. The gym teacher's eyes never left the deputy's, as the two continued to size each other up. As far as Parker could tell, no phone was ringing on Joe's body. *Then again, the phone could simply be off.* Parker stepped in. "It's fine," she said to Michaels. Parker gently put her hand on Joe's arm in an attempt to defuse the situation. "A beer sounds really good."

Joe flashed a sarcastic smirk to Michaels. "See? She'd like a beer." Joe nodded to Parker. "I'll get two and meet you back at the table."

Parker pushed out a smile as Joe waded through the crowd toward the bar, leaving her to Michaels.

"Sorry," said Michaels. "I didn't know if you were in trouble, or if I should step in or—"

"Your timing was perfect," said Parker. "Heller's killer is here. I've been getting texts from her phone."

Michaels furrowed his brow. "Well, who is it?" He nodded toward Joe at the bar. "Ranger boy?"

"I'm still working that—" Parker's sentence was interrupted by a huge cheer near the bar's entrance. A small crowd of teachers and PTA parents had encircled a new patron. Parker squinted for a better look but couldn't make anything out with the shifting bodies. "Stay sharp. I'll be right back."

Parker pushed her way to the front. To her surprise she discovered the fired music teacher, Gerome Bernstein, frantically hugging PTA'ers as though they were long lost family.

"It's so good to see you!" one PTA mother exclaimed.

"How have you been, Gerome?" another asked.

Parker closed in on the former music teacher to join the chorus. "Gerome Bernstein!" she shouted louder than anyone to take instant command of all conversation.

Gerome Bernstein blinked with a smile. "Parker Monroe!" he playfully shouted back.

The two met in an awkward embrace.

Bernstein took Parker's hands into his, then dropped his face into a concerned pout. "I'm so sorry to hear what happened to you the other day. Are you alright?"

Sure, you are. "I'm fine," Parker answered.

"And to think it happened not far from my home!"

"I *know!*" Parker gritted her teeth. She didn't have time to waste and went straight for the jugular. "What the fuck are you doing here, Gerome?"

Bernstein blinked again. "I was," he winced as if in pain. "I was invited!"

"By *who?*" Parker asked bluntly. *Because it sure as hell wasn't me!*

Bernstein stammered at Parker's question. "I uh—does it matter?" He grimaced. "Do you not want me here or something?" The PTA'ers around Parker began to sour on her.

"What the hell, Parker?" asked one.

"How rude!" proclaimed another.

"Of course, I want you here," said Parker in her worst patronizing voice.

The twinkle in Bernstein's eyes faded. "You don't trust me," he declared.

Parker dropped the facade. "It's not that simple," she answered solemnly.

Bernstein's face contorted into a mixture of fear and anger. "These people are my friends, Ms. Monroe," he stated, straightening his posture. "*They* trust me. And if you don't mind, I'm going to go spend some time with *my* friends." Bernstein pushed past Parker to disappear into the crowd.

Parker sighed and stared at the crossbeams of the ceiling. "Fuck!" she yelled, her cursing swallowed by the loud music. Her phone buzzed again. She scowled at Heller's latest text:

You should have left it alone.

Parker instantly pressed "call back" on her phone and scanned the crowd around her. Half of the PTA looked like they were on their phone, either taking selfies, texting their kids good night, or doing any of a thousand things that were unrelated. *FUCK!* Parker screamed in her head. Her eyes met with Michaels who stood next to the bar. He hunched his shoulders to match the puzzled look on his face. Parker mimicked him, mouthing the words: "What do you mean?" Then she saw it, or more accurately didn't see it -- Joe was not at the bar where he said he would be. In fact, Joe was nowhere in the bar.

Parker's phone buzzed again with a Heller text:

You made me do this.

84.

Parker's blood boiled.

If only she could reach through the phone, grab the neck of the killer, and yank it back so she could come face to face with him. Was it Joe? Did he have Heller's phone? Was he the one screwing with her this whole time? Why?

Parker pushed her way back to her table, only to find Julie sitting alone as she played a puzzle game on her phone. "Where's Glory?" asked Parker.

"Little boys room," said Julie. Hearing the intensity in Parker's voice, she sat up at attention. "Why? Is something going on? Something's going on, isn't it?"

"We need to split up and find Joe Ward. *Now!*"

Startled by her friend's assertiveness, Julie jumped up from her seat and saluted. "On it!" She held up her phone as she pushed into the crowd. "I'll text if I see him!"

Parker started to push in the other direction. The next several minutes of searching felt like a lifetime as she jostled for position through the crowd. When Slippery When Wet finally finished their encore, and the crowd jumped up and down screaming, Parker felt as if she were going to lose her mind. Now, Parker couldn't find Julie, Glory, Michaels, Joe *or* Bernstein. All the faces around her blended together. Parker shoved her way toward the long hallway that led to the bathrooms. The hall was empty save for the figure of a man running at her at full speed. Parker squinted. "Glory?"

Out of breath, Glory met Parker and grabbed her by the shoulders. "You gotta come quick! It's bad! It's really, really bad!"

Without looking, Parker instinctively grabbed a long neck beer bottle off a nearby waitress's serving tray. Her eyes finally locked onto Michaels, who appeared just yards away. "Michaels!" she yelled at the top of her lungs. "Michaels!" she screamed again, this time getting the off-duty deputy's attention. Parker pointed to the hallway. "Meet us over there!"

Michaels began to work his way toward Parker, but she refused to wait any longer. Parker ran down the hallway with Glory, who couldn't help but notice the beer in her hand. "This is no time for a beer!" he lectured.

"I agree," said Parker. She slammed the top of the bottle on the corner of the wall, spraying beer all over the floor. The action created a crude weapon of sharp and jagged edges.

The pair rounded the corner to find the bar's rear exit door wide open. The doorway revealed a small horrified crowd gathered around two men fighting on the black top. Parker blinked. It wasn't two men fighting. It was one large man, straddling a much smaller man as he wailed into his face with his fists.

Parker gasped as she recognized both of them. Joe Ward was beating Gerome Bernstein to within an inch of his life.

"Joe!" Parker shouted, pushing the onlookers out of the way. "Stop it! Joe what the hell are you doing?"

Joe did not heed her. A wild man enraged, the gym teacher smashed his knuckles repeatedly into Bernstein's bloodied face.

"Joe, stop it!" Parker tried again. She watched in horror as Bernstein's once flailing hands suddenly went limp and fell to his sides. Judging from the amount of blood flying into the air, the music teacher was either unconscious, or dead.

Parker threw her broken bottle at the back of Joe's head as hard as she could. The jolt gave Joe pause. He twisted, his blood-spattered face turning with wild eyes that now targeted Parker. Joe's muscles trembled, pumped to the brink of so much adrenaline that his fists actually shook, as if he couldn't control them. For a split second, Parker hoped she'd detected a hint of recognition and reason – as if Joe might have suddenly recognized the horror he had inflicted. If either had ever occurred to him, the thought had all but vanished in the next instant as Michaels barbaric yell came at him like a freight train.

The deputy charged through the crowd and bulled into Joe, throwing him off of Bernstein. The two men rolled onto the ground.

Parker and Glory rushed to Bernstein's body, checking for breathing of any sort. She wrapped her arm around his wrist.

Bernstein has got a pulse. He's barely breathing. But for how long?

Meanwhile, Michaels tried to get a punch in with the ex-ranger. But it was only seconds before Joe had trapped the deputy's wrist and twisted it around. A horrifying crunch sounded as Joe broke Michaels' arm, prompting the young man to release a cry of agony.

Joe followed up with a hammering punch to Michaels' nose. He shoved the deputy off and rolled over to glower at Parker, still hovering over Bernstein's body. Parker watched in horror as Joe climbed to his feet and lumbered towards her. "Joe, stay away!" shouted Parker. "You've lost control, you need to *calm down!*"

Joe shook his head angrily. "Get out of my way, Parker!" he growled. "He deserves it!" Joe leaned forward as if ready to pounce, when suddenly his entire body seized up.

Joe's eyes suddenly rolled up into the back of his head as a loud cracking noise emitted in the air. Joe dropped the ground, spasming from the fifty thousand volts injected into his body from two metal prongs launched via curly wires from Sheriff Bill's taser gun.

Bill stepped up to stand over Joe's paralyzed body. The Sheriff looked up at Parker, then down to Bernstein's bloodied face. "Sorry, I'm late."

"Jesus, Bill!" shouted Michaels, cradling his broken arm. "Are you ever!"

Ambulance sirens echoed throughout the night's sky.

Parker pointed to Glory who stood transfixed over Bernstein's body. "Glory, can you go and get some clean, wet rags or something from the bar?" She cradled Bernstein's bloodied head in her lap. The music teacher gasped for air. "Hold on, Bernstein. An ambulance is on its way." She watched Bill turn Joe's limp body over and pull his hands behind his back.

Joe managed a groan when Bill cuffed his hands together.

Then, Bill suddenly backed off, startled by something. "What the hell is that?"

Parker's eyes narrowed as she heard the buzzing noise. "Check his back pocket."

Bill winced as he moved his fingers inside of Joe's back pocket. He pulled out a black cell phone that buzzed loudly as if someone was ringing it. "Someone's calling his cell phone," informed Bill. He looked to Parker for an explanation. "Is that you?"

Parker blew out an exhausted breath from her puckered lips. "Yup," she answered. Parker lifted up her phone to reveal the number she was calling. "Only, I wasn't calling Joe's phone. I was calling Heller's."

85.

One hour, two ambulances, three patrol cars, and twenty witness statements later...

Parker found herself sitting in a small plastic chair across from the Sheriff's vacant desk. Her ass throbbed nearly as much as her head, and her stomach relentlessly growled over filling it with so much beer but no dinner to absorb it. Parker insisted she give her official statement after all the other witnesses had been interviewed – she wanted time to sort the night out in her head, plus a chance to question Joe Ward directly. Bill had reluctantly agreed only if she was willing to accompany him to the station.

Finally, Bill opened his windowed door and solemnly walked in carrying an evidence bag. He slumped into his chair—exhausted. "He sure was a handful," muttered Bill. The Sheriff reached up to massage the back of his neck, then adjusted his hat. "But Joe Ward has officially been processed and booked."

Parker anxiously leaned forward. "Aggravated assault."

Bill tried to smile at the presumption. "That, and murder one."

"Murder one?" Parker balked. "For Heller?"

"Yeah, for Heller." Bill's jaw dropped. "Oh, come on, Parker. It doesn't get more cut and dry. You said so yourself, whoever has Heller's phone killed her. Joe Ward had Heller's phone!"

"You're going to need more than a phone to convict him," Parker chastised. "Like *motive*. I'd been calling that phone all night. And the one time I get through it happens to be in his back pocket for everyone to see?"

Bill shifted in his chair. "You're saying somebody planted it on him? Come on, Parker, I thought you'd be relieved. The guy is obviously dangerous! Joe nearly beat a man to death! Right in front of you!"

"I know, I know and that's awful!" Parker gritted her teeth. She knew Bernstein was clinging to life in the ICU of St. James Memorial Hospital. *He certainly won't be giving any answers any time soon.* "But it doesn't make any sense! Why would Joe do that? Why would he do any of it? It's like the guy completely snapped!"

"Well, it wouldn't be the first time, would it?" challenged Bill. "Remember? He was dishonorably discharged from the Army for beating his commanding officer to within an inch of his life. War changes people, Parker. It breaks them. Don't ask me to explain crazy."

Parker wagged her finger. "Something triggered Joe. What did Bernstein do to him? Why play these phone games with me? I never even knew the guy before coming back to Oak Creek."

"Yeah," Bill slouched back in his chair. "About *that*." Bill reached opened his evidence folder and pulled out a clear plastic bag with a black phone in it. He placed the bag on his desk, then tossed Parker some blue latex gloves to put on.

"Is this Karen Heller's phone?" Parker snapped the gloves onto her hands.

"You mean the one I lifted from Joe's back pocket? Yes."

Parker carefully lifted the phone out of the bag and turned it on. It instantly displayed its home screen. "Odd – there's no password to unlock it."

"I am aware."

Parker ignored Bill's terseness as she tilted the phone around, tracing its edges. "It has a thumb print button. Like we thought, the killer could have used Heller's dead hand to unlock it initially. Then he would have full access to change anything."

366

"The killer? You mean Joe." Bill folded his hands together on his desk.

"The *suspect*," Parker corrected.

"Look at the photo album. You might find your motive in there."

"In a second," said Parker. She was busy perusing the call history. She found the log of her own unanswered calls to Heller's number, but everything else occurring before them had been deleted. It was the same with the text conversations. Every creepy text that had ever been sent to her from this phone was there, but nothing before. "Looks like most of Heller's history has been wiped."

"Yup. Noticed that too. You get to the photos yet?"

"Yeah, yeah," Parker thumbed over to the photo album, which listed a total of thirty-one. After blowing up the thumbnails, she started to swipe through what at first appeared to be random shots. To her horror, she recognized the woman featured in every picture. "Holy shit! He was taking pictures of *me*?"

Bill nodded. "Creeped out yet?"

"Oh god," Parker's empty stomach began to turn. There were pictures of her shot from across the parking lot at school. There were pictures of her getting coffee at The Bean. There was one of her and her family walking into the funeral home for Heller's service. But the pictures toward the end were the most startling, shot at night over the fence line of her mother's backyard. The last four pictures captured intimate glimpses of Parker undressing in her bedroom through the slats of her window. "Shit."

"I know. I'm sorry. It's awful."

"Yeah, it is!" Parker held up the phone screen to Bill, so he could get a better look of the photo where Parker was awkwardly trying to remove her shirt, but it was caught around her neck. "This is the best shot he could take? I look *terrible*!"

"Wait," Bill blinked. "That's what you're upset about?"

"Fuck Almighty!" Parker growled. "I can't even stand to look at myself! I mean, I know it's been a while since I hit the gym, but gahhhhhhhh! We gotta delete these before they go any further. I will not have this shit turn up in some court hearing. Fuck. THAT."

"Parker!" Bill slammed his fist onto the desk. "That's evidence tampering and you're missing the point! Joe was clearly obsessed with you!"

"Oh, settle down, Bill, I figured that out!" shouted Parker. "Fine! Whatever! Say he was -- it doesn't explain why he murdered Heller and stuffed her in the back seat of my stolen car!"

"Um, it kind of *does*," Bill whined. "And there's more. We searched Joe's car at the bar." Bill threw another evidence bag onto his desk. "We found this."

Parker lifted the bag to inspect a series of needles, pill bottles and a plastic bag containing what looked like brown powder. Parker frowned. "Heroin."

"Along with some stolen prescription bottles," Bill explained. "Joe is addicted to pain killers. I think Heller found out about it and was going to fire him. Joe needed the job -- so he murdered her in a fit of rage and tried to implicate you to cover it up."

"That's terrible."

"I know. But it's the only theory that makes sense to me."

"No, I mean, that's a *terrible theory*." Parker shot up from her chair. "Where's the gun that shot Heller? *That* hasn't turned up."

"I'm getting a warrant to search Joe's house. Maybe it will turn up there."

"Where is Joe's *other* phone?"

"His other phone?"

"You think he walked around making every day calls from a dead woman's phone when he knew you could locate him? No, he had a normal, Joe-Ward-non-dead-woman-phone. *His* phone. And if you don't have it, then it's still out there somewhere."

Bill clenched his jaw. "Parker, I know you're used to dealing with big city cops. But I'm *not* an idiot. Neither are my deputies."

Parker folded her arms. "I know that." *Sort of.*

"Well, you sure as hell don't talk like you do. I'm doing you a huge favor by showing you all this stuff. I thought it might help you get some closure. But, you're refusing to see what's right in front of you."

"And you are refusing to look for what *isn't!*"

Bill's cheeks flushed red. He held out his hand. "I'm going to need Heller's phone back now. And I think you should go home."

"You need to take my statement. And you said I could question Joe Ward directly."

"Not tonight," Bill said tersely. He blinked again and drew in a deep cleansing breath. "We sedated him."

Parker's eyes narrowed. *Convenient. Are you truly so sour because I don't buy your dumb-ass theory?*

As if noting Parker's suspicions, Bill unclenched his jaw. "We *had* to, Parker. You saw what he did to Michaels. Joe Ward is dangerous. Regardless, we can't question him. None of it would be admissible. Give it a day. Let's see how he is after he's had time to cool off in a cell. After we've *all* had time to cool off." Bill extended his hand. "The phone, please."

Parker looked at Heller's phone in her hand. It was the only tangible evidence that might yet contain clues to adequately explain Joe's outburst, Heller's murder and everything in between. Parker needed more time with it, but she didn't want to push Bill any further. Parker slowly picked up the empty evidence bag. "'What the eyes see, and the ears hear the mind believes'," quoted Parker.

369

Bill couldn't help but let out an unexpected chortle. "You're quoting Houdini, now?"

Parker carefully angled the phone's screen toward her chest as she placed it back inside the evidence bag. "Believe it or not, I've tried to learn a little more about magic," admitted Parker. She paused, sheepishly looking down at Bill's desk. "You know, in an effort to understand *you* better."

"Uh huh. I'm flattered. And what have you learned?"

"It's still incredibly lame," Parker closed the evidence bag. "But I'll give you another quote: 'When a magician let's you notice something on your own, his lies become impenetrable.'"

"That's Teller, of Penn and Teller," attributed Bill. "Are you trying to steal Heller's phone from my evidence bag?"

"I wouldn't *dream* of it," Parker placed the clear plastic bag with Heller's phone securely in it on the desk. "I'm simply pointing out the idea that maybe, just maybe, my stolen car, Heller's murder, Joe's assault, the cat and mouse game on this damn phone – it's all hand waving. It's all a distraction."

Intrigued, Bill leaned forward. "From what?"

Parker swallowed. "I don't know. Yet."

Bill smirked and shook his head. "Go home, Parker Monroe. Rest easy knowing you helped catch a murderer tonight."

Later, as Parker walked to her minivan in the Sheriff's parking lot, her phone buzzed to life multiple times -- thirty-one to be precise. She smiled, knowing exactly what the incoming notifications were hailing. Parker lifted her phone to confirm she had received all pictures from Heller's album. While she was distracting Bill with magic quotes, she had secretly forwarded them as a mass text – a simple procedure since her own number was the last that Heller's phone had interacted with. Then, she clicked the screen off,

370

making it appear as if the phone was completely turned off, when in fact, it was quietly transmitting the data.

Maybe magic isn't so bad after all.

86.

Parker marveled at her mother's poise and grace at such a late hour.

If Valerie was tired, no red veins or bags under her eyes betrayed the fact. Her hair was perfectly combed, and the edges of her satin robes glided across the floor as she carried two bottles of wine to the kitchen table. Parker knew her mother looked good at any hour, but she couldn't help but to wonder if Valerie had taken extra care lately as if to dazzle anyone who might pop into the house in the middle of the night, be it a deputy, burglar, peeping tom, murderer or murder witness. Parker couldn't have cared less. She scratched her frizzy, unkept hair and unbuttoned the top of her jeans to breathe better before slouching over the kitchen table. With her arms outstretched and phone in her hand, she relentlessly swiped through the thirty-one photos looking for something, *anything* that might explain Joe Ward's behavior.

Valerie presented the first bottle. "Amarone," she said. "If you feel congratulations are in order."

Parker shot her mother an annoyed glare.

Valerie switched bottles. "Valpolicella it is, then, to take the edge off." Her manicured fingers immediately went to work with a corkscrew. Valerie plopped herself into the seat across from Parker, so she was sure to catch her peripheral. "You certainly don't seem very pleased for someone who helped crack a murder case wide open."

"Bleh," mumbled Parker, her speech impeded by her jaw weighing the table down.

Valerie popped open the cork. "You're not convinced Joe Ward killed Karen Heller."

"No."

"Why?"

Parker shifted uncomfortably. "I don't know. Something's off. I won't know until I question Joe."

Valerie arched a brow. "I wonder if that will be enough."

Parker glared at her mother again. "Enough for what?"

Valerie poured two glasses and gently pushed one to Parker. "Say Joe confesses. To everything. What then?"

Parker grimaced. "He won't."

"Say he does. And the Sheriff finds the murder weapon in his house. Say the evidence is irrefutable. What then?"

Parker threw her hands in the air. "Then it's over. We all go back to our lives."

"And you're okay with that?"

Not really. Parker pressed her lips tightly together as she quietly stared at her mother.

Valerie smirked as she sipped her wine. "I already know the answer. I was just curious if you could admit it."

Parker sat up. "You think I see this all as some kind of game?"

"Some girls like being chased, but not you. You've always been the chaser. It didn't matter what you were chasing, as long as you could run at it full speed. As a young girl whenever you solved a problem, or a puzzle, or won a game of tag, you'd be satisfied for all of five seconds before you looked for something new. You told me once there was no sadder death than that of a mystery's. I think you were twelve."

"I was *fucking poetic*, was what I was." Parker took a gulp of her wine and belched. "What do you think? You think Joe did it?"

"I think if I were quicker on the trigger the other night, you wouldn't have to ask." Valerie held her wine glass close to her heart. "Still, it's a shame, isn't it? The way Joe brutalized Mr. Bernstein. And if he did take those pictures, well—here I thought he was a decent man. Especially after his talk with Maddy. He struck me as more of the protective type. Maddy will be so disappointed."

Parker winced. "Wait – say that again?"

"Maddy will be disappointed."

"No, you used another word – 'protective'."

Valerie took a long sip. "Well, isn't that what soldiers are supposed to do? Protect. Defend."

Parker drummed her fingers impatiently on the table. "That's supposed to be the job, anyhow." A job Parker once had the impression Joe Ward took very seriously. Even a warped and distorted idea of "protecting" might help explain his violent behavior. *Joe said Bernstein "deserved it." Why?*

Valerie relished a gentle sip of her wine. "When are you going to tell Maddy?"

"Right -- *that,*" Parker poured more wine into her glass until it nearly overflowed. "Ideally, after I've had a chance to question Joe. But I don't think Bill's going to be able to keep his arrest quiet. Especially since all of the PTA watched him beat the shit out of Bernstein. I'll talk to Maddy after school tomorrow."

Valerie nodded. "Do you think all this drama will affect your Boo Fest?"

Parker dropped her head between her shoulders. "Oh hell."

"It's set for next Friday, isn't it?"

"Sure is. One week." Parker buried her face in her palms. "Gah, there's still so much to do and I can't get the image of Holly's panties wrapped around her bony ankles out of my head! I don't even want to deal with it. What's even the point now, anyway?"

Valerie slowly shook her head as if to cast judging shame over her daughter. "Music," she declared. "You made a pledge to your daughter, the PTA and the entire school to fund a music program for the children of Oak Creek. That applies with or without Bernstein. With or without Holly's panties, whatever that's about. And with or without murder. Well, preferably without any more murder."

Parker held up her hands dramatically as if to shield herself from the words. "Ugh! Stop talking so much sense!"

Valerie finished her wine, and stood up from the table, a clear sign she was ready to retire, but not without first dropping another mother-load bomb of wisdom. "I know it's not nearly as exciting as solving a murder," she started. "But the money you raise at this Boo Fest event will touch countless more lives and accomplish more for the community. You want to chase something? Chase that."

"I know, you're right," admitted Parker. She didn't bother pouring another glass of wine, instead taking the bottle directly into her mouth to chug the last of it.

Alright, Holly, let's finish this.

87.

"You're going to have to look at me eventually, Holly."

Parker issued her demand as gently as she could. She and the PTA President had bumped into one another in front of the school entrance the next morning, likely because Holly refused to make eye contact with anyone around her. As the last of the children and parents dispersed, the two ladies stood across from each other like an odd pair of gunslingers refusing to draw. Parker grimaced. *"Please*, can you look at me? We have to be able to work together if Boo Fest has any chance of succeeding. Maybe try a quick glance, like you're checking out my boobs without looking like you're checking out my boobs."

Holly threw her hand down to glare at Parker. "I would never do that!"

Parker cringed at the sight of Holly's insane eye twitching. It was the worst she'd ever seen. "Oh shit! *Wow!* That thing is really going isn't it?" It became obvious that Holly wasn't avoiding direct eye contact so much as trying to hide her malady.

"Damnit!" Holly's eyes welled up. "It is bad, isn't it?"

"It's like there's some kind of gnat trying to crack open the side of your face with a miniature jack hammer."

"Really?"

"Or you're trying to wink Flight of the Bumblebee in Morse code."

"Oh god!"

"You fell asleep face down on a taser during an earthquake."

"Parker!"

"I'm sorry, they're just coming to me."

"It's been like this since last night!" Holly sniffled. "It won't let up! Please, *please*, say you didn't tell anyone about me and Brad! Especially not Julie! She would spread it everywhere!"

I only told my mom. "Of course not!" *And maybe Julie and Glory after all this has blown over. We'll see.* "What can we do about this? How can we settle you down?"

Holly rolled one of her eyes. The other wouldn't cooperate. "Well, normally, Brad—"

"*Without* Brad," Parker insisted. *I'm not going to condone your having an affair. Though, if Brad was your husband I'd encourage him to bang you six ways to Sunday if that's what it takes to finish Boo Fest.* "What about weed? You ever smoke weed? I hear it's legal in California these days."

"I voted *against* that!"

Parker drew in a long, deep breath. "Maybe, you're just overly stressed because I saw you in a highly compromising position?"

"You think?" Holly blasted.

Parker ground her teeth. "What if I evened the odds?"

Holly paused. "What do you mean?"

Parker lifted her phone and swiped to the picture she had forwarded from Heller's phone. The one of her taking her shirt off in a most compromising position. "I'm only going to show you this once. So, drink it in." Parker held the phone up to Holly, giving her a twitching eyeful.

"Is that – *you*?" Holly held back a chortle.

"Yup."

"Oh my, you look—" Holly caught herself. The more the PTA president looked at the photo, the less her eye seemed to twitch.

Her face suddenly twisted into an expression of disgust. "Why would you take a picture like that?"

Parker yanked the phone away. "I didn't!" she snapped. "It's a long story. You feel better now?"

"I feel--confused." Holly pressed a finger to her eye, as if testing the skin's elasticity. The twitching had settled considerably, at least for the moment.

"Let's call that an improvement," said Parker. She swiped to her to-do list app on her phone. "Now, I went over our notes, and we need to remind Mendez to send out a list serv announcement, we've got ten volunteer shifts yet to account for, we need to make a down payment to the carnival ride company, we need to find a balloon artist, a face painter and build and place twenty signs around town this weekend to ensure maximum exposure. What can you handle?"

Holly nodded. "I'll cut the check and make some calls about the volunteers. I could also handle probably half of those signs."

"Perfect," Parker put her hand on Holly's shoulder. "We got this, Holly."

Holly winced. "Is that all? Don't you want to talk about what happened last night? I mean, when I heard what Joe Ward did—"

"Shhhhhhh," Parker gently pressed her finger to Holly's lips. "Don't tempt me. I've got to focus now and chit chat with our esteemed principal."

88.

"Shall I just walk into Mendez's office unannounced, or can you give me a little fanfare this time?"

asked Parker as she sidled up to the Silver Fox's desk.

"Principal Mendez is not in," Silver Fox stated formally as she madly typed away at her computer.

"What do you mean she's not in?" *And what are you typing about all the time? What do you even do all day?*

Fox paused her typing to swivel in her chair and address Parker more directly. "I don't know how much clearer I can be. I guess the alternative would be to say that 'she's out.'"

Parker gleefully clasped her hands together. "Oh good, we're bantering now. I *love* banter. When will she be back?"

"Monday—maybe."

"*Maybe* Monday?"

"Or Tuesday."

"Tuesday!" Parker repeated with feigned astonishment, pumping her fists in the air.

"Maybe."

"You *don't* say!"

"I *can't* say, really."

"You can't say, or you won't?"

"*She* didn't say, therefore I *won't*." Fox's eyes slyly narrowed. "Huh. Banter *is* fun." She began to type away on her keyboard again, ignoring Parker.

"Yeah?" Parker refused to be ignored. "You put a lot of banter into the smutty romance novel you've been writing during office hours?"

Fox's eyes flashed with anger. "I don't know what you're talking about!" Her finger reached for her monitor's power button.

Parker intercepted Fox's move, and quickly turned her monitor to the side so she could better read it. "Yeah?" her eyes scanned the screen as her arm fended off Fox's hands. "Well, the Glamazons of Uranus beg to differ!" Parker read further down the page. "Oh, wow, they're begging for a lot more than that!"

Fox shot up from her chair. "How dare you!"

"How dare *me*?" Parker balked while reading a few more lines. "You know, I was just bluffing before, but this really isn't half bad! Though, I doubt the Superintendent's Office would appreciate you using a school computer to write adult material."

Fox threw her hands on her hips. "What do you want, Ms. Monroe?"

Parker twisted the monitor back into place. "I want to know where the hell Mendez has been all this time!"

"I don't know! Okay?" yelled Fox. She huffed and puffed. "She comes, and she goes, she never explains herself, and she's hardly ever in her office! I'm the one who had to arrange for Mr. Ward's substitute today. Not her! Never her! I do all the work, and Mendez is a terrible, terrible Principal!"

Parker smiled calmly, satisfied with the shade of red in Fox's face. "Alright then. If you see her, please let her know she needs to send a list serv out about Boo Fest next Friday."

Fox blinked as she tried to reclaim her breath. "That's it?"

Parker headed toward the door. "What's your pen name for your smutty novel?"

Fox rolled her eyes. "Veronica Naples."

"I look forward to reading your finished work, Veronica." Parker pressed the door open. "Now, I've got to go see a man about balloons."

89.

"Can you not make it look like a man's penis?"

Parker asked Glory after he presented his meticulously crafted balloon sword in the Bean Coffee Shop later that morning. The arrangement of the double rings around the sword's hilt gave Parker the strong impression of a man's genitals, and the placement of the tie at the top of the blade was practically sperm coming out of the tip. Parker couldn't discern as to whether Glory intentionally had made the balloon to look so phallic, or whether it was some unconscious reflection of something deeper.

"A man's penis?" Glory's eyes widened, confused by the question. "Are there other kinds?"

Citing no other patrons in the shop to be offended, Bearded Man-Child couldn't help but to interject into the conversation from behind the safety of his bar as he mixed a drink. "If you include the entirety of the animal kingdom, there are several kinds," informed Man-Child.

Glory appeared concerned by this new revelation, as if somehow these other penises might mean more competition for his own. "Woah."

Parker tried to stay on task. "Can you just remove one of the ball sacks and then flip the blade around?"

"Oh, sure." Glory did as instructed, and in no time, his edited balloon appeared as a family friendly pirate sword. "How's this?"

"Perfect! What else can you make?"

Glory held out his hand to count on his fingers. "I can do princess crowns, elephants, horses, poodles, and a bunch of other crap."

Parker sighed. Her bet that somewhere in Glory's wide array of useless talents was a master balloon sculptor had paid off. "You're hired."

"Wow, really? The gig pays?"

"No. I didn't mention it was volunteer work for the school?"

"Uh, no," Glory looked down at the floor.

"But, I'll buy you a coffee," offered Parker.

Glory smiled brightly. "*Alright!*"

Parker turned to Man-Child. "My friend would like a drink. What do you want, Glory?"

"I'll have whatever Parker's having!" Glory declared.

Man-Child nodded. "So, a caramel Frappuccino with whipped cream, a shot of determination and sprinkles of hope?"

Glory blinked. "Uh, yeah. That."

"Coming right up."

Glory turned to Parker. "Say, you haven't mentioned anything about what happened last night. I've been dying to talk to you about it!"

Parker slowly shook her head. "Nope! I'm waiting to hear Joe's side of it. And Bernstein's. The Sheriff's already made up *his* mind."

Glory hunched his shoulders. "I know, but it's so crazy!" he clenched his fingers. "I don't know what that phone call was about but whatever it was, it like, turned Joe into some kind of wild man!"

Parker's eyes narrowed. She spun on her heel to face Glory directly. *Come on, Parker, you need to focus.* "*What* phone call?"

"I was talking with some people after the Sheriff left, and they said before all the shit went down between Joe and Bernstein, somebody saw Joe reading his phone while waiting at the bar. He got super agitated after some text, like with crazy eyes and all that, and then he bolted toward the bathrooms. That's where he found Bernstein and the two just started going at it!"

"Who told you this?"

"That lame third grade teacher who was trying to hang out with us. Billy! Bob?"

"*Brad?*" Parker nearly choked on the name.

"Yeah! Brad!"

Parker closed her eyes. *Well, I can't not follow up on a lead like that – right?*

90.

"How's Holly?"

asked Brad solemnly at his desk during his lunch break at school. He played with his ham sandwich, as if food had lost all taste after being separated from his lover. "Has she said anything about me? I feel like it's been forever since I've felt her touch."

Parker folded her arms. "You touched her plenty last night. Are you going to elaborate on what Glory told me or sit there and stew like a star-crossed twit?"

"Harsh," Brad gulped. "Well, like Glory said, I saw Joe start pushing Bernstein around just outside of the bathroom. I couldn't hear what he was saying, but Joe was pointing at him threateningly. Then he shows Bernstein something on his phone, and Bernstein's eyes get super big. Like golf ball big. You play golf?"

"No."

"Holly and I used to play golf together."

"Focus, *Brad*." Parker emphasized the teacher's name as if it was some awful word used to describe the lowliest of miscreants in ancient times.

"So, Bernstein starts yelling back at Joe, and knocks the phone out of his hand. Joe flips out and then pushes Bernstein into the back alley. A bunch of us follow, a crowd forms around them, but no one dares get in Joe's way. He starts wailing on the poor guy. And well, you saw what happened next. I couldn't believe it!"

Parker's blood began to boil. *How did I not hear about this?* "Was all this in your statement to the Sheriff?"

"I didn't make a statement."

"Why the fuck not, *Brad*?" Parker clenched her fists.

"I panicked. I couldn't find Holly. I looked everywhere for her. I just wanted to make sure she was okay. By the time I got her text telling me she'd gone home, the Sheriff and his deputies had left the scene."

Parker slammed her hands down onto Brad's desk, startling him. "You're going to go down to the Sheriff's office and make your goddamn statement. Today. You got that, *Brad*?"

Brad gulped. "Yeah. Sure."

Without a word, Parker turned and marched toward the classroom exit.

"What are you going to do?" asked Brad with wide eyes, as if watching a super hero about to jump off the ledge of a rooftop to fight an upswelling of crime.

Parker flashed back an angry glare. "I gotta see a woman about painting faces."

91.

"You want me to do what?"

Julie didn't even bother glancing at Parker. Instead, she kept her eyes focused on the spin class instructor at the head of the gym room full of exercise bikes.

"Come on, people!" the instructor yelled. He wore a bright purple spandex unitard that revealed his over-accentuated pectorals that could have served as a life-model for any comic book character. "Pump those legs! Move! Pump! Move! Pump!"

Parker panted uncontrollably on her stationary bike, her feet rotating at barely a fourth the speed of Julie's. "I want you to," she gulped air, then wiped the sweat off her forehead. "I want you to paint unicorns and flowers and shit on tiny faces for Boo Fest!"

"Parker, I *hate* kids!" shouted Julie.

"Don't you *have* kids?" Parker panted.

"Yeah, but they're mine! Everybody else's suck!" Julie lifted her butt off her bike's seat to get better leverage and cycle twice as fast. "I thought you wanted to talk about last night!"

The instructor pointed Julie out to the rest of the class. "You go, Julie! You show us how it's done!" shouted the instructor. His finger aimed at Parker. "Your momma must be so proud!"

Parker winced as she realized the instructor was talking about her. "What – *me*? I'm not her mom! We're the same age!"

"That's right! You're as young as you feel!" the instructor agreed. "Wooooooooooooo!"

Parker's legs felt like jelly. Defeated, she started to dismount.

"What, you're leaving?" Julie balked. "You said you wanted to make a change! Come on, I thought this would be fun to do together!"

Parker rolled her eyes. The picture on Heller's phone had certainly helped inspire this moment of insanity, but one spin class wasn't going to erase a decade of decadence. "But, I'm so tired," gasped Parker.

Julie frowned. "Fine! I'll do the face painting thing!"

Parker perked up. "You will?"

"But you have to woman up and finish this class!"

Forty grueling minutes later, Parker slowly trailed Julie into the locker room. "Sweet mother of fuck, you do this every day?" Parker whined.

Julie bounced over to her locker. "Every other day. You gotta mix it up. Three hours in the gym plus yoga six days a week can help you look like *this*!" Julie turned around and struck a model's pose completely naked.

"Holy!" Parker held up her hands to cover her eyes. "How did you undress so quickly?"

"I'm not ashamed of my body."

Parker tossed Julie a towel. "Impressive, but my eyes are still reeling from what I saw last night."

Julie scowled. "What do you mean? You mean Joe whomping on Bernstein? Or did you see something *else*?"

Just Holly grinding on Brad. "Of course, I mean Joe and Bernstein. Didn't you see it?"

"I arrived late to the fight," explained Julie. "I got my phone out so I could snap some shots, but everyone was pushing and shoving so much, I dropped it. So, I pick it up, but I can't unlock the damn thing. Then, I realize I picked up the *wrong* phone, so I had to wait for everybody to clear the hallway, so I could find *my* phone."

Parker's eyes bulged. "You picked up the wrong phone?"

Julie wrapped the towel around her chest. "Yeah, but it's okay because I found *my* phone." She retrieved it from her locker, showing off its spider cracked screen. "Stupid thing got stepped on, so now I got to have *that* fixed."

Parker waved her hands. "What about the *other* phone?"

"You mean the not-*my*-phone?"

"Yes. What did you do with the not-your-phone?"

Julie pulled out another phone from her purse. "I kept it in case it belonged to one of your dorky PTA friends. I was going to post it under the school's lost and found and hold it for ransom." Julie felt the phone buzzing in her hand. "Holy shit, it's ringing!"

Parker lifted her own phone. "That's because I'm calling it. I'm calling Joe Ward's number. You found Joe Ward's phone!" Parker's heart raced. She could hardly believe her luck. "God, Julie, this is *huge!* I'm so excited, I could kiss you!"

Julie held up her index finger in protest. "Hey. I don't do that. Not since college."

Parker held out her hand. "Can I have that phone, please?"

Julie gladly handed the phone over. "What do you think is on it?"

"Whatever it is, it could go a long way to explaining what happened between Joe and Bernstein," answered Parker. She tried accessing the phone, but it was locked with a six-digit passcode. "Shit. Of course, *this* phone is locked."

"Are you going to turn it in to the Sheriff?"

Parker continued to examine the outside of the phone as she mulled the question over. If she surrendered the phone now, before she had a look inside, it was unlikely she'd get another crack at it. Then again, if she waited too long, Bill would get mad and technically she could be charged with obstruction of justice.

He wouldn't do that – would he?

92.

"Bill!"

hailed Parker over her minivan's speaker phone as she raced back to Oak Creek to pick up her kids. "I need to talk with Joe Ward as soon as possible. Can you get me in to see him today?"

"Parker?" Bill fumbled. "Listen, I—"

"Come on, man, haven't the drugs worn off?" she blasted. "He's had all night and all day!"

"You found something didn't you?" asked Bill. "What is it?"

Parker pulled into the car line, six or seven cars behind the pick-up area. She hesitated, not wanting to give up Joe Ward's phone just yet. But she had to give him something. "Brad Somebody-Somebody is going to be coming down to your station today to make an official statement."

"Brad Somebody-Somebody?"

Parker pulled her car up to keep pace with the line. "I forget his last name. He teaches third grade at Oak Creek Elementary. He was a witness you guys didn't get to interview last night. Brad is going to tell you a compelling story about a phone call Joe Ward received before he went nuts on Bernstein. I think it might—"

"Parker, it doesn't matter."

"What do you mean it doesn't matter?" Parker slammed on her brakes to keep from ramming the car in front of her. "Bill? Explain. *You* found something, didn't you?"

"We searched Joe's apartment this morning. We found a hand gun hidden in a loose floorboard."

"Okay, and—"

391

"The ballistics match the gun that shot Karen Heller."

Parker's heart sank. *Shit. Bill was right this whole time?* Time slowed down as she searched for another explanation. Any other explanation. A car honking from behind returned her to the moment at hand. "I got it!" she yelled at the car behind her. Parker slowly pulled forward, watching Maddy and Drew emerge from the crowd of children.

"Parker?" asked Bill, breaking the silence.

Parker swallowed. "I need to speak with Joe Ward. I need to understand why."

"You and I both. But he's not talking, Parker. He's made it clear he won't see anyone, you included, until his lawyer arrives."

"When is that going to be?"

"Probably Monday at the earliest. She's coming in from San Diego. We don't have anyone in the county qualified to handle this."

"Damnit," Parker bowed her head. Maddy and Drew would get in the car any second. "Okay. I have to go. Can I call you later?"

"Of course. And Parker? I'm sorry."

93.

"This doesn't make any sense!"

cried Maddy, wiping her tears away. She sat at the kitchen table with Valerie and Parker at her sides, each resting a hand on her shoulder in an attempt to comfort her. "Why would Mr. Ward do any of that?"

Parker gently massaged her daughter's back. "I'm sorry, Maddy. I don't understand it myself. I just thought it would be better for you to hear it from me. Before everyone started talking about it at school."

Maddy sniffled. "We all knew something was up when we got a sub for gym. Some of the kids said their parents talked about how Mr. Ward went crazy. I thought they were joking. But killing Principal Heller?"

Vice Principal. Parker lifted her hands in surrender. "I don't get it, either!"

"But!" Maddy wiped her nose on her sleeve.

"Don't do that dear," Valerie pulled a handkerchief from the cleave of her bosom and handed it to her granddaughter. "Use this."

"Sorry," Maddy blew her nose in the handkerchief. "What proof do they even have?"

"They found the gun used to kill Heller in Mr. Ward's apartment," explained Parker. "They found Heller's phone on his person when they arrested him. And they claim he was obsessed with yours truly."

"God, *of course*, he was," Maddy moaned with a roll of her eyes.

What is that supposed to mean?

393

"And how was he *obsessed* with you?"

"He took pictures of me with Heller's phone. Picking you up at school, walking into the funeral home, even from the fence line of *our own backyard*." Parker noted the tone of her own voice. *Am I starting to buy into this explanation too?*

Maddy wiped the last of her tears away as she sat up in her chair. "The funeral home?"

"Yeah, that was one of them."

Maddy ruffled her brows. "Was the picture outside or inside?"

Parker blinked. She pulled out her phone and swiped to the single shot taken at the funeral home. The picture was taken from across the street, as Parker and her family walked toward the front doors of the home. Everyone's back was facing the photographer.

Maddy breathed a sigh of relief. "Mom, Mr. Ward didn't take that picture. He couldn't have."

"How do you know?"

"Because he was inside the entryway when we walked in. Don't you remember?"

"No," said Parker, slightly ashamed that she didn't. "To be honest, I was distracted over having to give Heller's speech."

"Well, I remember *very* clearly," declared Maddy. "I was trying to work up the nerve to talk to him. We even made eye contact. He didn't take *that* picture."

Parker and Valerie looked at each other in sheer astonishment.

"Maddy," Valerie offered a soft golf clap. "Very nice work. But, if Joe didn't take it, who did?"

"He was set up!" Maddy exclaimed.

"You want to reach for a conclusion, not jump to one." Parker drummed her finger tips on the kitchen table. "We arrived late.

Most everyone was already inside the home by the time we got there. Who was missing? Mendez and Bernstein never showed. Bernstein claimed he was sick. Mendez told me it was none of my business. Bill said the texts from Heller's phone were coming from the funeral home after I gave my speech. That's when he started suspecting Joe. Then Joe gets into a huge fight with Bernstein last night."

"Set up!" Maddy reiterated in a sing song voice. "Set up, set up, set up!"

"Stop!" Parker closed her eyes. "I'm trying to think!"

"Set up." Maddy whispered under a small cough.

Parker pulled out the phone Julie had given her. "Joe got a call or a text or something while he was getting beers at the bar. Whatever it was, it served as a catalyst for attacking Bernstein. And the damn thing is password protected."

"Yet Heller's phone wasn't," added Valerie. "Making those *really embarrassing* pictures of you accessible to you and the Sheriff."

"Thanks," Parker frowned. "That set up the warrant to search Joe's place, where Bill and his guys found the murder weapon." Parker's eyes bulged. "Joe was set up!"

"Oh, wow, really?" Maddy scoffed. *"No duh!"*

"But it's messy," said Parker. "The whole thing feels *really* messy."

Maddy plucked Joe's phone out of Parker's hands. "What do you think is on this phone?"

"Without the password, we can't know." Parker kneaded her fingers together. "But there's a music teacher sitting in a hospital bed on the other side of town who does know."

Maddy's jaw dropped at the revelation that Mr. Bernstein was still at the center of the storm. There was no denying it.

Parker eyed her daughter carefully, unsure if she was about to scream or burst into tears.

"Well, what are you waiting for?" asked Maddy. "Are you going to find out what Bernstein knows or just sit there?"

Parker leaned back. "You're – okay with this?"

"You're so close to figuring it all out, Mom! I can feel it!"

Parker checked her watch. "It's getting late, visiting hours will be over soon."

"Then you better move, woman!"

Parker stood up, staring at her daughter with a mixture of pride and fear. "Maddy. This isn't a game. A man is in jail, another was nearly beaten death, and your vice principal may have been shot because of what is on this phone. Learning its secret could put us all in terrible danger. Do you understand?"

"Who knows you have that phone?" asked Valerie.

"Only Julie. I didn't want to tell Bill about it and have to surrender it just yet. I still don't."

"You need backup," stated Valerie.

"You need a plan," added Maddy.

Parker pushed her hands together as if in prayer. "I need something more important than either of those."

94.

With all the traffic lights and turns...

Memorial Hospital was easily a twenty-minute drive through the city of Oak Creek from Valerie's house. The Sheriff's department was located on the opposite side of town, also twenty minutes away, making each of the three locations an edge of a perfect triangle. As Parker drove the route crowded with the last of the day's commuter traffic, she couldn't help but wonder how quickly an ambulance could make the same trip with the sirens on. Valerie's house might be picturesque, but hardly the ideal setting for an emergency response.

Let's hope we don't need it.

Visiting hours ended at 8pm, leaving Parker a good fifteen minutes by the time she'd parked and rode the elevator up to the 3rd floor. The nurse at the desk informed her that Gerome Bernstein's condition had stabilized, and he'd been moved from ICU to a standard hospital bed. "Room 351, at the corner down the hall," a young and bubbly blonde nurse informed. "He's still very weak, so don't get him too excited."

Parker smirked. *You have no idea.* She glanced down the empty corridor, as most nurses had gone home for the night. "Does he share a room with another patient?"

"No, he's in a single." The nurse presented a sign-in book. "Please write your name, who you're visiting and the date and time."

"I suppose there's been a steady stream of visitors today," mused Parker.

"Oh, sure, a lot of teachers have dropped by showing their support. Gerome is such a sweet guy."

Parker quickly scanned the sign-in log, noting the names. As the nurse had stated, teachers had filed in one after the other since school rang out. Parker flipped the page back and forth, pretending to misunderstand where to sign as she double checked the names. "I'm sorry, where do I sign this thing?"

The nurse pointed to the latest blank entry and chuckled.

"Thanks. I hope his wife brought him some of her world-famous lemonade."

The nurse tilted her head. "Oh. Probably. I didn't realize he was married."

Parker could not find Imelda's name anywhere on the log-in.

The nurse looked off to the side, trying to recall. "But I met his brother," she added. "Or was it his half-brother, maybe?"

Parker's memory flashed back to the Sheriff's office, where she had met Victor, presumed brother to Imelda, uncle to Pedro. Sure enough, Parker located the name Victor Cortez near the end of the ledger. He'd signed in almost an hour ago. "Victor," stated Parker. "Brother-in-law." Parker finished signing her name.

"Thanks. You'll have about fifteen minutes, okay?"

Parker nodded and slowly walked toward the end of the hallway. The tall and thin window in the door framed a pathetic portrait of a sleeping Bernstein tucked into the covers of a metal framed bed with the back angled up. Oxygen tubes curled around his purple ears and into a nose protected by a metal guard. Gerome's right eye was completely covered with white gauze wrapped around his skull. Three lines of stitches marked his forehead, one on his cheek. A large mandible type cover protected his jaw. His skin boasted a depressing rainbow of blue, black, green and purple shades.

Parker gently pushed the door open and walked into the room, allowing it to close behind her. The loud clicking of the door latch announced her presence. "Hello, Mr. Bernstein."

Bernstein's one eye opened. With a tired groan, he tried to turn his head to better identify his visitor. "You," he grumbled with a slur. "Visiting hours are over."

"I'm told I've got fifteen minutes."

"Go away." His hand reached for the corded call button with which to call the nurse.

Parker gently pulled the button away. "I need to ask you some questions first."

"Nurse!" Bernstein tried screaming, but his lungs could barely muster a whimper as he cringed with pain. "Nurse!" he cried in a whisper. The exertion proved to be too much.

Parker's ears caught a spike of Bernstein's pulse beeping on the heart monitor. But it settled when he took a breath. "If you want the nurse to come in I can go get her," offered Parker. "She might want to see what I brought to show you." Parker lifted Joe Ward's cell phone in front of Gerome's good eye. She pressed the home button to activate the main screen, which prompted a password over a picture of Joe and his Ranger platoon posing somewhere in a desert.

Bernstein's eye widened.

"That's right," said Parker. "Joe Ward gave me his phone." She lowered the phone and turned it to face her. Her thumbs jabbed at the screen as she pretended to unlock it.

Bernstein's pulse steadily rose.

"Now, I've seen some crazy shit in my time," continued Parker. "But I can admit when I don't understand something." Parker contorted her face into an expression of disgust as she pretended to swipe through pictures on the phone. "Help me understand, Mr. Bernstein. What is this all about?"

Bernstein's pulse spiked, as a tear welled up in his eye. His lips trembled. "You don't understand," he whined.

"I want to. Help me understand."

Bernstein began to sob uncontrollably. "I never hurt any of them! I would never do that!"

Parker tried not to react. She needed more. "I want to believe you."

"I loved them! I loved each of those boys!"

Parker's stomach wrenched into knots. *Oh hell. Is this what I think it is?* "Who are these boys?" she demanded.

"They were asleep the whole time. They never felt anything, I promise you! I wouldn't hurt them! I loved them!"

"Give me names."

Bernstein's expression twisted from sadness to abject terror. "Oh no! They'll kill me!" he gasped.

"Who will? Joe? A cartel?" Parker gritted her teeth. She needed more information but couldn't tip her hand. "I can get you protection, Gerome, but you have to tell me who you need it from!"

Bernstein shook his head no. "No, no, no, no, no, no they'll kill me!"

"Give me a name!"

Bernstein sobbed, shaking his head back and forth. He writhed in agony, until finally, his lips parted to utter two words.

One name.

A revelation that pierced Parker's heart like a dagger of ice.

95.

"What is going on in here?"

yelled the nurse as she charged into Bernstein's room. "His heart rate is off the charts!"

Parker slowly stood up, numbed by the information she'd just received.

Bernstein cried uncontrollably.

"Get out!" shouted the nurse. She pointed to the door. "Get out of here, now!"

Parker walked out of the hospital room, brushing shoulders with two other nurses who rushed in to tend to Bernstein.

This changes everything.

Parker's heart thumped against her chest wall so hard it hurt. She gently pressed her hand to her breast in an attempt to slow it down, as she wandered aimlessly down the hall. She was excited, terrified and mortified all at the same time.

The last piece of the puzzle. It's all starting to make sense now!

"Parker?" asked a familiar voice. "Are you okay? You look like you've seen a ghost!"

Parker looked up to see Sheriff Bill standing directly in her path. His eyes darted every which way as he scanned her.

"Are you hurt?" asked the Sheriff.

Parker swallowed. "I'm in -- shock."

Bill took a deep breath. "You're scaring me, Parker. What happened? What are you doing here?"

"What are you doing here?" Parker asked back.

"The teacher came to the station and made his statement. I thought I'd follow up with Bernstein to ask him about what he saw on Joe Ward's phone." Bill's eyes narrowed. "Did Bernstein tell you something?"

It's too soon. I can't blow this.

Parker's mind raced with new scenarios and explanations. She remapped puzzle pieces, trying new configurations to slot them in. As the picture began to coalesce, one thing was glaringly obvious. "Danger," she whispered.

"Danger?"

Parker blinked. She pointed back to Bernstein's room. "Bernstein's life is in danger. You need to put a guard at his door. Tonight."

"Joe Ward can't hurt him anymore."

"He's not worried about Joe Ward."

Bill clenched his jaw. "You're acting really funny, Parker. What did Bernstein say?"

"You're not going to believe me."

"Try me."

"No," Parker slowly shook her head. "I have to *show* you."

"Okay."

"I'll step you through it. Every point. But I need my notes. They're in my house."

Bill pulled up on his belt buckle. He looked Parker up and down, as if still trying to assess her state of mind. "Alright. If that's what you need." He said calmly. "How about I follow you back to your house? You get your notes, then we'll go to the station."

Parker nodded. "First, you need to put a guard at that man's door." She pointed back to Bernstein's room.

Bill offered a complicit smile. "Whatever you say, Parker." He reached to his shoulder walkie and called it in, never taking his eyes off Parker. "Okay, now, let's get you home."

Parker remained quiet as she and Bill rode the elevator down to the main lobby. Bill kept his distance, not wanting to upset her even more. When they hopped in their respective cars, Parker led the way back through town. Twenty minutes exactly.

A lot can happen in twenty minutes. I just hope it's long enough.

When Parker finally pulled into her driveway, her eyes scanned across an unfamiliar car parked in front of the house. A tall and slender woman was knocking at Valerie's door. No one answered.

Parker eased her minivan to a halt, flanked by the Sheriff's car next to her. As the two of them climbed out of their cars, Bill looked to Parker. He put one hand on his gun holster, then directed his gaze toward the woman at the door. The woman spun on her heel to face the Sheriff, a puzzled expression on her face.

"Principal Mendez," greeted Bill. "What are you doing here?"

96.

Mendez's eyes narrowed as she looked the Sheriff over.

She nodded to Parker. "Ms. Monroe invited me," she answered calmly. "I'm a bit surprised to see *you*, Sheriff."

Parker turned to Bill to explain. "I texted Mendez on the drive over. I thought she would want to hear what I have to say."

"Parker, I don't know if that is such a good idea," said Bill.

I don't know if it is either, thought Parker. *But I've already rolled the dice.*

"No one is home," stated Mendez. She pointed to the darkened windows. "Where is your family?"

"They must have gone out," answered Parker, moving toward the front door. Her keys jingled as she retrieved them from her purse. "It's better that way. No one will interrupt us." Parker unlocked the door and pushed it open. She turned back to find a puzzled Mendez and Bill standing at the top of the driveway. "Are you coming?"

Bill extended his hand for Mendez to go first. The two quietly followed Parker into the dark entryway. A shaft of light from the back of the house served as a guide through the front room and into the kitchen. Parker plucked a handwritten note off the refrigerator:

Took the kids to a movie — Val

Mendez examined the crude crayoned colorings on index cards spread about the kitchen table. "Your children's artwork?"

Parker reached for the cupboard. "They're Ally's. Either of you thirsty? A lemonade perhaps?"

Bill let out an impatient sigh. "Parker, what is this about? You said you needed your notes."

"You're looking at them." Parker grabbed three glasses from the cupboard.

"These?" Mendez chose one of Ally's colorings to better inspect it. The drawing was an erratic black circle of crayon scribbles.

"That one is of *you*, Principal Mendez." Parker swooped over to the fridge and retrieved a cold glass pitcher of lemonade. She filled each glass on the counter top. "I think Ally did a hell of a job capturing your -- essence."

"It's a black hole," noted Mendez.

"Right?"

Bill placed his hands over his nose in an attempt to hide his scowl. He failed. "Parker, why don't we go down to the station? Principal Mendez can go home, and you and I can have a long talk."

Parker pushed the lemonade glasses toward her guests. "Let's have a drink first." Parker's eyes reddened. "I *insist*."

"I'll pass," said Bill tersely.

Mendez lifted her hands in gentle protest. "No, thank you."

"Neither of you took the glass," noted Parker. "Maybe you don't trust me. Maybe you think I put something in it." She lifted a glass and took a few gulps. "Date rape drugs are so advanced these days, you'd never know if your drink was spiked until it was too late. You'd wake up disoriented, usually with no memory of what happened other than a foreboding sense of not feeling quite right. But you know what? You offer lemonade to a child? Or a drink that tasted just as sweet? They'd drink that shit almost every time. Most of them wouldn't even care where it came from. Especially if it was from a trusted music teacher who, unbeknownst to them, had sick urges to molest little boys."

"What?" Mendez gasped angrily. "Are you saying--?"

"Gerome Bernstein is a serial pedophile. He confessed as much to me tonight."

Bill cringed. "Why would he confess *that*?"

Parker tossed a phone onto the kitchen table. "Because, I showed him what was on Joe Ward's cell phone." *If the lie can work once, it can work twice.*

Mendez and Bill stared at the cell phone on the table in stunned silence. Parker folded her arms, watching each of them carefully.

Mendez picked up the phone and held it. "Well? Show us what's on the phone!"

Parker frowned. She angrily opened the fridge again to return the pitcher of lemonade. "Why don't you ask the Sheriff?"

Bill's jaw clenched. He blurted out an awkward laugh. "What? How the hell would *I* know?"

Parker closed the refrigerator door, revealing the small six-shot revolver in her hand. She aimed the gun directly at Bill's head. "Because you sent what's on Joe's phone from *yours*."

97.

Parker firmed her grip on the revolver.

The same revolver she'd asked Valerie to stash in the refrigerator before evacuating the kids from the house on her drive back from the hospital.

Mendez threw her hands in the air at the sight of the gun. "Ms. Monroe!"

Bill let out a calm but annoyed snort. He kept his hands to his sides. "You're bluffing. You don't even know what's on that phone, do you?"

Parker swallowed. "I'm guessing they're pictures. Shocking pictures of Gerome with young boys he claimed to 'love.' Sick pictures that would throw Joe Ward into a blind rage. You read his file. You knew of his violent history, you even told me about it. All Joe needed was a push. Then, when you tasered and cuffed him, you slipped Heller's phone into his back pocket to make it look like he'd had it the whole time."

Bill smirked. "Parker, you have no idea what you're doing."

"And *you* have no idea how *pissed off I am*," growled Parker. "I hate guns, and for me to be holding one on you? Right now? Chafes my ass in the *worst fucking way*."

Bill extended his hand for the pistol. "Come on. Hand it over. Before someone gets hurt."

Parker expertly cocked the hammer of the colt .38. "My mother has been a member of the NRA for over forty years. Against all reasonable judgment, she saw fit to have me trained to shoot by the age of ten. You go ahead and try me, Bill, or you can finally admit that you royally fucked up."

Bill smirk widened. "I didn't fuck up."

"You did. You fucked with *me*."

"Parker, look around you!" Bill threw his arms open wide to the room. "You're holding a gun on an officer of the law and the principal of an elementary school! You've presented a two-year old's crayon drawings as evidence of – *what* exactly?" He turned to Mendez. "This looks crazy, right?"

"How's *this* for crazy?" asked Parker. "There was only one person tied to every aspect of Heller's murder more than Bernstein, and that person was *you*. You had access to my Highlander when it was impounded at your office with plenty of time to crack the alarm. You were at the PTA meeting the night Heller was murdered. You were always first on the scene when things got hairy, acting like some goddamn hero. God, as sheriff you had access to *everything*!"

"Parker!" Mendez pleaded. "Why would the Sheriff be involved with any of that?"

"Yes, Parker," added Bill. "Why?"

Parker adjusted her grip on her gun. "It goes back to that sappy, bullshit story you told me about when you caught Bernstein smuggling a young boy and his mother into the country. Yeah, you didn't turn them in, but not because you felt 'conflicted.' You saw Bernstein as an 'opportunity.' You saw him as a future partner."

Mendez's eyes widened. "A partner for what?"

Parker swallowed. The very idea made her sick. "Human trafficking."

"Wow," Bill slowly reached for a chair at the kitchen table. "This is a *fascinating* story. Even Mendez is starting to buy it. You mind if I sit down?"

"Keep standing," Parker ordered, jabbing the gun in Bill's direction. "Bernstein's ranch is the perfect way-station to funnel illegals especially when the local law enforcement is ordered to steer clear.

Bernstein and his wife already had the connections you needed. Traffickers could run their operation without any harassment in exchange for a piece of the pie. You've gamed both sides of the law this whole time."

Bill frowned, unimpressed. "That's quite a stretch."

"Not really. When Heller stumbled onto the truth, you murdered her. You tried to frame me for it, and when that didn't work, you framed Joe."

"And you can prove all this how?"

"Bernstein implicated your name at the hospital. It's over."

Bill chuckled. "You're taking the word of a man hopped up on pain killers?"

"The real evidence is locked away on the phone Mendez is holding." Parker pointed to Joe Ward's cell phone in the principal's hand. "I bet if we marched down to the station right now and presented Joe with it, he'd have no qualms unlocking it for us, that is, if he isn't still sedated to keep from talking. So in the meantime, your phone will do just fine, Sheriff. Care to show us what's on it?"

"You want me to show *you* what's on *my* phone?" scoffed Bill. "To prove, what, I'm some kind of criminal mastermind?"

"*Please*, you've been playing the last few weeks by the seat of your pants," answered Parker. "Trying to distract me. Sending me on wild goose chases. Feeding me bullshit leads to keep me off your scent. You've been scrambling. Running scared. You're no mastermind. You're a fucking *hack*."

Bill took a long deep breath and stared at the floor. "Heh," he laughed awkwardly. "I'm a hack?" His face turned beat red. "*I'm* the hack?" Bill jabbed his finger angrily at Parker, losing his cool for the first time ever in Parker's presence. "I played you, Parker. Played! You! *You're* the goddam hack!"

"So, it's true?" gasped Mendez. "*You* murdered Karen?"

"Oh, look who just did the math?" spat Bill. "Shall I spell it out? I-killed-Karen-Heller!" Bill proudly announced, as if he were yodeling from the top of a mountain. "I shot her in the back of the head. Pop! She never saw it coming. Good luck proving any of it!" Bill took a deep breath to calm himself, realizing his mistake. He pulled out a chair and slowly sat himself down.

"I told you to keep standing," ordered Parker.

Bill smiled. "You're not going to shoot me." Bill laced his hands behind his head and placed his feet onto the table, shoving Ally's pictures onto the floor with the soles of his boots. "You would've done it already if you had the balls. Besides, you're curious. You think you've got the who, the what and the when, but you're still not sure about the how."

Parker's eyes narrowed. "When Heller left the PTA meeting, she was rushing off to meet with you. To give you what her investigator found on Bernstein."

"Don't strain yourself," scoffed Bill. "*Bernstein* insisted on meeting Heller that night. He couldn't understand why after all those years of working together, Heller would fire him because of 'budget cuts.' He wanted to confront her face to face."

"But she was afraid of how Bernstein might react, so she asked you to come for protection, is that it?" added Parker.

"Ironic, right? I'll admit I didn't know the extent of what Heller's investigator had dug up. I even broke into the school looking for the files."

"Ah hell, of course!" Parker wanted to kick herself. "You ransacked the music room and stole instruments to divert attention from what you were actually looking for! Heller's files on Bernstein!"

Bill dismissed Parker with a wave of his hand. "Turns out they weren't much. Just some complaints of parents of former music students who came home feeling woozy after lessons with Bernstein. Still, it was all circumstantial. But when Heller

410

confronted him about it that night, Bernstein got all emotional and whiny. He started crying, then practically admitted to Heller he loves little boys. Always has. Once that came out, I had no choice. I had to kill her. Heller knew enough to ruin years of my work."

"So, it's true!" Mendez snapped to Parker. "We need to call the police!"

"Yeah, *do* that!" chuckled Bill. "Oh wait! Shit, they're already here!" Bill clapped his hands together as he laser focused on Parker. "The truth is, Parker could've done that on the car ride over, but she didn't. Because after what Bernstein told her in the hospital, she didn't know how deep the well went. She didn't know who she could trust. She *still* doesn't. But she called you, didn't she, Mendez? I wonder, what's so special about *you*?"

"I needed another witness to your confession," Parker explained.

"All you did was add to tonight's body count," said Bill. "Now I've got to take care of you, your family and Mendez. It's not going to be pretty."

A thunderous crack sounded as Parker's gun exploded to life, startling both Mendez and Bill as a hole tore into the kitchen ceiling. "I'm the one with the gun!" Parker reminded.

Mendez held a trembling hand to her forehead. "Oh god!"

Bill smiled. "Fine. What's your next move? You going to shoot me?" He pointed to his face. "Better aim for the head, because you know the vest I'm wearing is gonna stop what's coming out of that pop gun. Maybe you should call the Highway Patrol? Or the San Diego County Sheriff? Of course, they'll both check in with my office first which won't bode so well with you."

"Shut up," demanded Parker.

"See, I don't think you thought this all the way through," Bill continued to muse. "But I have. A good magician is always two steps ahead of the audience."

411

"Your magic sucks. It's always sucked."

"I fooled an entire city for years. And what's more, Parker? I fooled you." Bill sat forward in his chair. "The key to a great trick is to keep your audience engaged. A little dazzled, sometimes confused. But always misdirected so they see what you want them to see. When really, all you're doing is buying *time*."

Parker heard the sound of a gun being cocked behind her head. She felt the cold steel of a barrel press against her hair. "Drop your weapon, Ms. Monroe," said a man's voice.

Parker's stomach wrenched into knots.

Bill smiled. "Every great magician works with an equally great assistant."

98.

"Shit,"

Parker slowly lifted her revolver toward the ceiling, until it was plucked out of her hand. A powerful arm shoved her toward Mendez. She spun on her heels to find Deputy Michaels out of uniform, his broken arm in a sling, with his good hand holding a Beretta pistol aimed at her heart.

Bill stood up from the kitchen table. He openly applauded Deputy Michaels. "Perfect timing, Deputy."

Michaels nodded appreciatively.

Parker stared up at the ceiling. "Of course, there were *two* of you!" she growled. "Michaels was with Ken Heller when he thought he was getting texts from his wife! All he had to do was feed you the answers to Ken's questions."

"You don't get any points for figuring that out now," teased Bill. He unholstered his own gun and trained it on Mendez. "In high school you were always so fucking annoying telling us all how smart you are but it was all just talk."

"Fuck you." Parker growled as she put her hands in the air.

Bill checked his watch and turned back to Michaels. "Are we clear?"

"I searched the perimeter and checked the house. Place is clean. No witnesses. Neighbors called about the gunshot. I told them I would investigate."

"How did you get in?"

"Forced the side garage door."

Bill frowned. "Before or *after* the gunshot?"

413

Michaels grimaced. "I'm—not sure. Is that important?"

"There's a motion camera covering that alley. If you broke in before the gunshot, then you're on camera doing something weird. We'll have to clean that up."

"There was no camera," retorted Michaels. "I checked."

"There *is* a camera," insisted Bill. "I noted it when I was here the other night."

Parker glanced at Mendez.

"Fine. There's a camera." said Michaels. "Whatever."

Bill turned from his partner to stare Parker up and down. "Unless," he angrily marched around the kitchen. "Shit. Where the hell did you put it, Parker?"

Parker innocently hunched her shoulders. "Put what?"

Bill back handed Parker across the face, throwing her back against the wall. "Don't play dumb with me!"

Parker's head rung like a bell. *Fuck, that hurt!* She collected herself and glared at Bill. "You just made a *huge* mistake."

"Shut up!" Bill finally spotted it. He reached above the refrigerator to pull down a battery powered motion sensor camera—the same one Glory had installed to cover the alley side door. "Shit!" He threw the camera onto the tile floor, blasting open the case and bouncing parts into the next room.

Parker parted her bloody lips into a smirk. "Oh dear, do you think it was recording this whole time?"

"Fuck!" cursed Michaels. "What do we do?"

Bill hammered his fist into Parker's face so hard her nose spurted blood. He shoved her into a kitchen chair and snapped his fingers. "Gimme the bag!" Bill leveraged his body to pin Parker as he handcuffed her wrists to the armrests of the chair.

Turning his gun on Mendez, Michaels tossed Bill a small bag. The Sheriff pulled out a needle and syringe as he bore his weight down on Parker. "Stop struggling!"

Parker's head still spun like crazy as she tried to resist Bill's strength. She felt a small stinging in her arm, followed by a burning sensation — and then suddenly, all the pain seemed to float away. As angry as she was at Bill, her heart rate only seemed to slow. "What?" she gasped breathlessly. "What — are you doing?"

"Pure heroin," explained Bill.

"Oh god," gasped Mendez, nearly in tears.

Parker struggled to keep her eyes open. She could barely lift her hands.

"But you, Parker Monroe, we're going to blast you with so much of it you overdose," said Bill. "See, you're just a junkie. You got into this because of your friend, Joe Ward. And then you went and lost your shit tonight, pulled a gun on me and the principal, and shot her in the face before I could shoot you. How's *that* for a story?"

Parker's head started to get lighter. She tipped out of her chair and fell onto the floor. "It sucks."

Bill snapped his fingers at Michaels. "You got another dose ready yet?"

"Coming up," Michaels traded Bill syringes for another one full of heroin.

Parker shook her drowsy head and started to laugh as Bill straddled her, armed with another needle.

"You think this is funny?" asked Bill. "You're going to die, Parker."

"You're so fucking stupid," panted Parker.

Bill smiled. "Yeah? Well, I played you, Parker. And I won."

"You played me," moaned Parker as she felt around the tile. Her brain had never worked like this before. Everything was upside down. She was somehow furious and sad, without her body capable of expressing the emotion. The room spun. She couldn't even feel the blood rushing down from her nose. All she could do is laugh as she tried to get one last point across. "You played me, and she played us."

"She?" Bill paused. "Who? *Heller*?"

Parker's bloodied smile widened. "Mendez."

Mendez's eyes shifted from abject terror to a blaze of sheer hellfire. "Damn you, Parker!"

Before Bill or Michaels could even react, Mendez had jabbed a stiletto heel into Michael's left calf while pulling his gun hand across her stomach and directly toward Bill. As Michael's body crumpled from the pain in his left calf, he fired by accident. The bullet grazed Bill's arm and shattered the window behind him. Mendez pressed her attack by using her free hand to tug on Michael's ear so hard she detached the lobe from his head. He yelled, but not before Mendez adjusted her grip and threw his forehead into the edge of the kitchen table.

I knew it, Mendez! You <u>are</u> undercover FBI!

Michaels' head ricocheted back into the air, loosening his hold on the gun. Mendez kicked the gun away, while lifting her skirt to reveal her own concealed handgun strapped to her inner thigh. She trained her FBI standard issued Glock 22 promptly on Bill, who in turn, trained his gun on her, forcing each to grapple the other's weapon with their free hand.

Parker could still barely lift her own torso off the floor. Through blurry eyes, she found Michaels reeling on the floor across from her. Bill and Mendez struggled to dominate each other, inadvertently aiming one of the guns directly at Parker. The gun's barrel exploded with flame and thunder.

Parker watched in disbelief as her right thigh exploded with blood. *Holy balls, I've been shot! And I can't even feel it!*

The gun's aim swung wildly toward Michaels. It fired again, blowing off a chunk of his head.

Oh fiddle-fuck, I bet he felt that!

Horrified at his own mistake, Bill smashed his forehead into Mendez's, startling her to drop her Glock. Mendez backed away, desperately searching the counter space behind her. Bill started to raise his gun to aim at Mendez's face, but not before her fingers had locked onto the kitchen's knife block. She flung a steak knife into Bill's gun arm, then grabbed the butcher knife and sliced open Bill's gun wrist, forcing him to drop his gun onto the tile.

Bill, in turn, wildly grabbed for anything in the sink next to him and found the rim of a ceramic bowl. As Mendez pressed forward with her knife, Bill cold-cocked her with the bowl on the side of her skull, sending her reeling into the kitchen table. Mendez slipped on the blood on the floor. Bill loomed over the would-be principal and tossed the ceramic bowl into the back of her neck.

Mendez struggled to push herself back up. "Goddam, Mendez, you got some moves!" He kicked her in the small of the back, slamming her body down onto the floor. He reached down for the gun he'd dropped earlier, only to find it wasn't there.

"Looking for this?" panted Parker. She didn't bother waiting for Bill's answer. It took every bit of strength she had left just to pull the trigger. The gun exploded to life, and Bill crumpled over, grabbing his bleeding crotch.

Damnit. I was aiming for his head!

"Shit--!" Bill cried, wincing in immeasurable pain. He stumbled out of the kitchen toward the front of the house to throw the front door open.

"He's getting—" Parker panted to Mendez, who continued to groan on the floor. "He's getting away!"

Exhausted, high as a kite, and gushing blood out of her leg, Parker crawled on all fours through her mother's house in her attempt to pursue Bill. To her surprise, when she reached the doorway, she found the entire street crowded with cars, emergency response vehicles and people.

Parker would later learn, that her last-minute gamble had worked almost perfectly. At Parker's request, when Valerie had set up the motion camera in the kitchen, she'd also emailed everyone on the school's PTA registry a live link to the camera. Some people ignored the link, thinking it was spam. But for those who did watch, word spread like wildfire. Bill's confession was witnessed by hundreds of people on social media in Oak Creek.

When Bill exited Valerie's house, nearly the entire PTA stood to meet him at the curb, along with the state highway patrol, a few FBI field agents and even some of Bill's own confused deputies. At the forefront of the group stood Julie, Glory and Valerie who angrily aimed a shotgun at Bill's head.

When Bill asked them who the hell they thought they were, Julie proudly replied: "We're the mother-fucking PTA."

Bill passed out from his blood loss only seconds before Parker did.

Then everything went black.

99.

Parker's eyes opened to the soft morning light of a hospital room and the hard aching of her entire body.

Each beat of her heart caused a sharp and powerful throbbing in the bridge of her nose, cheek bones and right thigh.

I guess the heroin wore off.

Parker couldn't believe the power of that drug. Under its influence, she literally couldn't feel anything, good or bad. For those with nothing but misery and pain in their life, she could understand how so many could be tempted by it. But the price to be paid simply wasn't worth it. In a strange way, Parker missed her pain. Without it, she didn't quite feel whole. Parker looked down at her left arm to note the IV running into it. "Blehk," she grumbled, disgusted by the sight.

"You blew my cover, Ms. Monroe," said a voice from her right.

The statement startled Parker, which prompted another shock of pain. Parker slowly turned her aching head to find Principal Mendez sitting in a chair next to her. Of course, even with the bruises on her face, Mendez still looked picture perfect. "Have you just been sitting there, waiting for me to wake up so that you could tell me that?" asked Parker. "Creepy."

"I ran into your family as they were leaving for lunch," said Mendez. "I offered to say with you until they got back."

"Ah hell, I missed them?" Parker tried sitting up in her bed, which prompted even more aches and pain. *Gah, maybe that heroin wasn't so bad?* "I could really use some hugs right now." Parker gave her best puppy dog eyes to Mendez. She grimaced as she outstretched her arms. "Unless?"

419

"No." Mendez defiantly crossed her arms.

"But we, like, went through some *serious shit* together! *You* got beat up. *I* got beat up."

"I'm not a hugger."

"We both shot people. We bonded, man! Bring it in." Parker opened her arms wider, ready to receive Mendez.

"Ms. Monroe," Mendez cleared her throat in an attempt to change the subject. "You took an incredible risk the other night texting me to come over."

"The other night? How many has it been?"

"Two," answered Mendez. "How did you know I was undercover FBI?"

Parker waved the question away as if it were no big deal. "I knew you had to be *something* undercover. You are a terrible principal. And you obviously hate kids. And you practically begged me to investigate Bernstein's ranch. And you came when I messaged you 911."

Mendez allowed herself a small grin. "So, you *hoped* I was undercover FBI."

Parker shrugged. "When Bill turned up at the hospital, you were my best bet. I couldn't call the local authorities. I didn't know how deep things went. Even if I was wrong and you simply were just a terrible principal, your presence doubled my chances of survival. The worst that could happen was that Bill killed both of us. I simply *hate* the idea of dying alone." Parker winced. *Even my toes hurt! Why do my toes hurt?* "How much did the feds know about everything going on?"

"Oak Creek has had an unrealistically low-crime rate for years," answered Mendez. "But we had no evidence that the Sheriff was doing anything wrong. My assignment was to look for signs of trafficking within the school system. We'd busted a ring last year that clued us in that there might be activity within this county."

"But Heller never knew about you, did she?"

"No. Only the superintendent. Maybe that's why Karen never trusted me. If she had, it might have saved her life."

"I don't think Karen felt she could trust anyone," added Parker. "She'd been Bernstein's greatest advocate. They'd built the music program together. His secret would have destroyed the both of them."

"Bernstein hid it all very well. I had a few leads, but it wasn't until you unmasked everyone the other night that the dots started to connect. You'll be pleased to know we raided Mr. Bernstein's ranch this morning and arrested his wife as an accomplice. She revealed an underground tunnel hidden beneath a false floor in their barn. It ran three miles to an outhouse across the border. The longest ever discovered. But it's all shut down now. Johnson, Bernstein and his wife, and her brother Victor Cortez whose dealership provided transport for migrants will be behind bars for a very, *very* long time."

"Prison is too good for them."

Mendez stood up and rested her hand gently on Parker's. "I like to believe there's a special place in hell for human traffickers. They are the worst of the worst."

Parker smiled. "Aww, you *do* have emotions!" Her smile suddenly dissolved. "What about Pedro?"

"He'll become a ward of the state. We can't locate his mother anywhere."

Parker's eyes lit up. "He has a great grandmother, here, in the States. Her name is Cecelia. She's been searching for him."

"Interesting," Mendez nodded. "I wasn't aware of that. I'll look into it, okay?" Mendez looked up toward the door. "I can hear your

421

family down the hall. Your son keeps shouting about ghosts in the hospital or something." She patted Parker on the arm. "Good luck to you, Ms. Monroe. I wish you a speedy recovery."

Parker frowned. "Wait. You're leaving? Like, forever leaving?"

"Oak Creek Elementary deserves a real principal. It's about time it got one."

"You could at least stay through Boo Fest! We're short volunteers! We could really use your help!"

Mendez's smile widened. "I have no doubt Boo Fest will be a roaring success."

100.

"Boo Fest is a fucking disaster,"

grumbled a green-faced witch-costumed Parker. The make-up did a remarkable job hiding her swollen nose and black eye, a poor consolation when Parker surveyed the sparse crowd of costumed kids and their parents exploring the lavish Halloween themed carnival sprawled about the school's grounds. There was literally no waiting in line at the Ferris wheel, the tilt-a-whirl, or the zipper rides on this hot and arid Friday afternoon. *Slippery When Wet* jammed in front of only twelve die-hard Bon Jovi fans, which included the dancing train wreck of Cray-Cray who proudly wore her child's undersized Boo Fest t-shirt "because it fit like a glove" – if the glove was meant to announce to the world she wasn't wearing a bra.

Parker took some solace in the fact that those families who did show, arrived in elaborate Halloween costumes. The Power Rangers, Frankensteins, Pokémon' handlers, Hobbits, Fobbits and Harry Potter clones appeared to genuinely enjoy the event. But the math was obvious. Such a poor turnout meant the fundraiser was well below hitting the break-even point. Parker angrily adjusted her pointed witch's hat that perfectly accessorized her lavish purple satin costume rental for the umpteenth time. "All this work, and for what?"

Valerie, appearing as a regal Cleopatra, gently patted her daughter on the shoulder, causing her to cringe from her days old bruises. "I'm rather surprised anyone showed up at all," she stated blatantly.

"Thanks, Mom."

"I mean, who wants to give money to save a music program started by a pedophile?"

"Maybe ask that a *little* louder," Parker tried smiling at the shocked constituents who passed by.

"Still," Valerie smiled. "You should be proud. And if you aren't, I'll be proud enough for the both of us."

Parker and Valerie began to walk and survey the grounds, with Parker doing her best to hide her limp.

"Do you think you should be walking so much?" pressed Valerie.

"Sure," Parker waved her mother off. "Walking is good for a bullet wound."

"Really?"

"I don't know. I'm hopped up on pain killers."

Parker waved to Glory, who had perfected his non-penis balloon swords that children chased each other with. She waved to Maddy, who patiently (for once) guided Drew and Ally along to the kiddie dragon themed roller coaster. She smiled at Julie who painted a young girls' face into an alarming rendition of Kiss's Gene Simmons. The young girl stuck her unusually long tongue out at Parker. Then there was Brad wrapping his arms around Holly at a carnival game. He pretended to help her aim the stream of a water pistol into the mechanical clown's mouth. *God, if that isn't a pathetic suggestion.* Parker tried to shield her eyes from the display. It was only when her mother and her reached the end of the fairway, that Parker finally spotted *him.*

"Mom, can you give me a minute?" asked Parker.

"Is something wrong?" replied Valerie.

"No. I just need to have a quick conversation with the Grim Reaper." Parker parted from her mother's side and circled around the back of the dunk tank's shack. About a minute later, the skull-faced Grim Reaper rounded the corner to stand silently before the witch. He gently laid his scythe against the back wall.

"How are you feeling?" asked Joe Ward as he pulled off his skull mask.

"The pain killers the doctors gave me aren't nearly as effective at killing pain as that heroin Bill shot me up with," answered Parker.

"It's powerful stuff," said Joe. "I nearly got hooked on it years ago after I got shot in Afghanistan. Stay away from it."

"Yes, sir." Parker offered a sarcastic salute. She paused as her eyes met Joe's. In the past she'd always tried to read him and gauge as to whether he was telling her the truth. Without all that distraction, now she searched his eyes for something else. "Your text was rather vague. What did you want to talk to me about?"

"I wanted to thank you. In person." Joe drew a long, deep breath. "And I wanted to apologize."

"For what?"

"I didn't mean to lose it on Bernstein the way I did," Joe looked to the ground in shame. "That must have been awful to witness. I was out of control."

"Yeah, you were." Parker didn't mince her words. "You have a serious problem."

Joe nodded. "I thought I was doing better. It's been years. But when I got those pictures of Bernstein with those boys – it all came flooding back."

Parker looked Joe up and down. She finally found what she was looking for. "You were abused," she deduced.

"No," Joe shook his head. "Not me." He looked up to the afternoon's cloudy sky. "Funny, I don't even know what his name was. But he served as a 'tea boy' on base in Afghanistan. There was a commander in the local police militia, a guy the Rangers were partnering with for Christ's sake who had a real interest in this boy."

425

"You're talking about *bacha bazi*," stated Parker.

"You've heard of it?"

Parker swallowed. "I've read about it. Roughly translated, it means 'boy play.' Young boys are sold to prominent men in Afghanistan for entertainment. Of course, it's all just cover for them to be sexually abused."

"They're sex slaves," added Joe. "At night, on base, you could hear them crying from time to time. And their abusers were men we had to work with the next day. It made us all sick. But we were ordered to stand down. It wasn't our culture. It wasn't our place get involved. There were rules to abide by."

Parker folded her arms. "So, what did you do?"

"Nothing," answered Joe. "And that kid who served my coffee every morning? He took my inaction as being complicit. He saw it as the Americans giving permission for him to be abused. So, one morning, after suffering a particularly brutal episode from the local police chief, that boy didn't serve me coffee. He served me a bullet." Joe pointed to his chest. "Missed my heart by an inch."

"I'm sorry, Joe. That's awful."

"I couldn't blame the kid. He was right to be angry with me. I failed him." Joe clenched his fist. "We went over to protect these people from the Taliban, and some of the assholes who replaced them were just as bad. After weeks of recovery, I was still pissed. I took it up with my CO. He gave me the same spiel about our mission. The rules of engagement. How we needed that Afghan police chief to continue doing his job, so we could win. And I lost it. Just – lost it. I took all my rage, I channeled it through these fists," Joe held up his hands, and curled them tightly until his knuckles were white. "And I beat the living crap out of my CO. Just like I did with Bernstein. Both times, it cost me my job."

Parker's eyes widened. "You're being fired?" she gasped.

"I'm resigning," admitted Joe. "All the teachers saw what I did. They're frightened of me. Who could blame them? This school has enough issues. It needs a fresh start. Without me."

Parker sighed. *And you were just starting to get interesting.* "What are you going to do?"

"I don't know," said Joe. He lowered his fists and took another cleansing breath, then offered a smile to Parker. "Whatever it is, I just wanted you to know why."

101.

Later in the evening...

hours after the Boo Fest had closed down, Parker answered the doorbell in her mother's home. She couldn't help but to smile at the small, elderly man in front of her. "Good evening, Mr. Heller."

Heller's lips parted into a tired smile. "You look ghastly," he greeted.

Parker took a wet cloth to her face, continuing her effort to rub off the last of the green make up, and revealing the black and blue bruises beneath. "Not all of this color is make-up, unfortunately," she chuckled. "Please, come in. Mom nearly has dinner ready."

"It smells delicious," said Heller, slowly shuffling his feet into the entryway. "How was your fundraiser?"

Parker's heart sank. "It was fine," she lied, not really wanting to talk about it.

"Fine?"

"It was good."

"Good," Ken nodded, apparently satisfied with Parker's last descriptor. "I'm sorry I couldn't make it down there today."

"I imagine you've had a lot to process."

"You could say that," Ken paused to stare at the floor. When he looked up, his eyes were glassy. "Karen tried to do the right thing, you know. I truly believe that."

"I know."

"She could just be so stubborn sometimes in asking for help."

I know that too. Parker put her hand on Ken's shoulder. "No one blames your wife for what happened."

Ken swallowed. "I don't want people to remember her as the champion of some pedophile. Or the victim of a crooked cop." He reached into his pocket and pulled out a small mail envelope. "Her legacy needs to be about her passion for helping kids. So, I'm making a donation in her name to the music program. It's not much, but there's more to come."

"That's not necessary," Parker tried to smile as she received the envelope. "But, thank you. I'll make sure Karen gets due credit."

"Thank you," Ken smiled and slowly turned for the door. "Good bye, Ms. Monroe."

"Wait, you aren't staying for dinner?"

"I'm very tired tonight."

Parker frowned. "Suit yourself. But my mom opted to make duck again when she heard you were stopping by." The statement gave Ken pause. "And Maddy would very much like to play for you again. If that's alright with you. But if you're tired, we can certainly take a rain check."

Ken turned his head back with a slight twinkle in his eye. "Well," he said. "Maybe for just a little bit."

The dinner proved to be as enjoyable as Ken's first visit. Valerie's bottle of a '04 Premier Cru paired perfectly with her broiled duck. Drew and Ally regaled the table with ideas as to how to get the most candy during the upcoming night of trick-or-treating. Maddy pointed out how the bullet hole in the ceiling above the kitchen table went straight into her bedroom. Ken drank it all in, enjoying every moment. Afterwards, Maddy played several songs at the piano, prompting more requests from Ken. Did she know any Scarlatti? Schubert? Maddy eagerly accepted every challenge, digging into musty music books in the cabinet nearby that hadn't been opened for years.

The piano playing drew long into the night, several hours after Drew and Ally had gone to bed. Valerie had retired to the kitchen to wash some of the dishes, leaving a very relaxed Ken and Parker to enjoy Maddy's latest music selection. When the clock approached ten, Parker excused herself to check on her mother.

Parker found Valerie at the sink, drying a plate as she looked out the window. "You were drying that same dish the last time I came in here. You sure you don't want any help?"

Valerie smiled at her daughter. "I've just been enjoying the music. When you were a child, I'd do the same thing. I'd come in here, do the dishes and listen to music on the radio. It was my way of unwinding from the day."

Parker looked back toward the front room where Maddy played. Parker recognized the next piece – Moonlight Sonata. But when she played it this time, it was different. It told a story. It told Maddy's story, with all the emotional up's and down's only a real musician could express. Parker wiped a tear from her eye. "She's pretty great, isn't she?"

"She takes after her mother."

Parker let out a chortle. "No, this music stuff is all her father." She smiled as she rubbed away more tears dribbling down rosy cheeks. "Too bad Boo Fest was such a shit show. I guess we'll have to go the private lessons route again."

"*I've* yet to donate."

"Yeah? You got thirty thousand dollars you're willing to part with?"

"Oh my," Valerie frowned at the suggestion. "You're that short? I suppose I *could*."

"No," Parker shook her head. "No, I can't ask you to donate so much. That's really nice and all, but it's not sustainable. This thing has to stand on its own."

"Well, what did Ken donate?"

Parker grimaced. She pulled out Ken's envelope from her pocket and tore it open. Inside she found a check folded between three papers stapled together. "Ken wrote a check for five hundred dollars."

"That's nice of him."

"It is," Parker's voice trailed off as she examined the papers.

"What is that?" asked Valerie. She gently placed her dish onto the counter and moved to her daughter's side. "A letter?"

Parker's eyes scanned the text. "Legal documents." She flipped to the last page. "Signed today." Parker looked up, realizing she no longer heard Maddy playing the piano. After she'd finished Moonlight Sonata, a gentle silence reined over the house.

Parker and Valerie walked into the piano room to find Maddy standing in front of Ken's chair. Maddy turned to address her mother, stepping away to give a clear view of Ken's face. His eyes were closed, his face locked into a small smile. Maddy put a finger to her lips. "He fell asleep," she whispered.

Valerie cupped her hand over her mouth as tears welled up.

Parker slowly approached Ken and Maddy, looking for any signs of shallow breathing. When she couldn't detect any, Parker reached out to touch Ken's bony hand that rested on his lap. Ken's fingers were cold and unresponsive. Parker wrapped her hand around his wrist. There was no pulse to be found.

"He's not asleep, is he?" asked Maddy calmly.

"No," answered Parker. She watched Maddy carefully. This would be the second dead body she'd witnessed in a month. "I'm sorry, Maddy. Are you--?"

"I'm okay," said Maddy. She nodded to Ken's body. "He looks – at peace." A sharp contrast to Maddy's discovery of Karen's body.

We should all be so lucky to go like this. "Yeah. He does." *Ken told me he wanted to know who his wife's killer was before he died. Was he holding on just long enough for that?* The thought prompted Parker to give another look at the stapled papers in her hand. *And then he delivered this.* Parker lifted them, squinting to read the fine print.

The papers detailed a copy of Ken Heller's newly revised will. With no children or living relatives to inherit his estate, all property was to be liquidated and resulting monies donated to Oak Creek Elementary under one singular condition—

--it be used to fund a music program in the name of Karen Heller.

Parker smiled. "I can work with that."

The end.

Acknowledgements:

This story is an ode to mothers everywhere trying their best to take care of their families, raise their kids right and navigate the organized chaos that is our public school system -- all the while trying to keep their own sanity and sense of self worth intact. That's a pretty tall order, but my life has been blessed with strong women who do that and so much more everyday.

Emily Cravens, my wife of over twenty years, is one of several real life inspirations for Parker Monroe. Her experience as a mother and volunteer was invaluable. It's hard to believe what started off as an off-color joke about a Unicorn Killer blossomed into such a thrilling mystery. Most importantly, Em gave me space for me to be me – an essential ingredient for any writer looking to create something authentic.

Ann Truxaw Ramirez, another inspiration, put up with a lot of random texts about crazy ideas, possible book titles, characters names, etc. for the past two years. She was a great one to bounce ideas off, and did an incredible job proofreading the final draft before print!

Colleen Graff eagerly read every draft of this book and I always appreciated her insightful feedback.

Erin Potter not only read all four drafts of the book, but was often one of the first to get back to me with constructive feedback and follow up questions. Her enthusiasm was invaluable.

Emma Somers' blunt language and honesty was not only a source of inspiration for Parker, but desperately needed when parsing the words I threw at her.

George Castro never read the book, but he was often the first person I'd try ideas out on our afternoon coffee runs. I guess he got the audio version. If George is blown away by an idea, you might have something.

Stacey Burns, my favorite East Coast redhead, served as another great inspiration for Parker. Parker's love for all things Bon Jovi definitely comes from Stacey. Her insight into my writing surprised me time and time again.

Kim Wilson Holst has become one of my favorite test readers over the years. She is always timely and professional as well as a good friend.

Chuck Yager for all of his excellent wine selections!

Natalie Wang, Andy Marchi, Lisa Oelkers Daak, Carrie Mayo Clift, Amanda Davis, Nancy Shubsda and *Chris Elliott*, all of you, thank you so much for taking precious time out of your day to read and help hone this experience into what it was meant to be!

Of course, thank you to all the real life teachers and PTA'ers who work tirelessly to make our kids' future as bright as it can be. I have some fun with all of you in this book, so I hope you enjoy it.

Finally, I'd be horribly remiss without thanking my mother, *Suzanne Flora Cravens*. Mom followed every draft of this book, and would always, without fail, get me feedback on new chapters within minutes after reading them. Her encouragement was often the shot in the arm I needed to push through to the next chapter. Sadly, she died before I could publish this work. She never knew the title I landed on, or saw the final cover. But I know she's looking down on it, proud of what she had helped to accomplish in her own way.

Mom was my first true fan.

Made in the USA
Middletown, DE
28 June 2019